The First Apocalypse

Table of Contents

Chapter 1 – Open Arms
Chapter 2 – Ilkin's Alliance
Chapter 3 – Honor for the Sethites
Chapter 4 – Battle with the Oka
Chapter 5 – Attack in the Marshes
Chapter 6 – Designing the Ark
Chapter 7 – News from Bura
Chapter 8 – Ham Returns
Chapter 9 – Warrior Angel
Chapter 10 – The Nephilim
Chapter 11 – Farewell to a Hero
Chapter 12 – The Grand Union
Chapter 13 – Meet the Nephilim
Chapter 14 – Life among the Ugric
Chapter 15 – Incognito
Chapter 16 – Shem's Return
Chapter 17 – A New Direction
Chapter 18 – Schemes and Dreams
Chapter 19 – Back to Baku
Chapter 20 – The Silent Killer
Chapter 21 – Strong Drink
Chapter 22 – Ugric Big Village
Chapter 23 – Sound the Alarm
Chapter 24 – Return of the Dead
Chapter 25 – Birth of War
Chapter 26 – Eye of the Storm
Chapter 27 – Final Conquest
Chapter 28 – New Love
Chapter 29 – The Beginning of the End
Chapter 30 – A Bad Omen
Chapter 31 - Ararat Gives a Warning
Chapter 32 – City Life Carries On
Chapter 33 -- The Animals
Chapter 34 – Final Warning
Chapter 35 – Waters Pour Forth
Chapter 36 – Beginning Again

Note from the Author

Shem has taken us on many exciting adventures in *Tuball: The Lost City*. When we first met him, he was an impatient young man who escaped simple farming life and headed north with his uncle Zakho into strange new lands. Shem battled fierce creatures and contended with an infamous people known as the Cainites (those descended from Adam's son, Cain). On his quest to find a great city called Tuball he fell in love with a brilliant and beautiful girl named Kara. Ultimately, Shem reached the magnificent city only to be sentenced to death by a suspicious and guarded people. Despite his predicament, he fought for the people of the city when they came under siege by a horde of brutes known as the Okan. His respect for men and faith in his God gave him the power to defeat the Okans.

The Sanctuary took us to present day Azerbaijan, where a spirited petroleum expert named Rebecca Belmont discovered an ancient underwater city in the Caspian Sea, the same city Shem lived in thousands of years earlier. Rebecca and her colleagues struggled to uncover the secrets of the ruins, despite mysterious and lethal setbacks. During the exploration, uncovered artifacts revealed the history of Shem and his tribe known as the Sethites (those descend from Adam's son).

Shem returned to his homeland and was widely respected for his mighty deeds. However, his people's crops were ruined by a pestilence that forced them to the brink of starvation. Shem and Kara were bound to lead the Sethites to a refuge where food was abundant—the city of Tuball. Hundreds of Sethites moved from southern Mesopotamia, over mountains through dangerous territory such as the wild forest fire event, to ultimately arrive in the safe boundaries of Tuball.

A war between tribes of the north and the south must be fought to determine who will rise to supreme power in *The First Apocalypse*. These are the last years of pre-diluvian history. The Earth is on the verge of a cataclysmic event, and Shem, his family, and the rest of mankind will soon be at its mercy.

Final Note

Some of my Christian colleagues may have some difficulty with this novel if they are of the early-earth persuasion, but they shouldn't. I do try to blend both science and faith into good fiction. Additionally, I have taken great efforts to exclude any insinuated facts that may contradict the Bible.

What truly happened thousands of years ago is tricky business—ask any archeologist. The bottom line is that no-one can prove without a doubt that they are correct. We should trust laws and be leery of theories. Laws are the foundation of science, but theories are not.

Therefore, I am neutral on the issue of an early or a long earth. I love my faith and I enjoy my science and I will not have them fighting with one another. What I try to emphasize in my books is the common ground between science and faith. What I am trying to accomplish in my writing is to produce a fun story, critical thinking on morality, and uncommon trivia.

The First Apocalypse
Prologue

Millions of miles above, among the celestial lights, lurked the wandering star. This was no ordinary star, but rather a gigantic comet of loosely packed chunks of ice, dirt, and ore. Its fragile gravity prevented the small ocean of frozen water with house-sized boulders from flying apart.

An eon in time had passed since its inception, and the comet crept methodically throughout the heavens on a trajectory determined by the gravitational forces of interstellar bodies. After thousands of years drifting through space the journey has finally come to an end. It had raced passed the Sun's outer planets and through the solar system's asteroid belt, shedding fragments of its mass as it collided with cosmic debris. This comet could have easily been destroyed by a distant planet, or even a rogue asteroid. Instead, it would either fall to its destruction into the Sun's fiery, hydrogen furnace, or to a nearby planet…Earth.

Chapter 1
Open Arms
78 years before the end

The ram's horn blew from the top of the city walls. "Uuwaaaaaah!"

Shem looked up toward the sound of the horn from his rope-laced stretcher, then over to Kara. She was walking beside the stretcher, casting concerned glances down to him.

"Worry not. We will find the healer soon," she reassured, likely comforting only herself.

"Uwah, uwaaaaah!" The horns blew louder.

Shem grumbled. "Let me off this thing. I can stand. It is only a shallow head wound."

"You speak false words," she scolded.

He fidgeted, then sat up on his elbows. "I am a man, and wish to walk in on my own feet."

She pressed her hands against his chest. "You are a foolish man who should listen to the wisdom I speak."

He flopped back down. "Why is it you worry so, Kara?"

"Do you think I wish to see my future husband die?" Her eyes welled up and she quickly took out a cloth and dabbed his face.

Shem pulled back and saw red on the fabric. He glanced at the blood that had trickled down his shirt. He touched his nose to see red on his finger tips. Soon spots appeared before him. *What is this? I do not understand.* Shem tightened his grip on the wooden poles of the stretcher. *Have I brought my people out from their woes, only for me to suffer? This should not be. It is my time to bond with Kara.*

The gigantic wooden gate began to crack open. The ram's horn continued to blast as the thick pine doors pivoted on a stone base that took two men per door to move.

"Hurry!" she called out harshly to the carriers. "His nose bleeds."

The men on each side of Shem's litter trotted quicker.

When the doors swung wide, a cheering throng of people spilled out from the city. Like an ocean wave, the citizens of the city surged around Shem with their hands out to touch him. He lay helpless, flat on the stretcher, unable to stop them from crushing in on him.

"Honor to Shem—his people—his God!" the citizens shouted.

Cymbals clanged, drums pounded, horns blared. Shem winced at the cacophony of noisy exaltation. Instead of acknowledging them, he covered his face with his hands. The shouts of joy were too harsh, too loud. His litter bobbed through the crowd, into the open courtyard toward the healer's chambers.

"Hurry, I say!" Kara shouted over the roar of the crowd.

The spots before him grew into darkness—sounds became muffled. "Kara? I know you are there." His voice faded, the multitudes melted away, and he drifted into unconsciousness.

Chapter 2
Ilkin's Alliance

Ilkin was desperate, dying of hunger, and suffering from a plague of open sores. He had little skill for hunting. The city life of Tuball had taken its toll on the exiled son of the grand elder. He gathered berries, dug roots, and skulked about in secret to steal food from travelers and villagers. A hopeless sight of a man of skin and bones, Ilkin still trusted no one. His energy was virtually gone and yet he had enough strength to make one last desperate attempt to save himself—even if it meant discarding his pride.

"I cannot live this way. May the gods have mercy on me and spare my life of this pain." He staggered out of the woods to see several lights in the distance. He shuffled his way toward them. At the edge of the camp he fell down and crawled to where most of the people had gathered.

Disheveled and exhausted, Ilkin reached out toward some figures in front of him. As he crawled on his hands and knees, he felt his hair tighten; his head began being pulled upward. From the corner of his eye, he saw a yellow haired warrior staring down at him with disdain.

The warrior let go of Ilkin's head.

He slumped to the ground in a heap.

The big man reached out and ripped off Ilkin's ornate necklace with a symbol of the ziggurat on the bottom.

"This man is from Tuball," he announced to the others, showing off the emblem. The big man then spat down on Ilkin. "Your people only bring trouble." The warrior took hold of a large club and raised it up.

Assured of certain death, Ilkin shook his feeble head. "No, I am not one of them. Show me favor and I will show you how to defeat them."

The large warrior smirked at him, but set the club down anyway. "You lie. I hold the truth in my hand," he said, displaying the necklace.

"No!" Ilkin gave a raspy shout. "No! I have been banished. I am not with them."

The warrior turned to another man for a judgment on Ilkin's well being. "What say you, Agul?"

The man was barrel-chested and wore a wolf pelt around his shoulders. He raised an eyebrow and shook his head. "Balkar, do not kill this one…yet. He may have other uses. Bring him to my house."

Balkar signaled two younger warriors in leather loin cloths and fur leggings to follow the elder's orders. They grabbed Ilkin's arms and dragged him to a stone house with a thatched roof. Once inside, a woman pointed for the men to put him on a pile of straw so she could feed him and attend to his wounds. They threw him down and she went to work, cleaning him and applying salve on his open sores, then leaving him until morning. For the first time in many nights, Ilkin slept soundly with a roof over his head.

The next morning Ilkin woke abruptly to the crash of wood falling outside his room. He glanced about to see a fire started in a stone fire pit, but no one else. He crept up to the window. A boy of about thirteen years was thrown onto a pile of firewood. The man named Balkar picked up a large round chunk of wood and set it down. He reached for the boy's wrist and laid it onto the wood. The boy's face was calm, but his eyes widened with fear.

Balkar looked straight into the eyes of the boy. "You know what I must do."

The boy nodded.

Balkar then picked up his club and slung it over his head.

The boy kept his hand steady on the stump.

The club came down hard. It smashed the boy's hand with a crunch, indicating that at least some of the boy's fingers were broken.

The boy groaned. A single tear dropped down his cheek.

Ilkin didn't wait to see what else was to occur. He shrunk down and crawled back to the straw pile, trembling.

Ilkin closed his eyes tightly. *If this is what they do to their own, what of me? Why am I here? My own people threw me away! How could they? I was to be in line as their leader and they threw me out like spoiled meat. My god, El! You must protect me! I have done no wrong…it was my mother! Be cruel to her but not me, please.* At the sound of the creaking door, he opened his eyes.

A man ambled into the room, with a woman following with a plate of food. "I am Agul, leader of my tribe. She is my woman. It is time to talk."

Ilkin sat on the straw, curled up in fear, his arms wrapped around his knees. The woman shoved a plate of gruel over to Ilkin across the flat stone floor. He took the slop with a bow of his head. As he shoveled the food with his hand, the elder sat down in a chair carved out of a stout pine tree trunk.

The chieftain leaned his head against the back of the chair and raised a pointed thick finger toward Ilkin. "Who are you?"

Ilkin swallowed. "I am Ilkin, son of Erti, the grand elder of Tuball." He continued eating.

"Are you?" the elder asked with a pompous laugh. He rose from his seat and walked to the fire, then bent down to adjust the logs.

"Yes," said Ilkin between mouthfuls of gruel. "And you are someone important?"

The elder shook his head in disbelief and picked up a burning stick that was red hot at the tip. "You insult me and are a liar. I am the leader of the Oka people, strong and full," he said, patting his big belly. "You have no meat on your bones and look nothing like the son of any grand elder." He turned to his wife. "I must show this one what we do with liars."

The woman gazed at the burning stick and absently touched her lips where a scar lay.

"It is true!" pleaded Ilkin. "I will prove it to you."

Ilkin set his empty bowl down and spent time expounding his knowledge of the city, its people, and even secrets that the common man wouldn't know.

The demeanor of the elder changed. He tossed the stick back into the fire, then stroked his beard while Ilkin finished an extensive self defense. After Ilkin's mouth ran dry, he sat perfectly still to wait for the verdict. The Oka leader eyed Ilkin a moment, turned, and, without a word, left the room. As Agul's wife followed, she glanced back and gave a favorable nod to Ilkin.

Ilkin closed his eyes and relaxed. *I believe my life has been spared; and the Oka will have me as a new ally. Once I get these dumb beasts to follow me, Bulla will soon feel woes that I have suffered. Yes, Bulla will pay!* He crawled over to the window and peeked out to see Balkar waiting for Agul.

Balkar stepped back from door when the Oka elder walked out of his home. "What do you say, Master?"

"You heard us?" Balkar nodded. "You have been in the city of Tuball. Does he tell the truth?"

Balkar leaned on his club. "He seems to know much of the city and its workings."

The elder spit on the ground. "I do not like this one. He slithers around like a snake."

"I could smash the snake to be safe. But snakes are good if we can use them to bite others. Let me talk to this Ilkin to confirm the truth. I need ask one question."

"So be it. Be quick."

Ilkin fell back from the window and scurried over to scrape food out of the pot near the fire.

Balkar stepped inside with his club over his shoulder. "You, Tuballite pig! Speak with me!"

Ilkin dropped the bowl and bowed. "What is it you wish to learn?"

"You said to Agul that you were the grand elder's son."

"Yes, that is the truth."

"Who is your mother?"

"Seleen."

Balkar raised his eyebrows. "Seleen? Where is she?"

Ilkin's eyes narrowed. "She was murdered by Bulla, my own brother. He is now grand elder."

Balkar didn't reply. He walked out, and then slammed the door behind him. Ilkin crawled back to the door and peeked through a crack.

Agul was waiting outside. "Well?"

Balkar leaned against the wall. "He speaks the truth, Master. We have fought hard against the Tuballite warriors and have lost many of our good men. Maybe this one will bring us victory against the southern pigs."

"Why would this man help us?"

"Seleen was the woman who helped me and my men enter the city. I promised her a seat in high power if we defeated the Tuballites. This Ilkin is her son. He says she was murdered and he was banished. I see anger in his eyes toward them. Anger we may be able to use against them...anger *and* secrets." Balkar smashed his club to the ground. "I too have anger and wish to return it to them."

Agul put his hand on Balkar's shoulder and lowered his voice. "With Erti dead, we must have a feast. We must treat this one kindly. For much knowledge can be gained to fight against our enemies. They have many warriors that protect their cities. Can we get the Tuballites to come to us?"

"They will not come to us without good reason."

"Then we will give them a reason."

Balkar scratched his beard. "Master Agul, There is another we must be wary of. His name is Shem, a Sethite from beyond the southern borders of Tuball. If it were not for Shem and his God we would rule Tuball now."

Agul tapped a finger on Balkar's chest. "Was Shem not the one who asked his God to call fire down to the earth?"

"Yes. He is the one. If Bulla unleashes all his men and Shem's God upon us, we may lose, even with this Ilkin pig."

"Do you know this Shem?"

"No. I never set eyes on him."

"Hmmm. We will see whose god is stronger. Maybe it is time we set aside our ill will with our cousins to the far north. With their great beasts on our side, not even this Shem and his God could stop us."

Ilkin took his ear from the door and grinned smugly.

Chapter 3
Honor for the Sethites

Shem opened his eyes.

Kara pulled back her long dark hair and then examined the bandage Shem had around his head. He reached out and touched her smooth oval face. She held his hand a moment and her smile glowed. She tucked the bandage in and walked over to the fireplace where water was boiling. He recognized the room as the one he had lived in several seasons ago. It was the same spacious rooftop chamber that let in the cool breeze from the sea.

"My head has stopped spinning," said Shem with relief. "But my body is stiff."

"Thank the healer. You have slept through two nights. Your face has color—it is a good sign. I have told my brothers about our bonding. They are anxious to have you as their brother."

Shem lay with his head sideways on the bed watching her tend to him. Her brothers Itsu, the metal worker, and Bura, now a new warrior in the army, were honorable and hard workers. "I too wish to have them as my brothers. They are good men."

She brought him some black tea mixed with healing herbs. "Here, drink." She helped him sit up.

Shem winced and reached up to feel the knot on his head. "That evil Sevag hit me hard. He is—"

"Dead." Kara finished Shem's sentence through clenched teeth and a hardened stare. "Much dead. He will not trouble anyone else again."

"And my people are safe now?"

"Yes, most are, but not all escaped the fire. A few were like stones staring at the flames. Your big cousin, Torak, tried to coax them out but they would not move."

Shem closed his eyes tightly. "Why did their fear take such hold of them? Why did they not run?"

Kara put her arm around his back and tried to comfort him. "I have heard of it before. Only Mo—I mean only God knows why they were as stones."

Shem half heard her comments. He took his hand away from the bump on his head. "What did you say?"

"Only God knows why they were as stones."

"No, before that."

Kara just shrugged, but Shem's face withered. "You said Mot. Mot! Your other god!" He shook his head in anguish. "That burns as much as a wild fire."

She took a step back. "How can you say that, Shem?"

He sat upright to face her. "My heart! It burns when you speak so! You have not left your gods! How can we share our lives with them in between us?"

"How can I leave my gods so quickly? I have known them my whole life. It will be fine...rest easy. My mother said that I could have my gods and your God too."

Shem wrinkled his face with disgust. "No! My father would never accept that! You cannot serve two masters, can you?"

She hung her head in humility. "I had not thought of that. I know you feel much pain from the death of your kinsmen. Please, do not pass it on to me. I will change. Can you be patient?"

Shem took a deep breath. "Let me think on this." He twisted around and put his feet to the stone floor. "Is Bulla in the city?"

"I heard he has returned from the sea."

Shem dizzily stood up and put his hand on the wall for stability. "I must speak with him."

Kara went to his side and reached around his waist to support him. "You must heal, Shem. Please lie down. I will tell him you wish to talk with him."

Shem looked down as she leaned her head to his chest. He rested the side of his face on her head and sighed. "I love you too much to unhand you, Kara...I will be patient."

Kara looked up with a smile. "You are a good man, Shem." She kissed his cheek and patted his face. "I will send word to Bulla."

Shem sat back down on the edge of the bed with Kara's help. She walked to the door and, before shutting it, glanced back with a meek smile. After she left, Shem rested his elbows on his knees and dropped his head. "Maker of creation, help Kara...change." He took a deep breath and lay down. "Uhhh, *Mot*! How could she?"

Within the hour, there was a knock at Shem's door and it quickly opened. It was the fair minded Ozias, leader of the southern Sethite clans. The grey-haired yet robust man with the one withered eye smiled broadly as he entered. Shem hardly had time to get up before Ozias strode forward and embraced him.

"Shem! By the Almighty! You have not died on us yet. Ha!"

Behind him stood his shorter, stouter uncle, Tabas. Shem assumed that he had taken the torch as leader of the northern Sethite clans. Tabas still carried his spear as if he was ready for another animal kill. He smiled and took his turn to embrace Shem.

"Greetings, Nephew. It is good to see you again. Your brother Ham sends his greetings. He is testing the many foods in the city marketplace."

Shem shifted on the edge of his bed. "It is good to see you both well. Are our people being cared for?"

"Yes, yes. These Tuballites are a helpful tribe," Tabas assured.

Tabas and Ozias then looked at each other awkwardly, motioning for the other to speak.

Shem was puzzled. "What is it?"

Ozias pulled over a nearby wooden stool and sat next to Shem's bed. "There has been talk within our clans that I take the lead of our people and that Tabas be my second."

Shem shrugged. "I think either of you would do well. Then so be it. Is that all?"

Ozias cleared his throat and combed his beard with one pass. "There is another matter." He glanced at Tabas then back at Shem. "Our people also wish it that we settle outside the city...we work with the earth. Except your cousin, Torak, who took up with the Tuball warriors. We have the auroch bulls to plow the soil, but we may need seed."

Shem straightened up a bit. "Plow outside the city? But the Tuballites will let you stay here. Our kinsmen will not have to do the hard work in the fields."

"Yes, that may be true." Ozias cleared his throat. "You see, we know you are familiar with the gods of Tuball, and it does not offend you. But our people—"

"You mean Mordu," interrupted Tabas. "He has been causing nothing but trouble since we arrived. Stirring up anger, and um...." Unwilling to slander his cousin, he tousled his head of hair and let out a growl.

Ozias nodded. "Yes...it is Mordu pushing us. As I have said, these people have been kind to us. Yet we do not want to cause division in our own clans. They have customs that the Creator would not approve of. Women wear ashes and scents that seduce men, stories of the festival that honors relations out of marriage, and other things. That is why we feel it best not to mix with them as of yet."

"I do not agree with their gods, Ozias. And yet I know how our people must feel on this." Shem held his forehead. It was starting to ache. "Do as you see fit."

Ozias stood up. "Many thanks. We did not want you to think we hated these people. May the Almighty heal you quickly."

The two men said their goodbyes and opened the door to leave. Bulla, the grand elder, stood in front of them with his fist up, ready to knock. Shem saw Bulla and smiled. Bulla, still the same stoic, strong warrior, this time dressed in a simple layered tunic. Tabas and Ozias bowed deeply to the highest leader of the city, then stepped back to let him in. Bulla bowed back to them and entered Shem's chambers.

Shem held up a hand from his bed. "Bulla, it is good to see you again!"

"And you too, my friend."

"Bulla, this is my uncle, Tabas, and Ozias, leader of our clans."

Bulla shook wrists with both men and they reciprocated.

Ozias raised his hand. "We will leave you two now. We must tend to our people."

The two men walked out and shut the door. Bulla took a few steps and sat down on the stool near Shem's bed. "How are you, my friend?"

Shem was nonchalant. "I will heal."

"You must meet with my personal healer. No one has died in his hands."

Shem laughed. "I do not intend to die. I have been well cared for, Bulla. Worry not for me."

"As you wish. But you must be well on the third day from now for I have ordered a ceremony for your people. Many of my people have taken on your God, since last you were here."

"It is not needed."

"It was not your fight, when you called for the power of the heavens to defeat the Oka. It is right that we honor you and your tribe."

Shem sighed. "As you wish."

"What about your people? What may I do for them?"

Shem straightened up and leaned forward. "We wish not to be a burden on you."

Bulla frowned. "I do not understand. If you are my guest, then they are my guests."

"I have spoken with Ozias, the man with the one good eye you just met. He said it is best that they live outside the city."

"There is no need to stall outside the walls of the city. I will instruct the master builder to make homes for them inside the city."

Shem shifted uncomfortably. "Some do not wish your kindness. They feel it better to be in the fields and work the land."

"But they can have all they want within the safety of the city walls."

Shem lowered his voice a notch. "They are worried your gods may corrupt them."

Bulla scratched a mosquito bite on his neck under his beard for a moment. "I see." He shrugged. "If that is what your people wish, then that is what will be. I will instruct my masters to assist them in any way. I must point out, I cannot ensure their safety if they stay outside the walls of Tuball."

Shem smiled slightly. "I beg forgiveness Bulla, but even I, your friend, who trusts you with my life, do not put complete faith in the safety of the city."

Bulla rose from his stool. "What happened with the Oka will never happen again. I have vowed it."

Shem knew Bulla meant it, but doubted the reality of it. "To know this, you must have talked with a magus."

"I do not need to. My father was correct in his thoughts to bundle local tribes as one." Bulla became more animated with his gestures. "I intend to push north and do the same to the Oka and others."

"You want to include your enemies who hate you? That is like asking the insects to be kind to the fruit."

"For the safety of my people, I must."

Bulla walked a few steps to a model of the city on a granite table. "Have you seen this?"

Shem noticed the replica for the first time. "No. But someone must have spent much labor on such a great little city."

Bulla motioned Shem to come to him. Shem got up and hobbled over to examine the model. It was a duplicate of the city with the ziggurat in the outer courtyard and the Tuballite citizens with their accommodations, workplaces, and worship temple enclosed in the inner walls.

Bulla circled a hand over the model. "This is where we will build. It will hold many more people and protect us from invaders. I am building a third defensive wall around the eastern side. My masters have told me that the shallow waters, along a ridge to the east, are now dry. We may begin a new trade route by strengthening the soft ground. But you are correct; even high walls do not protect us. That is why I must conquer them and turn my enemies into friends. Once they are friends, they will be part of the family of Bundled Tribes."

Shem leaned against the table and mused at the idea. "A family?"

"Yes, and a family will not fight itself," Bulla added.

"That is a mighty and clever plan, Bulla."

Bulla gazed down at the model. "I have my doubts it will work. Yet I see it working in my dreams. My counsel, Olum, says that when we conquer them, we should make them slaves…as my father would have done. I have seen the anger in a slave's eyes and it is not good. So I will win them over before they ever become slaves."

Shem admired his ambition. "That is a worthy goal."

"I have dreamed it already. And now I will make it real." Bulla forced a smile. "Enough of this talk. I must let you heal." He started walking to the door. "I hear you are to be bonded with Kara."

Shem beamed and, forgetting his injuries, pushed off from holding the table. "Yes. It is true. I have received my and her father's blessings." He hobbled to the door.

Bulla reached out to support Shem by the elbow. "Will Kargi bond the two of you?"

Shem shook his head. "No. He is a good man, but I wish my father do it. He is a holy man of our God."

"He must be a great man, your father. I wish to meet him some day."

Shem knew Bulla had lost a father he had never known well. Noah had showed Shem a strong love and kind discipline that most men craved. "I wish for that as well, my friend."

* * *

A few days had passed and Shem was practically as good as his young self. He relished getting out, smelling the scents, and hearing the sounds of the market from memories of past seasons. It was good fortune. He had his Sethite kinsmen in the city where they could live under the rule of his good friend Bulla. Shem and Kara had their parents' blessing for marriage. In time, he hoped Kara would grow to respect his God and bear many children…then he would truly know the greatest of good fortune.

At the insistence of Bulla, Shem and the Sethite leaders were to be honored. The Sethite tribesmen had moved outside the city walls and entered the city to trade for food and clothing. However, this was a time for the Ceremony of Jubilation, with tribes around the region gathered around the ziggurat for the event.

As Shem made his way through the crowds, people bowed to him reverently. If the ceremony didn't make him uneasy, the adulation surely did. When he arrived at the base of the step pyramid, he took slow methodical paces up the steep stones. As he did so, the Tuballite citizens gave a tremendous shout.

"Exalted are Shem and his great God who delivered us from our enemies! Exalted are Shem and his God who delivered us from our enemies!"

Shem continued up the steps, ignoring their cheers. Kargi, the great spirit master, stood next to Bulla in front of the people. Kargi bent forward, listing to one side, holding a wooden stick to compensate. Bulla, in contrast, was a physical specimen of muscle and mind, a commanding presence dressed in his military leathers. Shem approached a wide shelf in front of the ziggurat entrance. He positioned himself next to the Sethite elders who were clothed in purple, one-piece linen garments.

Bulla raised his hands to quiet the crowds so Kargi could address the people. Kargi spoke of the Sethites with admiration and promised that the alliance would be a good one for their people. He then led Shem and the elders up to the chambers of the ziggurat temple while festivities continued in the open arena. Shem had visited the worship temple in the inner city, but never within the sacred ziggurat. They walked through the wide opening and into a passage that was lit by reflected sunlight off polished metal from above the corridor. Shem tried to analyze the design of the reflecting sun through the passageways, but Kargi urged them on to two large doors. Armed guards stood steady with their bronze-tipped spears. The soldiers stepped aside and Kargi turned to face Shem and the others.

Kargi tapped on the front of the wood. "Soon we will etch in these great doors the tales of how your people left your homeland

and journeyed over the mountains, fought hardships, and arrived at the city gates."

When the spiritual leader approached, the guards took hold of the large metal handles on the doors and swung them open for their guests to enter. The first thing Shem saw was the light at the top of the ziggurat piercing down into a square room many paces wide. Again, he tried to determine how the light filled the room without an opening. The room was almost as bright as the day and spilled over four statues that lay before them.

Kargi turned to face his guests. "This is El, our supreme god." He pointed to a twenty-five foot high stone statue of a robed man stood with his right hand outstretched as if giving a blessing. "His spirit lives within. Be reverent to him."

El's solemn face showed thick eyebrows atop mysterious dark eyes and he wore a cone shaped crown on his head. Mordu, the wiry man who assumed spiritual guide to the Sethites, gave a suspicious glance to Ozias and Tabas, saying nothing, but meaning much.

Kargi continued. "On each side of our god El is his daughter Anat, goddess of fertility and war." He pointed to a pregnant woman with a spear in hand. "On the right is his son Baal, god of storms and crops." A statue of a man with a ring on his arm was raised up with a small cloud in his hand. At El's feet was another statue laying on its side as if slinking to its prey. "And this is El's son Mot, the god of death."

Shem and the other Sethites looked with curiosity at the statues but were not impressed.

"What does this have to do with us, Master Kargi?" asked Shem. "You know we believe in the one unseen God."

"Ah yes. *Your* God. That is why I brought you here. Because of the many great things your God has done, we cannot leave him out of this precious place. We wish to build another statue in his honor."

Mordu stepped forward with bluster. "But He is not to be seen."

Kargi smiled. "My thoughts are with you on that. But should not the Tuballites have something to bow down to?" The spirit master thought for a moment. "What if we keep his face without form? We could bow down to him, yet still not see his face."

The Sethite elders huddled and conducted an impromptu private exchange on the matter. A moment later, they broke up their discussion and Ozias spoke for them. "We see your thoughts as a good answer, Master Kargi."

"Then it is done. I will have the stone master and his workers build it as you see fit."

Shem smiled at the decision. He noticed three small stone plaques hanging on the wall next to some type of access and went to inspect.

Kargi came to his side. "I see you have noticed the sacred chambers. They store our greatest treasures." He walked and pointed at each cover-plate as he spoke. "Wheat, barley, and," stopping at the last stone cover, "riches." He put his hand into a small slot on the cover and pulled. The door swung open and a sliver of light shot out from within the chamber. Shem saw small sparkling gold statues, urns, and other objects lined up on a shelf. The other Sethites moved close, but before the men could enter the treasure room, Kargi held them back. He closed the access and bowed. "This room is too precious to enter. Only I and a few others may enter and care for this chamber. I have shown you this to prove our alliance. I trust you will keep this knowledge secret."

Kargi thanked the men for coming and showed them out of the sanctuary. With the assistance of his cane, he led them down the passage and outside to the steps of the ziggurat. He stood for a moment, while the men gathered around.

The spiritual leader gazed over the city to the eastern waters. "From here we can see a split in the Twin Seas. The seas have always been fully cut off from each other. That is until this year. They are separated no more. The masters of the city have told me that the waters have been dropping each season for a generation." Kargi pointed to the thin strip of land between the two waters with his cane. "The late Grand Elder Erti had a vision that we would reach the east through the two seas by that bridge of land. It will be our destiny to follow it and use it as a way of including other tribes into our own. Now, you Sethites *must* join us in the great destiny of Tuball: to welcome in all the peoples of the world."

Shem desired to bond with the Tuballites in their grand quest, but he remembered the words of his father. *Beware of those who offer good fortune without offering good hardship.*

Chapter 4
Battle with the Oka

Bulla watched from his window to see Shem's people separate themselves from the city dwellers. The Sethites had settled outside the city, building makeshift earthen homes with local materials. It would be hard during the cold season, and even if this one was moderate, some could perish. Bulla turned from the window. A guard opened the door and announced that Tobanis wished to speak with the grand elder. Bulla instructed the guard to show him in.

Tobanis was tough from years of fighting, hardened by war, and a faithful aide to Bulla for many years. With Bulla assuming the position of grand elder, Tobanis took the temporary role of grand protector, leader of all the military forces.

Tobanis wore the standard leather vest and leggings. He bowed to Bulla and rested his palm on the handle of his short sword at his waist. "Grand Elder, I have been sent word that the Oka have again raided our people's lands. They burn homes, take food, and have their way with our women. When our warriors arrive to fight them they flee to the north—like cowards."

Bulla's jaw tightened. "With these endless raids, how can I hope to settle the anger between us and them?"

Tobanis spat on the stone floor. "They are like leaches, sucking the blood from us till we are too weak to go on."

Bulla tapped his fist to his square bearded chin and paced the floor, trying to calm himself. "Order a war council. Tell them I will be there to speak."

"Yes, Grand Elder." Tobanis bowed and left.

* * *

Within an hour, the war council had assembled with Bulla at the head of a large wooden table. Most were Tuballite ministers of trade. They had complained of the loss of goods and services and the future of the city. Bulla then told them he was about to send a force of 500 men to stabilize the area and that trade may get worse before it got better. He didn't need the council's approval, but as a courtesy wanted to inform them of his intentions. The council, still wary and fearful of the Oka, had no choice but to agree with what the grand elder suggested. Even while the meeting continued, Tobanis was at work rounding up warriors from around the city.

Two days later, Tobanis returned and met Bulla at the top of his roof home. He bowed to Bulla. "We are ready. I have 500 men with me and have sent a runner to Baku for more."

"How many men are in Baku?"

"Over three thousand."

"Proceed with the 500. Send word to Baku if the battle does not go well."

"Yes, Master Bulla. Do you wish us to push the invaders out of our borders?"

Bulla stared beyond the walls. "Ask them to join us or die."

"Ask? Can we talk with something we cannot see? They run like children at the first sign of danger," said Tobanis.

"If they run, push them up to the Ugric in the far north. Then trade will resume."

"But when our men march back to the city, the invaders will again return to burn villages."

Bulla face became red with anger. "Then we will not leave! Build a wall around the villages to hold them back. It is important that we keep our ground. If we have to build a strong wall from the mountains to the sea for safety, we will!" Bulla spat on the ground. "I tire of these Oka. It is doubtful that they will ever bundle with us. If they wish to die, kill them. If they wish to surrender, keep them as slaves. The council has given me power to do as I see fit, and I will."

"Yes, Bulla." Tobanis bowed his head and backed his way to the exit.

* * *

Shem was heading up the steps as Tobanis was coming down. "Tobanis! It is good to see you," said Shem, reaching out to shake his old friend's wrist. "I have heard you lead the Tuballite warriors as protectorate."

The war hardened soldier downplayed the compliment. "It is an honor to stand in place of Bulla, until he decides on a new grand protector. There are many good warriors." Tobanis looked keenly at Shem. "You are one of them. I could use you with me."

Shem drew back. "My full strength has only now returned to me. I fear I would only be a burden."

"You would not be fighting, my friend. I want what is in your head. You have fought the Oka before and know their methods. Of course your mighty God will be of help, too."

Shem considered his time away from Kara. "How long do you plan to be away?"

"With over five hundred of my warriors, I expect we will settle the northern villages in a moon."

"When do you leave?"

"When the sun rises."

Shem's stomach flipped "Sunrise?" *That is much too soon!*

Tobanis smiled at Shem's reaction. "I know it is short notice. We have to stop the Oka before any more villages are destroyed."

Shem rubbed the back of his head. *Something draws me with him. Is it the Oka? They are evil and must be destroyed. Or is it something else? Almighty God, are you telling me to do this?* Shem could see Tobanis needed an answer quickly. "If you see me in the morning, I will go with you," he blurted out.

"Fair enough." Tobanis slapped Shem's shoulder and trotted down the steps.

Shem watched Tobanis leave and thought about his time away from Kara. Could he bear to delay their bonding again? Could he also bear to see any one of the Sethites living outside the city killed by the Oka? When that thought came to Shem, his mind was made up. He bounced to the top of the stairs, and raised his palm to the guards at the door. "Please tell the grand elder that Shem, son of Noah, wishes to speak with him.

Bulla was passing through the entry hall. "Do I hear Shem's voice?" Shem entered and bowed to the grand elder. Bulla shook his wrist. "Come in and have some tea." He motioned for Shem to enter a large room with windows facing the south sea. He signaled for a servant to bring some drink. "How are your people, my friend?"

Shem walked toward the window. "They have tents or mud houses to live in outside the southern walls of the city on the land that you have provided. But they have little to eat on and need more seed to start planting."

"I will have provisions sent to them." Bulla pondered a moment. "This will be very hard for them with the cold season still strong. If it becomes too hard for them, they may enter the city at any time."

"Many thanks, Bulla. I will tell them." Shem paused and looked down at the floor. "Bulla, I have decided to go with Tobanis."

Bulla frowned. "With Tobanis? Have you hit your head again? You only have a fresh body as of today."

"I just thought of the idea," said Shem. "I am thinking of my people and wish to ensure that they are safe."

"And I do not want you dead, my good friend."

"Nor do I wish death. But Tobanis says I will not have to fight. He said he wants my counsel."

Bulla squinted sourly. "Counsel? That has a grand sound. But I will not allow it unless that is *all* you will do."

Shem felt like he was talking to his dominant older brother, Japheth. "I cannot make that promise. But I will try my best. When I am gone, would you take care of Kara so I do not worry for her?"

"Will you not tell her of your plan to leave?"

"You must tell her for me, Bulla. I do not have time and…I fear she will not allow it."

Bulla laughed. "Not even bonded and you already fear her." He shook his head. "Fine, I will tell her. But remember—counsel only." Shem bowed to leave. As Shem was shutting the door, Bulla called out, "Counsel only!"

* * *

Shem and the Tuballite forces arrived at the first village north of the city. All was as it should be. Farmers plowed their barley fields and families moved through the town without worry. A day's walk north, they approached the burned ruins of the second village. Dejected survivors rummaged through the rubble.

Scouts spotted a few Oka men in the woods and the Tuballites immediately followed. It wasn't long before they entered a clearing where a large band of Oka warriors was abandoning camp. Shem stood next to Tobanis as the battle began. Tobanis sent out Ismet, his second-in-command—a mighty warrior stout and fearless—with two hundred of his toughest warriors. The more than a hundred Oka fighters were not ready for an organized fight. The big brutes responded with the use of their clubs and other blunt instruments. The Tuballites attacked like a moving wall with sturdy shields and spears affixed.

Tobanis did not have Bulla's ideals of grandeur for diplomacy and peace. He yelled out, "Surrender or die!"

The Oka were not effective. They threw a few spears that bounced off shields, then ran north. Behind the wall of Tuballite soldiers were the long range spear throwers. They launched their spears from their throwing boards over a hundred yards and killed about forty of the fleeing Oka.

The Tuballite warriors accomplished their task effectively. Only a handful of Oka escaped into the deep woods. To pursue the men would be a waste of time, so Tobanis called his men back to regroup and camp. As the sun set, two scouts returned with a message that one of the main Oka forces was a day north, another Oka group to the west. Tobanis did not know how many bands were in the area. He sent scouts to the east and west to ensure that the Oka did not outflank them.

In the early morning light, the Tuballite army moved quickly north. As expected, the Oka tribe had spread into three groups, but Tobanis was clever enough to attack one group with enough reserves held behind to thwart a split offensive. The Oka must have caught on to the plan…they vanished.

The spirits of the Tuballites were high when they reunited at camp. Shem sipped tea while he watched the warriors wrestle, tell grand stories of war, or sit and challenge each other to mind games with wooden playing boards and stones. Shem went to his tent and lit an oil lamp. He lay back on his sheep skin, watching from his tent and listening to the laughter and jeering of comrades. He was about to close the tent flap and extinguish his oil lamp when he noticed a young man with wavy brown hair approach his tent.

Shem picked up the oil lamp and stepped out of the tent. Were his eyes deceiving him? "Bura?"

There he was, just as Shem remembered him from the mountains, tall with strong forearms like his father and green eyes like his mother. It had been far too long since he had seen Kara's brother.

Bura smiled, arms folded proudly to his chest. "You did not know that I am a warrior now?"

"No. Yes. I mean, I knew they needed you, but I did not know it would be so soon. You are such a good woodsman. It does not seem right." Shem reached out and gave Bura a tight hug, then released him.

"Shem, you must know that Tuball gets what he wants. I must be faithful until my time is up. I am good with the spear-thrower weapon now," Bura stated proudly. "It is the best weapon to stay alive with."

"You saved me in the mountains when I was in need. I know they have chosen well. Come in to my little home."

Bura bent down through the opening. He found a three legged stool with a leather seat to sit on.

Shem brought in his oil lamp and sat down on a fleece.

Bura opened his waist pouch and reached inside, but stopped short. "I met with Kara before we left the city. She says Mother and Father have approved of your bonding. I will be happy to have you as a brother."

Shem smiled. "I, too, will be happy as your brother, Bura."

"But Kara was not happy that you did not tell her you were leaving, Shem."

Shem dropped his head. "I could not. She would not want me to go." He raised his head. "But I must protect my people from the Oka. I have fought them before and know what they will do. They are evil men."

"Yes they are. I am glad to be with you, Shem. I thought you a weak-headed man when I first saw you in the mountains. Now I know you as a man of honor. You have proven yourself worthy during the Oka battle at the city." Bura pulled out some parchment and a container with dye and handed them to Shem. "You must also keep your honor with Kara. Make your marks so that she will know your thoughts. I will send a runner back to the city when you finish. Yes?"

Shem accepted the writing instruments. "I will."

"Here is one more thing." Bura held out a closed fist.

Shem placed his open hand underneath and Bura dropped a necklace into Shem's palm. Without a word, Bura got up and stepped toward the tent's flap.

"You are a good man, Bura."

Bura bowed and left Shem alone. Shem brought the oil lamp close. He gazed at the stone inside the necklace. He had given it to Kara more than a year before, and she made it into a necklace. She told him she had never parted from it. It was his turn to keep it close.

* * *

For the next two days there was no trace of the Oka. It was puzzling but not surprising that they would use their well-known hit and run tactics. After the Tuballites passed through another devastated village, they entered a canyon that narrowed to twenty paces. The scout went forward and returned to report that the Oka had a full complement of men waiting for them—over three hundred in all. It now became a stalemate. The northern tribes with their superior offense of size and strength at the narrow point of the canyon matched the Tuballites' superior defense of shields and fighting formations.

Tobanis, Ismet, and Shem sat in a tent finishing their meal. Tobanis laid out a rudimentary map of the area and sat agonizing how they may deal with the enemy. "See here." He pointed to the topography of hills to his second. "Even with our many men, we cannot spread around them to crush them. The canyon walls prevent it."

"We can try a spear point of men through the center to break them, and allow the rest of the warriors to enter," suggested Ismet.

Tobanis shook his head. "That would be a costly venture. We would lose many men that way."

Shem knew that Tobanis' pride would not allow him to leave the battle without a victory.

"We should not rush this plan," said Shem. "God will help us. I have prayed for it. We have chased them from the borders of the city, up along the shore of the northern sea. Have we not done well?"

Tobanis glanced at his second then shook his head. "Shem, I would have thrown you out for such a plan. But knowing how your God once sent lightening down to defeat the Oka, I will let the comment go. My decision will be made when the sun rises. I want a victory that I can be proud to announce to Bulla. I do not want a win with heavy losses. If it were up to me, I would crush the Oka men and return to their villages and kill the women and young ones."

Shem hoped it would not come to that.

That night the Oka tribe infiltrated the Tuballite camp and picked off soldiers as they slept. Among the victims was Tobanis' second-in-command, Ismet, his head bashed in by a club. Morale in the camp was hit squarely. Rumors spread that the Oka sided with Mot's servants and the night gave them power. Tobanis cursed the Oka and wanted to avenge the death of his best warrior. Shem knew Tobanis held back so more men were not killed without good result.

At sunup, the troops were assembled. Shem walked behind Tobanis as he inspected the lines of soldiers.

Tobanis made comments such as, "Do not let fear be your counsel," or "A ready weapon is your greatest friend," and "Cool heads with hot metal win the day."

Tobanis stopped in front of a big man who held a unique spear throwing harness in his right hand. It was Shem's cousin, Torak. Torak was the tallest warrior in the camp, but new to the Tuballites. His wide shoulders contrasted his thin waist, indicating a man who ate in the absence of gluttony. Tobanis reached out to inspect the weapon. The big man held out the device and Tobanis took it. He laid it in his palm to find the balance point and examined it with admiration.

Shem had never seen such beautifully crafted, polished weapon with such intricate carvings. The spear throwing device had a smooth handle at one end and a sharp spur at the other. Just above the handle was a v-shaped support for the spear to rest upon. It wasn't unexpected to see his hunting cousin adapt to a new weapon and improve on it.

"Good weapon. I have never seen one like it. I expect it throws spears well," Tobanis praised. He tossed it back to the big soldier. Torak caught the device with a hint of satisfaction.

Shem pulled Tobanis aside. "You told me you wanted to give a grand speech to rally the troops. If this weapon works well, it could be a way to raise their hopes."

"I was thinking the same," said Tobanis. "Let us test this new weapon to see if it compares to the others."

Tobanis picked out Torak and a few of the best Tuballite throwers to compare their abilities. These weren't common spearmen. These were men who practiced from childhood on the spear-thrower weapon, flinging a spear dart with lethal accuracy at 100 paces. The thrower would set a spear onto a crafted board, then hold onto the board and slowly bring it behind him as if launching a harpoon. As the thrower launched his spear from the board, he would flick his wrist for a leverage thrust, propelling it twice the distance of a common spearman. Shem hoped his cousin would outshine them.

When the men were in place, Tobanis gave the order to throw. Once the order was given, the spears accelerated off the board and flew away in a controlled arc. Each of the spears landed within the expected range of 100 paces…all except one—Torak's. The dart he used landed almost twice the distance of the others. Many thought it was because of his mighty strength, but it was difficult to tell.

Tobanis' eyes grew in astonishment. The stout Tuballite leader called out to the tall man. "You, the big one."

Torak turned, eyebrows raised, and touched his chest with his finger.

"Yes you," Tobanis confirmed. "What magic do you use to make your spears fly so far?"

Torak smiled. "Come, I will show you, my master," he said with a deep bass voice.

Torak took out one of his own darts, then borrowed a dart from another soldier. He held them up to compare. "See how my spear bends. It is allowed to spring out of my board like a cat. The common spear is made of oak and can be used for big game, but my spears are made of more flexible wood, best to hit men at long range. There is no magic, just good tools."

Tobanis stood back. "Show me again." The other soldiers gathered around to watch.

Torak laid the dart on his board, leaned back, and launched the dart with tremendous force. A distinctive zipping sound erupted from the weapon when the dart was flung. All the soldiers were mesmerized as the long thin spear flew farther than his last throw.

Tobanis turned back to the big soldier. "If it is not magic, it is its equal. What is your name, man?"

"Torak, Master Tobanis. I am a Sethite."

"Torak, your weapon made a sound like a loud bee. Does it not scare off your prey?"

"Most prey are too far away to hear it."

"I want you to show the others what they must do to make their spears fly like yours."

"Yes, Master," said Torak with a nod. The other soldiers crowded around Torak to learn his secret.

Tobanis moved with Shem out of earshot. "What do you think of this man?"

Shem smiled like a proud father of a newborn. "Torak is a mighty man of our tribe from the south."

"Ah! That is why you smile so! Does he handle men as well as he does the spear?"

"He may. But he is the best hunter I know of....aside from you, Tobanis."

"Do not try to stroke me with your flattery. He may be of use to me. When did this Torak learn his skill of the spear and board?"

"When he came to the city."

Tobanis's mouth dropped open. "He learned to throw the weapon within a season?"

Shem swelled with pride. "As I said, he is a great hunter."

Tobanis turned and examined how Torak instructed the other men. "He is more than a great hunter. He is a quick learner and a leader. If only I had ten of him."

Shem took out his three winged iron weapon and threw it. It sliced into the air in an upward arc, then circled back and dropped in front of him. "I never did learn to use the spear-thrower weapon. I always liked my dove."

"I cannot see how you make that work." Tobanis reached down and picked up Shem's dove. "You know that it is not a weapon," he said as he handed it back to Shem.

Shem gave a sheepish shrug and hung it on his waist belt. "So I have been told."

"From the boats?"

Shem shrugged. "A boat master told me that the idea was taken from spinning maple seeds as they floated down to the earth. This iron thing was to be used to make the boats move. It did not work. It spins fast in the air when I throw it, but the boat master cannot spin it fast enough to move a boat. There are a few left. I have learned the skill in throwing them—I once cut the head of a deer clean off."

Tobanis took another look at Shem's dove. "That too may be of use some day. Now come and sit in my tent and hear what I have to say to Ismet's widow."

Shem sat down while Tobanis practiced the words. After reciting his speech a few times, he gave up and sat next to Shem. He opened the flap of the tent to admire Torak's demonstration of his throwing form to the other warriors.

Tobanis put his foot on the stool and tipped it back. "I do not like telling woman of their dead men."

"Does anyone?" asked Shem.

"No. I think not." Tobanis gazed out into the field. "I have chosen a new second."

"Who?" asked Shem.

"Torak." Tobanis didn't wait for a reply. "I trust your words are true about this Sethite. If we can stand back further to throw our spears, we will cut them down like seedlings. And he is a big man, so many will follow his lead."

Shem noticed Torak was experimenting with a wing-like stone to help balance his spear to throw better. "I think you have chosen well."

A day later Shem and Tobanis returned from observing the canyon walls. They wanted to glean every advantage when they attack the Oka. When they returned to camp, Torak approached Tobanis and bowed.

"Yes, Torak. What have you?"

"I must tell you of a new part of my weapon. It helps me throw the spear with ease and with a whisper. I strapped this wing stone to the middle of my board and the buzzing stopped. It also helps me to aim better. I see that there are young pines around us. We can cut and make many spears from them.

Tobanis looked intently at big man. "Torak, I want you to be my second during the next battle. Train my spear throwers as you have trained yourself. When we face our enemies, I think we will fare much better than the last time."

"You cannot ask that. You do not know me."

"I know enough."

Torak looked at Shem for a response, but Shem only smiled. "As you wish, Master."

"As my second, you must learn of my ways to fight the enemy. You must learn quickly as I have no other to depend on. If you cannot do that, then I will look for another." Tobanis thumped his chest twice to indicate he was done with the conversation.

Torak did the same. "I will not fail you."

"Good. I hate defeat." Tobanis turned back and whispered to Shem. "Do not think he will be my second so easily. I will watch and test him."

"That is wise. He should bring us good fortune."

Tobanis became somber. "I sense we will need good fortune against our enemy.

* * *

The next morning, the mist rolled across the ground, cloaking the Oka tribe's camp. As in the last several days, when the sun burned off the mist, both sides of the battle stood ready. Tobanis looked over to where he buried his second and took a deep breath. Each of the spear throwers only had time to make rudimentary adjustments to their weapons and cut a few new darts. Tobanis ordered his men to launch spear darts—Torak in front.

The spear throwers leaned back and pointed their left hand up at an angle. They held their right hand behind them, with their spear resting in its holder. Simultaneously, they launched their weapons high into the air. The enemy stood lazily at 120 paces, expecting the spears to land well in front of them. Many Oka even pointed accusing fingers and laughed at their folly. With amazing power from the new devices, most of the spears flew well within the third and fourth lines of men.

The effect was devastating. Out of 200 spears thrown, a majority of them hit a target. Many Oka fell instantly. Others were injured with punctures, some merely shocked with disbelief. Running away meant certain death.

Agul kept Balkar, Ilkin, and fifty others with him and ordered the rest of the men to charge. Tobanis' spear throwers only had one more long distant dart left. As the Oka men bolted across the land, the Tuballite spear throwers launched a second volley. Again, a large number of yellow haired brutes fell.

With the Oka warriors now exposed, Tobanis gave the order to swarm around the men and defeat them. "Good fight! Great death!" he shouted. The Tuballite spear throwers dropped back to allow the shielded warriors to effectively spread out and surround the Oka. They squeezed the enemy from three sides and used their long spears and shields to press in and kill.

Seeing his men decimated, Agul retreated with Balkar and the remaining warriors northward out of the narrow canyon.

Tobanis let out a loud whooping war cry. The Tuballite forces gave chase after Agul and his men for several hours, through thick brambles and trees. The Oka knew the forest well but the Tuballite force was close and not willing to abandon its pursuit so easily.

The sun was low in the sky when Agul and his men reached a high walled and gated village. The walls, made of fir trees as wide as a man's reach, topped forty feet. The heavy gate opened to let the Oka in. As the gates began closing, Tobanis sprinted forward with his hundreds of forces beside him—too late. The heavy doors closed with a thud and the surge of men slowed against it like an expiring wave. It closed to leave the Tuballites skidding to a halt outside and pondering how to break in.

Tobanis leaned against his spear, breathing heavily. He looked up at the large curved tusks that were mounted on the front of the gate doors and frowned "This is not an Oka village. It is Ugric. The old battles were fought here." He held up his arm and signaled his men to push back out of range of the spear throwers assigned to the top of the wall.

Shem stood next to him, panting heavily. "But we have almost five hundred men. We can ram the gate and capture our enemy."

Tobanis shook his head. "Not this time. We will rest and attack another day."

Shem unlatched and flung his dove. It flew in an angry arc at the gate, where it stuck deep. "We chased them so far and now you wish to leave? What do you fear from these old battles?"

Tobanis was not impressed. "It is not the Oka or the Ugric I fear. It is the behemoth."

* * *

After the gates closed, Agul and his men collapsed to the ground inside the fortress. Balkar strode over and with one hand picked Ilkin up by the neck. He pushed the Tuballite against the wall next to the main gate. "Many of my men died because of you!"

Ilkin cringed. "Why am I to blame? I did not know they could throw a spear that far. No one knew!"

"Balkar!" yelled Agul. "We did not feed this Tuballite two seasons just to end his life!"

With fury in his eyes, Balkar threw Ilkin down and faked a sword stabbing. "I should run this through your bones! But Agul thinks you still have use in you. You can thank your gods that you will live to see another day." He turned to a local Ugric warrior. "Take him away before I cut off his head."

The Ugric willingly obliged. He dragged Ilkin across the courtyard by his collar.

Balkar walked back to Agul, who stood gazing as if he could see through the gate. "What do we do now, master?"

Agul stroked his grey beard. "We have need of the Ugric."

Several other men approached. They resembled the Oka, but wore long hairy garments. The leader of the village strode up to Agul. He was just as tall as Agul, yet leaner with thinner cheekbones and bright green eyes.

The man's face was stern. "Why are you here, Agul?"

"We had no choice, Bek."

"To unite with us, you must bring more men than this!" he blurted out with scorn. "There are hundreds of Tuballite warriors out there. We cannot hold them back. I have less than a hundred men in this village."

Agul let out a deep breath. "I lost over two hundred men, Bek. The Tuballites have new tricks. I will need your beasts to defeat them."

"Why should I bother to help you? You do nothing for us but complain and ask for help. It does not matter. We do not have them here. They are up at our most high leader's village, to the north."

"Then the Tuballites will conquer all of us. They have more soldiers than what you see outside the gates. More than we have lice." Agul breathed deeply to calm himself.

Bek paced the grounds, walked to the gate to peer through a knot hole, then paced some more. He became even more agitated. "By the gods, why did I agree to help you? I should strike you down right now for bringing them here!"

Agul grinned, revealing a missing front tooth. He spread his arms in a welcome. "But we are kin."

Bek stepped close and pointed his finger. "The marriage of my niece and your nephew does not mean we are kin." Bek walked over to the gate and peeked out to see that the Tuballite's had gathered in a circle around their leader. He pounded the wall. "You leave me no choice. I will send a runner to ask for the beasts. But it will be for our defense. I cannot bring them here just to satisfy your hunger to kill these men."

Agul crossed his arms. "If the Tuballites unite with any more tribes, we will soon become their slaves. We must not only defend ourselves, we must conquer them fully."

Bek looked away from the hole and back at Agul. "I wish we could start the day again!" He walked to the water barrel and threw some water on his face. After he cooled down, he faced Agul once more. "I did not think I would say this, but you are right. They must be stopped. The Tuballites move farther north every season."

Agul grinned. "Now you talk well, my friend. I tire of living in the shadow of the southern pigs."

Bek gave Agul a hard stare. "Do not think we do this for you, Agul. You are our friend because they too are our enemy. Let us hope my great leader agrees with me."

* * *

The Tuballite warriors had formed a protective circle around their leaders, shields locked. A few scouts ran the outside perimeter of the village to find any weaknesses. The scouts surmised that it was impossible to penetrate without large battering rams.

Shem pulled Tobanis aside. "What is this behemoth you speak of?"

"It is the big beast that stops for no one…not even fifty men."

Shem surveyed the area with a skeptical eye. "I see no beasts. If they had them, we would have been attacked. I say we push down the gates and kill them now!"

Tobanis almost mocked Shem. "You are still young, Shem. Do not let your young mouth run your mind. We have done well and lost few men. To do what you ask would cost us far too many warriors."

"We did not follow them this far to let them go. We must finish off the Oka leaders or they will again return."

Torak overheard the conversation and stepped in. "Shem, give respect to Tobanis. He is your elder and leads us."

Tobanis nodded to Torak. "Torak speaks rightly. Learn from him. I say we go back to the last village and build a new wall. We have no quarrel against the Ugric."

Shem thought of shouting: *You asked me to advise you! Why am I here?* Instead he spoke as he was taught—with respect. "I fear this was our moment. But you must do as you see fit."

Tobanis softened. "Shem, it does not matter if I see fit to attack. I have consent from Bulla to fight the Oka and rid them from our northern villages, not the Ugric tribesmen. I will send word to Bulla about our dealings and it will be his to say if we fight. Come, let us take our warriors back to the last village. We will rebuild a defensive wall at the canyon's narrow point."

Chapter 5
Attack in the Marshes

Another week had passed and there was no word from the high leader of the Ugric. Ilkin saw Agul pacing atop the the gated walls of the Ugric village. His most recent concern was that the Tuballites had blocked the exit at the canyon to the south.

Ilkin made his way up to Agul's position when an Ugric runner returned to Bek's outpost with the reply from the high leader. He reported that four of the behemoths and a hundred men might be spared to repel the Tuballites. Snow had been scarcer in the last few decades and the beasts live best where the air is cool. Fewer and fewer of the beasts had survived the warming years. It seemed apparent that the Ugrics' power with the big beasts was coming to an end.

Chief Agul waved the runner off. "They *might* come? Without the behemoths, we will be helpless against the Tuballites," he muttered.

Ilkin cautiously came to his side. "Be paitent, Agul."

Agul put his hairy face in front of Ilkin. "You were the son of the grand elder. What do you know that will help us stop the Tuballites?"

Ilkin remained calm. "Your bonding with the Ugric was wise. It will aid in our victory. But it seems that the beasts you want are not as plentiful as you wish."

"I do not care about the scarce behemoth herds. I want to conquer the city of Tuball and become the new grand elder."

Ilkin squinted at Agul. *Is he to challenge me for ruling the city? It does not matter. Let him have it. I wish to rule over more than the city.* Ilkin bowed his head to the chief and let him spout his frustration.

As Agul was fretting the complications of war, a distant bellowing broke his concentration. From within the distant woods, the tops of trees shook.

Breaking through the forest edge were four large, thick shaggy creatures, with their trainers on top. Each beast had a high, peaked knoblike head and high shoulder hump. They bore curved tusks, wide at the sides, tips virtually touching. At the shoulder, the behemoths stood at least three times that of a man. Agul and his tribesmen trembled in awe.

As the animals lumbered on thick powerful legs, their long snouts rose up to smell what was before them. Agul confidently ordered his men ready for battle.

Ilkin smelled victory

* * *

Tobanis had blocked the canyon exit into the village, using tree poles as levers to dislodge huge boulders from above. The largest boulders were laid on the base with smaller rocks stacked on top. With the stone barrier completed, Tobanis commanded most of his men to stand guard on the top of it. Torak formed a secondary protective line of men above the canyon walls for a high point offensive.

Not long after the barrier was complete, Tobanis saw what he had dreaded. Oka warriors bravely walked beside a hundred Ugric warriors with four behemoths pounding the ground with each step.

Unfortunately for the northern allied tribes, even with enormous animals, it was a standstill. If they tried to enter the canyon and break down the heavy wall, they would be met with a heavy spear assault from above. On the other hand, the Tuballites wouldn't dare come down from the canyon walls and confront the enemy with such massive animals at their beckoning. Therefore, each side waited for the other to attack.

After two hours of waiting, the impetuous Balkar ordered fifty Oka men to navigate around the canyon to the east where they could be concealed.

Shem caught a glimpse of the maneuver and informed Tobanis. "If they get behind us, they can pick us off like insects."

Tobanis agreed. "Take a hundred men and climb down the cliff to cut them off from the side. I will have Torak lead another hundred from behind to pinch them in the middle."

Shem waved the company of men to follow him.

Bura stepped forward. "May I go with Shem, Master Tobanis?" Tobanis tipped his head for him to go and Bura bolted.

* * *

Balkar caught sight of Torak's men descending to the rear of the south canyon. With his sneak attack foiled, he abandoned the idea of climbing and retreated. On his return to the main body of his compatriots, Shem's troops cut off Balkar from the safety of the behemoths. With the north and south blocked, the fastest of the Tuballites threw their spears and picked off the fleeing Oka one by one. Balkar had no choice but to move his men east to the deadly wetlands. Many had entered, few had returned. It wouldn't be an easy escape, but it was the only escape.

With his warriors dropping in numbers, Balkar thought of a way to save himself—the sinking sand. It was the most deadly, yet most direct route. The seasoned warrior knew his men would follow their leader obediently into any place he ordered. And if it meant that they had to sacrifice themselves in order to kill a hundred of the Tuballites, so be it.

Within the hour, the Oka and his men entered the quick sand. Balkar cursed the mucky mess, yet urged his men forward. He and his men were able to pull on extended roots and grasses to pass the most dangerous areas, but they were still waist deep in the deadly mire.

The fastest of the Tuballites were right at the heels of the Oka and had followed straight into the sinking sand without thinking. Before they knew what was happening, the lead man was up to his neck in the quicksand.

Balkar grinned smugly. "I am pleased we are not alone in our peril."

"Shem!" yelled Bura, slipping down to his chest. "We are sinking! Stay back!"

"Shem? The great and mighty Shem?" Balkar whispered to himself.

One Oka warrior, up to his chin in the deadly ooze, discovered a small fallen tree and grabbed onto it. The others then took hold of each other and, like a chain, pulled themselves to the other side. Catching their breath from the ordeal, the Oka laid back to wipe sand from their faces. Now half of the original fifty lay safely on a bank of reeds and bushes.

Balkar got up on the opposing side to wait—taunting the Tuballites to come. "One of you is Shem?" he shouted, wiping the sandy slime from his face. "Call on your God to save you and walk through the wet sand!" he mocked. His companions laughed with him.

* * *

Shem stood on dry ground and watched with pity as his men struggled and ultimately sank below the surface. He threw a hemp rope out and retrieved one of the Tuballite warriors. Those warriors who followed the Oka too quickly and too far out died a slow death. Bura was the only one who successfully used a breast type stroke to pull himself back to shore.

Shem scanned the outer banks of the marsh for a way around to finish off the Oka. "Bura, we can reach them from up there—"

Before he could finish his sentence, the earth pounded beneath them. A willow grove just to their north on the edge of the marsh broke open—the behemoths! Four large beasts bellowed and thundered their way toward the Tuballites. Ugric trainers sat atop the animals, urging the beasts forward. Behind was a column of Ugric soldiers on foot. The Tuballite warriors froze in place. The warriors looked toward Shem for direction. Again the beasts gave a trumpeting bellow.

Shem glanced at Balkar and his men, who grinned gleefully from the other side of the pit. With the big beasts towering before them, pursuing Balkar would be fruitless. There were no other options. Shem gave the order to retreat to the south. Torak still had not arrived. In many ways Shem hoped, for their own safety, they would not.

The Tuballites did the only thing they could do, sprint as quickly as possible until they find a place of safety. The slower men dropped their shields to gain some speed, but it wasn't enough and soon they were trampled and killed. Retreating at a full run wasn't enough, so Shem made a quick decision to divide up his men—half to the south and half to the west.

Balkar and his men made their way around the sand and followed behind the behemoths for the counterattack. The Ugric also split up, two beasts west, the other two beasts and the rest of the enemy followed Shem's men. The thunderous pounding beasts did their damage and Tuballite warriors dwindled in numbers. The cries from slower men sounded off as they were being crunched underfoot by the behemoths. As huge feet pounded just steps behind Bura and three others, they somehow found strength to pick up their pace.

Shem glanced to his left and spotted soft ground with reeds and rushes. "To the marshes!" he shouted.

The men turned abruptly and hopped along stable clumps into the marshy land. One of the behemoths overshot the turn and kept going. The other beast navigated the turn, but sank its front feet deep into the soggy soil. The animal gave a loud bellow, tipped over, and landed a hand's width from Shem. A gigantic splash threw Shem across the marsh into a mucky mess. Bura ran and helped Shem out and over to semi-solid land.

Bura looked down at Shem's dove. The sharp edges had split halfway out of its harness. "You could have cut your leg off with that thing."

Shem patted it. "It brings good fortune. Hurry, the beast will be upon us."

A mud-caked Shem and the others wasted no time escaping from marshy to firm ground. The big animal lay helpless in the muck, struggling to get upright. The Ugric warriors had to use the other animal to help pull its friend out of the muck.

Shem ducked behind a stand of bushes to catch his breath and listen. An argument broke out between the Ugric and the Oka warriors. The Ugric beast masters checked over their animals once on solid ground, but they told Balkar they would not continue the chase. As the trainers remounted the behemoths, Balkar ridiculed the Ugric for their weakness. The Ugric gave some choice words in return. Shem could only hear bits of their debate. But after some heated words, the behemoths and a dozen Ugric foot soldiers began to leave.

Balkar shouted at his retreating comrades. "Shem, the evil one, may still be alive! We must kill him now!"

Balkar then challenged the Ugrics' courage, but it was no use. They ignored his insults and kept moving. Balkar cursed them, and then gruffly ordered his nineteen men follow and kill Shem and the four others.

Shem remembered seeing Balkar in the great battle at the city. He was a fierce and unrelenting man with wild eyes. He carried the same claws and animal teeth around his neck he had worn at the great city battle. Balkar had more men, but he hoped Torak would soon arrive with reinforcements. Shem and his men crept stealthily into the marshy woods, putting distance between themselves and the Oka. The next encounter worked to Shem's favor. He and his men found a group of bushes on each side of the trail. As the Oka passed through, they launched a crossfire of spears into the enemy, killing four and forcing the rest to retreat.

Instead of being deterred, Balkar was enraged—a rage he fed upon. Once Balkar had regrouped to a safe position, he sent several of his fastest four men in a wide arc to cut off Shem and the others. The surprise caused two of the Tuballites in front to be clubbed to death. Shem, Bura, and another warrior were still able to pierce two Oka in their bellies and escape into the marshy woods. They didn't look back. They knew the best way was to go back west where Torak and the others were, but Balkar was now using a wide line of men to cut them off from such an idea. As the sun dropped from on high, they found a rare rock formation to hide and rest. The Tuballite warrior stayed back to guard their rear.

Bura stared down at the three-winged weapon hung on Shem's side. "Why do you drag that iron thing with you?"

Shem glanced down and patted it. He breathed heavily. "It has served me well. But you are right...I must let it go so I can move faster." *Where is Torak? He should be here soon.* It dawned on Shem that death was now an option. *God has always rescued me from difficult situations before.* But something sour sat in his stomach.

He pulled out the red jewel from around his neck and admired its beauty. "I never told Kara of my love for her before I left for battle," whispered Shem, leaning against a willow.

Bura bent over with his hands on his knees. "I told her for you, Shem."

Shem smiled through a muddy face. "Many thanks, Bura."

Bura pulled some bark from a scraggly tree and started sucking on it. "This is not poisonous is it?"

"If you get sick, then I will know it is safe for me to eat," said Shem, coyly. Shem handed him and the other man some dried dirty berries from his pouch. "Why did you want to stay and fight alongside me, Bura? You were with Tobanis."

"I could see it no other way. I wanted to fight with my soon-to-be brother...even if he chooses to be stupid at times."

Shem raised an eyebrow. "Should I thank you for such loyalty?"

A crackling sounded in the bushes behind them. The Tuballite crept back. "Someone is coming," he whispered.

Shem stuffed the necklace inside his shirt and tipped his head to his men to leave quietly. The three started with a methodical trot, just enough to stay ahead of the enemy. Shem spotted two Oka in front—one looked like Balkar. Shem wasted no time and let go of his dove. It flew in a beautiful arc over the brush. He hoped that killing the leader would force the others to leave. Balkar saw the three-bladed weapon just in time, and tripped backward to save himself. The scout to his side wasn't so fortunate. The blades completely sliced off his head.

With Balkar on the ground, Shem ached to finish him off, but three other Oka appeared out of nowhere. Shem took his men obliquely through the woods, half wondering how he would find his way back. He kicked himself for losing the dove, and yet it was a relief to get rid of excess weight off his body. They were left with Shem's knife, the Tuballite warriors spear, and two of Bura's spear-thrower darts...not much to defeat the Oka with.

Shem and Bura picked up speed, now running side by side, like they had done in the mountains several seasons earlier. The Tuballite had slowed many paces behind.

"We will be caught if he does not hurry," whispered Bura.

"We could find a place to rest," suggested Shem, between pacing breaths.

"No. We must not rest. We will be killed for certain."

"Our chances are better with three of us." Shem pointed to a small hill. "There! A safe viewpoint to see our enemy and rest. We will go there."

Shem glanced over his shoulder. The Tuballite had vanished. Bura and Shem slowed, then retraced their steps cautiously. They stopped when they heard a groan. From behind cover they and saw the Tuballite a stone's throw behind, kneeling on the ground, grasping a spear tip that protruded through his stomach. He shook his head from side to side.

"He is telling us to go," whispered Bura."

Shem caught sight of yellow hair in the bushes nearby. "They expect us to return so they can kill us too," replied Shem.

Shem smiled at the injured Tuballite, gave a worthy nod, then skulked away with Bura. They began a sprint to the east. Never-ending sloshing footsteps kept them from resting. Sleep was not possible, catnaps weren't even an option. The Oka were on the move even through the dark of night. It seemed that Balkar had a mission and he would not stop before it was accomplished. Shem's will was fading. *Is it a mistake to think we could outrun the Oka?*

At night, they slept little. But to their credit, in the early morning light, Bura was able to turn and launch his remaining darts from his spear-throwing device. He killed an enemy warrior and maimed another. Yet with only small respites available, Bura and Shem had no time to make more darts.

The Oka had been whittled down to eleven, but Shem knew that with one knife left in his belt, it would be futile to try and kill all of them. Knowing that the Oka would stop at nothing to kill them, it was time to try something new and desperate.

"Bura, it is time we separate," whispered Shem, while they jogged.

Bura wiped his forehead of sweat and kept his steps in rhythm with Shem's. "What do you mean, separate?"

"The Oka do not tire and, by God, I do not know how they follow us at night. We may live if we are not together. I wish you to go south. I will head east. It is my hope that they will follow me and you will escape. Once you are safe, go west and find Torak."

Bura stared at Shem. "They will surely kill you if I leave."

"They will surely kill me if you do not leave. I know God will show me another way."

"I will not leave you, Shem."

Shem stopped behind some bushes, his lungs heaving. With a grimace, Bura set his hands on his waist and arched his back. Shem put his hands on Bura's shoulders and faced him.

"You must leave. You must leave now!" he whispered harshly, then looked back to see if the Oka were near. "I do not have time to explain, but we are in more danger together. I do not trust your gods. I only trust mine. Go! I will give the Oka something to think on. Run!"

Shem pushed Bura in the direction he should go and wished him good fortune. Shem covered Bura's footsteps and then proceeded forward to a knoll that overlooked the area behind him. He looked down to see about seven men approaching. He slid a dried date into his mouth and skulked north to a firm section of ground on the side that the men could not see. Shem slid down the knoll and headed for the last man in line. Shem stabbed the man in the neck and darted away.

* * *

Balkar moved steadfastly forward, following the footprints of Shem and Bura. The scout ahead of Balkar suddenly stopped. "Master, Balkar."

"What is it?"

"We are following one man, not two."

As Balkar bent down to examine the ground when a warrior at the end of line cried out. Balkar made his way back in time to see the warrior on his knees holding his neck. The man was his sister's husband. He stared at Balkar, dropped his hands to his side revealing a cut with blood spilling out profusely. He keeled over face down.

"Sethite dog!" Balkar yelled into the bushes. "I swear by the gods, this is the last man you shall get! You four, go back and find where the other man left the trail. Kill him before the sun sleeps! Go!". He panted heavily then swallowed. "The rest of you come with me. This man must be Shem. I feel it. If we do not bring him down before the sun sleeps again, it may be too late."

* * *

Bura angled off to the southwest, hoping to gain some ground. A pain in his side turned into a splitting jab. When Bura thought he was far enough away from his trackers, he stopped to rest. He bent down, spread away leaves from the water surface so he could drink. After one gulp, he heard the Oka warriors splashing through the marshes not far from him. He groaned, then pushed forward until he climbed upon a dry clump of reeds to rest again. Several leaches had attached themselves to him and he plucked them off for a quick snack.

Bura had just eaten the last leach when a handful of angry Oka warriors spotted him. They huffed through the water toward him. Beyond was a swamp with even deeper waters. Swimming was now his only option. Bura dove forward, glided away from the reeds, and began a freestyle swim through pond scum. The water was refreshingly cool against his overheated body. After about a few hundred strokes, he turned around and treaded water. To his amazement, the Oka weren't following. They clumsily clung together on the little patch of reeds he had just left.

"Ha!" he splashed a hand in the water at them. "You cannot swim! Come and fight me now…if you are brave enough! Ha!"

One of the men dove in the water and dog paddled several stokes before turning back. Bura knew he had the advantage. He started swimming southwest. Behind him he heard Oka curses, but the insults quieted the farther he swam. The swamp cleared in color and of scum and opened up into a larger expanse where there were waves. *How far can I go? I cannot go back. The evil ones will be there to kill me. Forward... forward. But it will be dark soon. Where will I sleep? Sleep?*

Bura swam onward.

* * *

Shem had spent an exorbitant amount of energy distracting the Oka, and hoped it would allow Bura to escape. With the loss of his reserve strength, panic crept in. *How am I to rid myself of six madmen who will never stop trying to kill me? I will never make it. I must make it...Kara.* He crossed large areas in the trees to avoid making tracks, but he couldn't shake the Oka. *God, where are you now?* Discouraged, alone, he had to move on.

Eventually, the muck began to give way to dry ground indicating that Shem had left the marshes behind. As the sun was setting, Shem's steps were now solid and steady, and he couldn't hear the sounds of the Oka. He made for a ridge and climbed slowly upward several hundred feet. At the top of the ridge, heart pounding, legs burning, his head felt ready to explode He fell down face first to rest and wait, grateful for an excellent view of the enemy's approach. Shem's eyelids dropped a few times and he almost fell asleep, but jerked himself awake at the thought of the killers.

Soon six Oka warriors came out of a woody patch and spotted Shem's footprints. They didn't hesitate to start their climb up the cliff. Shem hid himself at the top behind a fallen tree, but kept watch. When they were halfway up, Shem crawled over to a large boulder and jostled the stone slowly to the edge with a dried branch as a lever. The boulder slid and creaked over the cliff's edge. It bounced erratically down the hillside. The men looked up, but not in time. The rock glanced off one, knocking him senseless. Another was in its path. It crushed him to death. Shem began to hope he could survive.

He peeked over the edge and counted the men. *Three men still climbing, one man dead, one man badly hurt. But where is the sixth man?* Shem heard the crack of a stick behind him and turned around. Before he had time to react, a large club came down on his head and all went black.

* * *

Balkar and his men climbed to the top to meet up with their comrade. They walked over to Shem's limp body then stopped to catch their breath. Balkar kicked at his legs to see if there was life.

One of the men stabbed a deer antler into Shem's torso. "Curse this one to the depths of the earth! He has been nothing but a blight in our life!" Another man took his club out and swung it down on Shem's leg—*crack!*

The others nervously poked at him with their spears, still cautious of him. "Is this the man named Shem?" asked one of the men.

An angry man, who had lost his cousin by Shem's hand, pulled out an obsidian blade from his waist belt. "Let me cut off his finger to prove his death to Agul!"

The eerie cry of a wolf sounded out somewhere in the nearby trees.

"Wait!" Balkar gazed around at the hills. "The gods speak." More wolves howled.

One of the Oka warriors pointed to the woods. "Master Balkar. Look."

Balkar turned white. "By the gods!"

Balkar and his men shot off the cliff top and scrambled down the hillside as fast as their legs could take them. Moments later the howls of the wolves turned to yelps.

* * *

It was too late for Torak. The big man led a hundred warriors down the backside of the canyon to cut off Balkar's men, but no one was there. The behemoths bellowed from beyond. Torak ordered his warriors to move at a careful jog around the mountain base. Distant cries of men and the behemoth's trumpeting continued. All he could do was follow, catch up, and hope that somehow he could manage a successful battle against the beasts. One of Shem's men had escaped and ran into Torak's legion, out of breath and shaking uncontrollably.

"Where is the enemy?" asked Torak. Without a word, the man pointed behind him, his other hand clutching his heart. Torak led his men forward to a large boulder. He peeked around it to see two huge behemoths and several Ugric soldiers kicking stones and talking with one another. After a moment of debate, the Ugric turned around and walked slowly north. When Torak was sure the enemy had gone, he and the soldiers silently worked their way east. On the way, they walked around crushed and dismembered bodies.

"Search the dead and tell me if you see Shem's body," Torak ordered.

After the soldiers looked over the bodies, it was decided that Shem was not among them. A scout returned to the main group and pointed out tracks of many men heading east into the marshes.

Torak knelt down by his scouts and touched the ground. "Several Oka warriors are giving chase to a few Tuballite soldiers. I want you two to run ahead. Return when you find something. The mist will make it hard to follow the enemy, but we must defeat the Oka before they kill Shem and his men."

After a day of tracking, the scouts returned with nothing to show for it. Torak kicked a tree stump.

"You have failed me," Torak said, calmly, through gritted teeth. "Children could do better."

"There is too much water on the ground to find the foot tracks," pleaded one of the scouts.

"If we do not move quickly, it will be too late."

Torak looked over his men. He took thirty of the fittest and the fastest men with him and told the others to stay put until he was satisfied he had found signs of their trail. Torak spotted breaks in the marshy vegetation that led to a few bodies of both Oka and Tuballites. He found more bodies, signs that fierce skirmishes were waged throughout the marshes. He found an Oka warrior, recently killed by a cut to the throat.

Torak smiled. "We are on the right path."

With the good news in hand, Torak and his elite men took off at a run. They ran through the brush and eventually broke into a clearing. Ahead was a cliff, and at the base was a crushed Oka body under a boulder. Two other Oka lay alive, barely breathing. Torak and his men left them there. They sprinted to the cliff and started to climb.

At the top of the cliff, crows and seagulls cawed and squawked over small pieces of meat. No body, only blood and hair and bits of red meat splattered across the ground. Torak shooed them away and stood back to analyze what had happened. He spotted something glittering in the setting sun. It was a necklace with a red stone. He tucked the gem into his pocket. Torak had his men search the area, but when nothing turned up ordered them back to the outpost. He had been too late to save Shem.

Chapter 6
Designing the Ark

Noah held out the three foot long replica of the ark as if it were a masterpiece. In reality, it looked more like a wooden house on a barrel shaped dugout. Technically, the dimensions of the little boat were exactly reduced from the specifications he received in a vivid dream many years earlier, but practical application was another matter. Standing at the river bank, Noah lowered the model into the water and gave it a gentle push. He released the boat with an attached piece of twine so as not to lose it in the river's current.

He challenged the model. "Let see what you have for me."

Noah walked along the shore, keeping watch over the boat as it moved grandly out from the shallows, across the water, then downstream. The model came upon some ripples and rode safely up and over them as hoped. He smiled at the prospect of a secure ride for the building of a larger vessel. Then, without warning, a cross current turned the boat sideways. As quickly as it had started its journey, it rolled over broadside and took in water.

Noah slumped at his misfortune and reeled in the boat back before it completely went under.

Noah shook out the water from the small boat and looked to the sky. "Was I wrong in how I built this? No, it was a perfect measure. This should not have happened. Do I lack in faith somehow?"

He trudged back to his home, resenting the project more and more with every step. Noah's annoyance climaxed as he reached his work bench. He slammed the model down and glared at it. "I am not a boat builder! Is there not someone else to do this?"

His wife Naamah was picking out pieces of kindling from a box near the fire. She startled from the noise in the workroom. "Did you ask me something, Husband?"

Noah calmed himself. "No. I am talking to myself, woman."

Naamah frowned. "I do not like the way you said *woman*." She shook her head and walked away mumbling, "You and your silly toys."

Noah stared at the model but he didn't know how to fix it. He left the room and went up the mountain. There he sulked till long after time for the evening meal. He devoted hours to prayer for an answer to his frustration, but nothing came. The most difficult part of following God's direction was not knowing how or when to do that which he knew was true.

* * *

Days later, Noah and his niece Lily were using a lever to roll logs for construction of a smoke house. She was a few years younger than Ham. Oh how he wished she could work like Ham. Noah spotted two strangers at the house and gave her a rest. He went down to investigate and found out Naamah had invited them in for the midday meal. They sat on the dirt floor to eat and promised they would like to trade for the meat. The strangers were going east and would return on the same route.

The oldest of the men had a long, bushy, black beard and sturdy arms. He stood and addressed the patriarch. "Noah, I have heard of you and your people. I am Memar and this is my son, Sabira."

The son had strong arms like his father, wavy brown head of hair, and a short beard.

Noah extended a hand toward a low bench. "Please sit over here to finish your food."

They sat down on the bench. Noah leaned his shoulder against the wall. Still preoccupied with the day's work, he found nothing to say.

After an uncomfortable moment of quiet, Memar washed down some venison with goat's milk and looked up to Noah. "You are a Sethite, yes?" he asked.

"Yes, I am," replied Noah.

"Do you know that your people have reached the city of Tuball?"

Noah perked up. "Not until now. How are they?"

"They are well. The city is caring for them."

"Those are good words." Noah sat down near them. "I suspect you hear these things from your wanderings. Can you tell me more?"

"We are from the Kura River over the mountains toward the great city. The messages we receive are crude," said Memar. "I had heard that some died in the evil wild fire two seasons ago, but most fared well."

"Yes I remember that fire. Did you hear if my kin lives? Tabas is my brother. Ham and Shem are my sons."

"Shem?" He thought for a moment, and then smacked his forehead. "Yes, yes! The young leader. My son Sabira has met him. He was one of the men who went to the temple for a great honor.

The spirit master walked with Shem and your elders. I do not know of the others."

Noah's body relaxed. "That is very good to hear. So my wife tells me you wish to trade with us. What is it you wish from us?"

"Enough meat to see us to the next village. We have Anbar coins and some tools as trade. No doubt they will be of much use to you."

"What tools do you have?"

"We are boat builders and use tools that can carve wood."

Noah's face glowed. "You are boat builders?"

"Yes."

Noah stood up. "I will be back—do not leave." The two men looked at each other, shrugged, then continued eating. Noah bowed and scurried off.

Soon Noah returned with his model of the ark. He set it down on the floor in front of the men. "What do you think of this boat?"

Memar set down his bowl and picked up the wooden model. "It is a nice piece of work…for a start."

Noah started to gesture with his hands about what had happened with his model. "I pushed this boat in the water to see if it could float, but at the first ripple in the river it turned over."

Memar looked lengthwise at the vessel. "Yes, I see why."

Noah waited anxiously for an explanation.

Memar set the boat down. "It has much top to it, like a little house, and it is very round on the bottom. It needs to stay steady in rough water. It would help to widen the craft."

"But I cannot widen the boat, the Creator would not—I mean I have created this design with a special purpose for a larger one. Is there not another way to make this boat stay steady?"

The son picked up the boat and conferred with his father. "He could put a rib along the bottom, to keep it up right. Maybe add a point to the bow to keep it riding straight."

"Bow?" asked Noah.

"The front of the boat," Sabira informed.

Noah stroked his long silver beard. "Hmm, a point on the front and a rib below. Could you draw me what this rib looks like?"

Sabira took his finger and drew a picture on the dusty dirt floor of a boat with a line extending under the length of the craft.

"Yes, I can see how those things would help. Many thanks, my new friends."

"Does that mean you will trade with us?" asked Memar.

"How could I not?"

The two men got up, wiped their hands on their clothes and shook wrists with Noah. It was getting late, so Noah let them stay the night. They thanked Naamah for the food and went to sleep on the straw in the storage hut.

The next morning, Noah thanked them for their advice on the boat and told Naamah to give them all the meat they need for their trip. Memar left a metal chisel as a gesture of kindness, then he and his son moved on to the western villages.

Noah was excited to try out his new friends' techniques. He spent all morning trimming and squaring a small sapling to fit along the bottom of the boat as they had diagrammed. Next he chiseled two squared pieces—one for the front of the bow, and one for the bottom—then tacked the wooden accessories into place with small wooden pins. He set it down near the fire hearth that night and went to sleep imagining how it would float.

In the morning, Noah didn't even wait to eat. He picked up the model and took it down to the river. Again he tied a small string to it and let it out into the current as he had done before. It started out smoothly and then entered the little rapids. It didn't wobble nearly as much and it kept fairly straight. But after a few pitches up and down, the little ark started to wobble more and more. Before Noah knew it, the model was on its side. Noah puckered his lips tightly and yanked the boat to shore.

He looked up to the sky. "If you have any ideas, my door is open to you."

Once it was ashore he kicked the boat. It landed ten feet away and the roof flew off the main deck. Noah reached down and picked up the craft, about to throw it in the river, but stopped short. Noah felt a little silly, because he had added almost a full house on the craft, and he remembered that his dream said it was to be a window just above the main deck. He took the boat back to the shop and cut down the upper structure into a short wall with a narrow window holding up the roof. He hoped this would be his final test.

Back at the river, he let the boat out again; his confidence was waning from the previous failures. After letting the boat move through the little rapids without incident, Noah could feel himself breathe again. Once it passed through more moderate rapids, his spirits picked up. Finally, the boat moved around eddies and rocks, and even rougher waters, without tipping over. Noah did a little dance on the grass to celebrate. When the waters of the rivers calmed, he reeled in the craft and plucked it out. He stuck the boat under his arm and started his walk back home.

Grinning from ear to ear, he looked to the sky. "I knew we could do it."

* * *

Weeks later, Noah was much more confident of the project and ready to draw up a rough list of wood required for the structure. After computing the material list, he leaned back in his chair and picked up the tally. Noah squinted at it from arm's length and breathed a deep sigh. *This is a forest of wood. How am I to get all this?*

Just then, Naamah called out, "Noah, the boat men are back."

Noah dropped his tally and trotted out to retrieve his boat. When he returned to the main house, the men were handing Naamah a woven rug to cover the dirt floor. They exchanged pleasantries. Noah explained to them his proud accomplishment with the model. The men approved of his success, and their wisdom to guide him.

Noah now felt bold enough to reveal more to them. "What if I were to make a boat as long as you could throw a stone?"

The men laughed heartily.

Memar slapped Noah's back. "You are joking with us, Noah. I do not know what you would need a boat that size for."

"I am not deceiving you. I have a purpose."

Memar eyed Noah a moment then looked down at the model. "What you have done will work well for a small boat, but a large one would break apart at the first rough water. The stress of rough seas grows many times greater when the boat gets bigger. A boat that size would not be able to float in the Aras River, maybe the Black Sea."

Noah could not reveal too much of his plans. "You are correct. I plan to float it in large waters. What should I do?"

Memar squinted and looked up in thought. He squeezed his chin. "You may need strong ribbing to strengthen the sides, maybe even bronze or iron."

"Oh, yes. Iron and bronze. I have seen them. They are made from special stones."

Memar pointed to the little boat. "You see here, wooden sides on a bigger boat would break with any strong wave. We have used iron on large boats for the city, when joints are in need of support. Yet, for a boat of even greater size, it would take a lifetime to get enough metal. Why do you need a boat that big, Noah? Even if you build it here, you would never be able to move it to the Black Sea." The men began to laugh some more.

Noah did not crack a smile. "This bronze or iron is the only way?" asked Noah.

Their laughter subsided. "Yes, the same metal that the city uses for tools. It is very heavy and will give weight to the base of the boat, and to the ribs to add strength.

"Would I get this from the city of Tuball?" asked Noah.

"Unless you can make your own."

Noah looked down at the ground. "I do not know how to find and make iron or bronze." *My God, my God. I will do what you ask of me. If it is to build the boat to the measurements you have given me, I will. But if this man's words are true about metal stones—I know nothing of making it—and I do not wish to build this boat just to see us all drown.*

Memar's eyes brightened. "The Seva tribe has many stones that are used to make metal. Maybe you can talk with them."

Naamah came in and served some goat stew to the men. They dug in with wooden spoons. Noah looked out the window at the goat pen and another thought crossed his mind.

"My friends, I have noticed that my gate that opens to the goat pen is very wide. When I had mounted a piece of wood from the lower corner to the upper corner it holds the gate up. Would that work on the walls of the boat? And would it decrease the need for metal?"

The men thought for a moment. "Very clever, Noah," praised Memar. "We have never needed such a method on our boats, for they are too small. It would take up some space, but on your boat it may do well."

"I know nothing of boat building. Are you willing to show me how to construct such a thing? I am willing to pay you well. I have many goats and sheep to sell."

The two men had rarely eaten either lamb or goat and were enjoying their meal. They glanced at each other and simply said, "Yes."

Noah began to relax. "I and my kin will do the bulk of the labor. Your help will be for the skill of design."

Memar thought for a moment. "Very well, Noah, but first you must give us the measures by which we must build so we can return to our village and explain this bold plan of yours to our clan. We will add that which needs to be strengthened and subtract that which can be done without." Memar wiped his mouth with his sleeve and burped. "Your woman cooks well."

"Will you need some payment?" asked Noah.

"No—on our return. We must earn something for it."

Noah reached out to clasp their wrists. "God has brought you to me," he said, shaking them with excitement.

Memar set his plate on the table. He shook his finger in the air. "There is something else, Noah. I think I know of a man who can help you with the wood. His name is Vard...very skilled with timbers and such. He has a son that works with metals in the city, too. You may get two badgers with one spear."

Noah brightened up. "I know that name. It is the father of Kara. She is to wed my son."

Memar nodded. "Aah! Then it is as it should be. We will walk back through the Seva tribe and talk with Vard, and when I get home I will talk with my clan. We will return to show you the ways of boat building. If Vard agrees, I will bring him along as well.

Noah handed them the measures written on a parchment. The two men departed with a lamb pie from Naamah and waved goodbye. Noah watched as the men shrank into the horizon. He breathed a sigh of relief. For a second, Noah thought that they may take the idea themselves and never return. He was sure that was an idea from the devil and put it out of his mind. *All will be well*, he thought. *And when my sons return to help build the boat, it will be much better*

Chapter 7
News from Bura

Bura swam west along the shore, followed by the four Oka warriors. He cursed his luck and realized he would have to go south until he was out of sight. Soon it would be dark and any hope to be on dry land was bleak. He arms and legs were more than sore, his mind weak and searching. Streamline strokes became flapping splashes. His eyes grew weary, aching for a bit of sleep. Finally, the open waters calmed down and Bura turned over to float on his back. Rest at last! He looked upward to take in the brilliant stars contrasted against the black night.

On summer nights Bura used to swim with his best friend Pashi. They would lie on their backs and point to the lights that looked like animals. They would sip the sweet water of Lake Sevan as they floated. Bura was dreadfully thirsty and wished he could do that now, but he dare not drink from the salty sea. Nevertheless, he was thankful that he had a moment of peace and began to relax. Bura's eyes started to close, but startled him. *I must stay awake. I do not want to slip into the depths of this sea, so Mot will have himself another servant. Kara, Itsu, Father, and Mother would never know what happened to me.*

"Stay awake! I must stay awake!" Bura shouted to the stars. The sound carried across the water. Then all was calm, all was quiet. His mind drifted. "Father! Mother! Have I told you about my life in the city? I met Istu—you know—your other son." He chuckled. "I know *I* am the important one. Now that he has taught me the art of iron making, I can fashion my weapon *and* use it in battle…"

Bura rambled on about silly and useless things, talking to himself, desperately trying to stay conscious. He languished in the water, shivering on his back through the dark.

At dawn, rays of light pierced the fog. "Ah! The sun's precious heat! Thank the gods!"

With the early sunshine at his back, Bura turned over and started an overhand stroke. He was invigorated by the new day, another chance. When the sun was high, Bura took a break from swimming and treaded water He wiped his eyes to get a better view ahead. A wind stirred the waves. Land appeared a fair distance away…he wondered if he could make it. He had not eaten anything of substance in two days and his internal reserves were waning. He mustered up determined stroke after determined stroke and plowed into the water with a mission…land.

The moments dragged into hours. His arms ached from the endless movement. The waves pounded against him, over and over. He stopped to look at the shore ahead. *I am no further than before*! He was fighting against the wind and current, keeping virtually in the same spot in the sea. *Should I swim back and be killed by the Oka?* Bura wouldn't look behind. He kept to the west and pushed harder against the waves.

Bura's arms and legs began to cramp. "Aaaaa! Noooo!" He inhaled some water and coughed it up. He was completely exhausted. "Anat!" he called to the heavens. "I love your beauty but need your strength!" He took in more water. "Please, help!" Bura splashed and splashed erratically, torturing himself to stay afloat. He reached to the sky, but with little strength left sank below the waves. Bura succumbed to the depths of the sea, but something grabbed his hand and pulled him upward. It was Anat with a halo surrounding her shadowed face. She was strong and determined, hair of brown tied up on her head. He was glad it was Anat to take him to the other world and not Mot. Bura couldn't speak—he closed his eyes—it was time to leave his old life.

* * *

The young woman flipped her long, brown, braided hair to the side and, with muscled arms, worked to pull in her load. She bent over to grab onto the man's belt so as to haul him aboard. But his dead wet weight was too much for her. Her seal-skin shirt and trousers stretched to the brink of tearing.

"This is a big one, Father," groaned the fisherman's daughter.

"Is it a sturgeon?" asked the wiry, cynical fisherman. He kicked a pile of rope aside to get to the front of the boat.

She laughed. "No, a man."

"A man? This far out?"

"Yes. Help me with him. He is heavy."

She and her father tugged on Bura until they pulled him into the reed pontoon boat. They tossed him down next to a pile of the white fish known as *kutum*. When he landed on his stomach, water forced itself out from his lungs. Bura let out a groan. His eyes opened a slit. The young woman leaned her ear down to hear him.

"He has a breath," she said with hope in her voice.

"Then he may live." The fisherman scanned the surrounding water. "Why would a man swim this far out from shore?"

The woman brushed back Bura's hair. "We will ask him when he wakes fully." She picked up a cloth and wiped Bura's face. His eyes wandered in a dream state.

The fisherman was confounded. "It makes no sense." He shook his head and looked at the fine catch of fish in the boat. "He takes the space of many kutum. Now we *must* return to the village."

"Yes, Father."

"We cannot rightly throw him back into the sea, can we?" he grumbled.

"No, Father. We cannot do that." She chuckled.

The fisherman threw up his hands. "Well, stop gaping at the man and help me with the wings, Daughter."

The young woman set Bura's head on a fat fish, then took hold of the reed cordage attached to sparrow wing-shaped sails. The sails were hung on each side of a spar connected to the thick bundled, reed mast. She pulled on the cords attached to the end of the mast to let the morning breeze catch the sails. The fisherman steered the sailboat's rudder on a return course to the shore. When they reached land, the woman found some men from the fishing village to carry their unconscious visitor up to her father's home. She had them lay him on a bed of straw, remove his wet clothes, and cover him with a mountain goat fleece. Then she made a fire to warm him.

Her father came back with a fish in hand. She already had a healthy fire crackling in the pit. "Well, Daughter, we do not have the finest catch, but it will do. My brother will take the fish to sell." He peeked at the sleeping stranger then went to a table to fillet the fish. "That one will sleep a while."

"Will he die?" The young woman threw a large limb on the fire.

"Is he breathing?"

She listened to Bura's breathing. "Yes, he still breaths."

"Then he will live…and we must feed him," grumbled the fisherman. He chopped off the head of the fish with an obsidian cleaver.

* * *

Bura slowly opened his eyes to his new surroundings: bone-tipped spears, serrated harpoon tips, and nets hung along the wall.

58

He jolted to life. "Where am I?" He sprang up, suddenly aware he had no clothes on. Just as he stood up, the young fisherwoman came through the door with an arm load of wood. She caught sight of his naked body. She dropped the load of wood so she could cover her eyes. Bura grabbed a fleece and pulled it around himself.

The woman peeked through her fingers. "Are you covered?"

"Yes," said Bura. "Who are you? Where am I?"

She set her hands on her waist. "I am Kepenek and you are in my village. My father and I fished you out of the sea."

Bura sat down and realized his situation. "You were in my dreams. It was not Anat after all…it was you. I saw you before I went under the sea."

She bent down to pick up the wood. "I kept you from sinking. I thought it the right thing to do."

"Many thanks for your help."

Kepenek set the wood by the fire pit. "What is your name? And what were you doing in the sea so far from shore?"

"I am Bura, warrior from the city of Tuball." He rubbed his head. "I swam from the east marsh…for two suns."

"Two suns? That is too long. You must not be a very good warrior."

Bura defended himself. "The Oka were chasing me and—" Bura remembered his mission. "I must go back to Tuball. I must hurry!"

"You are too weak. You slept two days."

"Two days is enough rest. I need to go! Now where are my clothes?"

Kepenek walked over to where Bura's clothes had been drying by the fire, picked them up, then handed them to him. "Here."

"Again, many thanks," said Bura. He took the clothes with one hand and held the fleece around himself with the other. He stared at the clothes in his hand and frowned. "Did you undress me?"

Kepenek gave him a saucy smile. "What if I did?"

Bura glared. "Did you?"

"No, my cousins did. Ha!" She crossed her arms but did not leave.

Bura stared at her as she leaned against the wall. "Woman, will you let me be so I can cover myself? Or do you wish something else from me?" Bura did admire her strong form, and independence, but hoped she knew he was jesting.

Kepenek rolled her eyes. "Do not puff yourself up so." She turned and left the little house. Bura put on his clothes. She came back in as he was tightening his sandals. He stood up, took one step, then gazed straight ahead for a moment without moving. He saw light shrink into a fuzzy swirl of darkness. His legs quivered.

Kepenek chuckled. "You are going nowhere until you eat and drink something."

Bura reached out to hold onto something. "But I have…to…" He dropped to one knee. Kepenek caught his elbow and guided him to a wooden stump next to a chopping block.

"Sit. Have something to drink. Your head is light and your body is not well." Kepenek set some millet cakes on the wooden block and poured some water into a wooden cup.

Bura's sight came back, but his skin was pale. "Maybe a little water will do." He chomped down the cakes, then downed a cup full of water.

The fisherwoman refilled his water and scrounged around for some more food while he told her of his battle with the Oka. He explained to her that he had to get help to save Shem.

She listened. Kepenek offered another plan. "It is over a day's run to the city. I doubt you are well enough to walk that far. My father's fishing boat can take you the city before the sun is even high."

Bura calculated that rowing by hand or walking would take one or two days to get to the city, and even longer to get to Tobanis if he went north. He agreed with Kepenek, to the city by sailboat was a far better option. With food and drink in him, Bura gained new energy.

Kepenek convinced her father of Bura's urgency, and in the morning they were soon aboard the boat that would take them down the coast of the sea to the city. As they were skimming across the water, Kepenek maneuvered the crossbar on the mast to catch the wind while her father skillfully steered the vessel. Bura laid his body on the upturned prow of the boat and rested his chin on his hands. He felt the spray of the water on his face and the rays of the sun before him. He could also sense the eyes of Kepenek behind him. Bura was impressed with the speed of the craft and wished his clan by the lake had learned to master the sail.

After pulling on the sail cordage, Kepenek spoke up. "I saw warriors, as many as ants on a hill, pass our land at the last moon. Were you with them?" Bura turned and nodded. "Did you rid the villages of the Oka?" Bura nodded again. "Did you hear that, Father? This man helped save our village from the evil ones."

The fisherman gave Bura a sour glance and spat over the side of the boat. "Our village was spared the Oka's wrath, so he must have been of *some* use."

Bura hoped he had been of use, but he did not want to speak of his own deeds. He could only think of Shem's courage to sacrifice himself. Bura prayed to El that Shem would be spared his life until Bura could bring back help.

The wind was brisk and in their favor. In less than three hours they reached the stone wharf next to Tuball. Other larger vessels were tied up. Soldiers milled about.

Kepenek jumped out of the boat. Bura threw her a hemp rope to hold the vessel from drifting.

"Here you are, Bura," said Kepenek, extending her hand to the city walls. "May the gods be with you."

Bura bowed to the fisherman. "My thanks to you." He jumped out of the boat and looked into the young woman's inquisitive eyes. "Maybe I will see you again, Kepenek?"

"Maybe not." she said with an alluring smile.

Bura bowed to her, then walked back toward the eastern gate with its high walls. He heard Kepenek and her father as he walked.

"He is odd, that one," said the fisherman.

"He is not so odd. Did you know he swam for two days in the sea, Father?"

The fisherman spat. "Two days? He *is* an odd one."

* * *

Bura felt lightheaded as he neared the eastern gate. He stopped to catch his breath. He explained his situation with one of the two guards. They let him through the gate with an escort back to the barracks. After a debriefing with the warrior in charge, Bura was allowed to talk to his sister. He slowly climbed the steps up to Kara's home and pounded on the door. When Kara opened the door, her mouth hung open, eyes bulging.

"Brother, you are here." She stepped back. "Wait, why are you here, Bura? Have the other warriors returned? Are you hurt?" Kara looked him over.

Bura knew he was her favorite brother. "It is a scratch and bruise—nothing."

"Thanks the gods," she said. Then she slapped his arm. "You could have been killed. I heard of the great wild beasts crushing our men."

Bura did not want to scare her. "Yes. I saw them from afar." He tried not to look into her eyes or she would see the truth. "I had no choice, Sister. It was my duty as a warrior. I wanted to stay close to Shem."

"Shem!" she whispered loudly. "Is he here with you?"

Bura dropped his head. "No. He is not here. I left him in the marshlands."

"You left him where?"

"The marshlands above the North Sea. He told me to." Bura's face was pained as he looked into his sisters eyes. "Shem saved my life. He told me that we had to separate for greater chances. I do not know where he is. I came back for help. He said his God would save him."

Her face became stern. "Then where is he, Bura?"

"Shem's God is powerful, Kara. He will save Shem…Kara?"

Kara hardly heard a word. She had turned around and begun pacing the room, biting her fingernails. "I must go and find him."

"Sister! Do not act as a child. I almost did not survive. How would a woman?"

She turned and gave him an icy glare. "I am not thinking as a child. I am thinking as a wife! We are to be bonded! You abandoned him!"

"Kara, wait!" Bura wanted to tell her about the search party he was about to arrange.

* * *

Kara flew down the stairs, across the courtyard and through the market. She climbed the steps to the grand elder's outer chambers. In the foyer she was met and stopped by the elite citizen guards, in their long purple robes, holding brass-tipped spears. She explained the urgency and they relayed the message to Bulla.

Moments later, the guard escorted her from the foyer into Bulla's private room. Kara entered the room just as a messenger handed Bulla a small scroll and a leather pouch. The messenger bowed to Bulla and then left. Bulla set the scroll aside and opened the pouch to peek in. He cinched up the pouch and tucked it in his pocket. He picked up and unrolled the scroll, then read the message.

She strode over to him with purpose, but Bulla held up his hand as he read. Kara crossed her arms and fidgeted until he was finished. Bulla looked up from the paper, his face pale and sad. He rolled the scroll back up, set it on the table, and tipped his head for her to speak.

"We have to save Shem!" she blurted.

Bulla was calm. "From what, Kara?"

"Death!" She trotted to the window and pointed east. "He is out there right now, being chased by the Oka and wild beasts. If we do not go soon, he will die!" Bulla said nothing. "Did you not hear me?" she emphasized. "He will die?"

"I do not know if that is wise." His voice cracked.

"Grand Master Elder!" Kara stated with pompous condescension. "He saved your city from the Oka! If they find out who Shem is, he will die as surely as the sun is bright. You must do this!"

Bulla picked up a wooden chair and set it close to her. "Kara, please sit."

She shoved it aside and moved closer to Bulla. "No! We must go!"

Bulla turned around so as not to face her. "I, um, have just learned that Shem is dead." He spoke the words quickly.

Kara jolted back as if a spear had struck her. "What? No! We do not know that!"

Bulla turned back around and approached her. "Yes we do."

Kara backed up. "No. It is not true. My brother said he was alive."

Bulla lifted the pouch from his pocket and pulled out the garnet necklace. "A runner from Tobanis told me that they found this on a cliff and much blood was on the ground." Kara stepped forward, took it from his hand, and held it reverently. While she gazed at it, Bulla went to the table to get the scroll. He held it a moment, then gave it to her. "Tobanis found this in Shem's tent."

She took the scroll, unrolled it, and read:

My Kara Many thanks for the stone
I will keep it close to my heart as if you were here
And will guard it with my life
Much love to you   Shem

Kara stared at the words, looked back at the stone, then collapsed to the floor on her knees. With both items in hand, the evidence proved too much. Tears streamed down her cheeks. Bulla knelt down beside her and put his arm around her. Kara put her head on Bulla's shoulder and wept.

"I cannot live without him," sobbed Kara.

"He was my good friend. I will miss him," Bulla choked out.

Chapter 8
Ham Returns

Noah sat in the kitchen with Naamah, enjoying a lovely spring morning eating fried lamb and eggs. He could hear Lily outside pouring river water into the barrel next to the stone house. The other Sethite cousins had headed south over the mountains to help Japheth and Lamech with the fields. With but three workers, Noah was fortunate to adopt a rejected Seva family as members of the community and taught them how to herd animals. He ate his morning meal and listened to the bleating goats and sheep. He glanced out the window to see the animals move down the slope, and, squinting closer, noticed some figures by the river. He took his last bite and walked to the door.

Noah opened the door and shaded his eyes with his hand. "Lily, is there someone down by the river other than the Seva youths?"

Lily finished pouring water and brought her gaze toward the river. "It looks like Ham and another man."

Noah grinned. He took up his staff from the side of the house and trotted out to meet them. When he was closer, he saw them clearly. "Ham! Shinar!"

Ham ran to his father and they hugged one another. Noah turned and hugged Shinar as well. He put his arms around the younger men and escorted them back to the house. Lily set the water jug down and went inside to tell Naamah. While Lily set out some food, Naamah ran out to her son, kissed him, and cried over him. Ham rolled his eyes, but did not object. He released himself from his mother and stepped into the home where he plopped himself down on some goat skins.

Shinar followed behind and bowed to Lily. "Lily, it is very good to see you." He gave a second bashful bow, and then sat on a stool near Ham.

While Naamah found the honey for the bread, Noah found another stool to sit on. "How are the Sethites? How are Tabas, your sisters, and your brother Shem?" asked Noah. "Traders have told me that the city received them well."

Ham drank some goat's milk and held a hunk of bread in his hands. He glanced at Shinar who avoided eye contact, concentrating on eating the bread.

Ham feigned a smile. "The Sethite clans and my sisters are doing well. Tabas and Ozias lead our people. The Sethites stay outside the city, so as not to follow in the ways of the Cainites."

Noah smiled. "Very well done. I was worried for them. They have taken the right path. And your brother?"

Ham cleared his throat. "May I have some more milk?"

"Yes, here." Naamah filled up a ceramic cup. "If you wish it, I can have Lily get you some berry juice." She turned to Lily. "Lily, get some berries."

"I do not need the juice. This milk will do."

Naamah prodded Lily. "Niece, clean these plates and get some wood for the fire so we can cook some more lamb." Lily obediently stepped outside to get wood, but left the door open.

"So where were we?" said Noah. "What of your brother Shem?"

"Shem." Ham took a deep breath. "I will say this quickly. Shem may be dead."

Everyone was silent except for Lily, who dropped the plates outside when she heard the words. She came to the door with silent tears, trembling with disbelief.

Noah stood up. He thought he had heard wrong. "Did you say...dead?"

"Yes, Father." Ham kept his eyes averted.

"But that cannot be," replied Noah.

Ham spoke quickly. "He was fighting for the Tuballites in a battle with big yellow-haired men to the north. I was told that they killed him and the wolves ate his body."

"Why do you talk so plainly?" scolded Naamah. "He is your brother."

"I am just telling you what others have said, Mother. I do not know how to speak so it sounds good."

Noah stood erect, blinking slowly. "But that cannot be."

Ham fled to the door. He turned. "Do not think this has been easy for me. I have tried to blot it from my mind, but I could not." Ham brushed Lily aside and stormed away from the house and down the path.

Noah sat back down on the stool. "This was not to be."

Naamah held a cloth to her face and cried. Lily dashed over and buried her tear-streaked face into Naamah's shoulder. The two held each other and sobbed. Shinar stopped his eating and brushed the crumbs from his shirt. He glanced nervously around and slowly stood.

Shinar walked to the door. "I must talk with Ham."

No one but Noah noticed him leaving. Noah tailed Shinar on a path that led to a shade tree, where Ham sat stewing. Noah kept hidden and just within hearing range. Even with the horrid news, the patriarch had to learn what was on the mind of his youngest son.

Ham glanced up at Shinar, then threw a stone at a lone sheep. He missed. "I was not happy to bring back bad words of my great hero brother. I hope Father doesn't forget that I am his son, too."

"Their hearts are with you, Ham. You told them of your brother's death. Do you not expect them to mourn?" Ham said nothing. "Will you stay here or return to the city?"

"My mother will want me here more than ever. With Japheth tending to the land south for Grandfather and Shem dead, it is my duty to stay."

"Good. We will build a hut for ourselves. For I did not want to stay without you."

Ham grunted. "Not that Lily is here? She was all you spoke of on the trail home."

Shinar cracked a smile. "I do not know if she even thinks of me."

"Give her a season to warm up to you. She will come around."

Shinar looked back to the two stone houses with thatched roofs. "Maybe I should help her with the wood."

Ham shook his head. "Go," he said, throwing a pebble at Shinar. "Leave me to stew in my pain."

* * *

The bone-chilling news had penetrated the Sethite household deeply. It tore into their hearts. For the first couple days, Noah was distant and confused. All he had thought and knew was shattered. Wasn't Shem to be a part of the future? Could he doubt his God who has always been faithful? Maybe his visions should be doubted. *No, it is the devil! He is a liar! He roams the earth devouring our minds and hearts. It is the evil one who wants us to groan in pain. But I will not bend.*

Noah told no one of his thoughts. He continued his mission for the boat construction with his wife by his side. Ham was now home to assist in his father's work, Lily faithful in her duties to the family, and Shinar happy to be near Lily.

A week passed and Noah's countenance grew stronger, even cheerful. He even hummed a tune while he rolled a log into place for the support base of the future ship. Shinar and Ham had gone into the forest to fell a pine tree. Lily sat near him stripping maple splints for a basket she was going to weave. She set aside her work and sighed. Noah could see Lily had something on her mind, but waited for her to speak.

Lily picked up a gourd full of water and offered it to him. "Uncle Noah?"

Noah lifted the gourd to his lips. "Yes, Niece?" He took a big swig and set it down to continue his work.

"I have been watching you and see how you enjoy life so. After Shem's death, my belly went ill. Yet you have such a cheerful way about you. Did you not care for him, like I do?"

Noah backed off the lever and removed the rope from the log, then peered at her keen, slender face. "Maybe even more than you, Lily. Do you believe Shem is dead?"

"Yes, Uncle Noah. Ham told us so."

Noah crossed his arms. "Does that make it true?"

Her mouth pinched tight as she thought about it. "Do you doubt Ham?"

Noah shrugged. "No. I believe that Ham has told me what was told to him." He held out his forefinger. "But how do you know the truth?"

"I cannot know without seeing Shem's body."

"You are correct! We do not see the whole view, but someday we will. You can choose to believe he is dead or alive. Now…which thought is better to dwell upon?"

"That Shem is alive," she said with a breath of hope.

Noah touched her nose with his finger. "Me, too."

"My belly does not ache so much now. I will believe that way from now on, Uncle."

Noah smiled. "Very well. Let us keep this between the two of us, yes?"

"Yes, Uncle." Lily took a deep breath, grinned broadly, then went back to her work.

Noah beamed inside. Somehow, as hurtful as life can be, showing her a different perspective made it seem a little brighter.

Chapter 9
Warrior Angel

Shem opened his eyes to a howling wind slapping the thick threads of hair that curled across his face. The earth was far below him. His arms dangled loosely downward. He heard what sounded like a rug shaken, then glanced around to see that he was in the clutches of a mighty winged creature. The animal's bright, bronze talons dug deeply into his sides. Shem wanted to loosen the animal's painful grasp, but was more afraid of a fall far below. They flew over a wide valley and up to a cliff overlooking a wide expanse. At a precipice of a sheer rock cliff the winged creature released Shem onto a soft bed of grass. Shem rolled over and sat up to inspect his ribs. No blood.

Before he could speak, an eerie and powerful whisper echoed through his mind, like the sound of a rushing river flowing through a cave. "Shem, son of Noah!"

The creature stood erect, tucking its wings behind, its face radiating a brilliant light.

Shem covered his face with his hands and trembled. "Yes, Mighty one, Almighty God!" He knelt on the ground with his head down.

The creature's voice penetrated Shem's mind. "Stop! Do not worship me! I am a servant of the Holy One!"

Shem looked across the valley into the distant mountains. They glowed with vibrant hues—more than he had ever seen. He shook with fear inside, yet stayed as still as a stone. "Am I dead? Am I in the underworld?"

"No!" It spoke loudly with a thousand voices. "You are between worlds. Have no fear. I am here not to strike you down but to lift you up. I have come to warn you and tell you of your duty to the Holiest of Holies." The voice pierced his mind and yet soothed his soul.

Shem looked down at the bare talon feet on the creature, then up at its strong human-like form, and finally up to the face—a brilliant, heroic face, almost too bright to look upon. More than twice Shem's height, it took a few steps back, readjusted its wings, then stood erect with grace and majesty. It both terrified and compelled him.

A terrible shudder suddenly went through Shem. *How do I know you are not the evil one?*

The creature reared its head high and closed its eyes. Shem watched the creature stand erect and still like a statue. After a moment, it peered keenly at Shem. "I sense your doubt and have been given knowledge from the Cherubim. You will bear five sons: Elam, Asshur, Lud, Aram, and Arphaxad." The brilliance around the angel's head pulsed. "I have also been given knowledge of your father's deeds. Noah is to build a boat for your family. It was a command by the Creator to ensure human salvation."

Shem's memory shot back to Mt. Ararat, where he stood with Noah two seasons ago. *Father showed Ham and I a field of stone and said he was to build a great boat that was not to catch fish.* "That is why my father builds the boat?" he whispered to himself. Shem looked up. "Indeed you are from the Almighty God. Only He would know of my father's plans to build that boat." Shem carefully stood up and checked himself for wounds. "But did not the northern clans kill me?"

The creature's powerful whisper radiated into Shem's mind. "Your time has not yet come. You are safe in the realm between heaven and earth. Angels and demons battle in this domain. Man cannot last here and events move quickly, so I have little time to waste. Listen carefully to my words, Shem, son of Noah, for I must return to battle against the dark ones."

"Dark ones? Battle? Who are you?" Shem looked over the edge from the high place they stood on to see a deep unending gorge.

"I am an angel and do battle for the Most High. I live in the spirit world, not unlike your place of dreams. Your captors are no longer a concern. However, you must be aware of the daughters of man—for they will be corrupted. The days are on the edge of their reign."

Shem tried to cover his eyes to shade the brilliant light and see the angel. "I do not know of these 'daughters of man.' Who are they?"

"They are the ones who take the sons of God into themselves. Their offspring will turn your people away from the Holy one. It is I and others who must do battle in the hearts of men, and it is you who must do battle with the bodies of men."

"I do not understand."

The angel turned away as if to think. "I explain poorly, because I am a warrior, not a messenger. I happened to this place, so I stand here to provide aid. Do not try to understand." Its voice became stern. "You must stay strong. Do not lose sight of your father's teachings. He has been given a great honor to be used by the Holiest of Holies. Much is required of you, too, for you are of a righteous line of men; a child of the promise."

"May I ask when Kara and I will have our first son?"

"I sense your heart is burdened for her. Worry not for the things of the earth. There are greater tasks before you. Listen to those that see with their mind and soul, not their heart."

Far in the distance a roll of thunder beckoned to them. The angel turned to face the disturbance. Flashes of lightening spread vein-like along dark, forbidding, billowing clouds, rolling above a bright blue horizon. "A mighty wind is coming. I must leave for battle. Heed my words Shem, son of Noah, and obey the Creator." The winged creature moved forward to the edge of the cliff.

"Wait! Tell me more of this place and the heavens!" Shem implored.

"It is not for me to tell. I must go." The creature adjusted its wings ready for flight, stared far into the distance, then turned back to Shem. "When the days are calm and all is well, beware of the daughters of man! It follows the alliance with the Nephilim."

"Who are the Nephilim?"

"They cause fear in the hearts of men. You will know soon enough. I speak no more."

The creature reached out to Shem with gleaming hands, and cupped them around Shem's face. The angel's dark eyes pierced through the aura of his brightness and stared intently into Shem's mind. Heat from the creature's hands grew unbearable on Shem's cheeks, hotter and hotter until Shem thought his head would burst.

"Please, stop!" Shem cringed at the searing pain brought onto his head. "Please ... Aah! ... Stop!"

Shem passed out, then drifted into a dreamland of rushing wind and heat.

* * *

"Pull him out of the coals, I say!"

Shem's head went from unbearable heat to soothing cold. He envisioned himself falling down a waterfall, landing into and floating face down in the current of a stream. When Shem reached the bank of the stream, someone turned him over. He opened his eyes to see a fair-skinned woman hovering over him with a cool cloth.

Shem's eyes flickered.

"He is awake, Master," the woman said, dabbing his forehead. "His color is returning."

Shem lay flat on his back, beads of sweat rolling down his temples. He looked up to the sky to see patches of clouds in an early light. A cooking fire was a few feet away. But he could not see the people taking care of him.

"Good! Two days asleep like a stone is long enough," said a familiar voice. "How do you feel?" asked the man standing over him.

Shem moved his head carefully to observe his surroundings. His vision was blurry and his throat sore. "My head and the whole of my body aches. Did you say two days?" he asked in a raspy whisper.

"Yes, with the blow to your head, we thought you were dead, Shem. My woman sealed the wounds and put ointment on your face."

The man's voice was strangely familiar to Shem. "You know my name." Shem focused his eyes closer on the man. "Tatunna?"

"You remember me!"

Shem tried to twist around, but his side wounds kept him from doing so. "How could I not. Aah! Ow! My head, side, and leg!" He fell back down.

"As I said, you were hurt. Woman, give him more water."

The woman offered more water from an animal skin flask. Shem took in a good portion of it. He handed it back and struggled to sit up with the help of the woman. He reached out and grasped Tatunna's wrist. "Many thanks for your help, my friend," Shem whispered.

"Did you see the men who attacked me?"

"No," said Tatunna.

Shem waited a moment for a more elaborate answer, but nothing came. "It has been many moons. Where have you been, Tatunna?"

"I live with a tribe from the east of Tuball; south from this spot where you had your bad fall."

Shem smiled. "You will always be a poet."

Tatunna patted Shem's shoulder. "Well said, my friend."

Shem was gravely shaken, and drained. It seemed as though the flying creature was still nearby. "Where is the…angel?"

"Where is what, Shem?"

The presence of the creature was so vivid it was etched into Shem's memory. He knew it was not a dream, and convinced he had met a messenger from God. He wanted to explain about his encounter with the angel, but decided they would think him ill in his head too.

"If you speak of the northern tribesmen, they must have left you to die by the wolves. You truly had your God's blessing. For we had found you before all your blood leaked out."

"How did you find me?"

"We were walking on a trading route and something pulled inside me to come on this path. It was good that we found you, or you would be in the land beyond life. Now that you are awake we will take you back to our village…if you are strong enough."

Shem struggled to sit up and look around at the others. He saw several huge men almost twice his own height, each with a fresh wolf pelt around his shoulders. He gasped. His vision was still blurry but he knew this was real. "They are—giants!"

"They are my friends, Shem. They are called the Nephilim."

Chapter 10
The Nephilim

Shem's dizziness faded in and out. Tatunna waved for one of the Nephilim to pick him up. The big man's hands were the size of Shem's chest and lifted him as if he were a child. He moved in and out of dreams of angels and giants, while being carried along the trail. By the end of the day, they had reached the Nephilim village. Excitement bubbled throughout the community. Large women and children rushed up to Tatunna. Others chattered about Shem, the mighty one, in their midst. But Shem found it difficult to stay conscious. He eventually drifted off.

Shem awoke with a start in the arms of the giant carrying him into a house. He set Shem down to sit on the side of a bed. Shem's feet dangled above the floor.

Tatunna sat beside him. "Ah, I see you are awake again. You will be safe here among the Nephilim."

Shem shuddered at the mention of the Nephilim. It was the same word the angel had mentioned. He'd said that men would fear them, and he could see why. Five of the giants crowded in the room, all of them with a belly higher than the top of Shem's head. Only the woman was close to his height—a mere three hands width taller than Shem and Tatunna.

Shem scowled at the big men. "Leave me!" The large men bowed and left quietly. Shem dropped his head into his hands. It pounded like thunder. After a moment it subsided.

Tatunna squinted at Shem. "You do not need to shout at them."

Shem removed his hands from his head and looked up. "Did I shout?"

Tatunna's squint turned into a weak smile.

Shem swung his splinted leg a foot above the floor like a pendulum. "What are you doing on this side of the northern sea, Tatunna? With these big ones?"

"I am doing what I always do…spreading wisdom and knowledge to all who would like to hear."

Shem smiled at his old friend. "That is a swollen way of saying you get people to like you so they can take care of you."

Tatunna shook a finger. "You see through me too clearly, my friend. I do not know why, but they like to have me here. They would like to have you here, too, Shem. Rumor has it that your words are magic and your hands are the work of the heavens. No doubt from tales about the battle against the Oka in Tuball."

"I am sure you were the one to tell them the tales."

"Ha! See, your magic is at work again. Many would bow down to you if you let them."

Shem reached over and put his hand on Tatunna's shoulder. "I will not let them. Looking at the size of these people, they could not get down that low."

Tatunna chuckled. "That is true. I see your weak body does not stifle your humor. Do not let their size fool you, Shem. They fear you more than you do them. And they fear your God even more. It has been said that your God holds heaven and earth in his hands. I think many will follow your ways."

"Then let it be so. Now I must try to walk."

Before Tatunna could stop him, Shem slid off the high bed. He tried to stand, but felt dizzy. He twisted and dropped to the ground in a heap.

* * *

A day later, Shem awoke to the village healer tending to the large wound across the side of his head.

Shem jerked away. "Leave me! I do not need your help!"

Tatunna quickly came to Shem's side. "Shem, look at me. It is I, Tatunna, your friend."

Shem's eyes cleared. "Oh, Tatunna. Where did you go?"

The corners of Tatunna's lips dropped slightly. "I have not gone anywhere…but your mind has gone from here to there."

"What do you mean, Tatunna?"

"You have slept another day, and have talked strangely all the way."

"I feel fine. Do not worry for me."

Tatunna tapped his foot. "I will try not to, Shem. But for your own safety, you should let these people help you if you need something. You have a dented head, a stab wound, and a broken leg. You will take long to heal, my friend."

Shem relented. "You are right, Tatunna. But I must let Kara know where I am."

"That will have to wait. These people will not go to the city. They are shy and do not wish to make themselves known. I must leave now, to attend to other matters."

Shem grabbed Tatunna's arm. "No! Do not leave me with them."

"Worry not, worry not. I will stay. Depend less on me. The Nephilim are here to help you. Just call if you wish to go somewhere and they will carry you."

Shem looked up at the face of a bearded giant across the room and smiled squeamishly. The giant bowed his head respectfully. Shem adjusted himself on the straw bed.

Shem whispered to Tatunna. "Why would Bulla never mention these big people to me? They are not easy to hide."

Tatunna leaned close. "There have been many stories. Some tell of angels in heaven who came down to earth to lay with women who begot these giants. I do not know if it is true. The Tuballites know of and stay away from Ugric to the north. The Ugric know of and stay away from the Nephilim. And the Nephilim keep to themselves. So how was Bulla to know?" Tatunna chuckled. "When you return to the city, you will tell tall tales…very tall tales, I suspect."

Shem rolled his eyes. "So you say."

"I have not asked you of your uncle, Zakho. How is he? Does he have a woman?" Tatunna asked with genuine interest.

Shem put his hand over his face to still the emotion, but managed to choke out the words, "He is… dead. A big cat hurt him so bad, he could not heal." Shem then cried more than he should.

The cheerful poet's smile evaporated. "Calm yourself Shem."

"Why do I feel so sad? It has been two seasons ago."

"He was a good man. He helped me survive when…." Tatunna wiped a tear from his own eye. "I understand your pain, for I cannot trade again, with the wandering one that was more than a great man. He helped me out of filth and near death, and now he is gone while I still have breath."

Shem nodded. "He was a good uncle."

Tatunna smiled quickly. "Is it not right that I found you—to heal you? For it would not be right for me to lose the both of you." Tatunna stood up. "Now, you must rest, and so should I." Tatunna turned and walked out of the tall stone house.

The wounds to Shem's head, chest, and leg all needed time to heal. Later, Tatunna returned with a staff for Shem to lean on. Behind Tatunna was the chief of the village. The chief, like the others, was huge. He wore a simple soft feather pelt hat and animal pelts around his shoulders and waist. He was fascinated with the stories and mighty deeds that Shem had accomplished at Tuball and was honored to be his host. Shem leaned on his one good leg, bowed and, as soon as he did so, started to fall. Tatunna caught him and helped him into bed. They graciously left him alone to be cared for by Tatunna's woman and her healing herbs.

* * *

As the days passed, Shem's headaches came and went like the tide. Sitting idle made him restless. He was in his bed trying to occupy himself by twisting leather for a bolo, when he heard some laughter outside his window. He set down his work, dragged himself to a high stool next to the window, and climbed onto it. He rested his elbows on the sill and watched the life of the Nephilim.

Happiness dwelled in the village of giants. They were kind, milling about, eating, drinking, laughing, while tending to their work. It was odd to observe the young ones who were as tall as he.

Shem watched closely and was impressed at how gentle they were with one another. They seemed powerful, yet some of the older adults got breathless rather quickly after a spurt of running or strenuous work. Without warning, a tall young child stopped in front of the window.

"Hi," she said with a grin. The girl was as tall as Shem. "What is your name?"

"Greetings, I am Shem," replied Shem with a smile.

"I am Anna. How many years are you?" she asked.

"I am of twenty years."

"I am six."

Shem raised a brow. "You are a big child."

"What is twenty?"

Shem held his hands up, pulled them back and showed them again. "That many."

"Oh. You are small for an old one. Bye." She left as quickly as she came.

Shem puzzled over that. "Twenty is old?" He hopped over to the table, keeping his splinted leg from hitting the floor. He picked up some flatbread and a piece of pig meat, then hopped back to his bed.

Tatunna entered the room soon after with a jug of water. "Are you healing well, Shem?" He set the jug on the table.

"My side and leg hurt still, but my head has stopped striking me from the inside." Shem took a bite of the flatbread. He was about to take a bite of the meat when Tatunna took it away. Shem sat with an open mouth and a frown.

Tatunna smelled it and winced. "This is bad meat."

Shem took it back and smelled it. "I smell nothing." He looked at it closer, spotted some green color, and set it aside.

Tatunna pulled out a small onion from his pocket. "Can you smell this?" Shem took a deep sniff and shook his head. Tatunna scratched his chin. "You have lost your strength of smell."

Shem took a bite of flatbread. "Tatunna, a young girl said I was old at twenty. Why would she say that?"

"That may be true here, Shem. These people live to about thirty of years. They are big and powerful, but die quickly."

Shem swallowed. "Their lives *are* fleeting. Most Tuballites live at least twice that."

Tatunna spoke cautiously. "I have heard your people live even much longer. Very long. Is that true?"

Shem nodded. "Yes. Much longer if we do not get killed by spears or clubs."

Tatunna laughed, then put his hand on Shem's shoulder. "I know that you wish to get back to Tuball, but I suspect it will take a season before you will be able to walk."

Shem gasped. "Do not speak like that. I can make it by the next full moon."

"You are good only for wiping the floor. Let yourself heal. These are good people. They helped me when I needed it."

Shem conceded. "I will do as you say, Tatunna. But as soon as I can walk I will leave."

"I expect you to leave…when you fully mend."

Shem heard a scuffle outside and sat up to see Anna at the window. A boy, a head taller than her, was with her. The boy stood with his arms straight down. Through the window, Shem could only see his thin upper torso. Anna waved to Shem, then pointed to the boy.

"This is my brother, Nazar. He is nine years. He wanted to see you." The boy had a lanky body, with a head of dark-brown straight hair cut to his shoulders, a sharp nose and a jaw to match.

Shem held up his hand and waved it to the boy. "I am here, as always."

Anna giggled, but the boy just stared.

"What may I do for you?"

After a long pause, the girl giggled again, but the boy said nothing.

"Is your tongue stuck, Nazar?" Shem asked.

The boy shook his head. He pushed his sister. The two of them fell out of view.

"That boy was as tall as Torak," noted Shem.

"Children are curious, are they not?" said Tatunna.

Shem fell back on his bed. "I wish I knew how long I will have to stay."

"I will let you know when you are ready, Shem."

Shem sighed heavily. "As you say, *Master Healer*."

"I believe this house is too big for you. You will be moved to my house after the next sunrise." Tatunna patted Shem's shoulder, then left him to rest.

* * *

After Shem was moved to Tatunna's home, he began making sandals to occupy his time. It was soon after that the boy named Nazar again appeared in the window. At first, Shem tried to strike up a conversation with him. No luck. The boy just stared for a while. Then he left. He came back later in the day. This happened for several days in a row. After a while, Shem gave up. Sometimes he ignored the boy. Sometimes he would use him as a sounding board.

Days later, Shem finished his sandals and began to start a new bolo harness. Halfway through twisting the leather, he threw down the harness and picked up his walking stick. He hobbled to the door and ventured outside. Nazar soon appeared from out of nowhere.

Shem started down a dirt path. "Nazar, I am going to the water. You can come with me if you wish." He hobbled down to where the source of a stream bubbled up out of the ground. The boy followed close behind. Shem sat down and put his feet in the water. "Aaaah! That is the first clean water my feet have felt in a moon."

The boy was bold enough to sit close by. "When will you leave?"

Shem was startled to hear his voice. "So you speak!"

The boy continued as if they had spoken for years. "My mother and father died. My mother's sister cares for Anna and me."

Shem's joy abruptly turned into sympathy. "Are you sad?"

The boy picked up a stone and threw it in the bubbling water. "No. I cannot see their faces anymore."

"That is not important. The importance lies in how you remember them in your heart." They both sat still. Something gnawed at Shem's insides. "I take back part of what I said. Faces *are* important. Faces help remind us of who we love." He tried to view Kara in front of him…it was difficult.

Nazar looked out at the water a moment. "What does important mean?"

Shem chuckled. "Important means big and special."

"That is a good word. I want to be important."

They sat quietly, watching the meandering stream flow by. The sky was a hazy blue and a light wind blew across their faces. A big fish leaped out of the water a foot in the air and landed with a terrific splash.

While they sat on the bank, Anna came from behind. "There you are, Nazar."

Shem motioned with his hand. "Come, Anna. Sit with us." After she sat, Shem turned to Nazar. "Why did it take so long for you to speak with me?"

The boy shrugged.

Anna leaned over to Shem and whispered. "He does not speak to anyone."

Shem smiled lightly at Nazar. "You can speak. I heard you."

The boy said nothing. He threw a stone in the water.

Shem turned to Anna. "He spoke to *me*."

She giggled. "No he did not. He does not talk."

Shem glanced back at Nazar. He wondered if he had heard the boy or if his mind was playing tricks on him. Shem was having fewer headaches than before, but sometimes he still had strange visions and blackouts. Could this be one of those times? His mind drifted back to Tuball, where he assumed Kara waited for him with worry. *I must return soon.*

They threw stones in the water awhile and watched the sun move lower to the horizon.

Shem glanced at his companions. "It will be dark soon. We must get back."

When he propped himself up with the walking stick, the two Nephilim children sprang up and came along side to support him. As they started back toward the village, Anna chattered the whole way,

Nazar saying not a peep. After they arrived at Tatunna's home, Shem thanked the two tall ones for their assistance and entered the house.

Once inside, he spotted Tatunna preparing some soup. "Does it smell good?" asked Shem, kicking the door shut with his good leg.

Tatunna stirred the pot. "It needs more spices."

Shem took a seat on a stool. "Tatunna, would you be willing to bring news to my woman?"

"News?"

Shem set an elbow on the table and rested his head on his hand. "That I am alive and healing. I am sure she worries for me."

"It would take me two moons to get there and back. Would it not be better for you to heal and leave then?"

Shem rolled a wooden cup on the table with his free hand. "It may not take you that long to get there. There may be a shorter route between the seas…a bridge of land. I have seen some of it from the city."

Tatunna chuckled. "Many stories have been told of such a thing, but I doubt there is truth to bring."

"Could you try for me? My heart aches for Kara."

The poet added more spices to the soup. "Oh the pains of love, how they hurt so sweet. If it is so important, I will venture out to the shore and try to find this bridge of land. Will that do for you?"

Shem relaxed. "Many thanks."

Chapter 11
Farewell to a Hero

Kara paced her chambers. She ate little and her strength waned, yet lethargy didn't suppress her compulsion to kneel and pray to the gods. Bulla had made several attempts to see how she was coping with Shem's death, but she still wasn't willing to speak with him. Her brother Bura stayed with her and became a buffer between her and the outside world.

After a half moon, Bura confronted her. "Sister, you need to do some hard work. It will move your thoughts onward."

Kara leaned her elbows down on the stone opening and gazed out to the sea's horizon. "If your duty calls you, Brother, then tend to your work with the warriors," she said without inflection.

Bura crossed his arms. "You must know that I have told Bulla you are still ill. I have sent him away many times. Did you hear me? The *grand elder*! He will stop coming to the door altogether. Soon he will look up at your window from the street, just to see if you live. After that he will not care at all. Is that what you wish?"

"I cannot see him yet."

Bura sighed. "Bulla has confided to me that he promised Shem he would care for you. And yet he is helpless to fulfill the promise."

"Bulla need not do anything for me, Brother."

"Then tell him so."

"I cannot."

"He could make you leave here, if he wished it."

She glanced back. "But he would not."

"Agh! Women!" Bura strode away from her then turned around." Maybe you would be willing to talk to Itsu. Should I send for him?"

Kara shook her head. She stared out the window and across the sea. "No. I know he is our older brother, but he does not take the place of Father."

Bura let out a heavy sigh. "I have cared for you through your pain long enough, Sister. At least my warrior friends approve of my work." Bura picked up his traveling satchel and opened the door. "It is plain to see that you do not need me."

Kara ran to the door. She clasped his hand and kissed it. "Bura, do not be angry. You have been good to me." Her eyes welled with tears. "I do not deserve your kindness. Do not fault me. I will heal. You will see."

Bura gave a weak smile and patted her face. He freed his other hand from her grip, then closed the door behind him. Kara laid her palms on the door, squeezed her eyes, and took in a deep jerky sob. Time would heal her pain. Neither Bura's nor anyone else's advice would help. Maybe if she prayed harder to Anat or El, they would listen to her plea.

The death of Shem did not only affect Kara. She knew that it had affected the city people like a bitter winter breeze, especially the Sethite clans who knew him best. Shem had brought them from the verge of starvation into the city of Tuball where they could prosper. Some Sethites refused to believe he had died, but most had moved on with their new lives, accepting the fact that their champion was in a better place.

* * *

Time moved slowly for Kara. It was now the day of the summer equinox and still the gods had not removed her pain. In the late morning, she awoke to three knocks on her door. She stared at the stone ceiling, hoping whoever it was would go away. She had kept to herself for so many days that she was reluctant to see anyone. Food had regularly been left at her stoop, but never with a knock. At the second series of knocks, Kara got up and shuffled toward the entrance. Her knees were raw and sore from kneeling in prayer. She cracked opened the door to see a sophisticated woman in fine linen and jewelry, with painted eyes.

"Hello, Kara, my name is Almas."

"You know my name, Mistress?"

"Yes, I knew Shem."

Kara wasn't surprised. Shem knew many of the citizens. "What do you wish of me?"

"I was a good friend of Shem and heard of his fate. May I talk with you?"

Kara had not bathed in a week, her hair was like a rat's nest, and her slept-in clothing was strongly wrinkled. Seeing Almas with such beauty and smelling of rare perfume, Kara suddenly became aware of her own shortcomings. She hesitated to allow the woman in. Behind Almas, Bulla stood at the base of the steps, pretending not to notice her. It had been weeks, yet he still watched over her. Kara's curiosity overruled.

"Come in," said Kara. "I will make some tea."

Almas glided over to a window seat that overlooked the south sea. Kara returned with a cup of tea. For a long moment, there was an awkward silence. Then, Almas took the initiative, explaining how she grew up in the city. Kara, in turn, mentioned a few of her own experiences living in the Seva Mountains—how she nursed Shem back to health from a snow storm, how she felt warm at the thought of the days with Shem in the mountains. Kara suddenly remembered the present day and stopped mid-sentence.

Almas smiled with empathy. "Would you like to know about how I first met Shem?"

Kara wiped a tear from her eye. "Yes, Mistress."

"Shem was accused of bringing a bad omen to the city. No one wanted or cared for his view. It was only I who wanted to learn of his customs and background. So I convinced my husband to accept Shem into our home until the truth was learned. We found not a bad omen, but a blessing in him. During the battle against the Oka, Shem saved my injured husband. Now, whenever I see my husband's wounds, I do not see a disabled man, but the result of Shem's courage to save his life."

It was evident that Almas cared for Shem very much. They talked some more of family, culture, but most importantly, of friendships. Almas had offered Kara companionship, and Kara was grateful for her kindness, but she was still reticent to express the deep anguish that she had stored up. After their meeting, Kara led Almas to the door.

"I hope we will meet again," Almas said with a smile.

"As do I," replied Kara.

Almas walked gracefully down the stairs. She bowed to Bulla and moved on. He stood at the base of the stairs removing a sliver in his hand with a thin knife. He gave Almas a returning nod as she passed by.

Something stirred in Kara's heart. "Master Elder!" she called out.

Bulla jerked around as if someone jumped out suddenly from behind a wall. "Yes?"

"May I speak with you?"

Bulla sheathed his knife, then ran up the stairs to meet her at the top. He stood at attention before her, stiff and unprepared. "How may I be of service?"

Tears pooled in Kara's eyes. Here was the grand elder asking her, a lowly mountain woman, if he could serve her. "I know it was you who sent Almas to me."

"No, I—only mentioned it to Almas."

She rested the side of her face against his chest. She sobbed. Floodgates of tears, pent-up sorrow, and disappointment were finally released. Her body went limp, while her hands squeezed his military vest tightly. Bulla stroked her head. Then he picked her up and carried her inside. He found some goat skin fleeces and laid her down on them. Bulla stood and turned to leave.

"Please do not go," Kara asked, between shuddering breaths.

Bulla turned around and stood, statuesque. He clasped his hands behind the small of his back, like a good soldier waiting for his next order.

After Kara gained her composure, she wiped her eyes with her arm and moved her raw knees to the side. She sat in an awkward silence, twisting the hairs on the fleece. "Do you know why I did not receive you, Master Bulla?"

"You were angry that I sent Shem into battle?"

Kara shook her head. "No. Shem makes up his own mind. It was the pain of his death that has been too great for me to bear. When I see your face it reminds me of him. That is why I did not wish to see you. I know it was wrong to punish you in that way. You have been a truly good friend to Shem and me. I should be the one to be punished."

"I think you have punished yourself enough, Kara." Bulla walked to a table where small idols of her gods were lined up. He picked up the statue of Baal and set it back down. "I must tell you something. Do you know of the woman I was to be united to?"

"No. I always thought you were a warrior with no time for women."

Bulla chuckled. "Many have thought that." His face became somber. "Maral was her name. She was with my stepmother, Seleen, and my half brother, Ilkin. They were in a boat at sea when a terrible storm came out of the heavens. I was told that Ilkin saved his own life at the cost of Maral's." Bulla's voice became tight and bitter. "I still have not been able to forgive him of his misdeed, but it took many years to let go of my love for Maral. I cursed the gods and left the city, setting my anger upon anyone or any tribe that got in my way." Bulla turned around and squatted before her. His disposition softened. "I know how you feel about losing someone you love. It seems we have both lost great love. We have a common hurt now. Do we not?"

Kara nodded. "Yes, Master Bulla."

He raised her chin with a gentle hand. "With this in common, you do not have to be alone now."

She nodded again and looked into his eyes almost too long. She turned away. "Thank you."

Bulla cracked a small smile. "I promised Shem I would care for you. Anything you wish for will be granted." He stood to leave.

She grasped his hand, then let it go. "I will not shut myself away any more. I must see the day as new."

"That is a wise thing to do, Kara." Bulla gave a hint of a smile, bowed, then departed.

*　*　*

With the passing of days, Kara received Bulla regularly. He would check in on her and talked of how much good he saw in Shem and what he had done for the city. He convinced her to consider planning for a ceremony to commemorate Shem's heroic deeds. In the end, it was decided that a statue of him would be erected in the outer courtyard, so all visitors could appreciate him as a hero. By the next moon, and thanks to the detail provided by Kara to the stone master, a good likeness of Shem was completed and placed prominently for all to see. The process was a cleansing for her...a way to release some of his grip on her heart.

After the memorial, Bulla escorted Kara back to her abode and talked of the expansion of the city. Kara debated with him about how to care for and protect the people. She spoke of many ideas regarding political and cultural complications. Bulla mentioned his admiration for her ideas and promised to implement some of them.

In the following days, she was comfortable enough to give advice on how to integrate the Sethites with the Tuballites. Soon compromises were made in such a way that both cultures were in harmony. Bulla became a close friend and colleague.

At one point, Bulla had laid out a map of the future plans for the expansion of the land bridge separating the two seas. He stated how proud he was of the plan and felt there was nothing finer in the world.

After Bulla finished his speech, Kara pointed to a specific area on the map. "The master builders must remember to fill in this section of land or the people who build their homes on it will live on sinking ground."

Bulla dismissed her comments flippantly. "That is not needed."

"Yes it is," she replied. "Do not think just your ideas are the good ones, Bulla. This ground over here is weak, I tell you. I have walked the grounds!"

"How do you know that? The master builder has been working with stone all his life. And you are only a woman!"

"How dare you call me *only a woman*!" She swung her hand to hit him, but Bulla caught her arm.

He grinned. "Do you know you almost slapped the grand elder?"

The realization of her actions hit her. Her eyes got wide and she knelt down before him. "Forgive me, Master Bulla."

He picked her up. "I should be the sorry one, for making you as small as an animal." She tried to look away, but he took her hands and looked into her eyes. "Kara, you are worth more than half of my masters. You mind is keen and your heart is good. I do not know what I would do without you."

Kara blushed. "I…"

He let go of her hands quickly and turned back to the table to roll up the map. "I will take your suggestions to the masters and thinkers."

"Wait." She touched his arm and he stopped. He looked over his shoulder. "Thank you," she said keeping a hold on his arm.

He moved around to face her. She kept her eyes lowered. Bulla tossed away the map and reached up to hold her face in his hands. Kara started to bend down to pick up the map.

"Leave it."

Kara looked up into his powerful steady eyes. "But, Master." She couldn't find the words to say with him staring at her.

"You are not merely a woman, Kara. You are a woman of women."

She averted her eyes. "Please, don't."

Bulla gently clasped his hands around her cheeks before she could turn away. "Kara, we must not mourn the loss of Shem, but honor his victories. Are you not willing to do that?"

Kara nodded slowly. "Yes." She was now caught by his calm power.

"Do you know how much my heart aches for you to be near me?"

"Yes. You have been in my thoughts too," she replied, meekly. *Is it wrong of me to think of Bulla in this way?*

He grasped the small of her back and pulled her close. "Are you willing to take a new path away from Shem's?"

For once, she could see Bulla and not think of Shem. "Yes. I am."

"With me?" he whispered, their noses virtually touching.

Anat, is this your will that we risk our hearts for each other? He has lost his love and so have I. "Yes…with you."

His lips touched hers for the first time. She received his kiss and wrapped her arms tightly around him. They clung to one another and filled themselves with the moment, as if they might again lose another one so precious.

Chapter 12
The Grand Union

Shem hobbled to the edge of the village and looked far and wide for something new. The Nephilim roamed about at their rather slow and methodical pace. Here there was nothing like the rapid activity of the Tuballites in the city. Shem steered clear of the giants, even when they showed kindness to him. It had been weeks since Tatunna left for Tuball and Kara weighed heavy on his mind. Shem started back to the house for his evening meal when he spotted someone nearing the outskirts of the village. A few children ran down the dirt road and met up with the man. The group walked on each side of the man and supported his arms.

It was clear who the man was. "Tatunna! You have returned. Is all well? Did you get to the city?"

Tatunna laughed. "No, on both questions. I did not get to the city and I broke my leg tripping on a root of a tree." He stuck out his leg with a branch attached as a splint. "Now we are like brothers, you and I. Do not say I did not try." When he leaned up against a tree, the children let go of him to run and play.

Shem's shoulders slumped, but he tried to smile. "My thanks for your efforts, my friend. Now we are both stuck here for...too long."

"You are stuck here, I live my life here."

Shem put his arm around Tatunna and helped him back toward the house. Another irritating setback. Would he ever get back to Kara?

Tatunna glanced over at Shem with a twinkle in his eye. "Fret not. I did find the bridge of land you talked of."

* * *

With the summer in full swing, the northern villages of the Bundled Tribes were fortunate not to experience any fleeting attacks from the Oka. The clans of the villages cursed the Oka for burning their homes, and doubled their efforts to rebuild better than before. To ensure the ability to trade north, soldiers were assigned to rebuild the northern walled-in canyon with a strong protective gate that would still provide a protective buffer from invaders.

Tobanis vented to Torak as they walked. "The Oka and Ugric are biding their time…planning to gather enough forces and attack once more."

"What would you have us do, Master?"

Tobanis was first to his tent. He opened the flap. "I would have asked for a legion of men to defeat the northern tribes once and for all."

Torak entered the command tent behind Tobanis. The stout leader hovered over a map of where all the units of men were strategically placed across the region. A runner came in and handed Tobanis a parchment. Torak knew Tobanis could not read well.

Tobanis threw the parchment aside. "You have a voice. Speak!"

The runner held true great speed and great memory. He recited the message verbatim.

"From the Grand Elder of Tuball: My good friend and warrior, Tobanis. I have the honor of calling you back to the city to attend the bonding ceremony between Kara, from the mountains of Seva, and myself. Return to me before the next moon and stand beside me as my best. I wish that this be your choice. Your friend, Master Bulla."

The runner waited for a reply.

Tobanis absorbed the message for a moment. "How can I say no to the grand elder? Why would I say no? Tell Mater Bulla I will be there." He waved the runner away.

Torak had stood still as the message was announced. He blinked a few times and held his tongue.

Tobanis shook his head. "I thought he would never marry, after…his other woman died."

"Kara was to be bonded with Shem," Torak replied pensively.

"You know her?"

"I have met her. She is strong in mind and will."

Tobanis blew out some air. "She would have to be, to marry such a man as Bulla. And now that Shem is in the afterworld, and since Bulla is here…"

Torak said nothing. He did not indicate he was happy with the news.

Tobanis prodded. "Shem was a good man. Do you miss him? He was a bit wild, but very reliable."

"I did not know him that well. He was the nephew of my good friend Zakho. Now both are dead."

"You are kin. Good men die at bad times," replied Tobanis. He bent down and flattened the map out and pointed to it. "Look here. The villages are fit with strong men and good leaders. And your warning beacons atop the ridges here, here, and here, will allow us the time to respond to the Oka if they attack again."

Torak's gaze strayed to the side. "I failed to save him."

Tobanis gripped the side of Torak's strong arm and looked up to the big man. "You did your best to try and save Shem. You did honor to him. You did not fail in your duty."

Torak gritted his teeth. "But I did. And I do not like to fail."

"None of us do. Do not harbor the pain. Yes, it is a waste to see such a man as Shem die so early. But I know that in the afterworld his God will grant him great battles against evil. Stay planted within, my friend. Aside from Bulla, you are the best warrior I have ever fought beside. Will you come back with me to the city? I do not take well to bonding ceremonies."

"If you wish it," said Torak in a monotone.

Tobanis waved a finger. "I know. You have fought hard and need a woman to lie with. It does not cure, but it helps."

Torak almost smiled. "I thank you for your kindness, Master. But I only wish to see my people."

"Ah, the Sethites. Yes, I am sure there are women there, too."

Torak shook his head. "You have a good head for the field of battle, Tobanis. Please keep it there."

"If you say so, my friend. Come, let us make ready for a wedding. Yes?"

"I will do as you say, Master."

* * *

It was a beautiful summer day. Trade and commerce were suspended on this special day for the marriage of the grand elder. All the masters of the city had assembled at the steps of the pyramid and waited patiently. Kargi, the spirit master, limped up to the steps while conversing with other masters regarding the music and dance.

Bulla readied himself in his chambers with the help of Tobanis. Bulla strapped on his sandals and attached his finest leggings. He buckled his scabbard and sharp brilliant sword to his waist. Tobanis help him on with his gold breastplate then handed him his helmet.

Tobanis stood back to admire him. "Your golden armor indeed makes you appear worthy of the title of grand elder."

Bulla scrutinized himself in the polished silver plaque on the wall. "Gold will make anyone look fine." He turned to face Tobanis. "It is time, my friend, for you to stand with me at the sacred steps for my union. Go and I will be there soon. I must see Kara first."

Tobanis bowed and left the room. Bulla walked briskly out of his chambers and through the passages. Guards were positioned along the passage and up to Kara's quarters. He entered her room with his finest armor on, but the gold he wore was second to her splendor. Kara had been given his mother's finest white dress, laced with a red floral pattern. Around her neck, arms, and ankles, she wore gold nuggets within an array of colored jewels. Her new friend Almas had showed Kara how to paint her eyes to enhance her beauty. She stood holding the puzzle box her father had made. She polished it slowly with a cloth.

Bulla walked to Kara. He kissed the back of her head and breathed in her perfume. He walked around and tried to look into her eyes, but she didn't focus on him. "What is it, Kara? What is in the box?"

Kara set the box on a table and ran her hands along his gold armored chest plate. "Nothing." She paused, then looked up. "You know that if Shem were here….from all the other fine women in your city, why did you choose me?"

"Kara, solely *you* have been able to strengthen my mind and soften my heart. Other women want me for my position as grand elder, but you look through that veil. I did not think it would ever happen, but my memories of Maral have dimmed from my mind. I thought I would never remember her face again and believed that all love was lost from me." He breathed deeply. "Until I met you." Bulla stepped back and looked away toward the window. He didn't want to dwell on the past, but was compelled to bring it up. "I suspect that Shem is still fresh in your memories. But *we* are to be bonded today…at least that is what I wish. I hope it is what you wish too." He chuckled nervously. "Tell me if you have changed you mind. Your mother and father are waiting—and the people of the city—and many throughout the region of the Bundled Tribes."

"You are a very good man, Bulla. No other man could have a mind as strong or a heart so gentle." She walked to his side, grasped Bulla's muscled arm, leaned her head against his shoulder, and looked out across the sea.

Bulla weakened. "Shem was better for you."

Kara shook her head. "No. I know now he was not. He and I could never agree about our gods. He believes in the one invisible God and I believe in ours."

"His God is a powerful one. Many of my people now worship his God."

"Yes, but I could not leave El, or Anat, Baal, or even Mot. They are a part of me." She composed herself, then stood on her toes to give Bulla a kiss. "How could I *not* be happy with the grand elder as my own?"

Bulla's disposition brightened. He smiled, reached out to hold her cheeks, then kissed her smartly. "Let us go now and be done with this vanity."

Chapter 13
Meet the Nephilim

With the wedding behind them, Bulla and Kara relished their wedding night. Afterwards, they journeyed out to the extended lands west and south. The wedded couple chose to visit the lands of bundled clans and tribes. However, with more than twenty elite warriors as their escorts and fifteen servants to care for their needs, a traveling couple they weren't. They conducted a goodwill trip to collect ideas from the other tribes on issues of politics, trade, and security.

Upon their return to the city, Bulla dove back into issues of city development, applying ideas generated from the trip. One such idea was to broaden the few exploratory boats his cousin Ori commanded by turning them into a fleet of large transport vessels. Thus, he instructed Ori to commission the building of grand vessels for military and commercial use. Bulla himself had never ventured to the east and needed to know if the Ugric had spread their tentacles into the area. He had to know if peaceful tribes lived on the eastern side of the seas, so they may be enticed to be part of a great empire of the Bundled Tribes. But who would he send?

* * *

Torak had rested in Tuball for several weeks. He grew restless. The season was dry and difficult to grow crops. Road building on the strip of land between the seas became a new opportunity for work by which to survive. Sethite men found themselves laying stone instead of planting crops. Torak joined them. The masters of the city had predicted correctly that a solid roadway between the seas was possible. The northern route was solidly blocked by Ugric military supremacy, so this new road was vital for expansion.

Ozias, leader of the Sethites, patted Torak on the back. "It is good to see you with us, Cousin. Most warriors would stay at the city and play games."

Torak stood up from laying a stone. "I rest easier knowing the northern tribes have not attempted to breach the outpost."

"I do too. That great barrier you warriors built at the canyon would keep anyone back. So we are safe, yes?"

Torak wiped sweat from his forehead. "No. They may not choose the canyon. Their beasts cannot walk through the marshes. We must watch the northern mountain passes."

As they were speaking, a runner came up and thumped his own chest. "Master Torak?"

"Yes?" said Torak.

"The grand elder wishes to speak with you."

Torak left Ozias and talked with Bulla. He was offered the task to organize an expedition to prove the master's predictions that a land bridge from Tuball was connected to the east. Torak jumped at the opportunity. He had been idle too long and was relieved to be moving again.

Torak chose two hundred of his choicest men for the excursion—men he trusted in the battle at the marshes. Within two days, he and his men were on their journey. They marched over the flat stones laid down by Sethites for a day. Beyond the manmade road, the land was a mix of rock and dried, cracked mud. The land bridge had narrowed from two hundred feet wide at the city to less than half that, midway across. It was hoped that there would not be a dead end further to force them to return.

At dusk, Torak ordered his men to camp within a jumbled mess of boulders to reduce the amount of wind-driven sea spray. That evening, an unusual storm whipped up howling winds that tormented them through the night—penetrating their porous fortress with gusting whistles. Fires were difficult to start. Sleep was tolerable. The unspoken order was to cross to the other side quickly. Every man was in agreement. The next day they passed through a large stream cutting through the land from one sea to the other. A makeshift bridge got them over it. Torak worried the land bridge would end when solid ground narrowed to within ten feet between the seas, but his fears abated when it widened thereafter.

On the fourth day, Torak stepped onto the eastern mainland where the eastern mountains stood before them. He was relieved when his men found a healthy fresh water stream to fill their water jugs. Could the Ugric have villages on the eastern banks of the sea? Without further delay, Torak moved his men over the arid land.

At camp, a scout returned with uncertain news. He had spotted a large group of men encamped in a clearing over the next mountain. The scout had not gotten close enough for an exact count, but assumed there were about fifty Ugric warriors hemmed in by a secluded, woody basin. Torak estimated they could reach them before dark. He took the initiative and ordered his men to move out. With military efficiency, the men packed and were on their way at a fast trot.

The force of two hundred arrived near the enemy before sunset, sweating and out of breath from their four hour hike. Torak allowed his men to sleep, but without fire. They rested quietly, but the sounds of chants and shouts echoed throughout the night. In the morning, Torak took the best half of his men out of the woods, and left the others behind for security. He looked at the slope downward and saw the encampment of men blocked from escape by sheer rock walls. Torak hoped he would capture or kill all of the Ugric. They would pay for the death of Shem.

Torak waited for his men to be in place, then raised his spear above his head. He and his men gave a whooping cheer and strode out from the trees in a wide arc. They stopped but continued their shouts. The enemy immediately fled their tents and assembled in a line. Torak felt he had a comfortable advantage with his hundred on the high ground and the rest of his reinforcements in the woods. And yet he noticed that the Ugric men seemed different somehow.

The enemy wore head dresses and ornaments around their necks, wrists, and ankles. The northern tribesmen wore animal furs with few adornments. These warriors could be from another clan. Torak stood fast with his soldiers at a safe distance and tried to gauge the enemy's tactics. He closed his eyes. *God, I pray they do not have the behemoths in their midst. Grant us the victory over these men.*

A shout from the enemy stirred Torak from his thoughts. An opening in the long line of tribesmen appeared and a lone man stepped forward several paces. He had glittering wide bracelets and anklets with feathers, antler points strung on a necklace around his neck. His fur headdress glistened with gems. The other tribesmen closed ranks again and uttered an encouraging chant. The decorated warrior trotted rhythmically for several steps, then dropped to one knee. The warrior raised his arms with a spear in one hand and shouted out a defiant call. He quickly jumped up, took another step, and twirled around in a circle, pulling his arms inward for a rapid spin. He stopped and shouted again, his eyes fixed toward Torak's warriors.

Clearly, the enemy was taunting Torak's men to send out a warrior to fight. Torak did not want to waste any more time with a strongman challenge. He advised one of his best spear throwers to stand ready. After the decorated warrior finished a second dance, he stood upright, thrust out his chest, and planted his spear next to his side. The army behind him cheered.

Torak had had enough. He gave the signal to his subordinate, who promptly strode forward with his left arm pointed up at an angle and right arm ready with his spear resting in the launcher. As the northern warrior turned to grin back at his countrymen, a long straight dart was flung from the spear launcher up in a high arc that crossed over a hundred yards. When the enemy warrior turned around, the dart hit squarely into his bicep.

The soldier's mouth opened with shock. He stumbled back a step and instinctively grabbed at his impaled arm. He fell to his knees, groaning in pain. His kinsmen gasped at the unexpected spear launch and ran to surround the lone warrior.

Torak commanded his men to take a defensive stance and prepare for retaliation. Instead, the soldiers laid down their weapons and sat weeping. Torak was puzzled. The northern clans he knew of would not lay down weapons so easily. He ordered the rest of his men from the woods to flank both sides of the foreign warriors. They moved in a phalanx from opposite sides to surround the escape routes. With his men in place, Torak took a step forward, planted his spear, and raised his hands, empty of weapons, to indicate a peace talk.

An elder of the warriors walked through an opening in the enemy line toward Torak. As the man got closer, it was evident that he was much larger than previously thought—a big man! A giant!

When the elder was several paces away from the Tuballites, Torak inwardly gasped, but outwardly stood steady. Torak was as big as any of the northern clansmen, but this man—if he was one—was huge, more than twice Torak's height.

The giant had tears pouring down his cheeks and into his beard. "Why did you strike him?" asked the elder. His voice was deeper and more powerful than Torak's.

Torak held back his fear and took a step forward, his head level with the elder's stomach.

The giant wiped his tears away. "Why?"

Somehow the elder warrior seemed smaller. "We thought you were of an evil tribe and feared your warrior was to strike at us."

"But we danced well! Why did you not do the same?"

Torak was baffled. "Dance? We do not dance in battle. We fight."

The elder reached out toward Torak to explain the gravity of the situation. "Do you not know our customs? Those who dance the best are the victors."

Torak was not impressed. "Dancing will not protect men from harm," he chided, keeping his distance.

"But if we dance, we do not have to fight," replied the elder.

"I do not know of these traditions. Crueler men than us would laugh at this dancing." Torak glanced back at his men and shrugged. He then faced the giant and asked an almost absurd question. "Do you accept defeat?"

To Torak's dismay, the elder dropped his arms and nodded. "Yes. You have won."

Torak ordered his men forward. The decorated tribe of giants showed no sign of aggression and submitted to Torak and his men. The big warriors carried their injured soldier to the medicine man and led the Tuballites to their village. It was obvious now that the Tuballites had made a mistake. These innocent giants, known as the Nephilim, were not the barbaric Ugric. Torak also learned that the Nephilim warriors weren't there to attack. They were on a spirit march, bringing some of the younger men into manhood.

Word of defeat reached the Nephilim's chief before they arrived. It was almost comical to see Torak and 200 well-armed midgets escorting the towering Nephilim through their village. Size did not seem to matter to the people. When Torak arrived at the chief's home, he was greeted cordially, and offered a ceremonial spear as a sign of submission. Torak did not accept it. Instead he explained the mistake to the chief and apologized for the wounding of their warrior. The chief was impressed with Torak's honor and invited him to stay and rest in their home. While the chief's wife gave him food and drink, the chief excused himself from the room.

Torak was told by the chief's wife that the people had never had to use physical combat as a solution to differences. The dancing game was their only battle strategy, a ritual of theatrical display rather than a physical challenge. The best display meant the best warrior. In this way, no blood would be spilled. Torak surmised that their sheer size was what others most likely feared, and what allowed them to avoid conflict.

The thought that kept running through Torak's head was the hope that the Nephilim, with their great strength, would become friends and, eventually, allies. To his surprise, they had already become allies without his knowing. When the chief returned, he brought someone back with him.

A wiry man walked through the door and bowed to Torak. "Master Torak, is it?"

Torak returned the bow. "Yes. Who are you?"

"I am Tatunna, a friend of Shem, son of Noah."

Torak was puzzled. "Are there any more of us shorter people living with these giants? Why are you here?"

Tatunna smiled. "No. I am the only one to stay and not run."

"I have heard your name spoken. That you know the life of many tribes. Why are these people so large?"

Tatunna rubbed his thin beard. "I have heard of two stories. One in which heavenly beings looked desirous of human women and went into them. The result was these big people known as the Nephilim. Another story is that men from the line of Seth lay with women from the line of Cain…the unholy births begot the Nephilim. As for me, I do not care if any of these tales are true, for they have been kind and include me in all they do."

Torak leaned in. "It matters not to me as well. They are a kind people, though they look fearsome. So you were a friend of my cousin, Shem. I must tell you that I was too late to save him."

Tatunna frowned. "From what?"

"From death. I found a necklace of his and much blood on the ground where he fought."

Tatunna cocked his head. "When was this?"

Torak breathed out. "Over two season ago."

Tatunna gave a pitiful smile. "You are mistaken. Shem is alive."

A feather could have knocked Torak over. "Shem? Alive? But I saw his blood!"

"But I took his body," replied Tatunna. "We saw him near to death and took him away…many wounds he had for to pay."

Torak went back to the moment at the cliff in his mind. Shem's blood, pieces of meat and hair, Kara's necklace. "So you saved him?" Torak stood up. "If he is alive, take me to him."

"I cannot, he is gone."

"Where did he go?"

"Back to city, and I wish him much pity. His strength has just mended and his mind close behind it."

"When did he leave?"

"A day has past, since I saw him last."

"Then it is time I leave," said Torak.

"But you have just arrived. What of your win over the Nephilim? There must be a celebration."

Torak grunted. "Win? We are as playthings to them. We would not have won if they had not let us."

Chapter 14
Life among the Ugric

Ilkin did not feel much like the stepson of a grand elder. He had been taken up to the most northern village of the Ugric where, in the end, was given to the local shaman as a worker until they could figure out a use for him. Ilkin shivered and stared out at the huge animals called the behemoths. A herd of thirty of the domesticated beasts crowded around the rare event of a newborn calf. Jubilation of the calf's birth swept through the connected villages, but Ilkin was in no mood for celebrating.

"It is I who should rule these people," he mumbled. *El, why do you punish me so? I want to be strong, like you and Anat, and provide for the people I will rule someday. So why do you bring me here, to this cold filthy place?*

Ilkin turned from the window to pull out the flank of a wild pig roasting in the stone oven. He wrapped a cloth around his hands to remove the ceramic pot but managed to burn his forearm on the side of the hot rock wall. "Ouch! By the gods, I hate this place!" Ilkin dropped the food down on a slab table and sucked on the injury. He went back to the oven and kicked it hard, stubbed his toe, then hopped around holding his injured foot.

The pudgy male servant of the chief shaman walked in. "You dog! Stop acting like a youth. Get some more wood!"

Ilkin released his foot and pounded on the stone table. "I was the son of the grand elder of Tuball. I should not have to do this!"

The servant was short by Ugric standards but still as tall as Ilkin." You have no honor in this village, and you will do as I say!" He picked up a stick of wood and walked toward Ilkin. "Or do I have to beat you?"

No matter how Ilkin tried to prove himself to these barbarians, they still considered him an outcast—lowlier than even a servant of the Oka tribes. He wanted to thrash the head servant. But it would be a useless pleasure. He would be made an outcast at the least and dead at the most.

Ilkin held up both hands. "No...I will get the wood."

As Ilkin opened the door, the servant behind him call out. "Be happy that the master was not here; he would have put a spell on you."

Ilkin slammed the door behind him and closed his eyes. *Why do I stay with these pigs? They treat me like a slave, when it is I who should be their leader.* Ilkin opened his eyes and relaxed. Mansi, the daughter of the Ugric chief, stood before him. He had seen her pass by many times, and many times he tossed compliments to her. This time she wore a tight otter skin dress that fell just above her knees, her flaming red hair braided and pulled up into a bun. She was average in physical beauty and strength, but her station in life made her quite desirable. Mansi gave him a seductive invitation with her eyes.

"May the day be as bright as your smile is to my heart, Mistress." Ilkin spoke his flattery with a bow.

She giggled to a servant at her side, then gave a nod for him to approach. She leaned over and whispered in his ear. "It has been long enough. At sunset meet me by the thrushes behind the longboat."

Ilkin smiled from one corner of his mouth, then bowed again. The women left him to finish gathering wood. *At last! After a season of flattery, she asks for me. El, you have heard my plea!*

While Ilkin stood daydreaming, Agul and an Oka warrior walked up to him from behind.

"Ilkin, you dog!" Agul shouted.

Startled by the sudden gruffness in the Oka leader's voice, Ilkin jerked back and dropped half the wood. He set his hands on his waist. "Agul. Why did you give me to the shaman?"

"Ha! Be grateful I did not give you to another, *son of the grand elder*." He spoke to Ilkin with a hint of sarcasm.

Ilkin hated that Agul enjoyed seeing him in such a pitiful condition. "When can we leave this place?"

"You will stay here till all of the parts fall together. I have to go back to my village and other villages of those who hate the Tuballites. We need more warriors."

"You cannot leave me here. I am worth more to you than that!"

"Yes, true. But we will not be fighting the Tuballites until I can prove to the high leader of the Ugric it is worth the cost of battle. Once I win him over, then your knowledge of the city will be useful. I must be going. Good living to you…with the Shaman. Ha!"

Agul gave another sardonic farewell laugh and left Ilkin standing alone picking up kindling. Ilkin would have escaped from the Ugric people if he had decent survival skills to battle the wilderness. Instead, he concentrated on other options.

After the evening meal, the forlorn Tuballite finished his duties without complaint, and the Shaman allowed him time to himself. Ensuring no one was watching, Ilkin then crept down to the Volga River where the boats were kept. A familiar slender figure was silhouetted in front of the setting sun. He strolled up to her and leaned against a willow, then looked about, still wary that other Ugric may still be nearby.

"I have wondered if the passion inside you is as bright as your flowing hair," Ilkin flattered.

The chief's daughter moved slowly toward him with a seductive smile. She used her finger to twist the locks of her hair. "You have a gift with words, Ilkin. I made many paths by the shaman's home, just to hear your sweet talk."

"Sweet words, Mistress? It cannot be helped. I was taught well, being the son of a great chief."

She smiled. "It has been said that you were banished for an evil deed."

Ilkin's proud features twisted to a stern frown. "I was not to blame! I should be their leader as we speak!"

Mansi stepped nearer and put her hands on his chest. She looked straight into his eyes. "Calm yourself. I have waited long to be this close to you. My father never allows me to be alone, with *any* man."

"Does he know of me?"

"Yes. But he does not know of my interest in you."

"What does he think of me?"

"He does not think of you at all. He worries for our people and if the Tuballites will try to strike at us."

"Hmm. He has not spoken about me," said Ilkin, with disappointment in his voice.

"It does not matter," she said brushing his chest hair. "I am the one you should be asking about."

"Are we alone?" He kept his eyes on her, but feared an Ugric warrior might appear.

"Yes. I have arranged it so." She stroked his chest downward to his stomach. "Do you know what I want?"

Ilkin smiled. "I am a man and you are a woman. Do you need to say more?" He took her hand and kissed it. Ilkin looked down at her lithe body and grasped the back of her hair firmly, then kissed her lips. He reached around the back of her waist, but she pulled back.

"I need more than just your manhood from you."

"Oh?"

"I need you to take me away from here. Take me to your city, where there are great things...spices, foods, jewels. My people are backward and unrefined. You can show me many things."

Ilkin stroked her cheek with the back of his hand. "I thought there must be something else you wanted of me." He eyed her a moment, unsure how much truth he should share. "There *are* many things I can show you there. But I cannot go back yet. And yet, I cannot stay here as a servant. Can you talk to your father about freeing me from my duty with the shaman?"

"My father does not trust Tuballites. I will need time." Mansi continued to run her finger across his belly.

Ilkin drew close to her cheek. She closed her eyes, and he touched his lips lightly across her soft face. "I will help you and you will help me," he whispered into her ear. He kissed her on the neck and she leaned into it, then sucked on her ear and bit it lightly. Ilkin abruptly took hold of her face and kissed her lips passionately. He moved his hands down to her breasts, but she stopped him.

She glanced around. "Not here."

Mansi led him to a vacant hut near the river, then undressed herself. Ilkin did the same. The light was dim, but they had no trouble finding themselves the pleasure they had been looking for. After a lengthy surge of gratification, their bodies collapsed into a blissful slumber. When the black of night began to lighten, they dressed themselves and skulked back to their separate domiciles, careful to mention the secret rendezvous to no one.

When the opportunity presented itself, the two indulged themselves throughout the summer. The benefits of the venture paid off for Ilkin. The head servant of the shaman was contacted by Mansi, and the spiritual leader's hand was never again laid on the son of the grand elder. When Ilkin was not with Mansi, he spent much of his time building friendships with the warriors, espousing that if he was their leader, he would provide them with wealth and position. It was risky and mutinous, but the Tuballite outcast had little to lose. As expected, the warriors didn't reveal Ilkin's rebelliousness to the high leader, instead, kept in contact with Ilkin.

Bliss has a way of ending in disappointment. For on one summer night, a servant girl to the mistress had become suspicious when she noticed Mansi's absences in the evenings. She pretended to fall asleep and followed the mistress to the rendezvous point. The servant girl dutifully told the chief.

The Ugric leader sat on his throne in the great hall, furious at the information. "Where are they now?"

The servant girl shivered, kneeling with her face to the ground. "I saw them at the river by the boats. You will not harm my mistress?"

"I will do as I choose!" He stood up and strode down to the guard by the door. "Bring in my daughter and the Tuballite. They are at the boats. Go!"

The warriors found the lovers inside the hut and the affair was quickly ended. Ilkin was whipped with leather straps and thrown in a prison cave. He sat in a stone cell for two moons. Hopes of royalty now dashed before him. Mansi was now on a close watch and available for *proper* Ugric successors.

* * *

The relationship would have ended at the moment the two were found out, never to speak to one another ever again. However, Mansi began to experience nausea and vomiting. The signs of pregnancy gave them a second chance.

Mansi bowed before her father on his throne. He nodded for her to speak. "It has been over two moons since we have spoken. May I come to you, Father?"

Pity washed over his face. "Yes. It is time we speak. I have talked with the son of a good Ugric clan elder. He is willing to see me and talk…about you."

She stood up. "Oh?"

"Since it is your wish to have a man, I will find a good one for you."

"It is kind of you, Father. May I come closer?"

The high leader was puzzled. "If you wish."

She stepped up to the throne and whispered. "I am with child. Ilkin's child."

The Ugric leader's face turned white. He didn't even wish to set eyes upon the Tuballite. But with a child now in Mansi's womb, she had all rights that they be united, their customs demanded it. The high leader painfully relinquished.

Ilkin was, therefore, not only released from his confinement, but given Mansi in marriage…a discreet marriage between the two, hastily arranged before the next moon. The Tuballite outcast was now the husband to the chief's daughter and in a position where he was one step to true leadership. He also saw this as a new opportunity that would lead to greater things, and it was not his objective to ignore something as fortuitous as this.

Chapter 15
Incognito

The light was waning, so Shem laid down the tinder and pulled out his flint to start a fire. Once the fire was lit, he faced the flames...randomly scanning the road behind him. *Something is out there.* He shivered. For days he felt as though someone was watching him. Once the rocks turned red he laid a big sea perch upon them and listened to it sizzle. Again, Shem had an eerie feeling and turned around. The silhouette of a man stood a stone's throw away on the land mass flanked by both seas. The man raised an arm into the air and shouted, but the waves hitting the rocks muffled the sound.

Shem thought he recognized the voice. "Who are you?" The man came closer and Shem took hold of his spear. When the firelight hit the man's face Shem dropped his weapon. "Torak!"

Torak took several more paces then reached out his hand. "It is good to see you." He clasped Shem's wrist and shook it vigorously. Thanks be to the Creator for your life. Two seasons ago we followed the Oka, but did not find you. We had given you up for dead."

Shem smiled. "I knew you would not forget me, Torak. Come sit." Shem released Torak's grip to turn the fish over with a stick. Torak leaned against a nearby boulder to rest. "You breathe heavy. Have something to eat."

"Your friend Tatunna told me you were alive. I had to see if it was true."

Shem pulled up his shirt to show a thick scar above his waist. "I was hurt badly. My leg was broken and my head still gives me pain."

"I wish I could have saved you. Tatunna told me the big people took you away before I could get to you."

Shem smiled. "Many thanks. Tatunna and his giants saved my life."

Torak shook his head slowly. "We almost fought those big men. If we had even ten times our numbers, my men would have been squashed like insects."

Shem chuckled. "They are a gentle people. With Tatunna's help, I have become friends with them."

"With Tatunna's help, we *must* become good friends," added Torak in a serious tone. "I would never wish them as an enemy."

Shem moved the sea perch from the fire to a flat stone." Shem glanced back to the east. "You are alone?"

"My warriors are a day behind me."

"Why are you without your men?"

Torak cleared his throat. "I wanted to tell you something else of great concern." He eyes stared into the fire.

Shem smiled innocently. "You look as if someone died. What is it?" Torak did not return the smile.

Shem suddenly stood up in fear. "Is my father dead?"

Torak gained his composer and rested his big hands on Shem's shoulders. "No! He is in good health. Or so I have heard from traders."

"It is Kara! She is ill!"

"She, too, is well," Torak reassured.

Shem reached down and took a bite from the cooked perch. "Then what is it, cousin?"

"Kara thought you were dead, Shem." Torak was quiet a moment. "I do not know how to say it."

"Just say it, Torak."

Torak cleared his throat again. "She and Bulla are man and wife."

Shem choked on his food. His heart skipped a beat, and he looked about as if trying to find something he lost. He dropped his fish. "But we..." His legs became like fluid and he leaned precariously over the fire. Torak took hold of Shem and drew him back.

"She thought you were dead."

"But..." Tears began to trickle down from Shem's eyes, yet he made no effort to stop them. He did not sob or cry out. Shem gripped Torak's arm and stared at the embers. He stared with his mouth ajar. "No," he whispered.

Torak moved Shem away from the fire then led him to a large rock. "I wanted to tell you myself, before you reached the city." The big warrior stood quietly next to him.

Shem leaned his elbows on his knees and looked up at the outline of the city walls. A slit of red cut across the horizon. He stared at them for a long while "Does anyone else know I am alive, other than you, Torak?"

"Only Tatunna and I."

"Then you must not tell Kara or anyone else that I am alive."

Torak frowned. "I cannot do that, Shem. She needs to know."

"No, Torak! She must not know. Not now."

"Shem—"

"Promise me, Torak."

Torak pounded his chest once and hard. He grunted, as if to let out some tension. "I speak what I know. And they must know. What good will it serve?"

"You have to promise me, Torak. If you tell anyone I live then Bulla and Kara will feel shame. I do not want that to happen. I care for both of them too much." Shem started to choke out a sob, then contained it. "Promise me."

Torak took a deep breath. "They will find out, Shem."

"But not from you. I will let them know some other day, Torak. But not now."

Torak looked as if he wanted to shrug off a new flax shirt. "I do not like this. When your name arises I will ignore I heard it."

Shem spit out a piece of fish bone. "My thanks to you, cousin."

"What will you do, Shem?"

Shem looked over at the darkened city. "I do not know."

* * *

Torak had returned to his men and Shem was closer to the city now. He knew he could not avoid Kara. He had to see her again, even if it meant never seeing her from then on. She was what gave him strength when he was healing from his injuries. She is what he dreamed of when his mind wanted to shut down. She was the woman he expected would bear his children. Now all of that was to be thrown away?

The eastern walls stood stoically upright and steadfast. Shem covered his face with dirt and greyed his hair and beard with white chalk slurry he found near the sea. He had disguised himself as an old man with a worn, tattered black cloak and crooked walking pole. He ensured his hood was covering his head well from prying eyes.

Even with this new disguise Shem still had the feeling that something was behind him. *Torak has left me, so why do I sense I am being followed?* Shem pulled the hood tighter but kept watching to the side. Finally, he saw something—a shadow?—or someone?

Has Torak returned? If he has, why does he not show himself? It must be someone or something else.

Shem stopped to listen and think. He quietly snuck behind a large boulder and stayed still. After listening to the waves lap for half an hour on the shore, he almost gave up...then...light footsteps. Shem clasped his knife from his belt and stood ready. The figure passed quietly to the other side of the boulder. When Shem felt confident he had the upper hand he lunged forward to grab the man with his left hand and present the knife with his right.

The man squealed. "No, Master!"

It wasn't a man's voice at all. "Nazar?" It was the tall lanky Nephilim orphan boy, Shem had gotten to like before he left. "What are you doing here?"

The young Nephilim cowered at the harshness in Shem's voice. "I..." he tried to say something but nothing came forth. Nazar glanced up, then hunched down as if he expected to be beaten. "Who are you, Sir?"

Shem sheathed his knife and reached out to raise the boy to his feet. "It is alright. I will not hurt you. It is me, Shem."

"You do not look like the master Shem."

Shem softened his voice and pulled his hood back. "See. I am covering myself...it is a game. Why are you here?"

The boy spoke bashfully. "I followed you from the village. You are the only one who speaks well to me. I thought you could be my brother."

Shem displayed a pitiful smile. "Many thanks for your thoughts, Nazar. But you should stay with your own people. Your sister must be worried for you."

"No. She said I could go. I want to be with you."

"That will not do. Where I go is dangerous. You must return."

"What is the word, dangerous?"

Shem sighed. "It means fearsome and deadly."

"That is a good word. I want to be dangerous. I am not afraid of danger."

Shem walked over and picked up his traveling bag. "You sound like me when I was your age. Your bravery is not enough, though. You must learn many things before you leave your village."

"You can teach me more than they can." He had promise in his voice.

Shem lifted the bag over his shoulder. "I have greater things to do than teach a young Nephilim the ways of life."

Nazar dropped his head and sat down on the ground. "You hate me."

Shem rolled his eyes. "No, I do not hate you. But you are not my kin, and I cannot have you in my care. I promise that if you return to your people. I will come back and see you again."

Nazar lifted his head. "You promise?"

"Yes. I promise."The young man turned to leave.

Shem stopped him. "What did you live on these last few days?"

"What you left on the fire, Master Shem."

Shem handed Nazar the bag. "Here. There is enough food to get you home, and a fire starter. I am proud that you think of me so highly. May the one true God bless you on your way home."

Nazar nodded and walked east without another word. Shem shook his head and turned around for his westward journey.

* * *

Practicing elderly walking methods, Shem soon closed in on the newly laid stone road that formed a wide street. After awhile, the road ended at the eastern promenade by the gates. Many local tradespeople gathered in dense clusters, vying to enter the city to sell their goods. As Shem hobbled along the new street, he recognized Tabas and other Sethite cousins working with the stone. It was imperative that he find some people who would not know him; someone he could enter the gates with. He peeked out of his hood briefly, not daring to reveal himself to his friends. He spotted a fishing clan making its way to the gates. He headed toward them.

Shem approached the clan in his new role. "Good people, do you think you can help an old man find the city temple?" he asked, in his best raspy old voice. This was a good time to test out his acting. If this clan believed him, then surely the city folk would not recognize him.

A husband and wife bending forward with a net full of pike on their backs, stopped and turned around. They scanned the bent over figure and smiled. "Why yes, old man." said the fisherman. "Hold onto my arm and I will guide you in."

"Blessings upon you, my son. My eyes get worse every season," croaked Shem. He laid his cloak covered hand on the man's elbow.

With his grip on the fisherman's arm, they approached the guards, who inspected the goods as the people entered. They threw opened lids on pottery and stabbed their spears into baskets and bales. To enter the eastern gate, one had to be a citizen or have a seal representing a citizen's servant. The guards focused a close eye on the strong and mischievous young men. Shem, as an old man, was given a cursory glance. The fisherman showed the seal of a wealthy Tuballite they were bringing fish to. After being waved inside, Shem was led to the temple and left to fend for himself. He thanked the fisherman and his wife for their help and pushed open the large doors.

Shem stood alone inside the temple, with the exception of an acolyte praying in front of the statue of Anat. Shem stepped softly toward where Zakho had discovered the hidden door two years earlier. Feeling for the lever, Shem twisted it and slid open the door that made a small scraping sound. He slipped inside, found a mounted, unlit torch and pulled out his flint to ignite the fibers.

Once he had lit the torch, he stepped forward into the same passages that he had navigated during the Oka siege. After a series of turns, and a couple dead-ends, he found the secret entrance to the grand master's chambers. He tried to look through the peephole in the door, but this time it was blocked by some fabric. Shem split off a piece of his walking stick and poked it through the hole. He slid the cloth sideways and peered in. No one was in the room.

Shem unlatched the locking lever and entered the room. He heard voices in the adjoining chamber and went to investigate. He peeked around the corner to see two muscular guards standing watch at the door, while Kara and Bulla looked over some drawings. Shem's heart pounded when he saw Kara. She was more beautiful than he had ever seen her. She had long dark hair pulled back through a leather sheath, painted eyes and lips with a purple swath of gauze wrapped around her shoulders. Her dress was made of a loose weave that revealed her breasts, hips, and…stomach!

Shem swallowed hard, pinched his eyes tight, before looking again to confirm his observation. Her belly was extended larger than a melon. She was carrying a child! Kara turned sideways and her pregnancy was proven. This also meant that there was no denying her love for Bulla. Shem jumped when he felt something rub his leg. He glanced down to see a thin black cat. It meowed quietly. He shoved it away with his foot.

After a moment, Kara squeezed Bulla's arm and he wrapped a cloak around her. She said goodbye and exited through the archway with the guards following. Shem turned around and knocked over a figurine. He picked it up and set it back on the table, then crawled quickly across the room to the exit. After closing the door, he peered through the hole in the door. Bulla appeared in the room and looked around briefly. The cat rubbed up against the table and Bulla picked up the figurine. He left the room without suspicion.

Girding up his cloak, and with his stick under his arm, Shem hurried through the passage, stepping as lightly as possible. Emotions of love, hate, failure, and resignation flooded his veins while he maneuvered his way through the corridors. Finally, the tunnels ended at the outer courtyard of the city and he calmed himself. He readjusted his hooded cloak and slid the door open into the outer city where the colorful crowds would be able to camouflage his presence. Shem slipped into the throngs unnoticed and hobbled along, aided by his walking stick.

Traders sold their goods by calling out, "Fresh fruit! Fresh bread! Stones of beauty! Fine weaves!"

Shem continued his way through the people and up to the ziggurat where he could get a better view of his surroundings. However, after only a few steps up, he saw something that stunned him. There in front of God and men was a life-size effigy of himself.

Shem stared at the large iconic statue a moment then touched it to prove it real. He shook his head, squeezed his walking stick, then stepped back. A woman and her child stepped in front of him and set flowers down at the statues feet. They bowed reverently, mumbled some words, bowed again, and left.

How could so much happen since I have been away? This is not right! He took the heavy rod and swung it upward to weigh siege on the statue, but something behind him stopped him. He turned around and saw a wispy haired young man with a stack of papyrus under one arm, his other hand holding onto Shem's rod. He was a young man about Shem's age, thin, yet with bright excited eyes. The young man shifted his eyes and tipped his head to the right. Shem followed the direction of the man's eyes and lowered the rod. He looked over to see a beautifully dressed woman in articulately weaved sandals at the base of the ziggurat. It was Kara, climbing the steps, escorted by two guards. Shem looked back to address the young man, but he had disappeared.

The woman now stood in front of the memorial. "I walk by the statue every day." She said, looking over at Shem.

Shem bowed in her presence.

"Have you heard of him, old man?"

"No, Mistress. This is the first I have seen this," Shem croaked out.

"He was a great and kind hero to us."

Shem kept his head low. "I sense you knew him well, Mistress?"

"Yes. Yes, I did."

"What happened to him?"

"He died protecting our people." Kara caressed the side of the statue's face.

"And you loved him?"

"I will always love him." Kara wiped a tear from her eye.

The sound of footsteps interrupted their conversation. Shem could see Bura out of the corner of his hood. He was out of breath when he stood before Kara. Bura glanced at Shem then touched his sister's elbow. Shem pretended to turn his gaze elsewhere.

"Sister, I mean, *Grand Mistress*," he said with a twinkle in his eye. "Your servant said you wished to speak with me."

"Yes, Bura." She revealed the puzzle box that she had kept close to her for so long. "I want you to take this back home. To the mountains, where there is a safe place for it. I need it here no longer."

"The mountains of Seva? That is days away. What is so grand that I must do it now? I am a warrior."

"Many reasons. For one, you have not seen mother or father in two seasons. By taking this home for me you can do both these things. I will release you from your duties."

Bura waggled his head. "Fair enough." He took the box from her and tried to open it, but he hadn't learned the trick to access. "What is inside?"

"Nothing that I want to have here. There are too many memories in it."

Bura smirked. "Thoughts of Shem?"

"Please, Brother."

"I will do it, Sister. Should I say a word for you to Mother and Father?"

"Yes. Tell them I think of them often and will send for them soon."

Bura bowed. "As you wish, *Grand Mistress*." Bura glanced back at Shem, then trotted down the pyramid steps.

Shem heard every word and figured one of his letters must be inside the box. He still kept his head low, his body as still as stone, unable to leave.

"May I help you somewhere, old man?" asked Kara. She could only see a shadow of the scraggly bearded man.

Shem, however, could see every detail of her in the bright sunshine. He looked up from the ground to see some fine leather sandals flanked by set of military sandals. Her cloak covered her loosely woven virtually see-through dress. He admired the perfectly smooth complexion with dimples aside a welcoming smile. She wore the red garnet around her neck. The same one he had held in his hands when his head was bashed by the Oka. Her belly is what he had the most difficulty looking past.

"No mistress. I have seen enough. I beg to leave now." Shem bowed to her.

"So be it," she replied. "Live well, sir."

Shem bowed to her and then hobbled out through the controlled chaos. When Shem turned a corner, he looked back to see Kara's face once more but she was gone. He looked to the sky. *What shall I do now, Master Creator? I have nothing to live for.* Shem walked a few paces when the young man, who had stopped him from destroying the statue, reappeared. "You are the young man I saw on the temple steps."

"Old man. Come with me."

"Who are you and what do you want with a weak fellow such as I?" asked Shem.

"I am Tural and my master wishes to see you."

"And who is your master?"

"The great magus of the city."

"I do not want to see Olum." Olum was Bulla's number two. If he talked with the magus Olum, Bulla would know of Shem's arrival.

The young man shook his head. "No, not Olum. His skill as a magus does not compare to my master's. I am speaking of Master Berin."

"Berin?" Shem had heard of the wise man but never met him. "Why me? I am nothing."

"I was told to watch for a man with a walking stick at the statue of Shem the Sethite during this moon's life. That I was to bring him to my master."

Shem only wanted to leave the city. "I mean no disrespect, but I do not know you and I do not wish to go with you."

"I was told to show you this." The apprentice pulled out a shiny silver triangle with a wavy line running through it and handed it to Shem.

It's my mark! Shem thought. "Where did you get this?"

The young man extended his arm and pointed to a tower inside the inner city. "There. Where my master lives."

Shem pondered whether he should leave the city or investigate this great magus. Curiosity won over. "Lead on."

Tural guided Shem through the inner city up a series of steps to a chamber at the top of the tower. The apprentice knocked on the door and a voice beckoned them in. They entered a room where an old man was flipping through some leather pages of notes. He wore a loose-weaved wool cap on his bald head and was dressed in layers of colored cloaks. He walked over to a mechanical device made of wood and metal to make some adjustments. The old man muttered as he went about his business, completely ignoring his guests. Finally, the old magus looked up at Shem and Tural with glee.

"It will be here, in the next cycle."

"What will, Master?"

"The messenger star!" He shuffled some papers. "It is all here!"

The servant looked down at the papers. "What does it mean, Master Berin?"

"It means the prophecy will come true. It is all here. As it is seen, so shall it be written. As it is written so shall it come to pass."

Shem was mildly interested but did not care if it was true. Anything that was important to him didn't matter anymore. He gazed around at the many strange charts and objects hung on the walls, pretending to ignore the Thinker.

The old magus eyed his new visitor. "It seems that you have little care for your own life, sir...true?"

Shem kept his face in the shadow of his hood. "I am old. What do I have to look forward to?" Shem croaked out.

The magus chuckled. "Ah, as I expected. Come, sit, and rest yourself. Call me Berin." he directed Shem to a bench.

The cooing of a collared dove sounded outside the window ledge. The buff-grey bird with a black half collar on its nape waddled onto the workbench. The old man took off a piece of parchment from around its leg, opened a cage door, and put the bird inside. He squinted to read the message with a finely polished agate, grunted, then handed the strip of parchment to Tural. "Put that with the others."

Tural bowed and passed by rows of boxes until he found the one to slip it into.

"What is it you want of me?" Shem asked, with his creaking elder voice.

Berin let out a punctuated chuckle. "Do not pretend with me, Shem, son of Noah."

Shem looked down at the metal icon in his hand. After a moment, he realized his acting was foiled and it was useless to pretend any further. He pulled back his hood to reveal his mediocre disguise. Berin crossed his arms proudly. Tural however, was surprised and intrigued.

"How did you know it was me?" Shem asked the magus.

Berin shrugged. "You hold the answer in your hand."

"Yes, this is my mark. But how could you know where I would be?"

The magus reached over and picked up a scroll from the table. "It has been written, Master Shem. Do you think your father is the only one to receive visions? The Almighty will use whatever and whomever He wishes for His purposes."

"How do you know of my father and of the Almighty?"

"Many questions you have. Which one would you like me to answer first?"

Shem decided to find out the core beliefs of the magus. "You mentioned the Almighty's wishes. Do you believe in the one true God?"

Berin set the scroll down and leaned against the table. "I was sure a prophecy was fulfilled when Shem the Sethite fought the Oka and brought heaven's fire down on them. Upon reading many scrolls from the ancients who have had visions, I discovered there was one magus whose prophecies *always* came true. He was also the one who said a single creator rules the heavens and the ground. That is when I believed on the one true God. I read more of his writings and found out that there would be a day when a foreign hero would give his life for the Tuballites. This man would return as an old man with a walking stick to see his own image. Since the only foreign hero was Shem the Sethite, I had Tural watch for you. Do not ask how I knew when you would come. That, I will not tell you."

Shem held out the triangular metal. "How did you know this is the mark that my father gave me?"

"Know? I did not know. The prophecy showed that the symbol was the hero's. I had hoped it would lure you here, so to prove the prophecy…and lay my eyes on a man who had risen from the dead."

"I did not die. That was a mistake. I was injured badly, that is all." Shem lowered his gaze to look at the icon. "My father gave it to me, but never told me of its meaning."

The magus put on a small clever smile. "You will learn of it, I assure you." He then slapped Shem's shoulder. "But now there is much for you to do. With the writings proving true, I too am a part of the prophecy. It is I who must direct you to your next step."

"I do not want anyone else to know of my presence," said Shem. "I expect that you will tell other magi, like Olum, and he would tell Bulla, and …"

Berin scowled. "I tell Olum only what he needs to know. Olum is clever, and he has stolen many of my ideas to advance himself with the grand elder. Such a position means nothing to me. I am here, as is the spirit master, Kargi…to guide the people with knowledge." He spoke with casual indifference. "Olum need not know." Berin picked up a scroll. "There are other things written in here that even I do not understand as of yet. What I do understand is that you have a purpose."

Shem sat up. "A purpose?"

"Yes, a purpose, a calling. And I am the arrow to point you toward it."

"And what is my purpose?"

"You must go back to your father."

Shem looked as if he had bit into a lemon. "That is my purpose?"

"Yes. It is written, and so it shall be."

Shem slumped where he sat. "That is all?" It did not seem anything out of the ordinary. How could seeing his father be a purpose?

Berin raised a finger. "No. That is the easy part of your purpose. Hardship will follow you."

Chapter 16
Shem's Return

Shem began the morning with a journey back to the Ararat Valley. Berin had told him nothing of what was in store. Only that he must return to his father's home. He was alone and discouraged. When he crossed the Kura River, he replayed his dreams and future with Kara with all that could have been. With every step he took, the nightmare of reality set in. On the first night out from the city, he lay on his back and looked up at how the night lights shifted across the blackened sky. Again his thoughts drifted to memories of Kara, and silent tears began to rain down his face.

He eventually fell asleep, but he woke up with a start to the sounds of his own sobbing. Shem sat up and wiped his blurry eyes…something rustled in the bushes. He reached for his spear, moved into a crouched position, and held his breath poised ready to strike.

Out of the bushes stood a large figure of a man in the light of the moon. "Are you hurt, Master Shem?"

Shem jabbed his spear into the earth. "Nazar? I thought I told you to go back to your people!"

"I forgot where to go," Nazar replied, in a mousy tone.

"The way you came!" Shem waved his hand to the east. "How did you find me?"

"I waited for you outside the city. When I saw you, I followed." He smiled proudly. "You were dressed up like the old man, but I knew it was you."

"Very good, Nazar," Shem replied, without enthusiasm. "And how have you fed yourself?"

"The food you gave me. And people have been good to me. I ask for food and they give it to me."

"I see. Then it seems as if you can survive without me."

Shem wanted to send him away. But even though the boy of nine was taller than most men, and though city people donated out of their abundance, he would not have the knowledge to survive in the wilderness alone.

"I will be good. I know how to get wood and make fire and tear the feathers off of birds for eating and—"

"Stop! I will not send you away."

Nazar grinned broadly. "Thanks to you, Master Shem!"

"I must go over the mountains to be with my kin. My father has great wisdom. I will take you with me and let him decide what to do with you."

"What is the word, wisdom?"

Shem smiled inside. "It means knowing how to use what you know."

"That is a good word. I will learn to have wisdom. I will be good. You will see, my big brother."

"I am not your big brother. First, I am a Sethite and you are a Nephilim. Second, you are too tall to call me a big brother."

Nazar chuckled. "Oh, I may be taller, but you are bigger in heart."

"Or crazy to keep you with me," added Shem. "Come, I have laid out many tree boughs over here. You can sleep by me."

The boy grinned and huddled down next to Shem, quickly falling asleep. Shem's thoughts were in disarray and it took another hour for him to nod off.

The next morning Shem woke to the crackling of a fire. Nazar had already risen to stir up the coals and fill Shem's flask with water from the nearby stream. Shem pulled out a hare he had killed the day before and let Nazar skin it. For a brief moment, Shem appreciated the company. Nazar kept a silly grin on his face as he worked to skin the animal. Neither spoke much, leaving a critical part of their lives behind them, but the kindness between them seemed to speak volumes. It wasn't long before the two were on their way southwest and climbing over the mountains south of Lake Sevan.

Once over the mountains, Shem and Nazar bent down to sip from the Aras River. Shem gazed at his reflection with blankness. His emotional well was dry. But he continued to care for his guest. They followed the river up to the familiar conical shaped mountain, to a motley set of houses that were patched together haphazardly with wood and stone. No one was outside the houses, but Shem thought he saw some figures working at the base of the mountain.

While Nazar hid outside behind some bushes, Shem knocked on the door of his parents' home. He opened the door and stepped inside. His mother was slicing up some onions and his father was scribbling out some drawings on the low table. When Naamah looked over to see her son, she gasped and clutched her free hand to her breast, unable to speak.

She soon found her voice. "You are dead—and back here from the afterworld."

Noah looked up from his work and smiled smugly. "My son!"

Naamah ran to Shem and squeezed him tightly. Over and over, she blubbered her thanks to God. Noah walked up and wrapped his arms around them both. Once the reality of Shem's physical presence set in, they calmed down. They walked outside to enjoy the cool late summer breeze and sip some mountain berry juice, while he explained his story.

It wasn't long before they were spotted by the others. Parading down from the hill were Ham, Lily, Shinar, and a few from the Seva tribe.

Lily sped quickly to him. "I knew he was not dead!" She hit Shem with an embrace so hard he practically fell over.

He relinquished to her tight embrace. Ham was close behind and put his arm around his brother's shoulder. Shem chuckled and then laughed when Shinar and the others cheered and patted his back with fondness.

"This is the best gift I have been given in many seasons," Shem choked out, half smothered.

Ham shook his head. "The Almighty could not let you die? You have too much work here to do."

Shem laughed again. "Where is Japheth? Does he not help with the work?"

Ham stepped back. "No! He lives well at our old home with Grandfather Lamech. He tills the soil easily, while we have to make do with this stony ground. Father is turning us into vile woodsmen. It is so good to have you back, my brother."

Shem shook his head. "To share the load, eh?"

"We can wrestle too!" Ham grabbed Shem's leg and pulled him off his feet.

Shem laughed and held his stomach as lay on his back. "Not now, Ham! Later, for I am beat like an old fleece." Shem picked himself up. "I forgot something. You must meet Nazar."

"Who?" asked Noah.

"The tall boy that was with me."

"You were not alone?" asked Ham.

Shem looked around the hamlet of homes. "Nazar! Show yourself!" The gangly, shy boy, stepped out of the bushes with his head bowed. "Come. This is my family. You have nothing to fear."

"He is a youth? I would like to see his father," joked Ham.

Shem put his arm around Nazar. "His parents are dead. That is partly why he is with me."

But for the insects, it became unusually quiet. Nazar said nothing. Naamah greeted him kindly and led him inside where she brought him some food. The others followed them inside, where Namaah set out some food. Shem and the boy ate sheep steaks and bread to their fill.

"Have your sisters secured good Sethite husbands yet?" asked Naamah.

"They are well, Mother. I do not know about their men." Shem didn't have the heart to tell her two of the girls took to the city life. He described how the Sethite tribes are farming outside the city, cautious to highlight only the good events. He even mentioned the battle with the northern tribes, but failed to tell of his experience with the angel. Lily sat at Shem's feet, listening to every word he spoke. Shinar left the family abruptly between stories. Shem wondered if he said something to trouble his cousin. But with so much on his mind, Shem tried to relax and enjoy his reunion.

After giving a chronology of his latest adventures, Shem encouraged them to keep his existence a secret. Later in the evening, Shem and Nazar quickly went to sleep on a pile of sheepskins stacked in the corner—much cozier than the pebbles and earth they had laid upon during the trek from the city.

Shem slept hard that night. He woke to the sweet smells of Naamah's cooking and a good nudge from Nazar. After Shem stretched out, he got up to eat his meal. As he ate, he thought back to Shinar's quick disappearance the night before.

Shem had his fill of food, then excused himself to be alone. He walked down by the grinding wheel where Shinar was sharpening some metal. Shem kicked some stones to make a noise and let Shinar know he was coming—no response. Shem took a few steps and stood over Shinar as he sat turning the wheel, sharpening his axe.

"So when are you and Lily to be united?" Shem asked.

Shinar didn't look up. "When *you* leave again."

Shem was taken aback at his bluntness. "When I leave? What do you mean?"

Shinar stopped sharpening and held the axe up to Shem's face. "You and Lily! Do you not see it?"

Shem took a step back. "No. I do not. She has always been kind to me."

"She looked at you like a mother dotes on an infant. She loves you, Shem! Not me!" He paused. "She always has," he muttered.

"What!? No, she and I are only…."

"Like brother and sister? Do not pretend with me," Shinar countered. "I will never have her while you are here." Shinar glared at Shem. "Is that why you want your presence here to be a secret? So you can have Kara in the city and Lily here!?"

Shem was dismayed. Shinar slung the axe over his shoulder, and strode over to where the log pile was. Shem recalled how Kara told him of Lily's fondness for him, and yet he dismissed it. Was it true? He cared for her, but not in the way he admired Kara.

Shem decided he had to do something before things got out of hand. He had to go to Lily to set things straight. Lily was down by the river washing the family's clothes, humming a tune. He walked casually to the water upstream from her. She was unaware of his presence. He knelt on one knee to sip water from his cupped hand, and glanced furtively, while trying to find the words he should say.

Shem stood up and called out to her. "Lily!" He waved to her, as if he happened upon her.

Lily grinned broadly and stopped washing. Shem walked over and sat down on the river bank next to her. He wanted to clear things up quickly, but he didn't know how to go about it.

"I see you carry the burden of cleaning our filth."

Lily looked down at the pile by the water. "It needs to be done," she replied with humility.

Shem picked up a small stone and threw it into the river. "Lily, um…I need to talk to you about something."

She set her clothes down and tried to peer into Shem's eyes. "Yes?"

Shem felt awkward and didn't want to face her directly, but he couldn't *not* look at her. When he glanced up, Lily sat attentively, waiting for his words. Shem took her hand and she willingly let him. He decided to focus on her hand.

"Lily, you are a wonderful, I mean, Shinar tells me you are of great help around my family." Shem could not find the words. "What I wish to say is that when a man loves a woman he knows when it is right. And I do not wish to—"

Lily's cheeks perked up and her smile grew and grew. Before Shem could continue, she moved forward and planted a kiss squarely on Shem's lips. Shem tried to pull back, but she wrapped her arms around his neck tightly.

She kissed him on both cheeks as vigorously as he was trying to pull away. "Yes, Shem! I will be your wife!"

"Lily! No!"

Lily moved backward with a confused frown. "What is it, Shem? Were you not asking me?"

Shem shook his head with a wincing pain. "No."

Lily gulped hard, then looked down at her lap. "Oh."

"Lily, you are as a sister to me. Better than any of my own sisters, since they have taken to the ways of the city of Tuball. You are faithful and kind, but I will only see you like a heart-friend."

Lily turned beet red. "I...I am ashamed."

Shem raised her chin and was now brave enough to face her directly. "You should not be ashamed. There are other men who want you—like Shinar."

Lily looked up to where Shinar was chopping wood. "The elders always thought Shinar and I would be married. But Uncle Noah said you were still alive and I believed him. When I heard that Kara united with the Grand Elder of Tuball, I hoped you..."she bit the side of her lip, and fought back tears. "You are right, Shem. Shinar has been kind to me for so long and I have ignored him. Your heart has always been tied to Kara's. But you cannot have her now."

Shem's eyes welled up at the mention of Kara. He dabbed his eyes with his sleeve. "I know. But my heart is torn. You would not want a torn heart like mine."

Shem stood up and touched her face. She held his hand close for just a moment, kissed his palm, then released it. Lily turned around, picked up a piece of cloth, plunged it into the water, then pushed it hard against the flat stone.

Without a word, and with a pit in his belly, Shem walked away from her. He noticed Noah waving his hands around, while talking with Nazar. The two were walking up to the mountain base toward the worksite. No doubt Noah was instructing the boy about some lesson in morality.

Shem had an upset stomach from the meeting with Lily. Somehow all would work out for the best. He had always admired her as a young girl, but could not accept the idea of her being more than that. She was growing in beauty and form, a desirable woman for any Sethite man. But he could not shake his feelings away from Kara.

* * *

At the base of the mountain, the site for construction of Noah's boat was in limbo. Shem hopped across the arm's-wide logs, which had been laid parallel to each other on the ground, but in no distinctive pattern. It was if it were a splendid creature with no legs to move it along. Shem looked up at Mt. Ararat, which sat majestically above him like a sentinel watching over the valley. Voices from below caught his attention and he turned around.

"Son! Look who I have with me!" Noah called out from just outside the hamlet.

Noah walked with Ham and Vard, the woodsman and father of Kara. The strong and kind woodsman would have been a fine second father. Knowing that Vard must have attended the marriage of Kara and Bulla, Shem felt the urge to flee. Instead, he took a breath and stayed put.

When they arrived at the site, Vard reach out his hand. "Shem, it is good to see you."

Shem shook his wrist. "And you, Master Vard." Shem looked back at his father. "My secret is not so secret anymore."

"How was I to know you would come back alive, Son? I invited Vard to help me with the boat long before you arrived."

"I will not be the cause of trouble," said Vard. "I came to work."

Shem faced Vard. "You are a good man. I know you will keep this to yourself."

"I will not tell my daughter you live, until you say so. And you will not have to worry about my wife's tongue. She has gone into the city with Bura."

"Are we fine now?" asked Noah. Shem nodded. "Good. Let us learn from a master woodsman then."

Noah rolled out a parchment that had a drawing of the vessel and asked Vard what type of wood was necessary to begin construction. Vard explained that a scaffolding system would need building before the boat was started. He and Noah paced out the dimensions, talked for awhile, and then pointed to the forest that surrounded them. With a basic in motion, Vard promised to stay for a few months, so as to train the Sethites in the art of working with timber.

All through that season Shem, Ham, Shinar, and Nazar followed the directions of the woodsman. Huffing and puffing, they towed and lifted each timber into its proper place. Vard brought with him some metal tools to help speed up the process of cutting and splitting the trees from the local forest. Pine was tall and straight, and plentiful for the scaffold. Maple, linden, and beech, grew near the river, and were to be used later for the structure of the boat.

As the scaffold began to take shape, Shem had noticed that so too was the relationship between Shinar and Lily. Days went by where the young men would trudge back to their homes. There Lily waited with water for the men...she was diligent to serve Shinar first.

Within the next moon, Noah was performing a wedding ceremony for the two. It was a bittersweet moment for Shem. In the span of two seasons, he had lost the opportunity to wed two good women. Yet, and at the same time, was able to see them marry two solid men.

After the wedding, work on the scaffold was a good distraction, but it still didn't take away his pain. Shem's vigor had faded. He was confused about direction and purpose of life. His relationship with Kara was so crisp and so clear in his mind, and now his life seemed to be slipping away.

In a quiet moment, when the others had gone to their beds, Shem and Noah stood around the outside fire pit. Vard was soon to leave them and so they tossed around some ideas about the next stage of construction. Shem stirred the coals while his father poured some water on them. Their conversation veered into Shem's escapades from the behemoths, the Oka, and, finally, bemoaning the loss of Kara.

Shem sat with his elbows on his knees and his face in his hands. "Father, what shall I live for now? All was sweet and clear, now it is sour and cloudy. If we serve the Creator faithfully and yet receive hard work for it, how is our God any better than the Cainites'?"

Noah put his arm around Shem. "Not all of life is a mountaintop joy. You are in the depths of the rocky crags of life. Great joy comes through the path of suffering."

"I tire of suffering, Father. I want something more than that."

"Endure this, my son, and you will come through the other side stronger. Our faith is not one of the fast race, but a long journey. Do not get tripped up by the guile of the evil one." Noah paused. "Did you know that I always doubted news of your death?"

Shem sat up. "You did not believe Ham?"

"Oh, I believed Ham meant well. But, when I heard of your death, I knew it could not be true. For I remembered my vision from God that you would be on the big boat with me in the coming days. Was I to believe God or man? It was an easy choice. Our faith grows, my son. When we trust in the Almighty, he gives us more chances for our faith to strengthen and flourish."

The fire had turned to dimming coals and the stars were brilliant. They gazed up at them in silence. Shem threw some water on the coals, and they started back to their little houses. Shem guided Noah back toward his house with his hand under his father's elbow.

"Do you not miss the green fields, and the herd of goats and sheep, and the harvest days near the Tigris, Father?"

"Yes, my son. I do. But the Creator is planning my life so I may produce greater things." Noah reached for the handle of his door and turned to Shem. "Do you believe this?"

Shem squirmed. "The hand of the Almighty has protected me through all my pains. So I must believe."

Noah pointed a finger in the air. "The Almighty also works us through small trials so that we may be prepared for greater ones. I sense great things from you, my son. Listen to the small voice inside and it will lead you."

Shem tried to smile. "I shall try, Father."

"Good night, Son."

"Father? There is something else. Nazar has been with us for over a full moon. What shall we do with him?"

Noah chuckled. "That big one? I think he has grown a hand taller, since he has arrived. He is curious and asks many questions. I like him."

"Should he not go back to his own people?"

"You brought him here. It is up to you, Son." Noah shut the door.

Shem grimaced. "I thought you might say that."

Chapter 17
A New Direction

Time passed without incident in the tiny hamlet. Fall and winter passed and spring was showing blooms of the first field flowers. Nazar had become a close member of the community, sharing and contributing as well as anyone. He too had bloomed, and had grown more than two feet taller in one year to become a spectacle to visitors passing through the valley. This, however, did not give him any special privileges...quite the contrary; they expected him to do work equal to his size.

The foundation of the ark had not even been finished, and yet an acre of trees had been felled to build the supporting structure to house the boat. It looked like a huge cage with an open top and crisscrossing supports. Shem, Ham, and Nazar hoisted one of the last spars across the forward part of the scaffold.

"Have you got this end, Nazar?" asked Shem, letting go of his hold of the large log.

Nazar grunted. "Yes, Master Shem. They get lighter the more I handle them."

Shem reached down to pick up some hemp rope. "Hold it now, while I tie it off."

At the other end, Ham slipped and fell on a crossbeam, bruising his ribs. "Blight me!" he shouted, sitting up. He tested his ribs.

Shem recollected. "I remember how Uncle Zakho would say that. Oh, how I miss him and our times of wandering."

Ham grabbed onto a support bracket and pulled himself up. "What does it matter? Why are we here! I am sick of this!"

"Father told us to do it, and that is all," replied Shem.

"Has Father ever told you what this boat will be used for?"

Shem pointed toward the Aras River. "No. It does not make sense if we build here. It will be too far from the river." He then stepped back to examine the scope and size of the scaffolding. "If it is as big as Father says it will be, it could make a good place for safety...from an enemy."

"If that was true, then he would have us build a walled village." Ham moved closer and spoke quietly. "Do you think Father's mind is ill? What if this is truly all for nothing?"

Shem smiled coyly. "Oh, he knows what he is doing. You can rest easy on that thought."

Ham kicked at the wooden stanchion and rubbed his ribs. "I wish Japheth was here." He looked around. "Where is Shinar? He is always busy crawling after Lily. We spend all our lives building this cage and yet fail to lay one board of the boat! Why do we do this? I hate this work!" Ham slumped down to the ground with his back against the pole, then let out a long sigh.

Nazar walked over, sat down beside Ham. He put his long arm around him. "I know why we are here."

Ham removed Nazar's hand and rolled his eyes. "Tell us, oh Great One!"

"Master Noah told me this is where the boat must be built, because this is where it all began."

Ham raised an eyebrow. "Where all what began?"

"The Garden of Delight—Eden. The master told me that it was all in God's plan. When your people left for the city of Tuball, they walked right by the land of the garden."

Ham scowled. "I went with our people to Tuball, and saw no garden."

"Master Noah said that after the fall, man left to follow his own way. Man is blind to where the garden is."

"How is it that father told you all this, Nazar, and not me, Ham…his own son?"

Nazar shrugged his shoulders. "I do not know. You will have to ask him."

Shem secured the rope around the log and gave it a yank for certainty, then noticed a lone figure enter Noah's home. He scrutinized the man a moment, then climbed down to the ground to get a better view. Ham climbed back up and tested the other end of the log by jumping on top. With the scaffold virtually complete, Shem felt no urgency to stay around.

"Can you do without me, Ham?"

"Why? So you can rest easy like Shinar?"

"I want to talk with Father. But I will return."

"Make it soon. And bring us more water when you come back. And if you see Shinar, tell him we could use him, too."

Shem smirked. "But we are almost finished."

"Shinar does not know that."

Shem didn't reply. He trotted down the slope to investigate the visitor. By the time he had arrived, the person was gone. Shem leaned against the door frame and looked inside to see his father setting a birdcage to the side of his drawings.

Shem wiped his sweaty forehead. "Is Shinar near, Father? Ham wishes his help."

Noah waved a hand toward the valley. "He has taken to herding the sheep and goats. The herd does well at his hand. Ham can do without him."

"Ham does not think so. Ham says we labor long days and have not even started the boat. I think he misses Japheth, too."

Noah continued to examine his drawings without looking up. "Do not despise the day of small beginnings. Let each day take care of itself. I will send for Japheth soon enough."

"Ham was also not happy that you told Nazar about the garden—and not him."

Noah looked up with a satisfying recollection on his face. "Hmmm...the garden. Do you remember when I told you about Azarah?" Shem nodded. "After her death, I wandered the earth to find the first land of Adam. I needed to know where it all began. After many moons, I found the entrance of a beautiful arch, cut out of a rocky cliff. Through the arch I beheld a wonderful beauty of flowers and fruit trees feeding off a gentle stream...the likes I had never seen. As I drew near, two tall men with golden hair guarded the entrance with flaming swords. I asked what the land was and they said that it was a sacred garden. They warned me to leave. They were greatly handsome and may have been angels. I stepped closer to see deep within the fruitful land beyond the arch, but their eyes became like fire and they brought down their flaming swords to strike me. I was quick to move back from the fearsome ones and ran away, never to return."

Shem leaned close. "I too have seen an angel. It had wings like an eagle and its face was a bright as the sun."

"Angel? You must tell me more of this, Son...later."

Shem picked up a water flask hanging next to the table and took a drink. "Where did you see the garden, Father?"

Noah tipped his head southeast. "It was somewhere in that direction."

Shem's passion for new discoveries overwhelmed him. "Would you show me where it is?"

"Let it go. I think God gave me one look at it to satisfy my desire. We would never find it again."

Shem looked out the doorway. "Who was that man, Father?"

Noah looked out to see the diminishing figure crossing the footbridge by the river. "Oh, just a messenger."

"Was the message of value?"

"Of value to the Tuballites. It seems that the northern tribes have been quiet."

"Good," said Shem.

Noah shook his head. "No, not good. It has been too quiet. No one has heard or seen the Oka or Ugric people. It is feared that they are up to no good. Maybe even an attack on the city of Tuball. I think the same."

"And if they attack the city, our people…"

"Yes—*our* people will be attacked too." Noah peered at Shem with distress. "I would not be so concerned, if you had not told me of behemoths, Son. If the northerners use the animals' mighty strength, it could mean big trouble for the city of Tuball."

Shem watched as Noah tapped his fingers on the bird cage. "What are the doves in the cage for?"

Noah evaded the question. He stopped his tapping, then looked out the window and over where the scaffold stood like a rectangular skeleton. "It looks as if we can soon begin the boat walls now, yes?"

Shem nodded. "Yes. Ham, Nazar, and I have almost finished the last log.

"Good. I will send word to my boat friends beyond the mountains and they will guide us with the ship building. This boat will be an ark, a monument to others that we believe in the one true God who rescues us through the worst of times."

"Ham says that clans walk by, laugh, and tell us that our God is not so great if we have to build it ourselves.

"Worry not what the other clans say. They will not laugh when God takes out his anger on them."

"You did not answer my question about the doves, Father."

"I must inspect the framework now." Noah glanced back at the doves, walking out the door. "The birds? They have their use."

Unsure why Noah was so elusive, Shem watched his father step up the hill with his staff. Shem peered into the cage. "If he wanted to explain, he would have." Shem tapped the twigs that made up the cage walls. "Hmmm. I doubt you two are for eating; and he does not keep pets. So what is father up to?" Shem knew he would be thinking all night. Not so much about the doves, but about his Sethite kin, plowing the land and building the streets beyond the city. How would they fare living outside the city walls when the northern raiders descended on them?

During and after the evening meal, Shem was quiet. He sat on Noah's and Naamah's front stone stoop and looked at the four other houses nearby. Lily took out a cloth and wiped the sweat and dirt from Shinar's face. Shinar caught her hand and kissed it. She smiled, patted his cheek, then continued cleaning her husband's grime. Noah approached Shem and sat on a bench next to the house. The sun was setting and cast long shadows across the hamlet.

"You have not said much, my son. Is there something you wish to say or should I let you be?"

"Shem sighed and dropped his head. "I must go back, Father."

"Back where?"

"To Tuball."

"To more danger? Is that wise? We need you here, Shem. We will celebrate the work completed thus far, and then begin the new work on the boat."

"I cannot leave our people in Tuball with the threat of danger stalking them."

"You almost lost your life. Are you willing to risk it again?"

Shem massaged his head where the last serious blow landed. He still harbored daily headaches and it took a feat of strength for Shem to contain sudden outbursts of anger. "If I must, I must."

"If you expose yourself, Kara will know you live. She is the grand mistress and has new duties to follow; not the ones you and her had planned. I have also learned she has a boy child."

Shem gulped, then tapped the earth with his foot, not looking at his father. "So be it. As you said, Father, there are no plans for her anymore."

Noah sighed and peered out at the dwindling daylight. "Men were not meant to kill each other. Warring hearts will be the downfall." Noah cleared his throat. "I do not want you to leave me, Son. I fear more sadness will be added to your heart."

Shem reached out and rested his hand on his father's knee. "I promise I will be back after we defeat the northern tribes. With Bulla's headship it will be short, and I will return to help on this boat."

Noah massaged his eyes. "Do not make a promise, you cannot keep."

"I need to do this, Father."

"I see that trying to stop you would be like pushing back a river." Noah removed his hand from his eyes. He focused keenly on Shem. "If you must, will you stop at the warrior city of Baku, first?"

"Baku?"

"Yes. There is a magus—a seeker of the truth. I want you give him a message for me."

Shem looked into the bright yellow/green eyes of Noah. "You want me to speak to a magus?"

"Yes."

Shem had a puzzled frown. "But you always told me not to listen or even speak to a magus."

"This man is different. Besides, it is too late for that. Have you not already spoken to one?"

Shem thought back to Berin, the magus at the city of Tuball. "How did you know?"

"It does not matter. Some men are magi in name only and some are truth seekers. The magus in Baku is one such as these. Now listen; you must send him a message."

"What message?"

"Ask him for me: 'Will you guide my son, Shem, on his purpose?'"

Shem was startled. He remembered the words from the mystic Berin. He too said Shem had a purpose. Now his interest was piqued. His elders are sending him everywhere and telling him nothing. What possible reason could they have to hold back knowledge from him? Shem's curse was that he had an incurable sense of adventure and curiosity, while at the same time obediently captive to his father's wishes.

"I will do as you ask, Father."

Noah smiled. They both glanced at Lily and Shinar moving back into their home. "Someday, there will be a woman on your arm too. But only God knows when that will be."

"When I am old and grey," said Shem, despondently.

"Ha! I doubt a young man with your value will have long to wait." Noah ruffled Shem's head and laughed.

Shem threw a pebble across the path. "It seems that way to me. And what of Nazar, Father? Should I take him with me?"

"With you leaving, we will need his help. We will care well for him…as long as there is enough sheep to feed him," he added with a wink.

* * *

When boat makers had arrived, Shem escorted the men up to the scaffolding. They brought their new designs that integrated the size constraints that Noah had established. The boat makers decided that the local trees were plentiful and enough for their needs. Noah requested there be plenty of stalls in the ship. The boat makers calculated that hundreds of rooms could be built, within a vessel over 450 feet long, 75 feet wide, and 45 feet high. Ventilation and lighting was critical. The men came up with a unique design of slatted floors to allow airflow between decks and maximize light with upper sky hatch windows.

Shem felt his departure was timely. Most of the next season would be one of planning and measuring at the worksite. Harvesting and shaping timber would be an ongoing process that would extend for years. He stood in the hamlet said goodbye to a handful of transient workers, gave a big hug to his mother and father, punched Ham lightly, and shook wrists with Shinar. Lily stood a bashful half-step behind her husband. Shem bowed to Lily, strapped a bundle on his back and with spear in hand turned to leave. The only thing drawing him away was his concern for his Sethite brethren in the city. But can one man save them from invaders?

Chapter 18
Schemes and Dreams

Ilkin looked out the window of his log house to see if anyone was coming. He ducked back in and hurried over to a wrinkled old woman with ratty hair and disintegrating clothing. He traded several copper discs for a small bone vile of hers.

She cackled at the sound of the coins in her hand.

Ilkin opened the top to ensure the vial was full. He showed her to the door. The bent woman left and gave a wicked laugh that echoed through the streets. He shuddered and went inside to find a place for his purchase. Ilkin wanted a place where his woman, Mansi, wouldn't find it. Just when he spotted a crack between two logs, Mansi opened the door. Ilkin turned abruptly and slid the bone vile from his hand to his pocket.

"Was that not the maker of spells?" she asked, shutting the door.

Ilkin went to the window as if seeing the old woman for the first time. "Oh, yes. Yes, it was." He felt around for the crack to hide the vile but was unsuccessful.

"Did you speak with her?"

He turned around to face her. "Yes."

"What did you want with her? She deals in dark medicines."

Ilkin shrugged. "I had a pain that has been ailing me. She gave me something to be rid of it."

Mansi walked over and placed her hands on his face. "Stay away from her. I will send for my own healer if you need anything." She removed her hands from his face and embraced him.

Ilkin stroked her hair as she laid her head on his chest. "If that is what you wish, I will obey." Ilkin kissed her forehead, then put his hand on her belly. "He is growing fast."

She smiled and covered her hands over his. "How do you know it is a boy child?"

"My mother, and mother's mother, had many boys...all grew to men of greatness."

"It may be a woman of greatness," she offered.

Ilkin smiled. "It shall be a child of greatness, nonetheless. And speaking of greatness, has your father decided on my plan to attack the city of Tuball?"

Mansi's shoulders dropped and she let out a breath of discontent. "You men always want to defeat other tribes." She walked over to a bed of fox pelts and sat down to sulk. "I do not know."

Ilkin pounded his fist on the table. "Again he delays!"

She was startled by the blow. "Do not be angry, my husband. He will see highly of your ideas in time. Give thanks that Father does not scoff at the mention of your name anymore."

Ilkin paced. "He is growing too fat in his head. The Ugric people need more from a leader than to solve family squabbles or petty theft. They need a high leader that will rule over all the tribes of the world."

Mansi arched her back and adjusted her seating position. "Is this high leader *you*, my husband?"

Ilkin crossed his arms. "It may be. It could be your father if he would move faster than a slug."

"Do not be in such a hurry. As long as my father lives, we must live by his rulings, yes?"

Ilkin tried not to sound treasonous. "Yes. You are right. We must respect his wishes." Ilkin turned. "As long as he lives," he muttered under his breath. "But I must see your father about the Tuballites. I have many ideas."

Mansi rolled her eyes. "This talk of war never ends with you."

Ilkin looked at her with a pained disbelief. "Do you not understand what this means to me—and you? I wish to rule, yes. But do you not wish the grand things of the city? Have you not told me how you want fine scents and clothing and jewels?"

Mansi looked away with a half smile. "Yes."

He knelt down close to her. "These are our dreams. But they may be ruined if the Tuballites bring warriors and weapons to enslave us."

"But we have peace with them. Could we not just leave here and live in the city as any other?"

"I cannot go back that way, woman. They would surely kill me. Is that what you want? A fatherless son?"

"Or daughter?"

Ilkin jumped up. "Or daughter! It does not matter!" He took a breath to calm himself. "You will have nothing if we do not make the Tuballites kneel before us. Only then will we be able to live as we wish."

Mansi stood up and rubbed next to Ilkin like a cat. "Then do as you see fit, Husband. I see great things in you."

Ilkin grasped her waist and pulled her plump belly to his. He kissed her lips hard, then pulled back to focus into her eyes. "Someday, we will rule not just the Ugric tribes, but all the lands of the world."

* * *

Later that day, Ilkin leaned on his elbows over the wooden pen of the behemoths. He watched the beast masters sit high atop the long-curved tusked animals. The behemoths mumbled low rumbling sounds and stepped on the earth with gentle force. They had a high hairy hump which allowed the trainers to sit neatly between the hump and the head without falling off. The trainers gave a few grunting commands and used wooden sticks to tap the animals' heads for direction. Most of the behemoths were used to transport logs or big buckets of stone for building structures or roads. All of the beasts were available for battle at a moment's notice. Although the power of the animals was impressive during peace, it was staggering during war.

After watching the activity for awhile, Ilkin sought out the head beast master. The beast master was large and fat, but full of muscle. He had worked with the animals his whole life and was head over all the other trainers. He had just released an animal and was rolling up a hemp rope, when Ilkin came close. The Ugric grinned with a crooked set of teeth.

"Here comes the noble son of the high leader." The beast master bowed with disdain.

"Know your place, man!" said Ilkin.

The beast master softened. "What is it you wish, Master Ilkin?"

"You know as well as I that my father is soft on war. We have these great beasts and need to use them. The city of Tuball and all it has could be ours for the taking. Do you not see that?"

The beast master continued to roll up the rope. "Many of the warriors ache to go to battle, but it merely gets them killed. And then what would their women say?"

"They would say they died well," countered Ilkin.

The wide man's eyes narrowed. "You offer victory? But we are at peace. Why do you wish to stir up trouble?"

"I have lived in Tuball and know of the grand elder's plans. Do you not see how he expands his lands to rule over others? Clan after clan becomes part of the Bundled Tribes. If you want the Ugric to be slaves to the Tuballites, do nothing."

"What can I do about such things? I cannot venture out on my own. I obey the high leader."

"It is right that you obey," said Ilkin. "But we must always be prepared for an attack, no?"

"That makes sense. So how should we prepare?"

Ilkin thought for a moment. "How do you kill a behemoth?"

The beast master laughed. "Not easily."

"What is its weakest point?"

"Everyone knows that many spears to body, it could take. I expect a spear to the head would bring it down fast."

Ilkin wanted a solution. "I have seen how the size of the animal can scare men into running. But this will not last long. Tuballites will use that weak spot to their gain. Agul, the Okan, has told me that every year it gets harder to breed the behemoth. It is more important than ever to protect them."

The beast master walked over to one of the animals and looked up to it. He thought deeply and walked around the beast. Soon he turned back to Ilkin. "We could use wood to make a shield for the animal to protect its head."

Ilkin smiled with a squint. "Good. What would it take to stop them if you did that?"

"Nothing I can think on."

"If you are the *beast master*, should you not prepare for this? If there was a war, the high leader would praise your good thinking. You would save the lives of the beasts and your kin."

The heavy man scratched his scraggly beard. "I may have thought wrong of you, Master Ilkin."

Ilkin bowed to the beast master, then turned around. *These Ugric are so blind to the might of these beasts. They could conquer the world if they wished.* He strode away from the pen and back into the Big Village straight into the great hall. There the high leader sat on his throne settling a squabble with local clan elders.

The chief looked over at Ilkin as he approached. "What is it?"

Ilkin bowed his head. "I need to speak with you, High Leader."

The chief waved off the elders. "Is it for you or my daughter?"

"Neither and both. I have seen to it that the beasts are clad with wooden shields for when we attack the Tuballites."

"Clad with shields? Attack? Who said we were to attack the Tuballites?"

"If we do not they will hit first and with much force. If the animals are not prepared we will perish."

"It is a fine idea to protect the animals. But are you more concerned for your new people here or conquering your old friends that banished you?"

"We must do this!"

"Oh? We *must*? And when did you become high leader?" He turned to pick up a drink of watered-down mead from a tray a servant held out. "I do not trust you, Ilkin. You are as spoiled as a rotten egg, and will have to learn your place." He drank half the cup. "I do not know what my daughter sees in you, but I swear you will be tamed as the behemoth has been tamed. You may leave now." He turned away from Ilkin and set the cup on the armrest of the throne. He picked out some shelled mollusks from a tray at his side and ignored Ilkin.

Ilkin boiled inside, but held his composure. He walked rigidly out of the hall and into the market place. He kicked over a stand of fish, which slid out onto the cobbled stone pavement. "Out of my way!" he shouted.

A young girl crouched down in the street. In her hand, she stroked a bird with a broken wing. She held it up to him as he strode forward. He looked down at the bird and scooped it out of her hand. Ilkin held it for a moment then, with a squeeze, crushed the life out of the bird. "Only the strong can live," he admonished. The astonished child stood erect with a quivering chin and tearing eyes. He threw the bird down and stormed down the street.

The high leader had watched Ilkin stomp out. "He is trouble," said the chief, to anyone who could hear.

One of the advisers to the high leader had been listening and walked over to the chief. "Try not to anger him so, oh High Leader. The Oka chief, Agul, agrees with Ilkin. If his words are true about the Tuballites, we have much to fear."

The chief finished his drink. "Ilkin may know of the Tuballite ways, but he must be tamed. I fear for my daughter, and I fear for our tribe." He sighed. "Talk to the other clans and see what they say. If we are to go to war, I will be the one to make it so."

Chapter 19
Back to Baku

Days after leaving his parents' home, Shem topped the hill that faced the military city of Baku. The fortification was as he remembered it: high stone walls, sloping inward, spanning over a mile from each corner. Soldiers positioned themselves at each corner of the rectangular towers, and guards stood at the entrance of thick wooden gates, open wide for citizens to pass through.

Two years ago, he had arrived at the city inexperienced and ignorant about soldiers and their methods. Now he was a veteran of battle, bold and fearless. Shem first met Bulla in this city and became his friend. Some friend Bulla was, to take his woman. Shem fought back his thoughts of Kara. Some day he hoped he would not think of her at all. He covered himself with a cold blanket of emotional protection and moved onward.

As he started through the gates, a sturdy soldier with protective leathers thrust a spear across Shem's chest. "Your name and doings?"

Shem moved the spear to the side. "I am Shem, son of Noah. Here to see the magus."

The guard's face turned red. "Shem? The great one? I did not know. It is an honor to meet you. I will have a runner show you to the master." The guard bowed and whistled. Soon a young boy of ten years appeared. "Show Master Shem to the magus," said the soldier.

Shem nodded to the soldier then followed the boy through the city. The boy was quick and agile. They hopped over open sewage drains in the center of the market streets, side-stepped cattle droppings, passed around a troop of soldiers marching, and, finally, trotted up a series of stone steps to a lone tower at the eastern wall of the city. The young runner knocked on the door, bowed to Shem, then skipped back down the stairs.

For a long moment it was silent, and Shem considered that the boy may have been wrong. Shem started to knock again when a slot in the door slid open to reveal a wrinkled, red-veined eye, surrounding a brown iris.

"Yes?"

"I am Shem, son of Noah. I have come to see the magus."

"What is my name?" ask the old man, emotionless.

"Your name? Do you not know your own name?"

The man's voice was steady. "Yes, but I am asking if you know my name."

"How would I know your name? I have just met you."

"I have just met you, and yet I know you are Shem."

Shem scowled. "But I just told you *my* name."

"Yes, it does not seem fair, does it? I will give you three guesses?"

Shem sighed. "I do not wish to play games. Are you the magus of the city?"

"Do you think I am?"

Shem rolled his eyes. "How could you be? You act so silly."

"Are you saying that a magus cannot act silly?"

Shem slapped his forehead. "Let me in to see the magus or…"

"Or what?"

"Or I will break down this door!"

"It is a thick door. That, as well, does not seem fair to you. Would it not be better if I opened the door?"

"Yes!" Shem replied with fire in his eyes.

"If you had asked me, I would have done it," he responded, unlatching the lock.

When the door swung open, there stood an older man with a long white beard, clothed in a tattered robe. He smiled with a glint in his eye. He was wide, with red cheeks and nose that matched his red-veined eyes.

"So sorry for the questions…much work has worn on me. Yet…I already have learned much of you, young Shem, and you know nothing of me."

"That does not seem fair," said Shem, with an eyebrow raised.

"Ha! Yes, good for you, clever one. It is not. But you did not even try. You see, I have learned that you are not a patient man, which is vital when you are in trouble. I have learned that you need more compassion—to bond with others. I have learned that you do not like to play games, which is most important for casting off the evil that lurks within." The fat man poked Shem in the chest then stepped back with his arms proudly folded over his belly. "What say you now?"

Shem stood stupidly still and let all that was said sink in. "I like some games," he muttered. Shem looked down at the stone floor. "You are right. I am all of those things."

"And you are humble! A very good quality to gain wisdom."

The man put his arm around Shem and brought him into his workplace. It was a mess. Clothes, papers, food, all scattered about without rhyme or reason. A complete opposite to that of Tuball's magus, Berin, and his workshop. Next to the window was a cage that had a small dove inside.

Do all the magi of the world like birds? Shem moved some papers to sit on a stool. He propped his spear against the floor. "You did not tell me your name, sir."

"It is Rutul. Does that mean anything to you?"

"Should it?"

"Ah! You did not say yes or no, Shem. You are catching on. You have learned already to let others reveal themselves before they know about you. That will be of use when you are unsure of your adversary. If I say yes, it shows I think highly of myself. If I say no, it shows I do not." Rutul looked to the ceiling for a moment. "But what if I said, 'it may?' What would you say then?"

Shem played along. "I would say that you are a timid or cautious person, because you did not say yes or no."

"Very good. It may or may not be true, but it would certainly move me into exposing who I am by how I respond. Enough of my teachings. You came here to ask me something, yes?"

"Yes. My father told me to come to you and ask if you would help me on my purpose."

Rutul leaned over and whispered. "Did you know that I knew you would say that?"

Shem was puzzled. "How could you?"

Rutul pointed at the dove in the cage. "That bird. We strap writings to their legs and send messages to one another. I knew you would be here before you did."

It finally made sense to Shem. "Berin had a dove, too. You must have sent messages to him, too."

Rutul chuckled. "Yes. We are the three servants of the Almighty that watch over our people. It has been three seasons now, but it gives us a picture of what mischief is about. Did your father not tell you of this?" Shem shook his head. Rutul smiled with an open mouth. "Noah is very good at keeping secrets."

"Why did my father not tell me this? And now *you* tell me this…without even making me guess."

"He has his reasons—I have mine. My task is to prepare you for your purpose."

Shem leaned in. "What is my purpose?"

Rutul's smile faded. "You wish to stop the Ugric, yes?"

"Yes."

"Are you willing to do something you would never wish to do?"

Shem scowled. "I do not understand. Tell me what I must do to keep my people from dying at the hands of the Ugric and I will do it."

"I cannot say what you must do. To stop the Ugric will take plenty, maybe even killing a man such as the high leader. Could you do that?"

"You mean when he sleeps or is not looking at me?" he whispered.

The old man shrugged. "Those are two ways. There is a man that lives in the northern flatlands—Kalmyk. He shall be your guide to do this deed. He is skilled in the art of killing silently ... man or beast."

"I cannot go north. I have to return to Tuball and warn the grand elder, Bulla. My father says the Oka and Ugric may attack and my people live there."

The old man shook his head. "You are too young to know what is needed. The Ugric will not war with the Tuballites for some time, and Bulla may not need to prepare for battle. Sometimes just one man can do more than thousands of warriors. Would you be willing to be that one man?"

Shem struck his spear to the floor. "If it means to stop a war? Yes!"

"Then you must meet with Kalmyk and he will guide you. I sense you have lived much in your short years, but your wisdom still has not grown as it should."

"I do not know this Kalmyk. Why would he help me?"

Rutul opened a box and took out a copper cube and handed it to Shem. "Give this to him and he will help you."

Shem took the cube and put it in his traveling pouch. "How do I find this man?"

"Warriors from this city leave tomorrow in search for allies and enemies of the Bundled Tribes. You will walk with them as far as the most northern outpost. They will show you the path to Kalmyk. Sleep here tonight and go with them at sunlight. There is straw in the corner. I will talk with the warriors and let them know. Take care, clever one."

After Rutul left the room, Shem bedded down upon the straw. He took long to sleep, but it seemed a short one. He woke to a pounding on the door. Night had slipped by and the morning light was streaming through the window. Shem jumped to his feet and looked around for the magus, but he wasn't there. On the table were a raw yam and a slice of cooked pig. Again there was a pounding against the door. Shem went to open it. There stood a muscular soldier with a spear in his hand. He wore his military leathers on his chest, legs, and wrist.

"You are the one who wishes to find the silent killer?"

Shem nodded. "Will you take me to him?"

The man tipped his head to indicate Shem was to follow. Shem grabbed the yam and pork from the table and followed the warrior. Within minutes, a troop of over fifty armed men had assembled at the northern gate. They formed two columns with Shem at the rear. They moved at a fast march out of the northern gate, led by a big, bushy bearded, war-hardened leader. The troops kept at a good trot for many miles over hills and valleys, stopping to rest only if necessary. It was plain that every one of the muscle bound men was an elite fighter. Shem was no slouch when it came to prowess, but even he had to work hard to keep up the pace.

They moved north over small mountains and wound their way on an animal path until a great expanse opened up. Shem tried to strike up conversations with the men along the way, but they chose to say little. It was evident that the soldiers had spent time with one another. They flowed together, legs and arms rocking in sequence on the march. Shem wondered if they did battle as well as they marched.

It was on the fourth day out, on a cool crisp morning, that Shem found out their abilities. Two scouts were unseen and far in the lead when a shout was heard. The land was flat and the grass was as tall as a man's shoulder. Shem and the others waited. It wasn't long before the first scout sprinted back to the group with crazed eyes.

"The beast is upon us!" he shouted.

Shem turned to one of the warriors. "What is happening?" No one answered him.

The hulking leader whistled something and waved his spear in a circle. Instantly the men retreated back from the tall grass and formed a circle. The leader grabbed Shem by the arm and ran to the rear of the circle. The formation of men left an opening for the second scout to enter and stand alone in the center with his spear facing the opening. They waited, poised fiercely, weapons ready. The ground shook before them and the grasses trembled with the pounding. Shem stepped around the leader to get a better view. The pounding became louder and more intense. The tall grass spread open.

Before them entered a large, brown, woolly rhinoceros. Its back was higher than a man's head and its largest horn was as long as a man's leg. Its heavy hide was covered with long strings of hair that dangled like a thin curtain. The animal paused, sniffed the air, then snorted out a breath full of vapor. It rocked its head up and down and focused directly upon the scout, oblivious to the other warriors standing still as statues. The rhinoceros snorted, stomped, and advanced straight for the scout. The scout stood bravely in the center, shouting at the animal to come at him. The scout never had a chance. The beast skewered the man with his horn through his belly. Death was quick.

With the man's body lying on the face of the rhinoceros, the other warriors yelled out a war cry that startled the big herbivore. The animal shook off the dead man to locate the others' positions. The warriors began to throw their weapons. Spears flew in sequential rotation from the right front side of the circle, around to the back, and then back to the left front side of the circle, hitting the animal in the legs, the flank, and the neck repeatedly. The beast tried to face the source of the spears, but their systematic rotating launching confused it.

The warriors weren't in a hurry. They had three spears apiece and continued to accurately throw one at a time. As the rhinoceros continued to whirl around and to face his attackers, its body oozed blood. It had a thick hairy hide, but at this short distance, it didn't take long for the spears to yield a pool of red. The animal's short, stubby legs finally buckled after the third wave of spears. Without a word, the men stepped back, pulled knives from their belts, and stood at attention. The leader of the men was the last soldier with a spear. As he walked boldly up to the two ton animal, it fell on its side with a *thud*. The rhinoceros stared at its attacker, then blinked in submission, knowing what was about to come. The leader took his spear and drove it into the brain of the animal. It was over.

The men remained silent while the leader knelt down on one knee to inspect the creature. He tipped his head and the others ran to remove their spears.

The leader stood back. "Check the tall grass."

Two men ran back into the tall grass. He stood fast with his spear planted beside him, waiting for a clear confirmation. Shem kept close to the commanding soldier.

"Are there more?" asked Shem.

"The hairy beast should have been far to the north, where the snow lives long," the leader muttered, his eyes fixed forward.

Moments later, one of the warriors returned and waved an all clear signal. The men relaxed. Shem was amazed at the teamwork and skill of the soldiers. He'd never felt as safe as this moment with these men. The troops in the city of Tuball could certainly learn from them.

"What tribe do you come from?" Shem asked the leader.

His face was stolid and his body motionless. "Where we come from does not matter. Each man has his place and duty. It is ours to protect the edge of our borders from any and all who defy us. We will not, and do not, lose."

"I doubt you not," replied Shem.

The soldiers didn't have to say anything more to make their point. They spoke with their actions. And on the day they reached the outpost, Shem bowed to the commander of the men and shook his wrist. The leader gave Shem directions that pointed him on a path north. It would ultimately take him to the man the magus of Baku called the silent killer.

Chapter 20
The Silent Killer

The peak of the warm season brought out a good sweat over Shem's body, and yet with every day he traveled north, the nights became cooler. The face of the distant hills, from east to west, presented large swaths of ice, like white permanent masks. Shem shivered at the thought of crossing them and prayed the path he was on would not take him there.

Into the third day from the outpost, he passed through a grassy plain with blue lobelia flowers, and into a grove of oak trees. Halfway through the grove, the path paralleled a slow moving stream teeming with insects. As he swatted at the pests, he spotted a log home in front of some birch trees. When Shem neared the property, he noticed a young woman dipping a bucket in a well.

"Hello!" Shem called out.

The woman looked startled and ran inside the house with her bucket.

Shem walked toward the house and noticed a shed adjacent to it. Next to the shed was a pen with a few pigs and one with chickens. Except for the snorting of the pigs and the clucking of chickens, he heard and saw nothing else. He stopped to examine a wooden cart with wheels. Shem was impressed with the invention. He pushed on the cart and smiled at the ease of which the cart moved. Shem backed up the cart and was ready to push it once more when he felt the sharp point of a knife in the small of his back.

"Do not move, friend," said a man.

"Friend? My friends do not put knives to my back," replied Shem. "May I face you to speak?"

"You may...slowly. Tell me what it is you want here?"

Shem let go of the cart and turned around with his hands open. The man stepped back with his knife, poised in a state of readiness. He wore a fur hat, was taller than Shem by a head, had almond shaped eyes ... and no beard. Shem had never known a man to intentionally keep his face cut so clean. He was twice Shem's age, but very fit. He wore animal hide boots, leather trousers, and a woven wool shirt. His face spoke of a ruddy frankness with years of experience.

Shem rubbed his back with his hand to check for blood. "You did not need to use a weapon on me to ask that question."

"There has been trouble lately. I trust no one."

"What trouble?"

The man scowled at Shem, jutting the knife forward. "I ask the questions, friend."

Shem kept his hands low and exposed his palms to show he had no weapons. "You will not have trouble from me. I am Shem, son of Noah. And you?"

"Kalmyk."

Shem's eyes lit up. "That is why I did not hear you. You are the silent killer, yes?"

His face tightened. "I am but a hunter of the forest. Who told you that?"

"Rutul, the magus of Baku. He sent me here."

The man's face softened, but he was still skeptical. "How do I know you tell me the truth? Even my enemies know this."

Shem reached into his pouch, pulled out the copper cube, and presented it. "He told me to give this to you."

The stranger sheathed his knife, took the cube, and stepped a safe distance back. He inspected the markings on the copper, and stared at it a while as if recalling a series of lost memories. The man dropped the cube into his pants pocket then looked back up to Shem. "Come, friend, you must be hungry."

Shem was pressed forward to the log house. When they opened the wooden door, a young woman was taking a sip from a large wooden spoon out of a clay pot over a fire. She was dressed in a sleeveless deerskin dress, loosely fitted down over her knees.

Kalmyk pointed at the young woman. "This is Liazzat."

The young woman turned and greeted Kalmyk with a smile and Shem with a shy nod. She was close to Shem's age and agreeable to look at. Long, blond hair twisted in a braid that fell to the low part of her back. Her strong arms and calves showed she worked the land.

"Lia, give this man something to eat," Kalmyk said to the woman. He sat on a bench by a wooden table.

Kalmyk flung his hat across the room, where it landed against the wall on a wooden peg. His hair was short and reddish-brown. A tattoo of dots trailed down the side of his head, behind his neck. Shem tried not to stare at the peculiar markings, assuming the man would take offense. The woman set a cup of water on the table.

Shem sat on the opposite side of the bench and looked up at the woman. "Is this your daughter?"

"She is now. I found her abandoned by her people. They left her to be eaten by wolves."

"Why would they do that to their own daughter?"

The man spoke curtly. "You ask many questions. We are not here to talk about her. Do you wish something of her or me?"

Shem blushed. "Of you, sir."

Kalmyk patted his pocket. "I know Rutul. He would not give this cube back to me unless he wanted a favor. So what is it?"

Shem took a drink from the cup. "I do not know if you have heard of my people, the Sethites. We once lived far south of Anbar Market. Do you know of it?"

"I have heard of Anbar, but not of these Sethites."

"My people now live amongst the Tuballites, but are in danger."

"Danger from what?"

Shem became more animated. "*Being killed.* I was told Rutul would guide me in the ways I should go and he pointed me to you. There are rumors that the Ugric will attack the city of Tuball with their great beasts. I need your help to stop them. Maybe if I kill their leader, it will stop the battle?"

Kalmyk leaned back and smiled for the first time. "You want to kill the high leader of the Ugric?"

"Yes. I think so."

"It is easy to creep up behind someone and cut their throat, and harder to live with. But that would not be a wise thing to do."

"Why not?"

"First, I can see in your face you are not willing. Second, it would anger the Ugric even more. They would hunt and kill every outsider until they felt they had gotten revenge. It would bond them with the other surrounding smaller clans, making them bigger and stronger than before. In the end, the city of Tuball would still fall and at a heavier price."

Shem was stunned by Kalmyk's frank of opinion and paused to reflect on his points. "You are correct to say that I am not willing. But I will still do what I must to protect my people. If we kill the leader, would it not be like cutting off the head of a snake? Or maybe you are afraid to help me?"

Kalmyk narrowed his gaze at Shem. "There is nothing more I would like than to see the high leader dead, but I do not even know you. Do not test my courage." The two stared at one another a moment without a word.

Their silence was broken when Lia set down a bowl of badger stew. "Eat," she ordered.

Shem nodded his thanks to the young woman and closed his eyes to pray. As he ate Kalmyk sat still, sizing up the stranger like a caged animal. Shem ignored his host and he peered around the room. There was nothing of consequence. No idols or icons, no proof of an allegiance to a tribe.

Kalmyk kept a steely eye on Shem. "I see you pray, friend."

"Do you have a god?" Shem asked between bites.

"My belief in a god will not help you." Kalmyk glanced at Lia and got up. "After you eat, I want to show you something outside, friend." He opened the door and walked outside. The young woman followed and shut the door behind her.

Shem heard them talking, but he couldn't understand their words. Lia came back inside to clean some pots. Shem finished his food and thanked the young woman. He found Kalmyk outside near the shed. He waved for Shem to come to him, then led Shem inside where he stored various tools and weapons: axes, spears, slings, knives, short swords, and so on. All were well-crafted from animal bones or tusks, or obsidian stone.

"Pick one," he said exhibiting the weapons with his hands.

Shem pulled back. "I do not need a weapon now."

"Oh, yes, you do. I want you to pick one that will defeat me."

"I do not wish to fight you. It is the Ugric I seek."

The man put his face close to Shem's. "I am an Ugric! To fight me is to fight them. If you mean to save your people, pick a weapon."

Shem looked back at the weapons and wrestled with the idea of killing the man who was supposed to help him. He picked up a well-crafted, three stone bola. Shem dangled the weights from their braided leather cords to check it for balance. On closer inspection, the weights were not stones at all, but ivory, beautifully engraved around the sides. Shem speculated that something as marvelous as this must be able to fell a man and still not harm him.

"I will take this one," said Shem.

"Good. Then I will get my weapons." Kalmyk walked outside and picked up three stones from the ground and held them in his hand. "I will walk over there and we will see who will defeat who. But first, you must test out your weapon."

Shem glanced over to see the young woman peeking out the window, pretending to sweep. He was trying to decide what to throw his weapon against, when a rabbit darted across the grass. Shem instinctively brought the bolo up and rotated it two times before releasing it. The bolo surged forward and wrapped itself around the rabbit, causing the animal to tumble to the ground.

Liazzat squealed for joy when she observed Shem's marksmanship, then ducked back out of view before Shem could spot her.

Shem ran over to the animal and, with a grin, picked it up to display it. "It looks like we have the evening meal."

"Well done, my friend," said Kalmyk with his three stones in his hands. "Now let's see how you do with a man."

"It will be much easier," spouted Shem. "Men are bigger and slower." Shem broke the neck of the rabbit and dropped it to the ground. He bounced up from the dead animal to evaluate his older opponent from across the area. Kalmyk planted himself, then tossed up a stone, caught it, and repeated the process a few times. Shem chuckled at the thought of the man defeating him with a few stones. He raised his bolo to throw.

"I am going to teach you your first lesson, friend. First," he said, passing a stone to his other hand and throwing it before Shem could respond. "You must disarm your enemy."

The rock shot through the air like a lightning bolt at Shem's throwing hand. The stone hit his wrist, making him cry out and forcing him to drop the bolo.

"Second, you must ensure the enemy is not able to rearm," he said tossing another stone into his throwing hand.

Shem reached down to pick up the bolo, but the second rock hit his wrist. Shem rubbed the sore spot. He sprinted to a stone well, grabbed its wooden lid to protect his arms, then started back to retrieve his weapon. Shem snatched up his weapon with the wooden lid shielding him.

"Lastly, you must ensure they are not able to defend themselves. Only then can you subdue the enemy."

Shem lowered the shield to view his opponent. As he did, Kalmyk threw a stone directly at Shem's forehead. He dropped like a bag of wheat. When Shem woke, he was on the floor of the cabin with a cold rag on his head, and a rising bump to go with it. The young woman slipped a lump of rags under his head for comfort. Kalmyk sat on the bench with his feet on the table and his arms across his chest.

"The great warrior is alive," ridiculed Kalmyk.

Shem sat up and touched his forehead. "Ouch. Why is it always my head? How can one stone do so much?" He winced and slid back to the support of the wall. "And I was careful to use a weapon that would not hurt you."

"My friend, it would not matter which weapon you chose, you still would have ended up here on my floor."

"So do you wish to teach me how to fight with stones to beat the Ugric?"

Kalmyk sighed. "You were not listening."

Shem rubbed his head. "Yes I was. You said disarm your enemy, stop them from rearming, then keep them from defending themselves. I wish to learn how to fight as well as you."

"You said it well, but you do not get the meaning. It is late. Sleep, my friend, and we will talk in the new light."

Shem glanced at the fire and felt its warmth. "I am sure I will sleep well here."

"No, not here. You will sleep in the shed."

Shem reluctantly got up and made his way to the tool shed. He found some straw on the floor and lay down to sleep. In the morning, he woke to several drops of water Liazzat tipped out from a jug onto his eyelids. He flinched and looked up to her smiling face. She had brought him some boiled dove eggs and a chunk of crisp millet bread. She set the plate of food and water on the work table.

She stood by to watch him eat. "You are very skilled with the stone thrower weapon, Master Shem…but my father is better."

Shem tested the tenderness of the bump on his head. "I fear you must be right, since he bettered me with but a few stones. How long have you lived here with Master Kalmyk?" he asked, sitting up to set the platter of food on the floor.

"Longer than I know any other as home. I was told that my mother and father were killed by the high leader of the Ugric himself, when I was a small child. I do not know what their crime was. Kalmyk will not tell me. Alone and nowhere to live, he took me as his own. He is the only father I have known."

Shem sat up to eat the eggs and look up into her bright blue eyes. He had never seen such a color. Shem smiled and nodded, but couldn't speak with his mouth full. He looked down at her animal hide shoes and saw a gold bracelet around her ankle. A small stone dangled from the anklet.

Liazzat caught Shem's gaze. "This is beautiful, no?" Shem smiled and nodded between chews. "It was the one thing left of my mother's. I never take it off."

Shem consumed the eggs and cleared his throat with water. "The workmanship is very fine."

She walked closer to him and set her foot on the table to let him see it. "See there are marks on the inside. I do not know what they mean, but it must be of value."

Shem looked inside the finger-width band and peered at the markings. *My woman, my joy.* Shem decided it was best not tell her he could read. He turned it over to see elaborate filigree etched along the outside and a single pink jewel dangling from the band. He let go of the anklet, then took a bite of the millet bread.

"Your parents must have been of high rank."

Liazzat removed her foot from the table came closer. "I think so, too," she agreed with a loud whisper. "Kalmyk told me they were good people, but that is all. I think there is more. He protects me like his own."

Shem finished the last bite of bread and drink of water then set the wooden cup on the plate. "Kalmyk is a good man?"

"Yes, he does not beat me and is rightly firm when I disobey."

Shem was compelled to mention the obvious. "Your eyes are very bright—like the sky."

Liazzat accepted the compliment with a smile. I will leave you now." She bowed with a bashful smile, picked up the plate and mug, then walked toward the door.

Shem retested his cranial bump. "Many thanks for the food, Liazzat."

"You may call me Lia," she replied and closed the door.

Soon after Lia left, Kalmyk opened the door and strode over to get a bag of grain. "Have you thought what I said, my friend?"

Shem got to his feet and stretched to get the kinks out of his back. "Yes, but I do not know what it is you mean."

Kalmyk tipped his head for Shem to follow. "The best way for you to beat the Ugric is with your head. Disarm means to become friends with them." Kalmyk untied the top of the bag and started spreading the grain in the chicken pen. "Stop them from rearming is remove all their suspicions of you. In the end, you must weaken them by letting them think the Tuballites are not a threat." He set the bag down to get a read on Shem's face.

Shem did some quick calculations. "To befriend them? That may take many seasons."

"It may. Are you willing or not?"

"I do not know. But you do … you are one of them. Do you not want me to kill the high leader?"

Kalmyk rubbed his chin with the back of his fingers, his eyes looking beyond Shem with a deadly stare. "That is just what I would like. I would do it myself, for reasons you do not need to know, but I am an outcast and would not get far. I would not be able to set one foot inside the Big Village."

Shem starred at the bag of grain. "I cannot wait seasons, and I am sure the Oka will not waste time to attack again."

"The Oka?"

"Yes, they are allies with the Ugric."

"The Oka, eh? Hmmm. The Oka is an ugly tribe. They care little for their own and less for outsiders. For the Ugric to bind with them could be a bad omen."

Shem tensed. "Teach me the skills of fighting, to stop the Ugric leader before he starts the battle."

"Even if the Oka are involved, fighting does not solve all things."

"The northern tribes may be on the move as we speak," Shem added.

"You worry too much. They will not attack in the cold season. We will have to think on this. Put on some patience. Needless death—such as your own—from rushing in too soon will not save your friends. You must understand your enemy's mind too. I will teach you how they think first. I then *may* teach you how to fight." Kalmyk glanced at the sky. "The days will become much cooler. We must cut wood."

Kalmyk walked over to the wood pile and picked up an axe. He handed it to Shem and left. An hour later, Shem stopped cutting wood when his host returned with a flask of water. As they sat, Kalmyk drew out a map of the North Sea on the ground and pointed out the various clans that inhabited the land.

"There are many clans of the Ugric that live around the Volga River. The strongest clan lives in the Big Village, where the high leader lives. Decisions of weight are made in a place called the great hall ... here," Kalmyk said, pointing to a square at the center of the village. "This is where you will need to go to talk ... or fight if need be."

Shem wondered how Kalmyk knew so much of the inner places of the Big Village. Kalmyk later explained that it was because of the ample amount of business he had conducted with the high leader in the past. Shem believed there was more to the story, because Kalmyk would not reveal why he no longer was allowed into the village.

Chapter 21
Strong Drink

As the days progressed, all went smoothly between teacher and student. Shem listened closely and learned that rules from elders and gods must always be left out of a discussion. He also learned about the psychology of evil men's minds and how to use it against them. Kalmyk taught him that the best way to infiltrate the wariness of men was to develop friendships first and make no judgments. Judging too quickly does not allow one to get in the mind of others.

Shem thought back to the past, when spontaneous reactions and judgment of others had many times put him in danger. He would have gotten himself killed if it hadn't been for the hand of the Creator. Shem began to see the wisdom and cunning of his new mentor and learned many things. Kalmyk and Liazzat had become good for him. With a new mission, he was able to put away his past hurts and concentrate on the future.

One brisk cold morning, Shem warmed up by stacking wood near the shed. He paused to admire a small whirlwind scooping up red and yellow leaves into a funnel then out to a grass field.

Liazzat meandered over to him with a bucket of water. "This season has beauty to it." She took out a cup and plunged it into the bucket for a drink.

Shem smiled. "We can see great beauty even in common things."

Liazzat peered at Shem keenly, then handed the cup to him. "Do you think me of worth to a man?"

Shem took the cup and drank it. "You stay with your duties to the end. Any man would think well of you." He handed the cup back to her.

"That is what worries me," she replied, starring into the empty cup.

"Why would that worry you? Do you not want a man?"

"Yes, but there are none around. Do you?" she asked, shyly.

"Do I what?"

"Do you think highly of me?"

Shem began to pile more wood. "I have told you, yes."

Liazzat kept her head down, but her eyes ventured up. "Would you lay with me?"

Shem was so surprised by her forwardness, he slipped and fell against the pile of wood. Half the pile rolled down with him on it. Her remark sparked a memory of the women in the mountains, with no values, who exposed their breasts and used their bodies to seduce the men. How was he to respond to this woman? Lia was dedicated to her father, and a good worker. Why would she ask such a thing? He crawled off the pile of wood and brushed off his shirt.

Shem responded as frankly as he could. "There are at least three reasons why I cannot. One, I am on my way to do a greater deed. Two, I would need the blessing of my father and mother. And three, I do not even know you." Shem hoped that Kalmyk would have been proud of the logic he used.

Lia lowered her head. "You do not have to stay with me. I just need your seed for a child. You may leave after you lay with me."

Many emotions flowed through Shem's heart. He was partly embarrassed that she just wanted his seed and partly saddened for her that she had no one to help bear her a child. No one would ever know. His opportunities with Kara and Lily had vanished—and he could die fighting the Ugric anyway. Nevertheless, he realized no logic from Kalmyk would help win this argument. Shem relied instead on his father's training to keep him from capitalizing on her desire for a child.

From the other side of the house they heard Kalmyk's voice. "Shem! Where are you?"

"Over here, Master Kalmyk!" Shem called out with relief.

Shem spoke firmly and quietly to Lia. "I have a clear mind and my God would not bless me if I did such a thing. Do not ask again." Shem stepped away from the shed and didn't look back.

Kalmyk turned the corner and stood at the edge of the clearing. He waited with a long bone-tipped saw in his hand. "Today we will cut up a tree that I felled in the spring."

"We have much wood in the shed," Shem said.

"That is not enough. It will get much colder."

Shem glanced back to the wood pile where Lia slouched, the corners of her mouth turned down. As he followed Kalmyk, he replayed what she had said to him. Shem had a quest and it didn't involve another woman. On the way to the downed fir, Kalmyk stopped Shem to inspect a beehive in an old stump.

Kalmyk boldly reached down into the stump. "The bees are slow today." He pulled out a finger full of honey. His eyes closed in ecstasy as he swallowed the sticky sweetness. "Mmmm. Try some, Shem."

Shem slowly reached down until he pulled out a drippy piece of honey comb. He thwacked a bee from the comb, then licked and chewed on the sweet wax. "It is very good."

"Yes it is," agreed Kalmyk. "The strong drink that we make from it is very good as well. I will have to start a fire tomorrow to heat a brew. It may be the last in the season."

"How do you make this drink?"

"We heat up water from the stream, mix the honey into it, and set it to a boil. As it boils, we take off the foam, then let it cool till warm. That is when we add the magic dust. It was given to me by a healer," Kalmyk confided. "The dust is what gives it power. We cover it and keep it cool for half a moon. That is when you can smell its power. We then pour it into a large clay bottle and cap it tight. By the second moon we will have a good brew, but the longer the better," he said with a wink.

"I would not know. I have never had the drink."

Kalmyk was surprised. "No? Then you must try some. A batch should be ready soon. For now we must chop wood."

They cleaned their sticky hands and proceeded to cut up the delimbed fir. By the end of the day, they had cut over three cords of wood to be split later. Shem and Kalmyk stretched out their backs and headed home. Upon their return to the house, Lia had a large meal of pork ribs and roots waiting for them. The young woman avoided speaking to Shem all evening.

* * *

Days later, after sunset, Shem was buffing a tool in the shed by candlelight. Lia came to provide some food and to talk with him. She was in a pleasant and curious mood. As he ate, she handed him a large ceramic bottle for him to drink.

"The food is good," said Shem, "but the drink is powerful under my skin. What is it?"

"It is made from honey," she said. "Here, try some more. There is plenty."

Shem's taste buds were never quite the same after his head injury, but this drink seemed to vitalize him. After he drank the first cup, Lia poured him another. The more he drank, the more the room started to spin.

"What is this drink?"

"We call it mead."

Shem picked up the candle and made a loop with it. "Look at that. The light from the candle trails behind." He felt freer than he had ever been before, and became quite outspoken. His words flowed about his life, his family, his dreams.

Lia removed her coat. She wore clothing that clung tightly to her body. As she poured him the last of the mead from the pitcher, her countenance and beauty seemed to improve. Her long flowing hair, sky blue eyes, and revealed body drew him in.

Before he knew what was happening, she had untied her top garment to expose her breasts. Shem, dazed, was unsure of what he was seeing. She reached out to him. Instead of outrage, his thoughts turned to desire. He no longer saw Lia's, but Kara's body before him. His mind whirled back to memories of happiness with Kara, laughing, holding, and embracing one another. He undressed himself and found himself caressing and kissing Kara with forlorn passion. The embrace was spirited and willing as they pressed their naked bodies together, and it wasn't long before the emotional encounter turned into ecstasy. The two lay with one another until the wee hours of the morning. Shem hardly noticed a final kiss on his forehead.

The next day, Shem woke with a jolt! He was naked, only a fur covering him. *Where am I?* He glanced around his surroundings. "Kara?" *What had happened last night? Was it a dream?* Still groggy, he dressed himself and went outside the shed. Lia came around the corner of the house with some trout in a basket. They looked at one another, but Lia gave no indication anything had happened between them.

As Shem got close to her, he spoke quietly. "What did you feed me in the last meal?"

"Why, Master Shem. Do you feel ill?"

Shem looked uneasily at her. He had a splitting headache. "Did we..."

She peered at him with a blank expression. "Did we what, Master Shem?"

It must have been a dream. "Do not give me that drink again. My head is sore from it. It might be spoiled."

"As you wish, Master Shem." She smiled cordially and walked briskly into the house with the fish.

It must have been a dream. It had been many days since he had dreamed of Kara. This was a setback. He had to push her out of his mind and focus on the mission to save his people. Shem's mouth was dry and his head pounded. He promised not to touch the mead again.

* * *

The three had worked well to prepare for the cold that was now upon them. Shem became anxious when a light snow fell. Feelings of dread welled up at the thought of his near death experience in the Seva Mountains. Kalmyk eased his mind with the fact that the snowfall had lessened in the last decade. To pass the time, Shem and Kalmyk would play games; such as besting one another by throwing pebbles through a small hole in a target, or balancing a spear on the tip of their finger the longest.

As weeks passed, Shem noticed some peculiarities with Lia. She had become sick and vomited behind the house. Was it the woman's curse? When the weeks turned to months, Lia exhibited some unusual eating habits. She would eat moss or other oddities with her meal. Shem surmised it was because she was cooped up in the house too long in the cold season. All in all, the three began to function well together, performing their daily routine efficiently.

Kalymyk showed Shem how to work with ivory. On one particular day, he etched some final touches on a small ivory deer engraved in a chunk of rhinoceros tusk, while Kalmyk gave him tips regarding the Ugric culture. Shem held up the scrimshaw with admiration. "I chipped in Lia's name on the bottom. I think she will like it."

Kalmyk looked it over. "Nice work. Where did you learn the art of words?"

Shem's smile disappeared. His secret was out. He set the piece down and stared through it.

"It does not matter," said Kalmyk. "You should plan to leave here at the next full moon. I have gathered the choicest weapons for you to take with you. As a weapons trader, you will not attract much attention by the warriors, and it will allow you to get close to the great hall."

There was a thump on the door and Shem got up to get it. Lia had an armful of wood. Shem took the wood from her and set it by the fire. When Lia went to close the door, her work apron flew up to reveal a prominent belly. Kalmyk caught sight of it and flinched. When Lia started back to the cooking pot, Kalmyk set down his spoon and strode over to her. He took hold of her apron and lifted it up. Lia tried earnestly to step back to conceal her body, but her apron came off completely. There she was, protruding belly for the men to see. Her stomach wasn't huge, but it was big enough to indicate her pregnancy.

Kalmyk put his hand on her belly for confirmation. "This is not fat. You are carrying a child!" He whirled around and glared at Shem.

Speechless and in complete dismay, Shem's mouth dropped. His focus went from Lia's belly up to her face. Lia cupped her cheeks and glanced sideways at Kalmyk. It was slow motion for Shem. He suspected Kalmyk might think he had taken advantage of Lia. He feared Kalmyk would cast Lia out of the house or even kill the baby. Lia had betrayed him. Suddenly, the slow motion turned into a frantic chaos.

Kalmyk's fury erupted on Shem. "I trusted you into my home! And *this* is how you repay me?" he shouted, pointing at Lia's belly.

Shem stood up and pointed at Lia as well. "I knew it was not a dream! You turned my head with the strong drink. All you wanted was my seed!"

Lia covered her face and began to cry. Kalmyk turned back to Lia, confused and yet still angry. "Is this true? Was it you?"

She showed her teeth as if she had bitten a scorpion. "Do not be so angry," she wailed between sobs. "I would have been barren if I had not lain with Shem. There are no others."

Kalmyk weaved where he stood, as if in a stupor, then steadied himself against the wall. He massaged his face vigorously with his hands, as if trying to eliminate the information he just received. He clenched his fists then threw up his hands with a shout. "Why do the gods punish me so?"

Shem stood silent, guilt-ridden for his part in the pregnancy. His mind told him that it wasn't his fault and yet he felt awful for Lia. As Lia continued to sob, Shem knew she would have to bear her shame of deception. He also knew Kalmyk must feel a great wounding of his honor.

Kalmyk wobbled over to the table. "I have always tried to protect her," he moaned. He plopped himself down on the bench and rested his elbows on the table, his head in his hands. He took a deep breath and sat up straight. "Lia will have to eat medicine that will remove the child from her womb."

"No!" Shem shouted without thinking. He swallowed a lump in his throat and composed himself. "It is a life. We cannot do that."

Kalmyk looked up at Shem, perplexed. "But she deceived you. There is shame on you and her. The right way is to be rid of it."

"I will not allow the death of a baby. What God has granted, man must not take away. You have been kind to me, Kalmyk, and Lia has served me well—well, except this. My duty now is to be a father to Lia's child and bring it up in the ways it should go." Shem gulped at his own words. "If I am willing to accept this, so must you."

Kalmyk was speechless and scrutinized Shem as if he was a newcomer. "Most men would have run from news like this. But you are not most men. I have heard you say that you were faithful to your God. I see the truth of it now. It is easy to be of faith when things are well, but you have shown this to be true even when it is difficult." Kalmyk sighed. "As you wish. I will not have the child killed. But have your task with the Ugric. Once that is done, you can return to us." He looked over to see Lia's arms dangling at her side, eyes downcast, tears dripping off her chin. "I blame myself for this, Lia."

Lia lifted her head, wiped her tears with her hand, then gazed at Kalmyk in puzzlement. "Why? It was me, Father."

"I was wrong to protect you like a mother bear with cubs. You have been a good daughter and I should have listened to your pleas for a man. I see now how you thought that there was no other path to take." There was a long silence. "At least we know Shem's seed is good." A moment of shock turned to tittering by Lia. Kalmyk shook his head. "But, by the gods, why this?"

* * *

Shem didn't have a chance to digest the ramifications of Lia's pregnancy. The next day, Kalmyk helped Shem pack for the journey ahead. It was the end of the cold season and Shem was to head along the North Sea to the population center of the Ugric people. Once with the Ugric, Shem could fulfill his mission.

Shem stood aside the wheel cart full of provisions for the trek and the many customized weapons from the tool shed. He handed Lia the sculpted ivory and shook Kalmyk's wrist. Adorned in Ugric clothing and with knowledge of their customs, Shem said farewell and set off to the most northern part of the sea where the Volga River ends.

On his first night out, Shem sat by a fire, roasting an ermine on a spit, reflecting on his situation with Lia. He had given her the deer scrimshaw to ensure intentions of his return. *What have I done? I am not at fault! And what will Father say? I do deserve this. The fault lies with me.* As his new commitment to Lia began to sink in, he wept. Shem forced himself to eat, then had a miserable sleep with dreams that bordered on nightmare.

The morning woke Shem with a cold north wind. He finished off the rest of the ermine and looked east to where the Ugric lived. He had to force himself to leave his troubles and obligations behind and summon his strength for what lay ahead.

Chapter 22
Ugric Big Village

Shem followed the rough deer path until it turned into a well-worn road of compacted stones. Populated areas of the Ugric lay just ahead, so he played out what-if scenarios in his mind if confronted by the people. Would he have to kill the chief or would he have time to stop him with sly words? Shem's train of thought was broken when he heard a commotion down by a river. He pushed his cart forward until he caught sight of a young girl splashing frantically in the water.

"Help! He—" she called out, before submerging.

Shem watched her hands reach upward out of the fast moving current. Her head poked up momentarily then slipped back underwater. The current pulled her behind some bushes and out of view. Without thinking, Shem abandoned his cart and sprinted toward the water where he would anticipate her arrival. She passed between two large boulders straddling a torrent at the inlet of a deep hole. When she went through, her body sunk completely. At the bank of the river, Shem threw off his outer jacket and dove in to the cold icy water.

Shem swam out to the hole. He spotted her body just below the surface. The girl was being pushed down by the foaming whirlpool, her hands reaching toward the light. Shem swam up to the hole, grabbed one of her wrists, and pulled with all his strength to bring her to the surface. He put his arm around her waist and swam back to the main current. He kicked wildly to release himself from the rushing flow.

Several people had arrived to meet them at the bank. Shem dragged the girl over a muddy bank and up to a grassy spot. She laid lifeless and pale blue. A gush of weeping poured forth from one of the women. A tall blond man with long arms yanked the child up from the ground feet first to let her hang downward. Water spilled out of her mouth and she started coughing. The man set the girl down to the ground. Soon the color in her cheeks returned. The mother hugged and rocked the child in her arms.

The tall man was not so comforting. "Let this be a lesson to you, Daughter. Stay off the big stones in the river until you learn to swim." He then turned to Shem and exposed a bright set of healthy teeth. "And who is it that I should give thanks to, dark headed one?"

Shem wanted anonymity, so he used the first name he could think of. He didn't want to lie outright. "Call me—Zakho," he blurted out.

The long armed man bear hugged Shem as if they had been friends for years. "Many thanks, Zakho."

"Think nothing of it," Shem said, as his ribs squeezed tight.

"Nothing? Ha! I have two daughters and this little one was my wife's favorite. You have made her a happy woman. What brings you to the river?"

Shem shivered and held his arms close. "I am a trader from over the western mountains. I have goods to sell." Shem looked up at his cart where an older boy was poking around. "You! Those goods are mine!"

The tall blond man frowned at the young man. "Leave those, Son!" He readdressed Shem. "I am called Stog. I see you are tender to the cold. You can dry yourself by the fire. If you are in need of food, we would enjoy your presence for the late meal. My woman's cooking is best."

"That sounds good, Stog," said Shem. "I have been on the road for awhile and would savor a meal cooked by a woman."

Shem followed the man upstream until they arrived at a camp. Three lean-tos with thatched roofs supported by willow branches encircled a fire pit of glowing embers. A second young man was splitting firewood, a third untying a rope from a beast on the bank of the river, and an older girl mending clothing.

"You are fortunate to see us gather the eels."

"Eels?"

"Yes. We found this old doe dead on the banks…not good to eat, but good for bait. We put her in the river for a day and now she is ready."

"Ready for what?" Shem asked.

He chuckled. "I see you know nothing of this. Come."

Stog picked up a thick wooden rod and swung it onto the carcass. He beat at it several times until the body of the doe boiled with eels. The young men dashed over and yanked them off the carcass and stuffed them into leather bags. After gleaning the dead animal of eels, the boys took the bags back to the fire pit.

Stog held up one of the bags with a grin. "These will be good eating—and good selling."

Shem didn't have to worry about infiltrating the Ugric. This family welcomed him in and explained the Ugric ways. More importantly, they would vouch for him when they entered what they called the "Big Village." The woman provided Shem a fur to cover him until his clothes were dry and a corner of one of the shelters to sleep in. But being accepted by fishermen was not his worry. Would he be able to pass as a trader in the city?

* * *

After a morning meal of eel, the family led Shem to the Big Village. It was a large patchwork of homes enclosed by a protective wall of thick upright fir logs. The guards at the main gate gave an inquisitive look at the weapons on the cart, but let Shem pass when they saw he was with Stog. Within the village, Shem and his guides passed pens of domesticated boar, caged rabbits, pottery kilns, and several fish traders. Shem noticed no metal works of any consequence. Most of the homes were built with wood from the local birch forest. They were round wooden houses, spread out like spokes of a wheel in the village, with the great hall in the center. Around the great hall was an open area where many vendors sold their goods. A young behemoth was tethered to a stake by a rope. Sparse hairs dangled from its thick body, its long nose searching for food on the ground.

Stog went up to it and slapped it on the side. "Look at the young beast. A season ago, he was birthed and now he is up to my chest. Ha! He may be full grown by the end of the warm season."

Stog's children squeezed the animal's legs and pulled on its nose and tail. The animal squeaked out a light trumpeting noise and rocked itself to shake the children off. After losing interest, they darted off to make mischief elsewhere.

Shem stopped his cart and went over to pet the animal. "The underfur is soft. I have seen the cousin of this animal near the river of my birth. It did not have hair like this one, and was not as big." The young animal flapped his ears and touched Shem's face with his nose.

"Ha! I think he likes you, Zakho."

The animal stepped on Shem's foot. "Ow!" Shem used all his strength to push the creature away. "He is a heavy one, too," said Shem, limping backward. "Where are the others?"

Stog pointed to the east end of the village. "There is a large pen for over thirty behind the village walls. The beasts could easily break free from there, but choose not to. See how this one is tied down? He pulls and pulls, but cannot break free. In time he gives up and chooses not to pull. The masters of the beasts are good to them and so the behemoths stay with us. Once this one is used to the Ugric he will go back with the rest."

"Thirty or more? I would say one could do the work of fifty men," mused Shem.

"The market is yours, friend. Stay out of trouble." Stog waved to Shem and set off to sell his eels.

Kalmyk had told Shem that posing as a weapons trader would foster little suspicion since the Ugric had a sweet tooth for weapons. Shem had dark hair of a Tuballite, but no Tuballite had Shem's blue eyes, common among the Ugric. Kalmyk recommended Shem's story should be that he had an Ugric mother who bred with a Tuballite father—some Ugric blood is better than none. Shem chose to skirt the truth rather than give bold lies. Kalmyk did provide valuable information regarding customs and idioms, including a layout of the great hall of the high leader.

Shem moved from the open area to the outside wall of the great hall where guards were posted. After setting up his wares, it wasn't long before negotiations took place with a shaggy-haired Ugric warrior wanting a good price for a sword. Shem tried to look as though he was bartering wisely, but he was more intrigued with the comings and goings of the people into the great hall. The Oka leader, Agul, stepped out from the great hall with Ilkin at his side. It was not surprising to see Ilkin cozy up to the enemy. Shem turned his back to them, so Ilkin could not see his face.

"I tell you we must have more of the behemoths!" Ilkin demanded.

"The ice moves further north and the Ugric tell me it is harder to find the beasts," Agul responded. "Do you not think thirty of the beasts is enough?"

"There are never too many! If we are to attack before the warm season, we must have more."

Agul shook off the idea. "It will never happen. Many ancestors past told tales of the ice lands thick with the beasts—too many to count. They captured the animals when they were young and trained them in the Ugric ways. The ice is gone, the Ugric have learned how to breed the beasts, but their offspring come less and less. Unless the ice returns, these are the last of the behemoths."

Ilkin froze at the gravity of reality. "If the beasts cannot take the heat of the warm season, then we will have to take what we have and attack soon. Make plans with the leader of the Ugric warriors."

Agul frowned. "Do not order me about, young one. Remember it was I who saved your life. And while the high leader still lives, it is not up to you or me to tell him his duty."

Ilkin's body and mouth tensed. "My father is as slow as mud. This is not going as I wanted!" He stormed away from Agul and back into the great hall.

Shem had his hand on a large leather-handled, ivory knife. He was close enough to kill both Ilkin and Agul easily, but if he did, he would have to run. Then his mission to kill the high leader would be impossible. Shem decided to finish trading for the day and search for a way to find the high leader. He began to cover his wares to let the warrior know he should either buy or leave.

The purchasing warrior smiled, exposing two missing teeth. He raised the curved ivory short sword inlayed around the edges with black obsidian. "This will do well when we fight the Tuballites."

Shem ignored him, until he realized that the warrior might have some critical information. His first response was to ask directly when the fight would be, but his teachings from Kalmyk and Rutul taught him otherwise. Shem watched with interest as the hairy man gleefully swept the short sword in a battle experienced manner.

"Battle with the Tuballites?" Shem inquired.

"Yes," said the shaggy warrior with a hint of excitement. "I overheard our war leader talk with the Oka leader. They say the cool of the cold season or early in the planting season will be the time of battle."

"I see," said Shem.

The soldier continued. "We warriors are ready at any moment, but our high leader may not allow it."

"Not allow it?"

"No," he replied, tensing up. "He does not wish to break the calm. Peace with the Tuballites has been in place for many, many years."

Shem was confused. He was told that the high leader wished to attack. Maybe his information was wrong. *How could a lone Sethite get to speak with the high leader of the Ugric to find out the truth? Could I stop this madness of war just by speaking with him? And is there enough time to try?*

"Do you think others will buy my weapons, friend?"

The warrior raised his eyebrows a couple times. "Your fighting tools are of the best quality. Any man would be proud to use one."

"Would it be possible for me to show my wares to the high leader? I have a few very special weapons that I believe a high leader would like."

The warrior thought for a moment. "He does not receive many people, but I know his servant woman and she might speak to him. I will talk with her and call on you before dark."

"Many thanks, friend. My tent will be at the end of the village."

The warrior left with his new weapon and Shem returned to his animal skin tent with a glimmer of hope. Entering the great hall without having to fight his way in sounded much more pleasant than risking injury.

By evening, hope had turned to results. The warrior told Shem that the high leader had a weakness for new trinkets. He told Shem to meet the servant woman after the late meal, and she would bring him to face the leader. They shook wrists and the warrior went his way.

Shem looked over his weapons for something that could be useful, then proceeded with his cart to the great hall. When Shem was stopped by the guards, the servant woman came forward and invited him in.

The woman lifted the cover and gazed across the weapons. "Do you have any bangles or bracelets?"

Shem smiled sadly. "If my uncle were here, he would surely have some." He looked over his cart and spotted a small knife with a red gem in the handle. "Take this. It is the best I can do." Shem handed it to her, and she responded with a pleasant nod of thanks.

The servant woman then led him from the vestibule to a large open area with big, round wooden columns that supported the high ceiling. There stood two guards who escorted Shem forward into the torch-lit area. He estimated that hundreds of guests could be entertained here. Wooden sculptures of animals adorned the walls of the building all the way up to a high platform where the high leader sat on a throne. Behind the throne was a huge set of antlers with over seven points mounted on the wall. Shem pushed his cart over the flagstone floor, wheels thumping over the stone edges, until he came to the base of the platform.

The high leader was a burly man, but pale and bent. He had three columns of slotted dots tattooed along the side of his head and down around the back of his neck. Shem looked over to see Ilkin at the high leader's side, pouring a drink from a ceramic pitcher. He added something to the drink, then took it to the leader, careful not to glance toward Shem.

"Here is your medicine, Father."

The big man received it with a look of disdain. "I do not know which I dislike more, you or the drink." He looked at Ilkin for a reaction, but none came. The high leader guzzled the sour liquid quickly and gave the cup back to Ilkin. "Why does my daughter not do this for me?"

"She has pains in her belly, Father."

"Yes, yes, her child. Tell her I want to see her when she is well."

Shem kept his head down, removed a covering cloth, then sorted the magnificent weapons on the cart. *It sounds as if Ilkin has been busy since banishment from the city. A new wife and father, and a new baby all in a few seasons.*

The high leader swayed a bit and looked closer at the meticulously designed weapons on the cart. A pain flashed across his face. He buried into his hands. Shem glanced at the warriors to the side and realized he could easily throw a knife into the heart of the leader. Would the leader's death stop a war from starting? Stomething held Shem back.

The high leader uncovered his face and leaned forward with moisture-filled eyes. "I have done much wrong. Tell him to return."

Shem was confused at the statement. "Tell who, Master?"

The high leader continued speaking as if Shem was absent. "Tell him it is he that must return to the seat of power." He rubbed the moisture from his eyes and took in a difficult breath, then slumped back in his throne, disoriented. "It is too much for me to bear."

Shem felt the small knife he had inserted in his boot. *How can I do this to a man who is so near to death?* Shem grumbled and covered his wares with a cloth. "You are ill, Master. I will speak to you another time." He bowed to the chief, and started to back the cart away.

"Tell Kalmyk the seat is his," the chief wheezed. He grunted in pain and put his hand on his stomach.

Shem jerked his head up. "Who?" Shem tried to return to the high leader, but the guards were at his side pointing bone tipped spears at him. They waved him back. "Did you say Kalmyk, Master?" Shem called out as he backed up his cart.

The big man was asleep.

"Move away, trader," said one of the guards. "Can you not see he is tired?"

"I must know what name he said."

"Leave the great one!" the guard repeated sternly. "Go!"

Shem was caught off balance with the chief's last words. He obeyed the guards and left the great hall without accomplishing his goal. *What did the high leader mean? How did he know Kalmyk?* As Shem pushed his cart back to the tent, he was met by the shaggy-headed warrior.

"Did the high leader buy your goods?"

"No, he was sick or tired," said Shem, discouraged.

The warrior laughed. "Maybe another time, friend." He patted Shem on the back and started to leave.

"Wait," said Shem. "Do you know of a man named Kalmyk?" The soldier stopped dead in his tracks, and then slowly turned around with a curious calm stare.

"How do you know that name?"

Shem did not want to reveal too much. "The high leader spoke his name. Who is he?"

"He was the brother of the high leader. It was said that Kalmyk killed his eldest brother, wife, and daughter. It was also said that he wanted to take his older brother's place on the throne. Kalmyk was cast out of the land of the Ugric."

"He killed his eldest brother and wife?"

"Yes, I was about your age when I found her parents. Their necks were sliced like an animal's.

"And the daughter?"

"Liazzat. A young thing. Her little body was never found."

Shem was astounded and shaken at this news. *Would Kalmyk kill for the throne?* "Do you think Kalmyk killed them?"

The shaggy warrior glanced around furtively, then spoke in a hush tone. "I doubt he could. He was the best commander I have learned from. He has killed many men and was good at it. But he had no desire for the seat of power."

"Then who?" Shem asked.

"The killer knows—and the gods." The soldier drifted back in his thoughts. "Those were better days. After Kalmyk left and his younger brother became leader, life became dark and hard. Our people were not the same."

"I saw some marks on the great leader's neck. What do they mean?"

"What tribe do you come from? Have you not learned of these things?"

Shem held his breath and said nothing.

The warrior continued. "No matter. It is our custom for the healer to draw the dots of life and wisdom on the leaders of the tribe."

Shem thought of the same dots that Kalmyk had on his neck. "Only the leaders?"

"Only the males of the leader's family," specified the warrior.

* * *

Shem thanked the warrior and went back to his tent and lay awake. *If Kalmyk killed his older brother, why would he save Lia?* Shem shook his head. *Why do I think on these things? This is an Ugric problem. I need to think of my own people. And it has been made worse since she has my child!*

Shem tossed and turned on his sheepskin. Unable to sleep, he left his tent and, in the dark of night, slipped up to the great hall. The guards were sleepy and Shem easily evaded them. He snuck around to where a stack of wood was piled close to a high window. He stepped quietly up the stack, through the window, and entered the great hall.

Flames flickered across the walls from the torches. Shem stepped with stealth to a column and peeked around the empty room. Ilkin and Agul were in the middle of carrying the limp body of the great leader from his chair. Shem moved around the column. He brushed the side of an icon resting on a lamp stand. It dropped to the floor before he could catch it. In the quiet of the night, the icon hit the floor and echoed loudly. Ilkin and Agul instantly let down the body.

"Who is there?" called out Ilkin.

Shem ducked behind the column. He had to escape. Ilkin looked down at the body, then at Agul. He stepped forward with Agul and called out, "Guard! The enemy is here!"

Shem ran back to the window, but it was too high to jump to. He had no weapon, but saw a sacred rope that had two heavy jewels on each end. He coiled it up, then slunk along the side of the great hall in the shadows, hoping to evade a confrontation. When the guards enter the room, Ilkin pointed to the side wall.

"He is over there!" Ilkin directed.

The two guards spotted Shem and rushed him. Shem let out the rope with the weights and swung them in a circle around his head and let fly the rope like a bola. On his first try, he tripped and dropped the front warrior. Shem ran over, picked up the guard's sword, and threw it at the other guard. The sword flew end over end until it pinned the corner of the guard's collar and some skin to the column. Shem backed up to the entrance of the great hall, but an ivory blade inlayed with obsidian touched the side of his neck. Shem slowly turned his head to see the shaggy warrior. The warrior stood before him with the same weapon Shem had sold him earlier.

The hairy warrior shook his head. "I was told to watch you, Zakho." The two guards composed themselves and each grasped one of Shem's arms to hold him.

Ilkin strode forward. "This is not Zakho. It is Shem! The savior of the Tuballites! Ha! I almost did not know you with long hair. It was cut short at the city of Tuball. He has killed the great leader!"

"What?" said Shem with surprise.

Agul walked close behind, with a coy smile. "Very good, Ilkin," he whispered.

Ilkin smiled pompously at Shem. "Balkar will enjoy burning out your eyes, if others do not do it first."

"You did this, Ilkin!" Shem shouted.

"Me? You come here and murder our leader and then try to blame me? His son?" Ilkin waved his hand. "Take him away. Enjoy your last sleep, Sethite. I have many duties as the new high leader." He laughed blithely, then walked away with Agul.

The guards led Shem to a holding cell of cold stone walls near the great hall. Shem gave a silent plea to his shaggy warrior friend, who shook his head in disappointment. The door slammed shut.

Shem kicked at it, then huddled in a corner and wrapped his arms around himself to stay warm.

* * *

Night passed into day. The sun poked through a slit in the stone work, hitting Shem on the chin. The light rays moved up to his eye, and he jerked awake. He jumped up and looked through the hole. There, in front of the great hall, Ilkin stood on a platform. He was waving his hands to hundreds of people who had gathered.

Shem gave an audible gasp. *Ilkin is now high leader? This is a terrible day for all people.*

"Friends! People! I must speak of grave news. Our great leader is dead. He was a good and fair man who loved us all. His time had come, and we must mourn for him. As the sun sets we will honor him at the burning by the river. He has done his duty to serve you and now it is your duty to pay homage."

The door to Shem's cell opened and the shaggy warrior stood at the entrance with a bowl of deer stew. Another warrior set a torch on the wall and stood by the door with an ivory tipped spear. "This is your last meal, friend. They will burn you alive in the village market after dark."

"After Balkar burns out my eyes," Shem reminded.

"I do not know about that." The warrior held out the platter of food to Shem. "Why did you do it? I liked you."

Shem took the plate. "It was not me, I tell you. Ilkin is a pig. It was he that killed your high leader." Shem paced the room holding the bowl. "I knew your ruler was acting odd. They said he was sleepy, but I saw Ilkin give him something to drink."

"They said you drugged him with hemlock. The healer said it was so."

"How could I? I was away from him."

"So you did not wish to kill the high leader?"

"I did not wish it and did not do it!" Shem withered. *How can I tell him the truth? I will surely die either way.* Shem turned around and gave the stew back to the warrior. "I am not hungry. I may have been wrong about the leader. He wanted peace. It was Ilkin who wanted revenge. He was given a bad seed from his mother. Nothing matters to me now. Please leave."

The warrior set the food down and closed the door behind him.

* * *

Shem paced the cell. After a while, the door opened and the wild-eyed Balkar walked in, an evil smugness about him. Shem backed up to the wall and looked around on the floor for something to protect himself. He glanced around for a loose stone, then saw the food plate. *Could a man be killed with a plate?*

"Agul told me you were here," Balkar said with a twisted smile.

"What do you want?" asked Shem.

"I think you know." Balkar turned to the guard. "Bring him."

The guard grabbed Shem by the arm, led him out of the cell, and into an adjoining wooden building, a large, open dungeon with chains, spiked balls, axes, and other paraphernalia hanging on the walls. The guard tied Shem's hands with a long rope. He looped the rope through a metal ring hanging from the center ceiling beam. Shem was then hoisted up so that his toes just left the floor.

A flurry of emotions flooded Shem: Fear from the thought of torture, anger at Balkar, for following the likes of Ilkin, peace from knowing he had done his best to stop a war. Shem took a deep breath and breathed back out his fear and anger.

A fire had been burning coals red to white hot. Balkar walked over to the side of the fire where a metal poker lay. He picked it up and set the tip of the poker in the fire. "Ilkin has taken the people to the river. They set the high leader's body, a sacrificed deer, and his sacred belongings on a raft. The raft will be burned and sent down river to the afterworld. While the others spend their time paying homage to their leader, you and I can have some words together."

"It does not look as if it is words you wish to use on me."

Balkar puffed. "You killed many of my men; first back at the city and later by the marshes. I thought I had killed you, but here you are…alive! This will end soon. Before the Ugric return to burn up your body, Agul has promised me your eyes." Balkar took out the poker and held it up with a glowing red tip.

Shem closed his eyes and prayed. "My God, watch over my people. And let me die quickly."

Balkar let out a deep cackle. "I do not think you will die as quickly as you would like to, Shem, son of Noah."

As Balkar moved closer to Shem, a loud commotion took place outside. A *boom*! Then screams, yells, groans, and a frantic voice that said, "Look out!" More yelling and shouting ensued, then there was quiet.

"See what that is about," Balkar ordered the guard.

The guard went to peek through a knot in the door. He instantly backed up to the wall of the torture room. He shook his head and stared at the door.

"What is it!" shouted Balkar.

Before the guard could answer, the roof split apart and there above Shem stood his young Nephilim friend, Nazar. He was amazingly taller than the last time Shem had seen him. Nazar's face contorted when he spotted Balkar standing in front of Shem with the red hot poker.

Nazar cried out with a low booming voice. "No!"

Balkar, a big man himself relative to a Tuballite, was not even close to being a match against the Nephilim. Instinctively, Balkar jabbed the poker at the giant. The big young Nephilim swatted the metal rod aside and tore through the door frame. He wrapped his hands around Balkar like a doll and squeezed the breath out of him. Balkar tried to rip the giant's hands away, but it was useless. Nazar raised the Okan overhead and sent him in a flight that landed him through the roof of a nearby home. He then turned around to the guard with a dirty glare. The guard promptly fell prostrate and froze in that position. Nazar ignored the guard and tore off the ropes that bound Shem as if they were twine. He lifted Shem into his arms like a little child, and flipped him around to his back. Shem held his arms tightly around Nazar's neck, and the two bounded out of the village, people screaming and scattering away like roaches.

The warning horn sounded, but most of the warriors were down at the river. The few who were left men were easily kicked or squashed by the young Nephilim on his way out. Nazar's strides were four times that of the Ugric. In minutes he had traveled a considerable distance from the Big Village.

The horns grew fainter as Nazar sprinted up and over a knoll and then a hill. Descending into a small valley, Nazar slowed down to catch his breath. The young Nephilim was big, but his breathing was heavy and his face was red. He set Shem down and collapsed to his knees.

"You are not a runner, are you, Nazar? You should be a teacher or a grand elder. Something that does not need much breathing," Shem stated with sarcasm.

Nazar took deep wheezing breaths. "What is this…grand elder?"

"The ruler of a people."

Nazar shrugged. "I would like to be that."

Shem shook his head and chuckled. After Nazar rested a moment, the two of them sat on the ground together and laughed. In the distance, the horns from the village continued to blow. Not wishing to take any chances, Shem encouraged Nazar to get up and walk eastward for fear of reprisals from the Ugric. Soon they were back on their feet.

As they walked, Shem looked up at his companion. "If I did not know you, Nazar, I would be in terrible fear of your size. Since I first set eyes on you, you have grown twice your size."

"Others are taller than me," said Nazar humbly.

"Does it not hurt to grow that fast?"

"My bones ache often."

Shem breathed a sigh of relief. "I am glad we are friends."

"Me too."

Shem peered up to Nazar. "Why did you leave the place of my father, Nazar? And how did you find me?"

"Father Noah had a bad dream about you and I was afraid for you. I left them to help you. I went to the city of Baku and they told me where to go. I went north and soldiers told me where to go. I found Kalmyk and he told me where to go. I saw a fisherman named Stog and he told me where you were and that you would die. Everyone was very kind to me and always told me where I should go."

Shem chuckled. "They have to be kind to you, Nazar. You are twice as tall as the biggest Ugric. They thought you might step on them if they crossed you."

"I would never do that, Master Shem."

"I know. But they do not." Shem looked to the east. "What now? We cannot go east forever."

Nazar grinned. "We will go back to my people," he said, proudly.

Shem squinted at Nazar. "You wish to return?"

"It is time. And we will be safe with them."

"That is very wise and true, my friend." Shem thought for a minute and raised a finger. "Nazar, that is the best place to go! The Ugric will attack Tuball soon. We must ask your kin to help in the fight. If the Nephilim help the Tuballites, then the Ugric have not a chance, even with their beasts. I thought this was my worst day, but it may have been the best."

Chapter 23
Sound the Alarm

The visit with the Nephilim was not as productive as Shem had hoped. While the people welcomed back Nazar into the community, Shem spent some time alone with the chief. He implored the chief to become allies with the Tuballites and fight against the Ugric, but chief would have none of it. Killing others was a violation of their creed. In the end, the giant reminded Shem that they had begun to trade with the Tuballites and that that was a valuable start.

Shem stepped outside of the chief's home and was greeted by Tatunna. "Your face tells a tale of defeat."

Shem gave a sad nod. "Without your help, I feel in my bones that Tuball will fall. Do you think you can talk with the chief? He respects you."

"The chief listens to my stories, but not my advice, Shem. But I will do what I can. Will you stay awhile?"

"I cannot stand idle. I must return to the city." Shem came close and spoke softly. "You must help him see my way or my people will die."

"I will help him see your way, my friend. But are you blind to his?"

"But my people..." Shem knew his cause with them was lost. "Do your best, Tatunna."

* * *

The next morning, Shem gathered some traveling goods and bid farewell to Tatunna and the Nephilim. He started his journey back to Tuball en route on the land bridge. Nazar said he would walk with Shem as far as the shore of the North Sea. All through the forest and out to the plain, Shem kept quiet, his mind playing out pictures of war and death.

"You have not said a word since we left my village," said Nazar.

Shem looked up to his young friend. "If we do not have the help of your kin, I fear for my people."

"Killing is not our way."

"What of your trashing of the Ugric in the Big Village?"

Nazar's voice rose as if to defend himself. "My anger took over when I heard they were to hurt you. But did not kill them. I would never kill someone."

Shem smiled at his innocence. "That is good, at most times," he paused, "but when many more deaths will result, killing has its place. It is not good when a man enjoys the death of others…that is evil."

Nazar said nothing.

"I respect your people and am not angry with them. I only fear for the lives of my tribesmen."

"When you leave me, will you get yourself in trouble again, Master Shem?"

"I do not know. I have to do what is right in my sight."

Nazar sighed. "I guess I will have to save you if that happens."

Shem laughed. "I will miss you, Nazar."

They came to the edge of the sea and had to say goodbye. Nazar knelt down and hugged Shem lightly, so as not to crush him. The Nephilim then turned and started back to his village. Shem watched Nazar thump off in a trot. When Nazar was out of sight, Shem started a brisk jog along the shore. He estimated that the land bridge was a few hours away. He knew he had to tell Bulla of the attack. He most likely would see Kara, but that was the least of his problems. Many lives counted on him and it was his duty to warn them.

As Shem's breathing finally matched his pace, he moved into a comfortable rhythm that allowed him to gaze out at the waves. He started to imagine the slaughter of Sethites and Tuballites beneath the feet of the behemoths. *Why did this have to happen? My people did nothing to deserve this. Maybe it is time they left the city and found a new home. Cities may have wonderful things, but they also invite danger…like a flame that draws in a moth. Why are men so evil?*

Shem slowed down when he spotted a boat that was pulled up and onto the beach. The sun was in front of him. There was a silhouette of a woman in the boat and a man on the first sand dune, scanning the area. The man noticed Shem and waved to him.

Unsure of the person, Shem came to a stop. He wondered if the man was an enemy. *I cannot just stand here and I cannot run the other way. I have to get back to the city. Mighty God, let this man be a friend.* The man trotted up the shore, while Shem waited patiently.

As the man neared, he recognized Shem and ran. Shem stood his ground.

"Shem? Shem! It *is* you!"

Shem gave a hint of a smile. "Bura?"

Bura stopped at a few paces away, more than astonished. "Yes, it is you! I cannot believe my sight. You have been brought back to life! Your God is mighty in strength and deed—the most powerful one of all!"

Shem was unusually subdued. "The only one," he calmly replied.

"I now believe it. For here you are, alive and fit."

When Shem saw Bura, he thought of Kara. Grief, anger, and pain flooded his body. "Alive—yes. Fit—no."

Bura frowned. "No?"

Shem gave Bura a deadly stare. "Have you not seen the grand mistress?"

All of Bura's air spilled out of his lungs. "Oh. I am so sorry, Shem…I…am. I do not know what to say."

Shem shook his head. "Nothing. Say nothing. We have no time to dwell on that. There are other things that weigh heavy. What we must do is warn Bulla. The Ugric will be sending all their warriors and beasts to strike at Tuball."

"The Ugric? We have built the wall of strength and have men on mountain peaks to warn the city. We have no fear of them."

"You should have fear of them!" Shem reprimanded. "They will find a way. I was there! Ilkin is still alive and will lead them to us."

"I thought he was—"

"Dead? No!" Shem snapped. A pain shot through his skull. "And if you did not spend your free moments with village women, you would know this." Shem winced and rubbed his forehead. He brushed Bura aside and strode forward. "I cannot stand idle. I must go."

Bura stood frozen at the rebuke, then followed. "Women? Are you well, Shem?" he asked softly.

Shem heaved a heavy sigh. "I carry a heavy burden. I said I must go."

"Where to?"

"To the city."

"Then I will go with you."

Shem kept a stoic front.

"There is pain inside you, Shem. What has happened?"

Kara was lost to him, the Nephilim would not help, and Shem had not even been able to stop Ilkin from planning an assault. Shem stopped and turned to his friend. He explained of his exploits in the last several seasons. He mentioned his time with the Nephilim, preparing for the ark's construction, travels to the north, the pregnancy of Lia, infiltrating the Ugric, and the Nephilim's refusal to help.

After Shem spoke awhile, he relaxed. It was good to clear his mind of all that had happened. Bura stayed quiet, nodding and making affirming grunts as Shem revealed his deepest troubles.

"You are a good friend, Bura. I wish we could have been brothers." Shem hung his head and stirred the earth with a knife.

"It was not meant to be," replied Bura. "If your God is so good, why does he torture you so?"

"I do not question the one who has molded the heavens in his hands. I, I trust Him and obey." Shem's task flooded back into his mind. He jumped up with fear in his eyes. "We must hurry! The Ugric may be here by the next moon. I have to tell Bulla."

"Walking will be too slow. Let us take the boat," suggested Bura. "We can save three sunsets." Bura took Shem down to the water where Kepenek was folding some nets. "Kepenek, this is my good friend Shem. We must hurry and get the boat wings ready."

Shem leaped aboard the boat. Bura pushed off from shore, then jumped in. Bura briefly explained the impending danger from the Ugric to the fisherwoman. She bowed her head, smiled at Shem, then went back to gather the cords to the sails. Bura adjusted the rudder and soon a north wind filled the sails. Shem sat next to Bura and watched as the two skillfully directed the sailboat westward.

"Do you not fight alongside the warriors anymore, Bura?"

"Yes, but Torak saw I was friends with the fisherman and asked me to make a map of the land east of the North Sea, between the Nephilim and the Ugric. That is what I was doing when we met. If the northern tribes tried to attack us, we have our fast boat to make a quick escape."

"So who is the woman?"

Bura glanced back and grinned. "The beauty who saved my life when we ran from the Oka. If her father had not stopped to pull me out of the water, I would never have met her."

Shem dropped his head in shame. "I never once asked you how you fared."

"It is not worth your worry. You have been through much."

Shem watched the fit young woman handle the sails. "Do you wish her to be your woman?"

Bura grinned proudly. "She is. We will be bonded soon. I have been building a wood house near her village for us."

Shem shook his head. "Much has happened since we last talked, yes?" He looked up at the sails of the boat. "How do these boat wings work?"

Bura laughed. "They capture the wind that blows over the sea and moves the ship without having to paddle. Kepenek moves them to get the most of the wind. Her father taught me how to steer the ship with this flat wood over the side."

"Using the wind to move the boat is a fine thing."

"We have the fastest boat in the village. With this wind, we will reach the city before the sun sets."

The boat sailed out into the sea, parallel to the land bridge, riding the wind and the current. Bura brought Shem up to date on the goings-on of the city and the growing companionship between the Sethites and Tuballites. As Bura predicted, the sun was still up as they neared the city's docks. Kepenek stayed with the sailboat while Shem and Bura went up into the city.

As they got close to the eastern gates, Bura shouted with vigor. "The great Shem has risen from the dead!"

Some of the citizens recognized Shem. Soon a large group of people began to fawn over him. Shem glared at Bura.

Bura laughed and pushed him forward. "They love you, Shem. Enjoy it."

Chapter 24
Return of the Dead

Kara tried to admire herself in the mirror. It should have been easy, since the long, red wool dress was a very fine weave that accented her rounded lines. However, the constant rumors of war with the northern tribes were unsettling. She had recently come to the conclusion that if the world was governed by woman, there would be a more reliable hand at keeping the peace. If it were up to her, she would rule with a focus on food, not weapons; encouraging trading, instead of war.

Kara placed a jade necklace around her neck, while several rams' horns blew from the eastern walls of the city of Tuball. She picked up her baby boy from the wicker crib, put him against her shoulder, and walked out to the portico that jutted over the city streets. A throng of people were massing toward the eastern gate. Cheering and joyful shouting spread like a wave through the people. She couldn't see the source of the attraction. After watching a moment, she turned to a servant girl who had come alongside to investigate.

"Find out what is upsetting our people," Kara commanded. The servant girl bowed and left.

She took her baby with her inside to where Bulla was mulling over the model of the new city walls. "Do you know of the unrest at the eastern gate?"

Bulla looked up from his work. "There is my little warrior!" Bulla gently took the infant from Kara and lifted him up in the air. "I see you. I see you." He turned back to Kara. "Unrest?"

"Our people are rushing the eastern gates."

Bulla set the infant boy down in his crib, then walked briskly to the portico and looked down. "Yes, I see. Is it trouble?"

Kara shook her head, puzzled. "I think not. They seem happy."

The servant girl soon returned, out of breath, and approached from behind. "I have news Master and Mistress."

Bulla turned around. "What is it?"

The girl bowed her head. "Grand Master, there is news that Shem, son of Noah, is alive and at the city gates."

Kara shuddered as if someone dunked her in ice water. She blinked a few times, her mouth partly open. "But Shem is dead."

"No, Mistress. I have been told he walks the streets."

"That cannot be," Kara insisted.

"You will be punished for coming to us with wild tales," said Bulla, sternly.

The servant girl dropped to the floor, prostrate in front of them. "Do not punish me! I tell you the truth."

A huge cheer from outside broke their attention. Bulla and Kara looked back over the stone rail to watch the crowd move back toward the inner part of the city. Songs of joy rippled through the mob. In the center of the throngs was one person. Soon it was possible to see who it was.

Kara gasped. "Shem!" Blood drained from her head and she pressed her hand to the rail to steady herself.

Bulla shook his head with amazement. "Did Shem's God bring him back to life?"

As Shem pushed through the citizens, everyone in the city tried to see and touch him. *"Shem is mighty! He is mighty indeed! Make way for the conqueror of death!"* They shouted. When Shem was below the portico, he looked up and bowed his head to Bulla and Kara. In the midst of cheers and singing, Shem walked around to the steps that led up to the grand elder's chambers. Two guard escorts shoved the people back, trying to keep the path clear so Shem could move forward.

Kara ran back inside, down the hall, and to the main door. She put her hands to her mouth and waited in stunned silence, not able to make another move. The door opened and the guards entered with Shem behind. Kara's heart pounded. Her hands shook. Shem looked at her with a penetrating stare but said nothing. She wiped away the tears that trickled down her cheek.

"Greetings, Kara," Shem said, with a bow of his head.

Kara stood speechless.

Bulla walked around Kara and reached out to grasp Shem's shoulders. "Your God is great!"

A corner of Shem's lip turned up into a partial smile. "I have always tried to tell you so. It is good to see you, Bulla."

"And it is beyond good to see you alive, Shem. You indeed have come back from the dead."

"So it seems."

Kara, still in shock, finally found her voice. "You cannot be Shem! He is dead!" She blurted out. All of her feelings for Shem rushed throughout her body. She trembled and shook her head, her eyes pinched shut. "No! It cannot be!" Kara ran from the hall to her sleeping chambers. She dove onto her bed of duck down and sobbed uncontrollably. "It cannot be! It cannot be!" she shouted into the blankets of fur.

Her new life as the grand mistress had helped her focus on her duties. She had grown to love her role as mistress of the Tuballites and mother of her new baby. Now, Shem had returned and rekindled the feelings she had hoped to leave behind. *Why would the gods bring him back? To give me pain? Why?* She sorted through her thoughts but could not find a reason. Not until the sun moved from overhead to the horizon did she gather herself and get up from her bed. Kara went to the door and looked down the hall to see Bura and Shem talking near the south window.

Kara smoothed out her long, red dress, wiped her eyes, and walked as confidently as possible to where the men were deep in conversation. They stopped speaking and turned to see her approach. Kara calmed her nerves and stepped close to the men.

Kara bowed her head. "Forgive me for what I said, Shem."

Shem smiled with a kind gentleness. "There is nothing to forgive, Kara. It was…unexpected." Shem glanced over at the crib. "I see you have a young boy to be proud of."

Kara looked over at her boy with weak smile. "Yes, he is a fine boy." She kept her eyes on her child, afraid to address Shem.

Bulla looked at Shem, then Kara. "Shem has told me of many things, one of which is grave. I must deal with it now. Speak with him until I return."

Kara did not want to be left alone with Shem. "Where do you go, Husband?"

"I have to talk with my war council. Shem will explain." Bulla kissed Kara's hand and left.

Kara kept her gaze upon the tile floor. It was too painful to see him in the flesh.

"Kara? Look at me," Shem said.

Kara gave him a fleeting glance. "I have moved on, Shem."

"I do not know if I can do that, Kara."

Kara peered at Shem. A sudden thought of loving two men came to her. *El, is it possible to have two men? Even if Bulla would consent to such a thing, Shem would never hear of it. But I love them both!! I am out of my mind to even think such thoughts.* "Why did you not come back to me?"

"I tried, Kara. It took almost two seasons to heal from my wounds. And when I was returning to you, I found out you and Bulla had bonded. It does not matter now. You and he are meant to be together."

"You accept that I am Bulla's woman?"

Shem nodded. "Yes. It is as it should be. I know now that we could never bond with our separate gods."

"Then why do you return? To hurt me?"

"Hurt you? No. I stayed away as long as I could so I would not hurt you. But I had to return to warn Bulla of a danger to the city. The northern tribes have joined as one and will attack our people soon. We must prepare for war."

Kara sighed. "You have always done your duty to your God and your people. I will thank the gods that you were alive to warn us."

Shem smiled. "You see how you thank your gods. You cannot leave them. It never would have worked between us." He started to reach out to her, but stopped.

Kara sensed his intention and took hold of his hands. "I must tell you that my heart still aches for you. I could still give up my gods. Let us flee to the mountains where it is safe. No wars or talk of wars. We could be as we were."

Shem put his fingers before her lips. "No Kara. You know that is wrong. It would be too hard on both our hearts. And what of Bulla? Have you thought of him?"

"He worries more for the city and the people more than for me."

Shem shook his head. "There is something else. I have another woman."

Kara was stunned into silence. She took a step back and scanned the floor for a response. "Another?"

"She is an Ugric woman and carries my child. I must return to her."

Kara covered her face. "No," her voice muffled. She removed her hands and glared at him. "You should never have come back! Why? I never want to see you again!" Shem moved forward to catch her but was too late. She ran out of the room and down the passage. *Why did you let him come back to me! He should have stayed dead!* Kara ran out through the city gates and around to the sandy shore between the sea and the city walls. She walked to where the waves lapped quietly on the edge and sea birds called from above. The wind blew across her wet face as she dropped to her knees and sobbed.

*　*　*

Shem looked out the window to the sea shore to see the figure of a woman with a red dress blowing in the wind, bending over the water's edge. She rocked forward and back. He hated to bring up Lia, but he realized it was the only way to help Kara be practical. He would have given up Lia in an instant, but not at the expense of Bulla. This did not go as he had planned. He hoped they would be able to say farewell gracefully and now it was all for naught. He pulled himself away from the window at the sound of footsteps.

A guard had entered the room and was ordered to escort Shem to the war council. Shem followed the guard out of the chambers, along a passageway that led into a large private space where several masters and thinkers sat around a big table, murmuring to one another. They were discussing the dilemma of the Ugric attack and needed information about the people and their ways. Bulla sat at the head of the table and waved Shem forward.

"Shem, tell them what you told me," Bulla said.

Shem stood at the end of the table. "My friends, we have little time to waste before the Ugric and their beasts attack us. Ilkin has squirmed his way into the great leader's home and married his daughter."

"Ilkin?" asked the stone master.

"Yes. Ilkin is alive and wishes to take revenge on us."

"But we have an agreement with the high leader that he will stay north if we stay south," said the wood master.

Shem shook his head in disgust. "The high leader is dead. And I suspect Ilkin was behind it. They are are many Ugric and Oka. If their clans and tribes band together, it will be a mighty force against us."

"We now have ten new, large boats," mentioned the water master. "Could we not use them?"

Shem shook his head. "The behemoths are the danger. And they will be on land."

"What of your Nephilim friends?" asked Tobanis. "They are as big as trees and would do well in battle. We would conquer the Ugric easily."

187

"I talked with their chief less than two sunsets ago, and he told me they do not kill others. They will be of no use to us."

Bulla stood up. "Then we must plan for the northern tribes to come with their behemoths from the west side of the North Sea. How many of the animals do they have, Shem?"

"Maybe thirty large ones and some smaller."

Bulla turned to Tobanis. "You must send word to bring all our warriors from Baku. We will need all of our strength. Shem, speak to your Sethites and find out if they wish to help in battle. I will send word to the chiefs of the Bundled Tribes for able men. You masters, I will need all the tricks and traps you can think of. We must ready ourselves for when the northern tribes come. For if we do not, this may be the end of Tuball."

Chapter 25
Birth of War

Torak stood on the thick Barrier Gate at the entrance to the narrow canyon. Sheer walls rose nearly a hundred feet high on each side. The Barrier Gate was like a moving wall hung on heavy iron hinges attached to the cliffs. One layer of thick logs lined the front, earth and stone filled between, and a second layer of logs lined the back. The top was wide enough for two men to pass each other comfortably, and yet it took ten strong men just to open it. Torak paced the structure, waiting patiently for the Ugric to break through the forest. The pass around the canyon by the marshes was blocked by a recent landslide, leaving this the logical way for the animals to navigate south.

Shem and Bura walked together through the valley, then up the wide, carved stone steps that led to the top of the canyon walls. When they reached the top of the Barrier Gate, they saw Torak motioning orders, sending men to appointed positions on the cliffs. They reached the top of the steps of the cliff and stopped to rest.

Shem looked down through the canyon. "You have just returned from the northern waters with Kepenek. Did you learn when the Ugric would attack?"

Bura took a drink from his water flask. "We heard rumors. It should be soon." Bura capped his flask. "You have told me you are not a warrior, Shem. Do you feel honored to be Torak's second? There are other stronger men, yet he asked for you."

Shem shrugged. "It is a task, like any other...and he trusts me." Shem started to walk to the gate.

Bura's face became serious. "Do you hate Bulla?"

Shem jerked around. "What? No! He is a good friend. How could you ask that?"

"He stole my sister from you."

Shem was annoyed with such a thought. "He did not steal her from me. It is as it should be."

"Do you hate my sister?"

Shem grimaced. "I think you have been in the sun too long. For the first time in my life, someone else is asking all the strange questions."

"She could have waited for you."

Shem put his hands on his hips. "Why would she? You thought I was dead by Okan hands. Should I hate you, too?" Shem pointed to the north. "I do not even hate the Ugric. Our anger should be set on the Oka and Ilkin. They are the evil ones."

Bura kicked at the soil a bit. "It is only that I wanted you as a brother," he confided.

Shem smiled. "We are brothers at heart, yes?" Bura nodded. "Then let us have that. Come, we have a battle to win."

They continued over to the gate where Torak was leaning over a bronze-tipped spear. He gripped it tightly with his big hands like he hoped to squeeze out water. He stood like a statue, gazing out into the woods, anticipating the inevitable. Bura and Shem stopped at his side and looked down into the canyon.

"My insides tell me this will not be easy," said Torak staring into the deep woods.

Bura cleared his throat. "Master Torak? Why do the Ugric not go west around the mountains, instead of this narrow way? They must know we have a trap for them."

"West is a much longer route into our territory. With so much time, we could easily kill each man off with strike-and-run moves, like picking lice off a bald man. Shem knows of the good men we have to the west. The Ugric would rather risk a quicker frontal attack through their own lands."

"The season warms, and I was told the behemoth likes the cold. That, too, may be why they may want to hurry," added Shem.

Bura pointed down to the village, not far south of the gate. "We have done as you told us, Master Torak," said Bura. "The people have moved south, away from harm. Should I not warn the fishing village? They are but a day from here."

"That is where Kepenek lives, no?" asked Torak, with a raised eyebrow.

Bura grinned. "Yes."

"Save your woman. Go."

"Many thanks, Master Torak. I will see you at the eastern gates of Tuball," he said with a bow. He patted Shem's shoulder. "May the gods protect you, Shem."

Shem didn't want to debate the issue of theology, but added, "And may the one God Almighty protect you, Bura."

Bura laughed. "I may be the better protected, eh?" He dashed across the top of the gate and to the canyon wall.

As Bura scampered down the steps to the valley below, an object flew high across the canyon and floated down like a maple seed to them. Shem ran over, caught the object, and unwrapped it. He found a note with symbols of the behemoths and warriors with numbers to the side.

Shem walked up to Torak. "The Ugric draws near. They have a count of thirty and one beasts and too many warriors to count," said Shem.

Torak gazed out at the stillness of the forest. "This will not be easy." A flock of birds flew up from the furthest visible trees. Torak reached out to look at the note. "This mark shows Ugric." He scanned the area along the ridge to the west, then looked at the note again.

"What is wrong?" asked Shem. "What do you see?"

"I do not see the mark for the Oka. I have been a fool!" Torak gave a series of whistles across the canyon and immediately half of the men made their way back to the Gate then down the steps to the valley floor. "The Oka will hit from behind us."

"How do you know?"

"Trust me." Torak watched the hills carefully, then looked down at his men assembling into a protective semi-circle behind the gate. The formation of 500 Tuballites kept their shields close and their spears extended, waiting for the eventual onslaught. He looked back and up to the hills, and, sure enough, a mob of Oka had crested the top and began a decent. Torak estimated the Oka had three times the numbers. "Now the enemy has us at both ends."

A distant horn sounded within the forest and moments later the behemoths suddenly broke out of the woods. Trees parted with a loud shattering *crack—crack—crack*! The animals trumpeted a terrible bellow and began a fast pace toward the gate. Torak swung around, his faced reddened with veins.

"Ready yourselves!" Torak ordered, to his men on both sides of the gate. The Tuballites above the canyon raised up their spears, poised, ready to throw.

Shem looked back at the second line of warriors on the valley floor, and how they used the front of their shields to support the heel of the spears of the first line. Additional short swords hung on their hips for hand to hand combat.

Ten groups of Oka, fifteen strong, jogged down the sides of the hill carrying half logs in their arms, like cross bars, the remainder of troops not far behind. The Oka segments moved across the valley and straight toward the Tuballite phalanx like a side-winding snake. With the heavy logs in front, the Oka picked up speed and soon pushed through the first line of locked shields with a crushing blow. The first line of Tuballite offense was devastated, and the second line was crippled.

Back in the canyon, the behemoths hit the ground with a force of pounding thunder. Out into the open, they plodded steadily toward the gate. Behind the behemoths, at the tree line, 3,000 Ugric warriors took one step into view, but did not move any further. The Tuballites held steady with their spears in throwing position, ready for orders. Their orders were to focus their weapons at the animals' heads.

Shem almost admired the Ugric. "The warriors stay back. It seems they will let the beasts take the spears. But the Oka are fearless."

Torak watched as the Oka pressed in on his men on the valley floor. He returned his gaze to the approaching animals, then gasped when they closed to twice a stone's throw. "The beasts have a protection of wood over them!" Torak gave a series of loud whistles. His soldiers lowered their spears and ran back to the gate. They lined up on the south side of the canyon in three ranks.

"What are you doing, Torak?" asked Shem. "The beasts will break open the gate if your warriors do not kill them." The behemoths continued their speed and were closing in on the gate.

"It does not matter. Their coverings will stop our spears. But we may be able to save our warriors in the valley below."

The Tuballites stood with their spears, waiting for their orders. "Set your aim at the body of Oka just beyond our warriors. Ready yourselves!" The men raised their spears at a high angle onto their throwing boards. "Now!"

The Tuballites launched a volley of spears in the middle of the Oka, behind the front line. Like wheat at harvest, many were cut down instantly.

"Again!" shouted Torak. The second volley flew. "Again!" he ordered.

Another volley was launched, and many more Oka fell. More than a quarter of the Oka had been killed and still they kept moving forward.

Before they could muster another volley, four of the first large behemoths slammed into the gates with a *boom!* Torak, Shem, and several spear throwers almost fell from the blow. The back half of the Oka had been decimated by the spears, but the big Okan brutes in front with their stone axes and clubs could easily overcome the Tuballites in hand to hand combat.

"Torak, there are still too many Oka!" shouted Shem. "I will take these men down to keep the Oka from opening the gates."

"Stay with me. The Tuballites know their methods of war better than you."

The Oka and Tuballites were heavily intertwined. Torak ordered the warriors off the canyon walls to augment the ground troops. The Tuballite reinforcements reacted quickly to surround the Oka from the sides and behind. Torak's lead men pushed the additional forces steadily forward. A solid wall of shields and thrusting spears penned in the Okans from their rear. While the Oka smashed Tuballites' heads in front, the array of spears skewered the Okans from behind. Favor passed from the Oka.

Torak turned to the last of two men standing guard on the gate. They each held an axe in hand. "Ready yourselves with the fat."

The gates, as heavy and as thick as they were, groaned at the heaving behemoths. The beast masters whipped the animals to press harder. When the gates bent no more, the beast masters backed up the animals and ran the animals into the gates once again. *Boom!* The animals bellowed and the gates began to shift and bend. The big iron hinges bent at the force. With double thick walls, the gate's weak link was its hinges.

Torak couldn't wait any longer and gave the order. "Drop the fat!" he shouted to the two soldiers guarding the gates.

A few very large urns of animal fat had been set in position along the top of the gates, each with a small fire to heat them up to a boil. The guards picked up and swung their axes into each of the urns to release the bubbling oil. The hot oil spread down the front side of the gate and onto to the nearest of the animals. The guards pushed the fire onto the liquid and immediately a burst of flames flowed down to where the fat had spread. The gates and one behemoth with its master were set ablaze. The animal mournfully cried out as its head soaked up the fire. The other beast masters backed their animals to a safe distance.

"See how fire tastes!" shouted Torak, raising his fists to the enemy. He picked up his spear. "You guards, Shem, come."

The four men ran off the gate and down the steps to the valley floor to meet up with the other warriors. Shem spotted Agul at the top of the hill waving for his men to retreat. The Oka broke through the west side of the formation and scattered up to the hills, leaving the Tuballites in front of the gate. Torak gathered his men around and tended to those that could travel.

"Should we follow them?" Shem requested.

"No. They have the uphill strength."

Torak looked around at his valiant men. "Warriors! You have fought well!" The soldiers, dripping with blood and sweat, whooped and cheered at the limited victory. "But we cannot stay. Those too weak to follow us must hide in the caves. We will return for you. The rest of us must leave the Ugric and their beasts. We are no match."

"If we leave, will the Oka not return to open the gates?" asked Shem.

"I have thought of that," said Torak.

Torak tipped his head to the two men with axes and they rolled out two more ceramic barrels from a small shed. The two men picked up a barrel and threw it against one of the gates. It shattered and the warm fat melted down the exterior logs. The two men did the same against the other gate and stepped back. Licks of fire from the other side caught the dripping fat and soon both sides of the gate were on fire.

Torak looked up at the high gates where black smoke boiled over, and ragged flames leaped high. "The gates will burn for many hours and keep them back. That may give us time to regroup with our warriors in Tuball." He turned to a man with a ram's horn. "Signal the lookout." The man blew three long notes on the horn. Shortly thereafter, the sound of a distant note responded.

Torak raised a spear in his hand. Follow me!" Torak began the traditional chant as they did a fast march. "Ooh, ooh, ooh-eey-ya." He then pounded his spear to the ground with a thump.

The Tuballites filed into columns of two and echoed the chant. "Ooh, ooh, ooh-eey-ya—*thump*! Ooh, ooh, ooh-eey-ya—*thump*! Ooh, ooh, ooh-eey-ya—*thump*!" And on they went until the troops reached the next village.

* * *

Dark was setting in when the Tuballite troops slowed to a halt. Torak sent Shem and two others to investigate the village. It was quiet, except for a crow calling. Bits of smoke wafted up from abandoned fire pits. Two scouts returned with a large doe and proceeded to carve it up for the troops. Another rekindled the fires for cooking the evening meal.

Shem and the two others searched the village and then returned. "The village is empty," said Shem.

"Bura must have warned the elders of the danger and fled," Torak said.

"They left much dried food and water jugs in a storage hut."

"Good. Our warriors can restock their food supplies for the next few days."

The warriors cut off cooked portions of deer meat to eat. After filling their stomachs, they dispersed throughout the area to make camp and to occupy the vacant homes for rest. A few of the strongest warriors stood guard while the others slept.

All was quiet and calm. Then in the still dark of night, a fire on the top of a nearby ridge erupted into a tall controlled burn. A guard ran to the village elder's home, where Torak had just gotten comfortable on a pile of sheepskins, and informed him of the fire. Shem had found another bed on the other side of the room and slept soundly until Torak stirred. They rose and exited the home to see a blaze on the hilltop to the north. Not long after the first fire was lit, a second fire on a ridge many miles to the south came to life. The next mountain to the south then lit its warning fire. All the hills to the south would continue to light their fires until the last one near Tuball was lit.

Shem turned to Torak. "The Ugric have broken through?"

"It seems I have failed," Torak replied, disheartened. "Spread the word. We leave at the morning light," he said and went back into the house.

Shem stood alone, watching the warning fire burn on the mountain top. Like his comrades, Shem was disappointed the gate was breached, but was still proud of Torak's pragmatic reaction. Anyone else would have been annihilated by the onslaught.

Before the early light, the Tuballites were on their feet and assembled. Torak moved to the front of the troops and motioned them forward to march quietly in unison. As they marched onward, Torak was silent, his face somber, his eyes fixed on the path south.

Shem hoped that more than just one of the behemoths caught fire, because he was sure not one of the 3,000 Ugric warriors was even scratched. Nevertheless, he took solace knowing, in two days, they would be back to the city and regroup.

Shem peered over at Torak. "Did you think you would defeat the behemoths?"

"I plan for many outcomes," replied Torak, blandly.

"Do not blame yourself, Torak."

Torak kept his gaze straight ahead. "Then whom shall we blame, if not me?"

Shem had no answer. He knew Torak would take the burden of failure, no matter the situation. Shem was about to console his friend when Torak lifted his arm to halt the troops. Shem squinted ahead intently and followed Torak's gaze out into the morning mist. Someone stood several hundred yards ahead…stiff, not moving.

"Is it a trap?" asked Shem.

Torak tipped his head for Shem to go see. "Careful."

Shem trotted forward warily, looking to each side, suspecting the enemy may dash out. The figure was of a man who wore Ugric furs and boots. He stood as still as a stone, waiting. Shem's heart began to pump faster with every step. If one Ugric is here maybe others are close by. He glanced furtively around and gripped his knife. The mist dissipated and Shem finally got close enough to see who the man was. He was shocked.

"Kalmyk?" he whispered. Shem turned around and waved, "It is all good!" Shem then looked back at his Ugric mentor. "You are the last one I would expect out here."

"Hello, friend," said Kalmyk. He stepped forward and reached out to shake Shem's wrist.

The troops, with Torak at the lead, quickly met up with them, while Shem was reacquainting himself.

Shem smiled. "Torak, this is Kalmyk. I learned the Ugric ways from him."

Torak reached out and shook Kalmyk's wrist. "You are alone?"

"Yes," said Kalmyk, without expression. The two men held a strong grip on one another, peering intently into each other's eyes. "You must keep up your pace. The Ugric and their beasts are less than a day behind you."

Torak released his grip. "Is this why you are here?"

"No. I must speak with Shem—alone."

Torak checked Shem's nod. "Very well." Torak took his men on ahead at a slow march, and left Shem and Kalmyk to converse.

"Why are you here, Kalmyk?" asked Shem.

"To see how you fared."

"I was told that you killed your older brother, and that you took his child, and that you are wanted by your people."

"You were never one to wait patiently, were you Shem?"

"Did you do it? Tell me it is not true."

Kalmyk stopped and faced Shem. "No. It is true that Lia is my niece, but I did not kill my older brother. My younger brother killed him and vowed to kill Lia too, if I did not leave. To protect her, I left my people. That is when my younger brother took the throne as high leader. And that is why I could not go with you. I would not kill him, even if he did such an evil thing to one of his own."

Shem let it all sink in. "I see now how that is true."

Kalmyk turned to walk. "Come. We fall behind your men. I still harbor anger toward him. That is why I did not care if you killed him. It would have been just."

Shem followed. "I am glad I did not."

"I, too, have heard gossip about you, Shem. People have said that *you* were the one who killed my younger brother, the high leader."

"And you too have been told wrongly. Ilkin gave your brother a poison to drink and said I did it."

"It seems that lies have been told of both of us. And now my brother's evil earnings have been paid in full."

"I did not know your brother, but before he died, he admitted he had done many wrongs. He also said that the seat is yours. Kalmyk, you are rightfully the high leader of the Ugric."

"I suppose I should be pleased. But it is too late for that. I have learned that Ilkin has stirred up the other Ugric clans to fight, and promised them much in return. His grip on them is too strong. Caution by the village elders slowed him down. But it did not matter. He and Agul have gotten their wish to make war with the Tuballites."

"Why did he not listen to the elders?"

"Once you escaped, he used you as a reason to justify his plans…lying to the elders that you would tell the Tuballites to make war while the Ugric slept. Ilkin had the behemoths, and knowing the Tuballites could not defend themselves from them, convinced the elders to act first. With the warm season coming, it gave him another reason to move quickly."

Shem spat on the ground. "Ilkin! Nothing but evil and death follow him! Only Agul and I know Ilkin killed your brother." Shem paused to let his anger subside, then remembered Kalmyk had not fully answered him. "Are you ready to tell me the truth of why you came here, Kalmyk?"

Kalmyk cleared his throat. "I will speak plainly…Lia has lost the child."

Shem stared ahead at the column of troops putting more distance between them. "You must know that I would have returned."

Kalmyk put his hand on Shem's shoulder. "I know. You are a man of duty and would have made a good father to the child."

Shem almost smiled. "I believe you mean that, Kalmyk." Shem looked up at the northwestern mountain range, puzzled. "You came this far to tell me this?"

"Lia did not lose the child easily. I had taken her to a healer in an Ugric clan I could trust. When I heard of the death of my brother, I sought you out to see if you had succeeded in stopping the attack. I was not far from here when I heard of the Tuballite warriors marching to meet the behemoths and suspected you may be with them." He sighed. "The one good that has come from my brother was his ability to keep the peace with the Tuballites. That is plainly gone."

"What will you do now?"

Kalmyk looked to the sky as if searching for an answer. "I cannot go with you and fight against my own people, and I cannot fight beside my people, because I am an outcast. I will go back to Lia and to our old way of life. And now, Shem, you are free of your obligation. May your God keep you safe."

"I will pray He does the same for you."

Kalmyk started to walk a few steps, then turned. "Did you say Agul knew of Ilkin's filthy doings?"

"Yes," said Shem, pointing northwest. "I saw him on the ridge by the gate with his warriors."

"Goodbye, Shem."

With that, Kalmyk gave a quick bow and walked north, disappearing into the mist. In many ways, Shem would have liked to escape with Lia and Kalmyk, and live with the Ugric, away from all his troubles. But running would not solve his problems. It would offer temporary harbor of safety where responsibility would eventually search him out. The Almighty had other plans for Shem, and those plans pointed him south.

Chapter 26
Eye of the Storm

The master of the lookouts stood on the wall walk and leaned against one of the curved merlons that lined Tuball's stone parapets. A few torches at strategic corners of the city showed faint signs of life. The master yawned. He caught sight of a signal fire erupting on a local hilltop. "Send for a runner!" he cried.

Bulla couldn't sleep. He was pacing the halls of his chamber lit by the moonlight that spilled in from the stone windows. A guard approached with a torch, escorting a runner. He stood stolid and waited.

Bulla waved him over. "What is it?"

The runner stepped forward and bowed deeply. "Grand Elder, the closest ridge to us burns its message, says my master of the wall."

Moments later, Tobanis opened the door to the hallway and strode forward with a torch in hand. "Have you heard?"

Bulla dismissed the boy and the guards. "It is true then. The Barrier Gate has been breached, Tobanis. Who led the warriors at the gate?"

"Torak, the Sethite. He has proven worthy."

Bulla scratched at his beard. "The message fire says otherwise."

"We would not have the message if Torak had not thought of setting up the fires."

"But the gate has fallen."

"I told Torak to send the signal fire when the beasts have broken through. But if I know Torak, they would have lost many a beast if they did. Spears from above would have poured down on them like a waterfall. It was our plan that the Ugric would pay with much blood. The few that survive would be slaughtered by our troops."

Bulla shook his head. "I somehow do not think it was that easy. Now that the Ugric breached the gate, how long do you expect them to arrive?"

Tobanis wobbled his head and squinted to think. "The beast walks as fast as a man...three days?"

"Do you have your warriors in place?"

"Yes, Master Bulla. 3,000 skilled warriors are camped outside the north of the city and another 4,000 men from the Bundled Tribes waiting near the south shore of the sea."

"How many men do the Ugric have?"

"Our scouts say there may be up to 3,000 warriors."

"Warriors we can overcome. It is the behemoths I fear."

Tobanis puffed out his chest. "Even if the beasts are worth fifty men, we will still succeed. Torak must have killed several of them."

In the flickering light, Bulla gave Tobanis a steely stare. "The great fall not because of their skill, but from overconfidence. We do not know how many of the enemy there are, or how many of the beasts have died. And I do not wish to have victory with only a handful of the Bundled Tribesmen left standing. We must conquer them by a wide margin."

"I will send a runner to get word of the enemies' numbers," said Tobanis.

"Good." Bulla walked to the window, rested his hands on the sill, and gazed out across the early light. "Let us hope the magic of the masters will bring them down."

* * *

The next day, Bulla stepped out onto the dock to inspect the newly built military boats. The ships had bodies of cedar, rudders and mast of hardwood. They spanned over a hundred feet long and five paces wide, and could carry up to fifty warriors or more. A deck ran over the top of the rowers for protection and for a quick dismissal of troops during surprise attacks. With no wind, and with twenty-five rowers on each side, the ship could move as fast as a slow run. With a good wind, the large square sail mounted in the center could make the vessels match or exceed that speed.

Ori leapt off the largest of the vessels to meet with Bulla. His thin, wiry cousin was overjoyed to command the four mighty ships. "Bulla! What do you think of my fine boats?" Ori was high strung, but had a gift for naval concepts. At a young age, his interest in seafaring propelled him to design some of the sleekest and fastest vessels ever to sail.

Bulla was immensely pleased with Ori's fleet. Though the little fleet was experimental and the crews inexperienced, Ori was committed to using every available weapon in his arsenal to defeat the northern tribes with a commanding blow.

Bulla gave the vessels another look. "They are fine indeed. But the Ugric have no boats and will attack on land. How will we use them against the enemy?"

"I have thought about that. The ships can sweep against them from the sea and release the warriors on land to attack from behind."

"With four ships, that would mean about 200 men against 3,000 enemy warriors. Why not take the best of the warriors that use the spear throwing board? You can hit them from the sea without worry of a pursuit."

Ori's thin body shuddered with joy. "A good plan, Bulla. You are as sharp as a Tuballite short sword."

"If you say so."

"The best warriors. I have your word? For I must tell this to Tobanis...to take his men."

"Yes, you have my word."

"Then I will speak with him today. When shall I send out the boats?"

"I suspect you will need to leave in two mornings, before sunrise. Use the morning vapor to hide within. Once the sun rises, the vapor will vanish for your attack. You may be able to surprise them and do greater damage that way." Bulla looked east. "We would fare much better if the Nephilim were with us."

"One of our trading boats just returned from the eastern shore. They told me the giants want to help, but will not kill for us."

Bulla scoffed. "What good is that? They may as well be women who are with child. We have enough to worry about without convincing them to fight. It may not matter. By the time the enemy arrives it will be too late." Bulla leaned forward. "During the battle, look for my sign, then move the ships to the shore for the attack."

Ori nodded several times with respect. "As you wish, Bulla."

Bulla bowed and left Ori to prepare for the battle. He walked the shore of the North Sea and looked back at the tall stone walls of Tuball. "May the gods be with us." *We have done what we know we can do. If the behemoths reach the city gates, it will mean an end to Tuball. I cannot let the dream of my father and father's father vanish. It will all end here.* He gazed north, watching the future battle in his mind, playing the events as he expected them. Bulla had never lost a battle. For the first time, he doubted himself.

While Bulla scanned the land, he noticed a large group of fishing boats making for the dock and along the shore. Bura and Kepenek were in the lead boat that had just tied off. Bura's eyes met with Bulla's. He waited for his subordinate to come to him.

Bura quickly ran up to Bulla and bowed. "Grand Elder, I have brought the fishing clan here for safety."

Bulla cracked a smile. "Kara would be proud of her brother."

Although they were now brothers, Bura never strayed from his place and status. "Have I seen favor in your eyes too, Grand Elder?"

Bulla smiled. "Yes. You have done well. Bring them into the walls of the city. Do you know of the battle at the Barrier Gate?"

"No, Grand Elder. I left before the fight. But I had heard from a fisherman who saw the battle that the behemoths wore shields around their body."

Bulla grimaced. "Then I doubt Torak had much success against them. We will find out soon enough. Tend to your duties, Bura." Bura bowed and started to leave. "Bura. I am glad you are alive, for your sister's peace."

"Many thanks, Grand Elder," said Bura. He bowed again and raced to the docks.

* * *

Torak, Shem, and the 500 slowed from a jog to a march when they entered the frontal defenses an earshot north of Tuball. They passed through some tall barricades that the masters had almost completed at a narrow passage between the cliffs and the shore. Shem saw Tabas leading a large group of his Sethite kinsmen. They were hauling a fir log up to the barricade. He was impressed with the speed at which the masters had built the wall, or rather, supervised the Sethites to build the wall. Intermingled with the workforce were the soldiers of the Bundled Tribes. Shem had never seen so many warriors in one place, encamped, marching, and practicing their weapons. They were everywhere, to the north and south, and around the city walls.

As they neared the eastern gates, Torak turned to Shem. "There are many warriors here, Shem. But do not think even this many can stop the behemoths."

"Would the Almighty not favor us? All of the Sethites are here, and we are his children."

"The enemy passed through the once great Barrier Gate. The Almighty favors whoever wins," he smiled wryly.

"Then why do we fight?" wondered Shem.

"To protect the ones we love."

"Is that not what *they* do, Torak?"

Torak thought for a moment. "Maybe the Ugric, but the Oka care for how quickly they can claw their way to the top of the dung pile."

"You are right about the Oka. But we must have faith that our will is God's will and that our victory is His."

"You sound like your father, Noah. I hope you are right."

When Shem and the troops marched up to the gates, the guard let them in. Torak took the men to the barracks, while Shem went to inform Bulla of their exploits. Along the way, Shem spotted Kara. His stomach flipped sourly. He would have rather avoided her, but she saw him and waved to him. Shem stood at the base of the stairs up to Bulla's chambers and waited for her.

Dressed beautifully in a blue robe, Kara came humbly to him. "I must speak with you before the battle."

Shem gave a pleading look back to Torak who quickly moved out of sight. He started up the stairs, careful not to look at her. "I must inform Bulla of the enemy."

She touched the back of his arm. "Please." Shem stopped. "It was cruel of me to leave you with such hate on my lips."

Shem wanted to end the conversation before it started. "I know how—"

"Let me speak." Her black brows and dark eyes showed firm purpose. "You are very much right on all that you have said. I do have my duties here, and to Bulla, and my child. It was foolish of me to think of leaving. I do not hate you." Her eyes welled up. "There will always be a space for you in my heart, even if I cannot have you in body." A tear dropped down and off Kara's cheek. "I know that even if you live through the battle…you cannot stay."

Shem half turned his shoulder to view her. "I am glad you have let go of your hate for me."

Kara reached out and wrapped her arms around Shem, but he was stiff. "I never hated you. I was selfish and was not thinking clearly. But I will never forget you!" she said in a loud whisper. Kara squeezed him for a long moment, until his body relaxed. She breathed in his ruddy scent one last time, then released him to straighten herself and wipe her eyes.

Feelings of pity and empathy flowed through him, but not love. "I do not know what to say, Kara."

"You do not have to say anything. It was up to me to repair my cruel words to you." Kara took a few steps down. "May you and your woman live long and well."

Shem suddenly realized he had told no one about Lia's dead baby, or the release of his commitment to her. He dared not mention anything. It would complicate their feelings, and more importantly, their destiny. This exchange with Kara was what he had hoped for all along. Now he could let her go. "I wish the same for you."

He watched as Kara disappeared into the market crowds. The bittersweet weight was lifted from him. He had the peace of knowing Kara's bitter words were far behind, and yet what stood before him was the promise of war.

Chapter 27
Final Conquest

Bulla assembled his men on the outskirts of the city. To this point, all defenses had been useless. This was the moment of truth. The muted sound of animals trumpeting floated out from deep within the thick curtain of morning fog, like a dreadful forecast of doom. A rattled stillness filled the air among the expectant Tuballite warriors. The trumpeting of the beasts began once more to terrorize their opponents.

"Stand ready!" shouted Bulla from his high point.

He raised his hand to keep the Bundled Tribes from moving or making the slightest sound. Then a cool, gentle breeze from the north blew in to force the fog up and away to reveal the northern tribes with their behemoths. The Ugric halted and began strategically placing their warriors to the side and rear of the huge hairy beasts. The behemoths stood ready with their riders atop, sniffing the air with their trunks as if making an assessment of the enemy. Large oak shields hung from the animals' necks down to their knees. The Bundled Tribes of the south outnumbered the Ugric and their allies three to one, but made little difference against such huge creatures.

The first protective defense was a makeshift barricade, not unlike the Barrier Gate at the north canyon. This was not as tall or as stout, but its length spanned from the foothills to sea. The barricade was made of hardwood ten feet high, filled with sand and stone two feet thick. The wood and stone masters created a blockade that would have taken months had it not been for the additional work and dedication from the allied labor force. Additional spear throwers stood on the wall, ready to ambush the creatures when they approached.

Bulla hoped that the gate would withstand the impact of the animals' strength long enough to give the spear throwers a chance to pick off the advancing warriors.

Their wait was short. A ram horn blew long and hard from the rear of the Ugric warriors, where the upper echelon of leadership stood in safety. Thus came the signal for the beasts to advance, and so they did. After a few moments, Bulla dropped his arm with a cutting motion, and instantly heavy bass drums pounded. *Boom*! ...

Boom! ... *Boom*! The drums continued their beat in a slow, rhythmic pace. The commanders of each thousand men led their troops on a slow march forward to meet the enemy.

The behemoths moved slowly forward, with the northern clans of Ugric and Oka a few steps behind. The beasts came to within shouting distance of the barricade, then halted. Tobanis stood bravely with the Tuballite soldiers on the apex of the barricade. The spear throwers were poised to launch their spear darts when the beasts came to within throwing distance.

Tobanis turned to the nearest warrior. "Wait for the behemoths. Do not throw." His words were passed on to the other men down the line. "Aim for the masters of the beasts. A beast without a master has no mind."

Out from behind the beast stepped three hundred men spread out across the field—Ugric sling throwers. They carried leather slings and pouches full of baked clay bullets strapped to their waists. The slingers quickly placed a perfectly rounded bullet into the sling pocket and swung the weapon in a circle. When a ram horn blew, the slings released a volley of bullets at the spear throwers on top of the barricade. Although not as deadly as spear darts, the slings were able to launch a projectile almost twice the distance of a spear thrower.

The first volley of bullets pelted the exposed spear throwers with anticipated effectiveness. Even at that distance, the bullets tore into the flesh of the spear throwers' heads and limbs—not destructive enough to kill, but enough to cripple. The Tuballites lowered their weapons and crouched into a protective position as the second volley came. The slingers then started a run toward the barricade, firing their bullets as quickly as possible to keep the spear throwers off balance. A second horn blew and the behemoths began to move forward. At close range, the bullets were deadly. Any Tuballite daring to launch a spear was instantly struck down. The Tuballites waited to launch their spears between volleys, but the rapid reloading speed of the slingers forced them to keep refuge behind the barricade.

Tobanis held up his shield and peeked through a hole. "The slingers are out of stones! It is time!"

The Tuballites stood up and, with precision, launched their own volley of spear darts. The spears shot out and killed the first line of slingers. The remaining slingers retreated at a sprint, leaving the animals to confront the Tuballites. Spears thrown at the behemoths occasionally hit the animals' feet or stuck into the wooden breastplates. The beasts picked up their pace. Faster and faster they ran, until they stomped the earth at full speed toward the barricade. The spear throwers realized, too late, the power of the behemoths.

When the big animals hit the barricades, the sound of the impact echoed across the land. The crash sent the temporary wall tumbling over on top of the men behind it. Even if a few spear throwers were able to launch their weapons before they were knocked over, most were crushed by the falling debris. Tobanis was one of those fortunate enough to leap off the barricade and skewer a beast master through the neck. They tumbled together off the behemoth, leaving it confused and waiting for direction.

The behemoths stomped over the fallen men and portion of the wall, then moved forward in an arrowhead pattern, with the largest and strongest animal at the front. A thousand Tuballite warriors stood ready with their swords and shields, still hoping to avoid contact with the giant animals.

Tobanis removed his spear from the dead Ugric. He moved toward the beast and drove it repeatedly into the animal's rear legs. The animal bellowed and groaned loudly. It twisted around and kicked at the pesky attacker. With daring agility, Tobanis dodged the heavy legs and went straight to the underside of the animal's neck. He jabbed his spear up several times. Again the animal bellowed, but this time reached down and grabbed Tobanis with his trunk. The seasoned warrior pulled out his short sword and swiped at the behemoth's nose until it was severed, spurting blood. It dropped to its knees, blood spilling from its belly, neck, and snout. The stout fighter leaped away just as it fell on its flank.

Other Tuballites were not as successful. After the behemoths broke through the barricade, they mowed down warriors like wheat in a grinding stone. Destined to be squashed as the animals marched forward, the Tuballite warriors ran like children. The beast masters kept low, behind the wooden plates of the behemoths.

Bulla took a deep breath. "So much waste," he whispered, as he paced. He looked to the shore to see the fog hanging over the water. The ships were completely masked by the cloud. *They cannot fight what they cannot see.* "Blow away, will you!" he yelled.

Agitated, Bulla motioned a signal to his troops. A hundred men with torches ran up to a small stream that cut across the land in front of the beasts. The stream was a trench filled with lamp oil twenty feet wide, from the western ridge to the water. A wall of angry flames flew up across the valley. Tobanis and a few hundred remaining warriors in the first line were on the enemy side of the wall of flame, cut off from the main force. Bulla had to sacrifice the first line of warriors to save the second.

The fire, however, did not deter the animals' masters. Somehow, they knew what was to occur. The highly trained beasts dropped to their knees and used their tusks to push their breast shields into the ground. The shields became like shovels, tearing up the fire and earth before them. The blazing oil parted before the beasts, and within minutes the Ugric allies moved through the fire line untouched.

The fog blew out from the shoreline, but the spear throwers on the ships were out of range. Bulla cursed the disadvantage and hoped that Ori would have the sense to disembark and set loose the warriors. Bulla held his arm up to keep the second line in place, at attention, with their shields up, spears ready. The bulk of Bulla's forces waited in their standard phalanx formation. They were the elite, hardened men, always willing to stand their ground and sacrifice their life for the cause.

After the trainers and their beasts passed through the opening in the fire-line, they continued to advance at a fast speed. The behemoths were once again spreading out with the largest ones in front. Closer and closer they charged toward the second line of Tuballites. Bulla looked on as the second trap was tripped. The ground was not solid, but dressed with a topping of grass that released at the weight of the animal. The behemoth crashed down into a huge hole in the earth and onto a planting of sharpened poles. Animal and master were instantly skewered to death.

A second behemoth and his master couldn't stop the momentum, tumbled over into the trap, and also were killed. A blast on a ram's horn stopped the remaining animals in their tracks. For an instant, the Ugric froze, unsure where to step without dropping into a treacherous pit. Bulla saw his advantage and took it. He ordered a team of spear launchers to position themselves at the outer edge of the battlefield, to flank the Ugric and launch a series of darts.

The Ugric commanders were equally cunning and ordered all their warriors to intervene. A human wave of northern tribes quickly poured in and around the beasts to meet the opposing forces on the side. Bulla hesitated to send any of his forces directly forward, afraid to give away the safe ground to the guardians of the behemoths. But if he did not send them out, the launching teams would be overwhelmed. In the end, it didn't matter. One of the trainers took a chance and forced his animal straight up the middle toward the Tuballite troops, missing all of the randomly placed traps. Soon, the other beast masters followed behind in safety.

The second line of warriors threw spears at the approaching animals, but couldn't penetrate the wooden shields. The spear throwers on the flank side had some success, until the overwhelming Ugric and Oka responded. The warriors in the second line stood their ground in another solid phalanx. Nevertheless, the huge behemoth easily broke through and order turned to chaos. The Tuballites tried everything they could to evade the beasts' crushing feet. With the beasts spreading out, the Tuballites had little hope, and were soon smashed underfoot. The animals plodded methodically through the Bundled Tribes, the Ugric and Oka close behind to assist. The second line of warriors was demolished.

Bulla considered his options—a retreat to the safety of the city walls, which would ultimately lead to the city being starved out, or a push forward with an all out charge against the enemy. Bulla was taught by his father that when given a choice whether to fight or run, fewer men die when they charge. He looked at the third and final body of warriors and waved his arm forward.

A mass of men moved through the area from all sides. Swords, spears, and axes clashed against one another. Death between the two sides was a match. Whether it was the Ugric's razor-edged obsidian axes or the Tuballites' finely honed metal swords—severed heads, arms, and legs were strewn across the ground. The advantage leaned toward the guardians of the behemoth. Bulla's men tried to skirt around the beasts without effect. Fighting the enemy and dodging the huge legs from the beasts was futile. A wave of darkness spread across the southern tribes, as the Ugric forces advanced with their great beasts.

For the first time in Bulla's life, he believed he could be defeated. He looked to the sky. *I have never believed or trusted in you. But I have seen your power. If you are the God that Shem has declared the true one, I beg of you to spare my people.*

* * *

Shem stood next to Torak on the city walls and helplessly watched the battle. "Why did Bulla order us to stand in the city, Torak? What good are we here?"

Torak leaned on his spear. "I do not know. But if the Tuballites' tricks do not work, those beasts will break through the gates. I fear the northern tribes are favored on this one."

Shem glanced up at Torak. "Bulla has never lost a battle."

"There is always a first."

"Why do you talk like this? Do you not have faith in him?"

"My faith is not in Bulla. Faith works best with a weapon in my hand, and my Maker by my side. Without beasts of our own, we are doomed."

"Then we should help them. There are hundreds of good warriors here in the city that I know would go."

"You may leave, but leave alone. I was commanded to stay with my men, so I will stay. If the enemy reaches the city walls, warriors must be here to protect it."

"How can you protect it, if you do not believe you will win?"

"I was commanded to do so."

Shem groaned. "I cannot stand here and do nothing." He paced a bit, staring out at the battle. "Do what you must, Torak, but I must leave." He reached out his hand toward his friend.

Torak took it. "Fight well, Cousin Shem. Return alive."

Shem glanced solemnly to Torak as he turned the corner of the wall walk. He then flew down the steps and over to the eastern gate. Running with all his strength toward the battlefield, he realized how futile his presence would be. Nevertheless he sped onward, around the chaos of flailing swords, spears, and clubs. Shem spotted a high point to his left that he thought would give him a better view. He climbed up the boulders to a wide ledge to scan the battlefield and determine where he could best be used.

The behemoths were squashing men like rodents. The bigger northern tribesmen had penetrated any kind of defense the Tuballites assembled. He couldn't smell the stench of death, but cries from the angry warring parties were loud and clear. As Shem assessed the situation, he heard something to his left. Climbing up to the ledge was Balkar. Bits of human flesh clung to his red stained chest.

Balkar stood up. "It is Shem, son of Noah! I was smashing many heads—then I saw you, standing up here like a torch ready to be put out. I had hoped El would give you to me. Without your giant to help you, it is time to finish where we left off." A sinister grin grew across his blood-splattered face and beard.

"I hoped Nazar had thrown you to your death."

"Ha! It brings me joy to see you sad."

Shem realized he had left his bolo behind, but he had his three-bladed dove clipped on his waist belt and a short sword in his hand. He sheathed his sword and unclasped the dove as Balkar started toward him. Shem threw the weapon and it whirled directly toward Balkar's neck. Balkar instinctively lifted his obsidian axe. The dove sliced the handle in half. The cutting blade whizzed close by his head. He touched his ear and felt blood. It was cut deeply, but not completely off.

Balkar paused to absorb the effect. "Nice throw. Now you have a sword and I have a handle. It is too bad I am so much bigger than you, or I would say you had the better of me." He chuckled wickedly.

Shem knew he had no chance with hand to hand combat against the big experienced Okan, so he took his sword and threw it at him. End over end, the sword flew forward, but again Balkar blocked the sword, and it stuck tightly into the axe handle.

Balkar laughed loudly and threw away the handle. "Now it will be my hands against yours."

Shem looked to the ground for his third weapon. He grabbed a walnut-sized stone from the ground. As Balkar moved forward, Shem held up the small, round rock.

Balkar stopped and taunted him. "A stone? You wish to throw a small stone? Do it. I will stand still for you. Then this will be the last thing you throw at me before I break your neck." Balkar crossed his arms and stood still.

Adrenaline pumped through Shem's veins, but he breathed out slowly and calmly while raising his arm into position. He aimed as he had done at Kalmyk's home and threw it hard and accurately, just as he was taught. The stone flew on a perfect trajectory to the temple of the big Okan. Balkar flinched and dropped his arms loosely to his side, then crumbled to the earth. Shem covered his face with his hands. He turned around to the battle and squatted down with his elbows on his knees.

After his pulse had leveled out, Shem raised his hands to the sky. It was losing its bright blue color. "What do you wish of me now?"

Distant cries and rams horns could be heard. "I see. It is time to fight for my people."

"Not so fast," said a voice behind him.

Shem dropped his arms and started to turn, but a hairy arm tightly wrapped itself around his neck. Balkar breathed heavily, his ear dripping blood, his sweat streaming onto Shem's head.

"No more of your tricks," said Balkar, squeezing hard against Shem's throat.

Shem tried to pull against the Okan's arms, but it was useless. "Please," Shem choked out.

"You have slipped from my hands twice. Now you must say hello to Mot."

Shem tried to wrap his foot around Balkar's leg, but it was like trying to trip up a tree stump. Shem struggled, and then jabbed his elbow into Balkar, but that too was useless. Shem's vision turned spotty, but he could still see strength of the Tuballite forces fading. Why would the Creator do this to him? The angel had told him he had a purpose, the magi had told him he had a purpose, and his father had told him as well. Was this it? To see the Tuballites get defeated by the Ugric and himself die at the hands of a filthy Okan?

"You had better make it three times," said baritone voice from behind Balkar.

Shem heard a thump behind him. He and Balkar fell forward to the ground. Shem landed against the big man on his back. He would have had the wind knock out of himself if there had been any left. Shem shoved Balkar away and coughed. He blinked a few times to clear his vision. Torak stood before him. Shem cleared his throat, and coughed a few times before taking in some good breaths.

He rolled over to a seated position and rubbed his neck. "Torak," he said, motioning to Balkar. "Make sure he is dead."

Torak kicked at the Okan. "I think he has seen the last of life. I split his head well. The insides have spilled out. He will never heal."

Shem swallowed a lump in his throat. "Why are you here?" he said hoarsely.

Torak reached out and pulled Shem to his feet. "I could not let you go to die alone. I can see that it was good I came."

Shem coughed a couple more times. He pressed his head with his hands to squeeze out the pain that had suddenly emerged. "Many, many thanks, Cousin. But what of the warriors in the city? Will they not need you?"

Torak shook his head. "It is too late for that. I will go back soon enough. For now we will find a weak spot and do some damage." He grinned with one raised brow, then pointed his sword at a group of Ugric overwhelming some Tuballites. "There! That is a good place for us to fight."

Shem closed his eyes tightly and pressed on his temples. A splitting headache squeezed his brain. Shem grimaced but looked out to see where Torak was pointing across the battlefield. Something extraordinary was happening…something wasn't right. A cloud materialized from the sky and floated over the northern tribes. It wasn't a cloud, but a multitude of strange beings with contorted, hideous faces, imposing feathered wings, scaled chests, and muscular legs with leather shin guards over high laced sandals. Angels…with spears of a bright green hue that matched the radiance of their bodies, fallen angels with an eerie and evil presence. The angels leaned close to the men as if speaking into their ears. The Oka warriors seemed to respond to the urging of the fallen angels with curses and fierce grimaces.

Shem rubbed his eyes. *Am I in a dream?* His head still throbbed with pain. He pounded a fist on his forehead, but pointed to the soaring beings. "Who or what is that?"

Torak looked out into the battlefield. "What do you see?"

"Them! The flying creatures! They fight with the northern tribes. With the heavenly hosts on their side, our loss is sure." Shem staggered back and leaned against a boulder.

"I see nothing like that," said Torak straining to spot something. The sun was setting, but there was still good light to see the battlefield. "I think you have been hit hard. You must rest a moment."

"No, I can see them plainly! Can you not see it?" Shem rubbed his eyes again, but it still did not stop the vision he was having. There were no angels with the Bundled Tribes. It was a pathetic sight. *Does Torak not see this? How could he not? Am I sick?*

"You may be ill. Stay here." Torak pulled Shem's sword out of the axe handle and stuck it in the soil next to him. "Use this to protect yourself. I will return." Torak left Shem and climbed down to the battlefield.

Shem's headache subsided a bit, but the vision continued. He looked to the darkening sky. "Creator of the heavens! What am I seeing? Is this a dream?"

Without a sound, two hooded men stepped on each side of Shem. Suddenly aware of their presence, he grabbed at the short sword from the ground, and whirled around to strike. His heart pumped hard as he flashed his sword at them. With his feet planted squarely, he pointed the tip first to one man then the other. After a brief moment of peering into their dark hoods, he recognized the men and lowered his sword.

"You…are the twins…who guided me and my people over the mountains."

They bowed their heads without a word.

"Why are you here?"

"Do not lose heart, Shem, son of Noah. The day is not lost. See before you," they said, gazing out to the battlefield.

Shem looked back to the valley and saw some men to the rear of the Bundled Tribes. They were tall, very tall—giants. The giants stepped forth from the outskirts of the battle, as if out of nowhere. Their steps covered the ground quickly. They had no weapons, just their hands. But what they accomplished without armor or weapon was equally effective. The biggest Ugric was but a child to the giants, and posed little concern. Without a doubt, it was the Nephilim.

Accompanying the Nephilim overhead were a multitude of beautiful angels. They flew over the men with their mighty wings, brilliant and powerful. Over a hundred Nephilim ran quickly, kicking away any Ugric as they approached the behemoths. Four giants per animal positioned themselves on each side, standing equal to or higher than the hairy beasts. They reached up and grasped the long hairs and curved tusks, then rocked and pulled on the hairy animals until they lost their balance. As each beast was tipped over to hit the earth hard, it let out a groan.

The big animals were down, but the Nephilim took no chances. They tied ropes around the legs of the beasts so they could not move. The giants then spread out around the animal like a protective shield to stop the Ugric from reinstating their animals to battle. In the middle of a flurry of slashing and screaming and fighting, every man and beast suddenly stopped where they stood. For an instant there was silence. The men stood as statues on the battlefield. No one moved except Shem and the twins behind him.

"What is happening to them?"

"It is now a battle in the heavens," said one of the twins.

The earthly battle had stopped but the angelic conflict took its turn. The fallen angels moved forward from above the Ugric warriors to attack God's angels hovering over the giants. Bright flashes of green and yellow light clashed against one another. Shem shielded his eyes as best he could, but he dare not miss the heavenly fight. The angels flew gracefully, yet fiercely, at one another, green and yellow hues blasting above earth and man. As sword met sword, a singing of metal rang out like a sick melodic refrain. Some angels were stronger than others. Some were quicker. All were magnificent. The fallen angels screamed with anger and vengeance, while their opponents fought in concentrated silence. A pulsing light of yellow mystical bodies rapidly moved forward until they forced the fallen angels to retreat, their green glows diminishing as they withdrew.

Shem watched closely as the light of the angels grew faint. "Is it over?" he asked the twins.

"Wait," said one twin.

Shem's heart was beating wildly. He had never seen anything as incredible as this. This must be the spirit world at war. The green hues were almost extinguished by the yellow light. Shem took a deep breath. It seemed as though a complete suppression of the evil angels was achieved.

Shem looked up to the star-filled sky in thanks. There he spotted a tiny red dot. The dot of red grew larger. Brighter and quicker it came, until a sudden shaft of brilliant red shot down to earth. It pierced the center of the legion of good angels with an explosion that formed a blazing mix of orange, yellow, and red.

Shem covered his eyes. "What is it?"

"It is the evil one," the twins announced with disdain.

The red light reassembled itself into a huge, vigorous strong body of scarlet. It was a red angel. He sneered with fearless eyes, and raised a flaming blood-red sword. He swung his sword at the angels of God with a force that knocked their ranks askew. Reinvigorated, the green hues from his compatriots regrouped and the heavenly battle ensued.

With his flaming sword raised high, the fearsome one yelled out an intense ugly war cry that echoed and pierced the atmosphere near and far. The fallen angels swelled in color and intensity, confident they could clinch victory. The yellow angelic bodies retreated to form a semicircle, then turned their faces to the heavens. Shem looked to the sky to observe what they waited on.

Before the red leader could advance with his minions, the stars parted and a blue light streamed down like lightening. Another large being appeared before them...a beautiful archangel. The blue angel hovered face to face with his red counterpart. The blue angel glowed with brilliance. His chest and shins were plated with bright metal, his feet clad with gold. He held out a two-sided, bright blue sword that hummed as he waved it.

"Did I not banish you from our presence long ago, Lucifer?" the blue archangel called out with a voice of rushing waters.

"Aaaghh! Michael!" The red evil one flashed his sharp and shining teeth. He shouted back, "Only of heaven above! Only of heaven!"

"And the Holiest of Holies called you his light bearer! You are nothing but the prince of darkness. You failed Him then and you will fail Him now!"

"Leave me the humans! The humans are mine!" he blasted back.

Michael stood firm with his sword outstretched. "You are mistaken, dark-hearted one! Take your minions and leave, or feel God's wrath!" The powerful archangel held steady his blue pulsing sword.

The fearsome Lucifer glanced back at his followers then retaliated maniacally. "No! Not this time!"

The demented evil one lunged forward, but the mighty archangel of God met him with a blast of blue that struck Lucifer's arm, igniting a purple pulse that spread across his body. He lost his sword and cradled his wounded arm. Lucifer's red hue returned, but only at half the brightness. He charged the archangel of God, but Michael was prepared. He held out his sword with both hands and a blast of bright blue and piercing harmonics flooded the opposing forces. Lucifer fell back.

The angels of good responded by surrounding the opposing forces, inundating them with a blaze of yellow-white light. A swirl of color lit up the sky as the spiritual battle waged on. A great shouting of pain and anguish filled the air. Green and red hues began to fade. The bright blue and yellow-white light became brighter and brighter until the sky and earth were immersed in a pure white brilliant blaze. A piercing pitch of harmony grew louder and higher with every increase in light level, until it masked all of the demonic cries.

Shem pinched his eyes shut, put his hands to his ears, and fell face first to the ground. A great trembling raced within his soul, his breath virtually gone. Shem gritted his teeth, assured that this was his end…then the cacophony of sound and light abruptly ended. He felt a great force from behind. The ringing in his ears faded and he began to breathe again. He opened one eye and then the other. The angels had vanished and so had the twins. Shem turned over to see that the men on the battlefield standing still, but alive, not as statues. They had weapons in their hands and were looking around for commands. The exhausted Sethite took his hands away from his ears and stood up.

"Master Shem!" A deep low voice cried out from behind him.

Shem turned with astonished glee. "Nazar! You have returned!"

The young Nephilim ran to Shem and knelt down to give him a gentle squeeze. He was even larger than the last time they were together, and had a good start on his first beard. Shem reciprocated with a joyful embrace.

Nazar released Shem from his grip. "I felt sad when you left me. You get into trouble so much."

Shem laughed. "Yes. I do. I see your people found a way to help us."

Nazar blushed. "It came to me on my own."

"And not too soon," added Shem.

"Are you hurt, Master Shem? There is blood on your face."

"Worry not, Nazar. It is someone else's."

"I will not worry. I will carry you back, Master."

"No. You do not have to do that."

Nazar ignored his objection. He picked him up like a child and carried him back to the battlefield. The behemoths groaned as they lay flat on their sides, birds chirped from the trees, and yet not a whisper was heard from the warriors. The Ugric warriors had laid their weapons and shields to the ground, then fell prostrate in front of the giants.

Bulla made his way forward and climbed onto the shoulder of a dead behemoth. He stood in front of the Nephilim and raised his hands to the Ugric and Oka. "Men of the north, this war is no more! Show me your chief! He must accept defeat for your people!" No one answered. Bulla scanned the field to see if a leader would present himself. "Accept defeat or sacrifice your lives!" he shouted.

Gradually there came a murmuring response from a smattering of the Ugric. "We have no chief. We accept."

"I will deal with Ilkin later," muttered Bulla. He cupped his hands around his mouth. "If there is no chief, you all must speak as one voice! Who accepts defeat?"

Finally, as if on cue, all of the northern soldiers spoke up in unison. "We do." They spoke out as if to hear their own voice for the first time.

Bulla shouted again. "Say it with meaning!"

"We do!" It was a loud unanimous shout from the northern tribes.

"So be it!" yelled out Bulla. "Today is a new day! You men will now renounce your allegiance to the Ugric, Oka, or any other. Today you are part of the Bundled Tribes of Tuball! What we eat, you eat. What we build, you build. And what we have, you have. We. Are. One!" He words echoed resoundingly.

The men on both sides raised their fists and cheered like never before. In past battles, the victor killed or enslaved the enemy and took the defeated's fortune. But on this day, Bulla ensured that they would live together as one large tribe. The vision of Bulla's father had been spoken about for years, and now it was Bulla's day to see it come true. Goods from the north would be traded with goods from the south; wares from the east would be traded with wares from the west. All would be in good standing across the land.

* * *

Ilkin sat on the throne in the grand hall at the Big Village, sulking about his defeat when he heard more bad news. It was said that Agul somehow was missed from the battlefield, and later showed up in the Big Village with Kalmyk. For some unknown reason, Agul unexpectedly removed his allegiance from Ilkin and informed the elders that it was Ilkin—not Shem—who had poisoned the high leader. The elders had Ilkin apprehended and burned to death the next evening. After Ilkin's death, his wife, Mansi, was never seen again. Kalmyk then took his rightful place as high leader of the northern tribes, with Lia beside him as his daughter.

Nazar, the young Nephilim, grew up to become a great leader of his people. He became important and wise, bringing prosperity to his people during all his days. Bulla became a grand elder over all the

Bundled Tribes, in the regions north, south, east, and west; governing fairly for the rest of his days.

This was a time Shem was comforted knowing that men, with the right desire, could work with one another to be of one mind and live under one ruler. He knew that when he crossed into the heavens at his death, all the faithful would be there one under the loving and strong Great Ruler. However, peace and prosperity among man could last for only so long. To achieve purity and compassion in the fallen is like taking hold of a vapor.

Chapter 28
New Love
Eleven years before the end

The days turned into seasons, the seasons into years, and years into decades. Shem's hair had streaks of grey, but his body was as strong as his youth. He reached down to pick up the buckets he had just filled from the river. He laid a pole across his shoulders and hooked the buckets on each end. Before leaving, he looked up to see a silver-haired man and a young woman on the other side of the river. Shem walked toward the river to get a better look. The man wore city clothes. He used a rod to steady himself along the banks of the river. Something seemed strangely familiar about him.

The old fellow looked up, caught Shem's eyes, then waved. "Shem! Greetings!"

The voice was unmistakable. "Bura? Is that you?"

"Yes! It is I!"

"Go upstream to the bridge! I will meet you there!"

They walked on opposing sides of the river banks, then crossed over to the middle of a wooden footbridge where they embraced one another. It was like the reunion of two lost brothers. Bura held Shem out at arm's length to scrutinize him.

"Look at you, Shem! How is it you do not age? I am an old man with hair of white and you still have brown curls on head and chin!"

"Maybe it is the valley or the water. My father says it is a sacred place."

Bura beamed. "It is from the heavens, is what it is. I must drink of this water." He turned to the woman. "Shem, I want you to meet my niece, Seda. She has wanted to meet you for a long time. "

The woman bowed. "I am honored to meet you, Master Shem."

Shem bowed cordially. "It is my pleasure to meet you, Seda."

She smiled in a way that lifted Shem's spirit. The woman of over thirty years had long black hair that cascaded around strong, heroic cheekbones. Her mature body filled a finely-woven, burnt-red dress. A thin wool cloth wrapped around her shoulders and high leather boots hugged her calves. But it was her eyes that drew him in. There was something familiar about her.

He turned back to Bura and squeezed his forearms. "It is so good to see you once again, my friend. Come to my home and we will feed you." Shem collected the water barrels and escorted them back to the hamlet."

Bura walked with Shem and recounted the fine and difficult times they shared together in the past. After passing a cluster of pines and a few stone houses, they entered a clearing, and Bura's breath was taken away. He stopped to stare. He lost his balance for an instant, then steadied himself with his walking pole.

Bura pointed with his forefinger. "So this is the great boat I have heard of."

Living with it day after day, Shem forgot that it was even there. "Ah yes. Father calls it an ark." He set the buckets down and stretched out his back.

Shem led Bura toward the vessel. The closer they got to it, the more amazing it became. There were dozens of workers on and around the ship. Scaffolds surrounded the outside of the vessel like a spider web engulfing its prey. A large area of the interior ribbing was exposed with planks encasing the majority of the boat. Technology from the city was evident—crude wheelbarrows hauled materials to and fro, large wooden cranes extended out from the top of the scaffold, wooden pulleys hoisted large loads up to the top, and large metal brackets held crossbeams in place.

"So it is true." Bura gawked. "This is a boat of all boats!"

"Yes, it is true. Whether she will float or not will be up to God."

"I do not see how the river will raise to that level, my friend."

"Neither do I. You will have to take that up with my father."

Bura coughed once, then coughed a lengthy session that made his face turn bright red.

Shem patted Bura's back. "Are you well, my friend?"

Bura took a deep breath and put on a gallant smile. "That was a fierce one."

Shem glanced at Seda, who bore a worried look. "Come. My home is over here. You must rest inside." Seda took one arm of Bura's and Shem took the other.

Once inside his home, Shem brought out some sweet berries he had picked the day before. Bura sat down on a sheepskin chair and breathed deeply. Seda sat on a fleece on the floor. Shem handed the bowl to Bura, then pulled up a three legged stool.

"So Bura, you have not told me why you are here. Your brother Domo stays with your tribe in the mountains, but his son lives and works with us. Do you wish to see him?"

Bura patted his belly. "The fruit is fine. Many thanks." He cleared his throat. "I would like to see my nephew, but that is not why I am here. In short, after Kepenek died, I did not wish to stay with her people. They had taken up the ways of the city and, to speak freely, it is better to die with you and yours."

Shem almost fell off his stool. "Die? What talk is this?"

Bura shook his head. "I am old and will not last another season."

"That is foolishness. You will live many more years. What of your family? They surely would wish you to be with them."

"You mentioned Domo. He and Katcha have gone to the underworld, and I do not wish to stay with those who worship other gods. I wish to be with those who love the one true God Almighty."

Shem's mouth dropped, then a slow smile crept up on him. "Is this a trick?"

"No," Bura stated flatly. "I speak the truth."

Shem leaned forward. "How? Why?"

Bura looked to his side and patted the cheek of Seda. "My niece. She taught me how to submit and worship Him."

Shem looked at the woman. "From you? How did you learn of my God, Seda? I have heard the city wishes to follow their own gods. There are few left who speak openly about the Almighty."

Seda was poised and calm. "You speak truly. There are few who believe as we. But I owe it to my father."

"Who is your father?"

"Bulla. In my view, he is the last in the line of the grand elders."

Shem was pleasantly stunned. "You are Bulla's daughter?"

She nodded. "After he passed on, my brother tried to carry on the traditions of my father, but was killed by his own son, my nephew—who rules the city today."

"Bulla's *and* Kara's daughter?" He asked. She nodded again. "But Kara had her gods. Why would she allow this?"

Seda clasped her hands together. "As I said. It was my father. My mother died giving birth to me. She had many still births between my brother and me. I never knew her."

"I did," said Shem quietly. "You have missed much from her, Seda." Bura nodded solemnly.

Seda pursed her lips to keep from crying. She wiped a tear then continued. "Before my father died, he told me I must leave the city. The Truthsayer confided in my father. He saw a day of evil coming and my father was afraid for me. My nephew has ruled selfishly. For him, it is too late. His advisers have told him he should be called a son of the gods and there should be a law to say so."

Bura became agitated. "Can you believe such a thing? The grand elder now a god?"

Shem stroked his beard. "I did not expect so many surprises. But how did Bulla learn of my God? I said very little to him."

Seda cracked a smile. "My father learned of Him from your Sethite people outside the city. He pretended to inspect the roads that the Sethites built and would listen to their stories. After mother died, Father thought it best for me to learn of the unseen God. My aunts wished that I would bow down to El and the other gods, so he taught me in secret. All was well, until my father passed from this life and my nephew took hold of power. I had no reason to live in the city. After my father was laid in the sacred tombs, I went to the fishing village to live with Uncle Bura and his wife."

Shem lowered his head. "I could not be there to honor Bulla. He was a good friend." Shem looked up and shook his head with a mystified smile. "The daughter of the grand elder leaving the city. That must have pained your aunts." Shem looked back at Bura. "And you came to accept my faith from Seda?"

"She has a gift," said Bura, coyly.

"Gift?"

"Yes. I had rushing pains in my shoulder for years, due to the many blows during battles, no doubt. Seda laid her hands upon me and there have been no pains since. This is truly the work of the gods, I said to her. But she corrected me and told me it was from the one true God. I submitted to Him after that. My only son knew Him too. He drowned at sea…" A tear dripped from the corner of Bura's eye and he pulled together a painful smile. "Now that my family is gone, and the city continues to slide into the mud, we wish to live with you and yours. Do you have a place for us?"

Shem grimaced. "How can you ask such a thing? I would let you stay even if you did not believe as me. But now, you are adopted kin. I could not have wished for more!"

Bura breathed a contented sigh. "I did not know for many years how truly a blessed man I was to have a friend like you, Shem."

* * *

Noah and the others received Bura and Seda warmly, with songs of joy and friendship. They weren't considered guests, but members of the community. Bura and Seda were given a newly attached hut adjacent to the main complex of Sethite homes. They became diligent in their work on the land and the ark. A close bond developed between them and Noah's family.

It was a cycle of the moon later when Shem changed. For years Shem had been plagued with recurring headaches. One day he climbed the steps inside the ark. A shooting pain hit his head with so much force, it knocked him to the floor. It had been the third one in the week and this one was the fiercest. He was escorted back to his hut where he tried to lay down and rest. The pounding pain was excruciating, and local herbs were useless.

Shem looked upward. "Lord God! Take me now!"

Seda heard his shouting cry and entered the hut. "Master Shem?"

Shem sat up on the edge of his bed, his head between his hands, trying to press the pain away. Shem opened an eye a sliver. "Seda, please leave."

"No, I will stay with you. Tell me what you need."

"To watch me cry like a child? There is nothing you can do. It is my curse to have the insides of my head split open."

"I can help you if God wills it."

His strong headaches seemed his hateful and constant companions. He had prayed to God for relief, but was never granted it. "God has not willed it," he informed her.

"I have been given a gift of healing. Do you not want me to help you be rid of it?"

Yes! I want to be rid of it! "No. Leave me in peace," he replied, pressing on his temples. "I have grown to live with them."

The demure and mysterious woman touched his arm and peered up into Shem's eyes with unusual strength. "Please, let me do this. I sense it is time," she insisted.

Could this woman heal me? How could she? If it was meant to be, I would have been healed long ago. Shem shook his head "There is no need. It is my lot."

"Do not be so proud!" she stated firmly. "Can you not humble yourself to a woman, or do you wish to be a slave to pain?"

Shem flinched at her rebuke. He waved a hand for her to proceed. Seda stood before him with closed eyes, and extended her hands open in front of her. She kept her eyes closed and brought her hands out to the side of Shem's head. All Shem could see was an angel of beauty before him and felt the warmth of her breath. His heart beat stronger when she pressed her hands around his head. As she breathed loud and rhythmically it was difficult for Shem to take her seriously. But then he felt a tingling through his skull, from one ear to the other, and a slow heat flooded his head. Shem closed his eyes tightly and he groaned at the increasing pain.

"Ahhhh! I—uh...." Shem cringed at the searing heat. A sudden coolness then flooded his body and he fell limp in her hands.

Bura entered the room when Seda was helping Shem lay down on the sheepskins. "What do we have here?"

"May God heal you, Master Shem," whispered Seda.

"She touched you, Shem?"

Shem opened his eyes slowly. "I will accept whatever He gives," replied Shem, fully spent from the ordeal.

"If you felt the fire, it means the illness was mended," informed Bura. "Rest and let Seda care for you."

Shem sighed and laid back. Seda brought a cool wet cloth and set it on his forehead. She adjusted the cloth and patted his face. Shem became drowsy and fell asleep.

When he woke, it was morning and the sun was shining through the window. Seda was cooking a stew in his fireplace. Shem groaned and sat up on his elbows. He sniffed at the aroma of her cooking. Seda quickly went over to remove the cloth and touch his head. As she bent over, he smelled her sweet breath and the scent of jasmine around her.

Shem caught her hand, then kissed it. "The pain is gone, and I smell once more." Shem breathed in her perfume and smiled. "You truly have a gift." She turned over the cloth and their eyes met for a long moment. They held one another's gaze without turning away. Neither one spoke, but within their hearts a bonding was made.

Seda's cheeks turned red. "The stew is boiling." She dashed over to the pot.

Once again, Bura appeared at the door. "How is my good friend?"

Shem smiled. "Never better."

Bura beamed. "Is she not the best woman?"

Shem looked over at Seda, who barely glanced up from her cooking. "Yes...I believe you are right."

* * *

In the days that followed, Shem was astounded how his headaches had vanished. He had a new energy, a new life. Nevertheless, not all was well. Bura's health had diminished. His coughing became worse and worse, until one day he walked to the door and looked up at the blue sky for a long moment.

Shem walked by and slapped Bura's shoulder. "You cannot get things done gazing upon the sky."

"Remember the puzzle box Kara kept with her, Shem?"

Shem smiled slightly. "Yes. I recall she gave it to you to get rid of."

"I took it to the mountains of my youth and placed it in a cave, the same cave you and I stayed in when I first met you. It is still there. It has your words to Kara."

"But that was long ago. The meaning of those words is lost. It may as well be buried."

"With rumblings in those mountains it may very well be. And that is how it should be. It is time for both of us to move on." Bura caught Shem's hand and pulled him close. "Take care of her. She is meant for you."

Before Shem could respond, Bura collapsed to the ground with a smile on his face. Seda rushed out of the hut to attend to him. But even she could not heal his ailments. His heart had given out.

Bura was buried on knoll that overlooked the valley. Seda cried over her uncle's grave, with tears of mourning and of joy. She said that they would see one another again in the lands of the heavens. With Bura gone, Seda carried a sadness about her that she could not lift. She had no other family to go back to, so Shem was obliged to watch over her.

Shem would drop in and sit with her daily and converse about good memories of the city to cheer her up. Seda had forgotten many of the good times and thanked him for the visits. Shem was thankful that she had left the city. And it was not just her beauty that drew him to her, it was a wonderful blend of Bulla's strength, Kara's mind, and her own kind soul that he cherished. He sensed that God moved through her and he felt a peace whenever she was around. Was it true when Bura said she was meant for him?

Shem was her constant companion. He helped her regain her countenance and lift the pain of her uncle's death. But was Shem's attraction to her only because she reminded him of Kara? And did he feel obligated to Seda because she had used her gift to heal his headaches? When asked these questions, Shem would simply answer yes…and more. But it did not matter what the others thought. He loved her. Shem knew God had meant for her to be with him all along. By the time Shem announced to his family that Seda accepted his proposal, it was no real surprise. Their love was as solid as the earth beneath them. What was there that could shake a strong love such as this?

Chapter 29
The Beginning of the End
Nine weeks before the end

Shem breathed hard as he reached the summit of the ridge, a small hare hung on his waist belt. He pulled back his curly brown hair, streaked with grey, and tied it back with a leather strip. Then he found a nice flat boulder to rest upon. From the highest point on the plateau, the land and water in all directions were clear. In the distance, Shem spotted the large channel that connected the Great Western Sea to the Black Sea.

He looked up at a crow that had been following him. "So this is where people of the valley say the salty water mixes with the sweet. Tomorrow I will find out the truth. Why did I not insist on Ham coming with me? I am stuck with only you to speak with." The crow cawed. Shem chuckled. "I will spend the night here and inspect the waters in the morning. You can stay if you wish." The crow cawed again.

As the sun was setting, the dark blue twilight appeared above a deep red horizon. With the moon behind the earth, the stars quickly began to brighten in awesome splendor. Shem gazed upward at a large, long bright light. *I have seen that light before. With every night it grows bigger, and runs across the sky with its tail as if it has something to fear. Was this what Father worried of? Is this the time of mankind's doom?*

Shem gathered some twigs and arranged them in a pile. He removed his traveling pack from his back, set it on the ground, and took out a flint. He stuck the small hare on a spit and started a fire to cook the animal. Once it was cooked, he sat on his goat fleece with his back against a boulder and ate. The crow landed at the fringe of the campsite, so Shem tossed it scraps of meat. As he chewed, he looked up to the night lights. "I hope I did not fail you, God. I have talked and argued with the Cainites but few have listened. Now I must return home." He stared into the fire awhile, and soon let out a yawn. His eyes became heavy. He drifted into a slumber.

Shem awoke to the sound of quacking. He followed the sound to a duck's nest. After shooing away the mother, he took one of four eggs. Upon returning to camp, he stirred up the fire's coals with his spear and set the duck egg into his brass cup to boil. He stretched out the kinks in his back and combed his beard with his fingers. A few minutes later, he moved the fire around, tossed some fig leaves into the water, then slid the cup and the egg away from the heat.

He gazed down at the wide channel. His plan was to investigate the rumors that the great Western Sea had poisoned the Black Sea. Thoughts of his family in the Ararat Valley caused him to breathe a solemn sigh. He sorely missed his wife and daughter and would be glad to return to them. A flock of birds burst up from some distant trees. A cool breeze raised pimples across his arms.

He rubbed himself warm, lifted the egg out with a forked stick, then peeled the egg and ate it. He sipped his tea and heard a growl behind him. Turning slowly, Shem saw two large grey wolves, only a stone's throw away. Their teeth were bared. Saliva dripped from their lips.

Shem closed his eyes, breathed in and out, then opened his eyes. "I respect your desire for food. But I have a wife and daughter to get back to and do not intend to let you hungry beasts stop me."

Fear would have taken hold of him if he was younger, but years of battle against man and beast gave him steady nerves. He glanced down the path. Several leaps away was a wide stream that cut across the trail down to the channel. The animals moved forward in a chilling slow motion. He slung his travel pack over his shoulder, calmly slipped the cup inside, took a good firm hold of his spear, and carefully backed up.

"Stay where you are and I will not have to kill you. I have cut down beasts bigger and meaner than you," Shem warned. At the same pace he backed up, the wolves stepped forward...a third smaller wolf appeared among the trees.

This was his chance. Shem sprang to the trail in a sprint, quickly sidestepping roots, rocks, and branches. He dared not look to the rear, for any delay could be deadly. He hardly had time to breathe— snarls and barks drew closer and closer. All his senses, blood, and muscles were focused on the stream ahead. *When I get there, they will have to swim! I would like to see that!* Shem was only steps away from the bank, confident he would lose them in the water.

As Shem stepped onto the bank of the stream, he felt a hard tug on his pack. A wolf set its teeth into the strap of the pouch. It was a huge male with wild green eyes. Shem instinctively whirled his spear around and sliced off part of the animal's nose. The wolf yelped and released the strap just as Shem fell into the stream. The beast followed without thinking, and they both sank below the surface into a chest-deep pool.

The crazed wolf lunged for Shem but bit into the spear. The animal shook the spear from Shem's hand and spit it out into the current. Without hesitation, it lunged again and sunk its teeth into Shem's arm.

Shem screamed. He punched the animal on the head. The wolf released him. It swallowed some water and began to swim back toward the shore. Shem grimaced from the wound, but regained his footing and reached out for animal's ears. He plunged its head underwater until the wolf struggled and thrashed. Soon it was over. He released the unconscious beast into the water, allowing the current to drag the carcass away.

Shem staggered back and stood upright to catch his breath. His heart pounded, his hands shook, and blood trickled down his arm. The other two wolves crouched on the bank watching him with evil eyes, venting random growls. He stood for a moment, staring the two animals down. Two more wolves bounded up to their side.

Shem groaned. "Two more? I am sorry to disappoint, but one fight is enough for today."

He trudged through the water to the other side of the stream and plopped down, dripping wet, exhausted, and annoyed. He tore off a part of his shirt and wrapped it around his bleeding wound. He looked up to see the four whining wolves pacing along the bank, sniffing the water's edge.

Shem held his arm close. "Ugh! Why was I so proud?" After tending to his wound, Shem saw his spear and the wolf carcass floating in a tangled net of willow roots. He retrieved the spear and stuck it in the ground, then pulled the dead animal ashore. "I told you to leave me alone." He pulled out a knife, made a cut up the belly, and began removing large sections of meat. Once he obtained enough to travel with, he wrapped them in a pouch made from its own pelt.

Hours later, he stopped at the end of the channel that emptied into the Black Sea. He was pleased his arm had stopped bleeding. Now he could concentrate on his investigation. He stepped closer to the channel where saltwater spilled over and into a monstrous waterfall. Shem was mesmerized by the volumes of water that thundered over the edge and ate away at the cliff like a predator devouring its victim. Gigantic chunks of stone tore loose and flew down three hundred feet to the Black Sea.

"It is true," Shem spoke out loud. "At this rate, the two great waters will soon be one. And salt from the Great Sea will infect the Black's sweet fresh water."

To avoid any further contact with the wolf pack, Shem took a safer route along the southern coast of the Black Sea. At nightfall, he made a camp by the shore, where the moon reflected slivers of light across the waves. Exhausted from the day's adventure, he drifted off into a deep sleep and lapsed into a dream where he was flying over a fishing village he recognized from his travels as a youth. It was a quiet, happy village where there was order and joy. But on this day, the village chief was climbing the nearby hills with his clan in a panic. Rain was pouring down upon them hard. Many scrambled up with few belongings.

When the villagers came to the crest of the hill, they cursed the rain. "What have we done to deserve this?" they cried out to their gods.

The chief was exhausted and soaking wet but he knew panic was not the answer. He pleaded with them. "We must blame ourselves for this. Let us pray to Shem's God."

"You and Shem did this to us," the villagers replied. "We have never seen water like this from above or below. Our gods are angry to have known Shem. You should pay for this!"

"We must pray to Shem's God, I tell you!" he pleaded.

The chief walked to the edge of the overlook and knelt down to pray to the God of the Sethites. The villagers looked down from above as their homes were inundated by the rising waters. From the top of the cliff, the once gentle people of the sea became enraged and turned on their leader. Delirious with anger they grabbed their leader and threw him off the bluff down to the rocks below. Not a moment later, behind them was a thunderous roar of melted snow. A river of water, loosened trees, rock, and mud cascaded down upon them all. The once proud clan of the sea was washed off the edge and into the abyss forever. A wave of grief swept over Shem as he watched in horror.

"Wake up, Shem! Wake up and go! You must hurry!" a voice shouted.

Shem woke with a start. He sat up and looked about only to hear the sound of buzzing insects. "Who is there!" he called out. Shem waited for a response, but none came. *The voice seemed so real.* "Is anyone out there?"

He wiped beads of sweat from his forehead then reached over for his bronze tipped spear to pull himself up. He stood in a guarded position with his spear pointed forward. Since it wasn't yet daybreak, he strained to see his surroundings. Realizing he was alone, Shem shook it off and stabbed the spear into the ground. He gazed out upon the still sea. The peaceful sounds of sea birds overhead and the lapping of small waves on the shore were a splendid calm.

"My task is not finished. There is one more place I must go."

* * *

Ten more days passed before he spotted a familiar fishing community, the same one he had visited decades before. As he neared the village, he observed how the settlement had grown twice its size since his absence. Dugout boats were anchored along the shore, and many more were out in the water. Most of the houses were built of mud and thatch, with a few wealthier homes constructed with an intricate mix of reed roofs supported by hazelnut tree walls. Shem had opposing memories: one of fondness for friends he had made, another of danger for when he had killed the water creature called Leviathan.

An old man standing near the guards at the village greeted Shem kindly. He remembered Shem from when he was just a boy, during the reign of Ordu. The old man offered to escort him to Suray, the new chief. Suray was born from the union of Ordu and Tanga, the mountain woman that Shem's uncle Zakho had rescued years ago. Ordu and Tanga had died recently and left their son, Suray, to inherit the position as leader of the clan.

The old man brought Shem to the chief's home. Once inside, the old man introduced Shem to the chief. Suray had his father's large, rotund frame and wore Ordu's necklace of shells. He was a balding, sturdy man who stood next to his plain yet glamorous wife, many years his junior. They knew of the legendary Sethite as Shem, the gods' favored one, and of his grand feat to kill Leviathan. Shem recognized Suray as the chief in his dream.

"Master Shem." He bowed. "It is an honor to meet you. I see the gods have blessed you with health. I was birthed after you and yet you have the years of my youngest brother." Suray waited for a reply, but Shem only smiled politely.

Shem's youthful appearance was indeed a curiosity to the villagers, but they all understood it as the gods' blessings upon him. A crowd had begun to form around the home of the chief to bid Shem homage, but at Shem's noticeable discomfort from the accolades, the chief shooed them away.

Suray's wife gave their honored guest a refreshment of food and drink. After a pleasant conversation and rest, the chief led Shem to the shoreline next to the village. At the water's edge the chief's son squatted down and rapped on a stone with a heavy stick. Within a minute there was a splashing noise farther out from shore. Shem scanned the water. A hump formed and created a small wake behind it. The hump entered the cove, then disappeared. For a long moment there was nothing. An unexpected splash a stone's throw out, erupted from the calm, exposing the head of the infamous Leviathan.

Shem trembled at the site of the familiar head of scales and flaming eyes. The creature rose up, its long neck extended three times the height of a man, and glided toward them. Its hump rose out of the water to expose fin-like appendages that steered it to shore. As the animal approached, it let out a raspy bark and vapor spray. Shem backed away from the water. He instinctively grabbed his bronze-tipped spear, and unconsciously flipped it around into throwing position.

"Stand back!" shouted Shem, waving Suray back with his free hand.

The chief's son laughed, but Shem stayed focused, his weapon poised and ready. Suray reached over and lowered Shem's spear. Shem gave a look of astonishment at the chief's calm disposition. The creature slowed down and dropped its head when it reached the shore. Shem wasn't convinced it was safe to withdraw until the chief's son went forward and petted the animal.

Suray cracked a delightful grin. His belly quivered with joy. "I knew you would be surprised! My father said the gods were on our side after you showed them how to brave the task of killing of the first one. The one you killed was young, and its mother came back to find it."

"Mother?"

"Yes, and she was a big one. It took the whole village to take her down. She was carrying another within her belly, weak and ready to burst. I think that was how my father and the village were able to kill her at all."

Shem watched as the leviathan extended its head so the young man could stroke it from the shore. "Where did this one come from?"

"It is the offspring of the mother beast. When they were cutting her up for the meat, out came this young one." Suray pointed to the animal. "We do not know why, but it would not leave us."

Shem shook his head. "I would never have believed this would happen. It is good to see such a thing. Only God could have allowed this."

"My father knew you would think greatly of this."

Shem couldn't stop shaking his head. "Ordu was right. I do."

Suray slapped Shem's back. "Come now, it is time we celebrate your arrival here. You are our special guest."

The village wasted no time in conducting an impromptu celebration. It started with the evening meal of fish, nuts, wheat flatbread, and local berries. Shem sat down and ate while musicians played their drums, flutes, and sistrums that jangled with sea shells and copper rings. The tribe chanted and sang while the young women used nets and fishing spears as props in their dancing.

As the celebration wore on, Shem tried to pay attention to the festivities. Instead, he thought back to his dismal dream and the gigantic falls to the east. He suspected that with the amount of salt water entering from the Great Sea, local fishing would soon suffer. *Was their belief in foreign gods the cause of it? There is no hatred or cruelty in the village. Could it be their misguided faith that put them in peril?*

While the gaiety continued, Shem pulled the chief aside for a serious conversation. "Suray," said Shem, in a somber note. "I have some news that may not be kind to you."

The chief swallowed a few berries. "What is it, Shem?"

"My father tells me that our God's anger grows. He says that the end of man is soon." Shem pointed up to the night sky. "The sign is that star with the tail."

Suray gazed up at it. "We saw that star two seasons ago and it did us no harm. My shaman says it is a blessing to us, not doom. Do you not see how our gods have blessed us? Even the creatures of the sea are in our favor."

"I see that you have a kind and generous people. My father is a great shaman too. His words from God always come true. I trust what he says. If he says that the Creator brings doom, I would pay heed to it. The Creator is patient, but He will not be patient forever."

Suray eyed Shem. "How will this God of yours show his anger?"

Should I tell him of my dream? Why would he believe me? "I do not know. But I do know that there will be much death. My father says that only a few will be spared. Even as we speak, the salty water from the Great Sea has poured into your waters. It may be the first of His wrath."

A flash of indignation crossed the chief's face, but it quickly softened. The chief looked out across the sea. "In the last season I have seen how the water lost its sweetness, and our catches are smaller...it may be nothing." Suray stared into his cup. "I know you have been blessed, and you would not speak to me like this unless you believed strongly of it. If this is true, when is this to befall us?"

"I do not know, Suray. If you accept *my* God , He may spare you in the life after death." Shem put his hand on Suray's shoulder. "Your father was a good man and good to me. I am telling you this because of his kindness."

Suray looked at his tribe laughing and dancing. "To accept your God would mean renouncing the gods of our youth. It would be asking much." He sighed heavily and shook his head. "I will speak to my elders of this, and hope that we choose wisely. You are a great man. I would be a fool to ignore your words."

Shem reached out and shook the chief's wrist. "That is all I ask. I must get some sleep. I leave before first light to return to my people."

"Sleep in my home tonight and on my bed of feathers. It will help you travel well, my friend."

Shem gave him a grateful smile. "I will. Many thanks."

236

A heavy pit sat in Shem's stomach. He empathized for these happy and carefree people. He left the merrymaking and took up Suray's invitation to his soft bed. But the comfort of the bed did little to sooth his memory of the ominous dream. Shem was glad that he had given Suray an early warning, so his people could change their ways. He knew even a peaceful and kind people couldn't be spared the wrath that will soon fall upon the earth.

* * *

Shem left early in the morning, before the villagers woke to bid him farewell. He had said what needed to be said and was anxious to go home. He climbed the crest of the hills, then looked down upon the village. It was a peaceful hazy morning. Villagers stirred. Boats pushed off to their regular fishing places. Shem absorbed the picture of how he wanted to remember the fishing clan. He blinked away his water-filled eyes then turned and followed the trail home.

The closer Shem was to his home, the easier his steps felt beneath him. Before he knew it, the Ararat valley was upon him. In the distance, he could see the huge boat at the base of the mountain. Workers climbed around the ship like insects on a mound, pounding and sawing the last of what was required. The massive vessel stood like a monument on the hillside, one hundred fifty paces long and as high as a cedar tree. A long snout reached out low in front, a series of opening hatches were mounted on a short wall at the top deck, and a high vented wall towered over the stern. It was truly a marvel.

As Shem walked along the river, a girl in a wool smock, about ten years of age, balanced herself carefully along a low branch of an apricot tree. The girl hummed to herself while she picked and dropped fruit into her buckets on the ground below. She looked over to see Shem watching her. She jumped down to the ground and ran toward him with glee.

"Father! Father! You have returned!" she screeched with joy.

She looked so much like her mother—flowing hair, dark eyes, and brilliant smile. With the time of destruction at hand, Shem felt a comfort to be where it was safe and close to family. The girl raced as fast as her legs could carry her…out of breath, she cried out once more.

"Father!" She squeezed him around the stomach until she ached.

"What are you doing this far down the river alone, my sweetness?"

His daughter turned around and pointed to the two wooden buckets sitting near the trunk of the tree. "I was told to get fruit." She giggled. "But I ate many of them," she said, showing him three apricots in her pockets.

Shem smiled then took her hand. "Come, Cala, we will get the fruit together." He looked up valley to see a cluster of Cainite homes near the river. A gush of pain filled his belly. His eyes welled up.

"Why are you sad, Father? Are you not happy to see me?"

Shem looked down at his big-eyed beauty and cupped his hands around her cheeks. "How can I be sad when you are around, Cala?" Shem saw a large boulder by the river and veered toward it. "I was thinking of many seasons past before you were born. Would you like to hear of a story about me when I was young?"

She clasped her hands together. "Oh, yes! But what of the fruit?"

He brushed the hair from her face. "It can wait."

Shem planted his staff in the earth and leaned against the boulder. His daughter crawled up onto his lap. "The past is one of beauty *and* terror. Are you old enough to hear the bad parts too?"

She nodded vehemently to give Shem permission to scare her if necessary.

"Let me get some water first. My mouth is dry."

"I will get it!"

Cala grabbed his flask, unseated herself, ran to the water's edge, then skipped back to her father. She pulled out the three apricots she had in her dress pockets and gave two to Shem, keeping one for herself. Shem drank deeply, capped the flask, wiped his mouth, then popped the apricots in his mouth.

He looked upward and stroked his bearded chin. "I should begin with the evil Ilkin, son of the grand elder of Tuball, my time with the angel and the Nephilim. I was much younger then. But I had been injured badly and did not know if I would live."

She rolled her eyes. "But you did live, for here you are!"

"Yes I did. But nothing ever seems to go as we plan."

Shem told Cala an abridged version of history with plenty of action and adventure, holding back the parts unsuitable for a ten year old. After he finished telling the story to his daughter, he stood and stretched out some kinks in his back. The shadows from the trees by the river were long. He looked over at Cala lying prostrate toward him, chin on her hands, elbows to the ground. She had hung onto his every word.

She twisted a lock of long black hair with her finger. "I love that story, Father. Will I get an angel to help me some day?"

"I hope so, Daughter."

"Uncle Ham says our people who still live in Tuball have been bad."

Shem sighed deeply. "Even the strongest walls have cracks." He tapped his staff on the earth. "Our Sethite cousins have strayed, like lambs into thorny bushes. I do not know what is to become of them, but it cannot be good. Tuball was a great city. The Almighty has given them many chances, but they, in their prosperity and growth, have squandered it. Many a trip I have made to warn them. Only a few have listened."

Cala sprung up from the ground and took his hand into hers. "I should pray for them. Grandfather says 'we must always let Him hear our burdens.'"

Shem ruffled the top of her head. "You are such a treasure, my child. Grandfather is right. You must never stop."

It was desperately good for Shem to be home. He looked over Cala's head to see his wife near the river in the process of washing a bundle of clothing. She raised her head from her work and peered quizzically his way. When their eyes met, she displayed a beautiful set of teeth within a warm grin. She waved vigorously, set aside the bundle, and rose to meet him.

Shem squeezed Cala and kissed the top of her head. "Enough stories for now. Your mother has spotted us," he whispered loudly, pointing a thumb downriver.

"Will you tell me another one later, Father?"

Shem pinched her cheeks. "Yes, of course. Now go on to your chores before your mother blames me for keeping you."

Cala ran to her mother and said some words, then picked up the overturned fruit buckets to start filling them again. Shem gazed at his approaching wife. She was as beautiful as when he left her two seasons ago, a woman that he would never have planned for. Instead of settling for Kara, Lily, or even Lia, God had given him the woman that was the best for him.

"Husband!" she said, striding forward with open arms, her hair flowing behind. "Why did you not tell me you were here? I have ached for two seasons to see your face."

"*You* have ached? For a dusty, smelly man? I have ached much more for you, woman. Your beauty was the best thing that kept me going."

She wrapped her arms around Shem and planted a kiss on his dry lips. The two kissed warmly, then stopped to just hold one another for a long moment. Both of them somehow knew that they would not part from one another ever again, and they relished that thought.

"Cala tells me you stopped to tell her a grand story. Could you not wait? You have just returned from your travels."

Shem stepped back and looked into her eyes. "She loves them. As do you."

"I do not," she protested. "My head stays on the ground, where it should."

"And that is what I love about you most."

Cala poked her head around the tree. "Do I have to pick more fruit?"

Shem and Seda turned around. "Cala!"

They ran after and caught her. They tickled their daughter until her sides ached. Once the laughter ended, the threesome walked hand in hand back to their home.

At bedtime, Cala lay on her stuffed sheep fleece while Shem peered down at his daughter. He bent to kiss her forehead. "It is good to be with the two women I love." Seda sidled up to Shem and smiled.

Cala grinned up at Seda. "And you love Father, too, Mother?"

Seda kissed Shem on his cheek. "Oh yes. I saw your father's strength of duty and faith. He is a wonderful man of the Almighty."

Cala yawned and rolled to her side. Shem arched his back, stretched out his arms, and let out a yawning moan. As Shem gazed down at his precious child, he suddenly had a sinking feeling.

Shem rubbed his stomach and spoke softly. "Why do I have an ache in my belly?"

Seda covered Cala with a bed cloth. "You need some of my cooking to fill you. You are too thin."

He smiled. "I do need some meat on me. But no, there is something else."

"A storm?"

Shem went to the window. "There are many more tents and homes by the river since last I was here."

"It is like a village now. Mother Naamah and Ham have a good trade selling food to them. Our sheep and goats are so plentiful, the Cainites trade meat for work on the big boat."

"Father must be happy to have the help."

"He is. The boat is almost finished."

Shem looked down at his dozing daughter with a sympathetic gaze. "Good. It has taken a lifetime to build it."

Seda studied Shem's gloominess. "What is it, Shem? You have a wounded face."

"I do not know. I…" He peered at Cala.

"Have the head pains returned?"

"No. My head is as clear as a fresh stream."

"What then?"

Shem shook off his troubled mind, and beamed a bright smile at Seda. "Nothing. Let us think on the good."

"Yes," she whispered. "Think of the good." Seda put her forefinger to her lips. "Shhh."

She let her outer garment drop from her shoulders to the floor. She picked up the oil lamp with her and set it down on a stool in the adjoining space, then pulled a translucent curtain across the sleeping space. Seda peeked from behind the curtain with flirtatious eyes then returned to undress behind the screen. He chuckled softly when he saw the silhouette of her body through the curtain.

"As you said, Seda. I am a man of duty."

Chapter 30
A Bad Omen

Shem woke to Seda humming a soothing tune as she fixed the morning meal for him. He grinned with his eyes closed, then pulled himself out of bed. Before strapping on his sandals, he checked them for any creatures hiding inside, then went to the table and ate heartily. Afterward, he walked out of his hut to gaze up at the iconic vessel up the hillside. It stood like a monument at the base of the mountain, nearly complete, and dwarfing everything around it. He made a note to reacquaint himself with it.

Down the hill from the ark, the Aras Valley had become a major crossroads between Anbar and Tuball. With trade routed through Noah's valley, the Cainite presence grew. Even this early in the morning, people were journeying by, pointing and laughing at the ark. Shem frowned at them.

Seda walked up beside him and leaned her head against his shoulder. "They mock us, Husband."

He had seen this behavior in his travels to warn the world of the impending doom. His words fell on cluttered minds. Tuball's prosperity birthed success. With success came luxuries; with luxuries came pride; with pride came amnesia; with amnesia came self indulgence. Sexual pleasures were there for the taking. It was fashionable to own a slave, many of them Sethites who had not bowed down to the Tuballite gods. Even the calm and peaceful Nephilim had children who took on the ways of the Tuballites. They became fearsome warriors with a thirst for killing.

"I do not know why Father wanted me to warn the world of their evil deeds. They laughed and spouted threats," said Shem, shaking his head. "Why could I not come back to good news?"

Seda's eyes sparkled. "There is some good news! Japheth has a woman."

"Japheth? I thought he would end up alone, married to his duty."

Seda leaned in with excitement. "We thought the same. But after Grandfather Lamech passed on, your brother returned to us with a woman named Adataneses. I was told Japheth always loved her, and it took your mother to make him see that they should bond."

"Why did he wait?"

"I think he wanted you to return, so all of you could be present."

"He has more patience than any of us."

Noah stepped around the corner of their home. His mouth and eyes opened wide and looked Shem up and down, then reached out and squeezed Shem's shoulders. "I thought that was your voice! And here you are! You look well, Son."

"Yes, Father, I am fine. But lately I have had dreams of death and ruin."

Noah sighed. "I too have been disturbed by dreams. Have you seen how the star with the tail gets larger? I fear the end is near. Were there any out there who would listen?"

Shem shook his head. "Very few. I think it would be easier to move a mountain than to try and change the hearts of men. They have chosen the earthly gods and their selfish ways. And, as Seda said, they mock us."

Noah pointed at the pasture. "But they do not laugh at our large flocks of goat and sheep, and long fields of wheat, even in this sad soil. We are the envy of the surrounding tribes."

Seda looked up at Shem. "Many say Father wastes the profits on the building of the big boat. But that does not stop them from bargaining with him. Most people wait until they are out of his site to mock him of his odd affairs."

"Odd?" Noah rebuked her, pleasantly. "It is not so odd to have a boat the size of village sitting on dry land, is it?"

Cala came from inside and wrapped her arms around her mother's waist to listen.

Seda stroked her head. "Daughter, go and gather the rest of the fruit you started on."

Cala dropped her head and huffed. "Yes, Mother." She plodded off as if it was punishment.

Shem laughed, refreshed by her spunky childishness. His focus moved over to see his brother Ham, at the next hut a stones throw away, talking to a young woman by water barrel. Ham had cropped his beard short, in the fashion of the city. His clothing was of a fine weave. He extended his arm and flexed his bicep for the young woman to feel.

"Who is that woman?" asked Shem.

Seda stood solid and quiet, eyes darting from Noah to Shem, trying to hold back a smile with her hand.

243

Noah frowned with consternation and shook his head. "Ask *him*."

Shem excused himself to talk with his brother. When the woman saw him coming, she filled the jug of water and abruptly left. Ham folded his thick dark arms across his body and ogled at the departing young female.

Ham looked back to Shem. "So here is the great speaker and wanderer!" he teased.

"Stop it." Shem slapped his brother lightly on the cheek. He scooped a handful of barrel water and brought it to his lips. After he sipped the water from his hand, he splashed his face. "I think I have seen that woman with Domo the woodsman. Is that not his granddaughter?" The woman shyly glanced back over her shoulder on her way to the wood workers.

"Yes, Ne'elatama'uk. I call her Ne'uk."

"Ne'uk?" Shem asked, with a raised eyebrow. "Is there something you wish to tell me, Brother?"

"What can I tell you? The Sevan people found her abandoned as a child on the road to Anbar and raised her as their own. The Cainites are the only family she knows. That is all."

"That is all? You seem to show a desire for her."

"You, of all people, know of love outside the Sethite tribe," replied Ham. He waved his hand. "We do not even know if she is a Cainite. She could be a cousin from the far south."

"She is very young…and yet she likes you?"

Ham puffed up a bit. "I am as fit as any man half my age."

"But of more importance, does she believe in our God?"

Ham stood defiantly. "Did Kara?"

"That was long ago, Brother. And you are old enough to know better."

Ham sighed. "I have been over this with Father. Let me not bore you."

Shem shuffled around stone on the ground with his foot. "You are right to challenge me. I have no place to judge you or this Ne'uk."

"That is grand of you, Brother. So let us not dwell on this now. We will have much time later. Why not tell me of your travels."

Shem conceded and gave Ham a lengthy summary of his most recent exploits: The city's new trappings of advancement, the increased use of slaves, offerings to false gods, and Shem's generally expressed regret for the way morality had changed for the worse. Even outside the city, it was becoming exceedingly evil. Greed and sexual pleasure were common place—virtue nowhere to be found. Ham listened intently, but gave no indication of disapproval.

Shem's mind moved far away before he regained his senses. "It is good to be back with family."

"And it is good to have you back. We need you to help. So do not get lazy on us," Ham advised.

As they were speaking, a tall man with silver and blond hair approached them. He wore Ugric furs and leaned on a walking stick. "Good people, I have come from the city of Tuball and have heard of Shem, the son of Noah. Will you show him to me?"

Shem noticed a deep pain in the man's eyes. "I am the one you look for."

The man brightened. "Ah! Good. I have some news from the city. May we speak privately?"

"Is it urgent?" asked Shem. "I have just returned from a long journey and wish to spend time with my people."

The man shrugged. "No. But you will like what I have to tell you and I will not stay long."

"How long, man?"

He pointed down by the river. "I will be staying with friends in those tents for a day and then move on."

"Oh, then we must talk soon. And what is your name?"

"I am just a man. Come see me when you are ready." The man bowed and left.

Ham eyed the man and spoke softly to Shem. "I do not like him."

Shem chuckled. "But you like so few, Brother. Worry not. I will find out what he wants later."

"The boat is almost finished, you must go up and see it and talk with Japheth," said Ham. He glanced back in the direction of Ne'uk. "Japheth says he misses you."

Shem squinted at his brother. "Yes, I see you must attend to other things."

Ham raised his eyebrows up and down mischievously, then strode back to Ne'uk.

* * *

At Ham's suggestion, Shem went up the hill to inspect the ark. The scaffolding was removed and reused for building up the local houses. The massive vessel stood majestically with but a few support beams on each side. The vessel put to shame the largest of boats of Tuball, with its one four hundred fifty foot length and forty-five foot height. Planks over two feet wide and a fist thick wrapped the hulking exterior of the vessel. A long snout reached out low in front, a series of opening hatches were mounted on a short wall at the top deck, and a high vented wall towered over the stern. With the ark virtually complete, just one Sevan clan was left to finish wood detailing.

Shem walked inside, up the stairs, and out to the main deck. Japheth was testing out the sky hatches on the roof. Shem watched Japheth for a moment. Sometimes he thought of how his older brother, tall and fair, would have mixed easily with the Ugric.

Shem climbed out from one of the hatches and onto the deck. "Japheth?"

Japheth turned from his work. "Shem! Oh, it has been far too long." He gave Shem a lengthy bear hug, then stepped back with a slight melancholy on his face. "It is good you are here. Now I have someone I can talk with."

Shem sat down on one of the closed hatches. "You have Ham and Father."

Japheth almost scoffed. "I do not think you understand." He took hold of Shem's arm and led him around the deck to explain. "Ham spends too much time with the Seva men *and* women.

Shem cracked a smile. "I saw Ne'uk. Is it true, their love?"

"Only Ham knows. And see there," said Japheth, pointing to an overturned dingy. "Ham even has built a small boat with the Seva's help. If he is not with that woman or helping father, he works on that boat. And Father spends too much time looking over every little piece of wood on this big boat. So you see why it is good to have you back."

"Fair enough. But I hear there is good news—that you have a woman?"

Japheth grinned. "Adataneses. That is true. She is a good one. Mother and she are like peas in a pod."

"I hear you met her when you were with Grandfather. Do you miss working the land?"

Japheth took a deep breath, closed his eyes, and spoke with aversion. "I am not a boat builder." He extended his hand into a fist as if he were holding a precious stone. "I like the feel of the good soil in my hands." He opened his eyes and glared down at the ark. "Not cutting and pounding on wood."

"I sense you miss Grandfather and Grandmother, too."

Japheth glanced over at the southern mountains. "I do. When Lily and Shinar sent word that Grandfather and Grandmother had died, it was a sad day. I miss them greatly."

Shem stroked his beard. "We will be as a family in the heavens one day, yes?"

"Yes, but that does not make it any easier here."

"After Grandfather and Grandmother passed on, why did Shinar and Lily not return here?"

Japheth patted his belly. "Lily was fat with child and could not travel. It is warmer on the other side of the mountains and the fields bear much. That, and I think they wanted their own life together."

Shem walked to the short wall on the edge of the boat. "As much as I hated it when I was young, I miss the days we would plow the soil. Now we are surrounded by the Cainites. There are almost as many people here as in the city."

Japheth looked out at the travelers near the river. "This is the main road to Anbar. On some days, hundreds pass by. They line the banks with many homes to do much trading."

"What will happen after the boat is finished, Brother?"

Japheth paused. "Let Father answer that. With God's help the Cainites will all leave us and go back to where they came from."

"Or we could leave them here and go back to the Tigris?" added Shem.

"So be it, Brother. Tell me when, and I will follow." Japheth chuckled. "I would feel better just to throw stones at those that curse us."

Shem laughed. "We could, but I fear few would be coaxed to our views."

Japheth shook his head in disgust. "It would not matter. They will not listen. Father has talked to the Cainite clans till he is out of breath. It does no good. Look at them. They know how we worship our God and yet they carry on in their tents and homes by the river, flaunting their filthy acts at us...naked bodies, hurting each other, drinking odd and wild juices. The wild grapes are good to eat and drink, but the Cainites let them sit until the juice is strong and spins the head."

Shem thought back to the mead he had once drunk. "I know. What do they think of Father?"

"They say his mind is going mad. I secretly think it sometimes. But they say it to his face. Look!" Japheth pointed to a couple near one of the tents. "They mate openly. Do they not respect our views at all?"

Shem suddenly remembered the Ugric man, he spoke with earlier. "That reminds me. I must go, Brother. A man needs to speak with me about news from Tuball. We still have much to discuss…tonight?"

Japheth waved him on. "Yes, go…tonight."

Shem climbed down the stairs of the ark two levels and out the big access plank of the main door. He trotted down to the tents where the Ugric had mentioned he was staying. The older man was sitting outside the tent chewing on some dried venison.

The man waved when he saw Shem. "Ahh, you have come."

Shem glanced over at the couple that was openly copulating, a few tents away. They moaned and groaned in their sexual proclivity. Shem turned to the man. "Could you come up to my home?"

"If that is what you wish, Master Shem."

"I did not get your name," said Shem reaching out to shake the man's wrist.

The man kept his arm to himself. "My name does not matter. Let us go to your home. We will talk there."

Shem dismissed the odd rebuff as Cainite rudeness. He led the man back to his home, where Seda and Cala were outside shaking out fleeces. Seda motioned for Shem to talk with her alone. Shem left the man at the door and excused himself.

The man went over to a ceramic pitcher, cracked the lid, and put his nose close. "This is from the best of grapes," he commented aloud to no one.

Shem turned to Cala. "Daughter, pour some of the grape juice for him and I. We will drink it inside." Cala smiled happily and did as he requested.

Seda moved closer to Shem. "Who is this man, Husband?"

Shem kept his voice low. "I do not know. But he has some news from the city and wishes to speak with me."

Her eyes lit up. "He has secrets to tell? I will wait here. If you are in need of food, call out."

Shem held her chin. "You are such a gift." Shem whispered into her ear. "I will inform you of his precious *secrets* soon."

Cala bowed to the stranger, picked up the pitcher, and went inside while her parents talked. She came back out with an empty pitcher, walked to Naamah's home, and then headed back into her parents' home. Shem left Seda and approached the man, who waited patiently at the door. Shem looked inside to see Cala pouring the grape juice in his cup. He walked inside with the man close behind. Cala set down the pitcher and picked up Shem's mug.

"Here, Father!" she said, holding it out to him.

"My thanks, Daughter," Shem took the mug from her. "But what of my guest?"

"Sorry." She picked up the other cup and handed it to the Ugric.

"Many thanks." He took a drink and exhaled cheerfully. "That is very good drink!"

"This was freshly crushed," said Cala. "See!" She said, proudly showing the bottom of her blue feet.

"I see," said the man.

"Go now, Cala. We have some things to discuss," said Shem.

"Yes, Father." She bowed and shut the door as she left.

Shem and the man sat down on the sheepskins near the low table and finished their drinks.

"So what is it you wish to tell me?" asked Shem.

"I heard many stories of you from my mother."

"Oh? And who is your mother?"

"Her name was Mansi, wife to Ilkin."

Shem pondered the name a moment. "Ilkin, Ilkin." *He was the betrayer who led the Ugric to war against the Bundled Tribes.* Shem abruptly rose to his feet, his face stoic. "What do you want?"

"You see, I am half Ugric. My mother told me how you had poisoned my grandfather and robbed my father of his rule…to be burned like a thief!"

"That was a lie!" Shem reached to his side and rested his hand where his knife was kept. "I asked you what you wanted."

"As a tribute to you, I poisoned the juice outside. You and I will die before the night is out."

Shem peered down into his empty cup. "You are so angry you would poison the both of us?"

"I am not angry. I want what is fair. My life means nothing to me."

"But why now?"

"Why not now? I waited for the gods to raise Mother back to fine standing. But when that did not happen, and she died with nothing…" He paused to spit. "…It was my turn to right the wrongs for her. Now your woman will know what kind of pain my mother went through when Father Ilkin burned."

Shem felt his stomach. "I feel no pain."

The Ugric winced. "You will feel its effect soon—uggh!" The man gripped his belly.

Cala opened the door and peeked in. "Father, my tummy hurts."

Shem kept his focus on the man. "Not now, Cala."

She wrinkled her nose. "I will go to Mother."

"Wait!" Cala's words hit Shem's mind, but he didn't want to believe them. "Did you eat some sour berries, Cala?"

"No. I have not had food yet."

Shem looked down at his cup and then over at his daughter. "Did you drink from my cup?"

"No, Father. I poured the juice for the man and knocked your cup over. I went to get more for you from Nana."

Shem knew the man had drunk the poison. But why her? "So you did not drink the juice?"

"No. I sipped up what I had spilled on the table, Father."

Shem's heart skipped. He had seen firsthand how the Ugric High leader had died miserably and didn't want the same to happen to his precious child.

The man chuckled. "It seems that your pain will be to watch *her* die."

The old man fell to the floor and writhed in agony.

"Seda!" Shem shouted. "Come quick!"

Seda soon appeared. "What is it, Husband?"

"Cala has drunk a poison. You must heal her.

"What do you mean?"

"The man poisoned the juice for me to drink, but Cala drank from it." Seda started to weep. Shem grasped her shoulders. "We have no time to wail. Think clearly and heal our daughter."

Seda nodded and wiped back a tear. She looked down at the shriveling man. "What of him?"

"Leave him. This is all his doing. He will not last long."

"What kind of poison was it?"

Shem glared down at the man. "What was it? Tell me!"

The man, curled up into a ball and cackled out a painful laugh.

"Tell me, I say!" Shem bent down and shook the man like he was a rag doll, but he drifted off into delirium.

"Will I die, Father?" Cala asked, holding her stomach.

Shem gave a fearful glance at Seda, then tried to compose himself. "You had a little. You may just get sick. Come, rest here." He kicked the man out of the way, then lifted and carried Cala over to a bed of soft padded fleece.

Seda left and came back with some healing herbs and water. "Here drink this."

Cala drank, but as time went on her stomach ached even more, and soon she become dizzy.

"Can you use your gift from God to heal her?" Shem whispered.

"Only if He wills it." Seda put one hand on Cala's belly and the other on her feverish head. She closed her eyes and prayed to God as she had never done before. But Seda gave a desperate glance that indicated she sensed no healing.

"Father, please tell me a story." said Cala weakly, her eyelids heavy.

Shem doused a rag into a bucket of water and placed it on her forehead. "A story…about a young girl?" he asked. Cala nodded slowly, her body losing energy. "Many seasons ago there was a beautiful child of God."

"Like me?" she whispered.

Shem's eyes welled up. "Yes, just like you. And she was good and kind and loved others, and everyone loved her." Cala fell unconscious before he could continue.

Seda put her ear to Cala's mouth. "She still breathes—but not well."

It was a restless night, trying to pour healing drink down her and cool her head. As the sun started to rise, Cala spoke quietly. "I see the angels," she whispered, then closed her eyes.

Shem raised his head from being buried in his arms. "Is she better?"

Seda tried to listen for a breath. She shook her head, with silent tears. Cala spirit had passed on. Shem opened her eyes with his thumbs, but she didn't respond. He fell on her body and sobbed. In his sadness, he bolted up from her and looked down at the man on the floor—clearly dead. Shem dragged the man a couple steps from his home and dropped him hard. He then strode over to the woodpile where an axe was wedged in.

Shem unbound the axe from the wood and flung it over his shoulder. "They are evil and will die!"

Seda ran after him. "Who will die?"

"All of them!" he said striding toward the foreigners' camp.

"No, Husband!" She took hold of his arm, but he shook her off. She ran in front of him and pushed on him. "Please! This is not right!"

Shem ignored her. She reached up to his beard and pulled his face down to look at her. "Do not do this!" Her lips trembled. Tears streamed down her cheeks.

Shem mouth pinched tight and a lone tear dropped from his eye. He dropped his head, then took up the axe and threw it in a level trajectory across the way, where it stuck squarely in the door of a hut. He looked skyward with raised fists. "Why!" he shouted. "Why her? You should have taken me!"

Shem fell to his knees, covered his eyes, and heaved a sobbing cry. Seda wrapped her arms around him. They held one another tightly, their hearts torn.

Chapter 31
Ararat Gives a Warning
Three weeks before the end

Seda built up a sweat from hauling another basket of manure and mulch to the top of the ark. Noah had told her he wanted to ensure there was a supply of fresh vegetables for the future, and suggested she have a garden in the upper deck below the sky hatches. A raised garden was his way of distracting her from painful thoughts of Cala. Since the burial, a cycle of the moon had run its course, and yet a day had not gone by when Seda did not look around to call for her daughter.

She packed dirt around some seeds, then paused to look through the mulch. An emptiness filled her heart. Light from the opened sky hatches streamed down upon a few seedlings that had poked through the topsoil. It was as if God was telling her that Cala was safe with Him. She bent down to pick out some weeds, when it occurred to her that the morning was very quiet—no insects buzzing, no birds chirping, just the stirring of humans pursuing their work day.

Seda brushed off her hands, climbed the ladder to the roof, and stepped out to the upper deck and over to the low ship rail. She gazed around at the broad panoramic view of the green valley enclosed by blue white-tipped mountains. Shem was working below, not far from the ship, tying up a stalk of wheat. Shem looked up and his eyes met hers. In that moment, something about Cala was exchanged between them, and somehow their grief vanished. No words were spoken, and yet it was completely understood. At that moment, a peace filled her heart. They smiled to one another, then turned back to their chores.

As Seda took a step down the ladder, she felt a low rumble beneath her. She walked back to the ship rail and called down. "Shem, did you feel that?"

He tied a knot. "Feel what?"

Seda listened intently for a moment; and when nothing happened, she started back to her work. Before she could step down the ladder again, another more intense rumble passed through. Buckets of water splashed out and tipped over. She dropped to the deck as the vessel gently rocked to and fro. The support beams groaned under the weight of the vessel, and after a long tense moment the rocking and creaking ended.

Shem called up. "I felt that, woman! Hurry out to me!"

Seda didn't wait to be told twice. She flew down the steps.

Japheth had been blocking the remaining slivers of light that filtered through the walls with pitch, when the rumbling occurred. But he held a beam to keep the bucket from falling out of his hands. Naamah and Adataneses had pushed some dried vegetables into a large cabinet on the second level of the ark, slammed the cabinet shut, and leaned against it to keep food from falling out. Noah and Ham, who had been pouring seed into bins on the first level, dropped the bags to steady their oil lamps. The woodsmen, who were finishing up a gate assembly for the stalls, abandoned their tools and ran outside.

Seda didn't stop until she was in the arms of Shem. The silence lasted a few minutes before the mountain released a booming blast followed by a series of loud screeching hisses. Those remaining in the vessel spontaneously came to life. They all raced from the ship, down the ramp, and out to open ground to observe the spectacle.

The top of Mt. Ararat shot up a grey column of steam and ash. Sethite and Cainite alike covered their ears with their hands and helplessly gaped awestruck at the event. The steam blast burst forth. The screeching hisses abruptly ended, but an immense billowing cloud of ash pushed through the steam and ascended westward. They cautiously removed their hands from their ears. Other than the ringing in their heads, all earth's creatures were silent…the silence was deafening.

* * *

In total quiet, the cloud billowed up in a dark, foreboding slow motion, then moved westward. The cloud displayed a twisted beauty of dark cumulus shadows contrasted by a dazzling brilliance of sunlight. Noah, his sons, and the laborers were speechless, as they watched in helpless wonder.

Shem was the first to speak up. "This a sign."

The elder woodsman removed his hands from his face. He breathed a heavy sigh, but his eyes were wide with fear. "It is the anger of the mountain," said the woodsman, son of Domo.

"It is more than that," Shem rebuked. "You never believe my father's words! *Your* god is woodwork and idols!"

Noah stepped in front of Shem. "Calm yourself, Son."

Shem stared at Noah. "You know it is true, Father."

Noah looked to the mountain where a flickering flash lit up at the peak. After a few seconds, a crack of thunder broke the silence. He pointed at the mountain and spoke with credible intensity to the woodsman. "Do you still not believe in the one true God? Look at His fury. For if you do not now, you soon will."

The woodsman stared at the cloud formation, but did not answer. He tipped his head in to the north. "Come, we must go back to our village, to our women. Our work here is done."

Shem shook his head in disgust and crossed his arms.

Noah ended further discussion and reached out his hand. "Do not leave without our many thanks, my friend. You do not know how much we are in your debt."

The woodworker glanced over to the coin box at the ark's entrance. "Just pay us what we agreed to, Noah, and we will be on our way."

Noah dropped his hand, then stepped inside the ark. He removed a large pouch from the box and ambled up to where the men anxiously eyed the mountain. Noah started to remove several coins from the pouch then dropped them back inside. He cinched up the whole bag and tossed it to the woodsman.

The woodsman felt the weight of the bag. "That is too much, Noah!"

"It is worthless to me, now." Noah pointed north. "Go home. We will not see you again. Head my warnings, friend."

The woodsman took the coins without saying a word. He glanced up at the ash cloud, back to his kinsmen, then signaled them to leave. Ne'uk had just finished cleaning up the pottery used for the morning meal. She was halfway between her clan and the Sethites. She looked over at Ham and then to her father.

Ne'uk didn't move. "Are we to leave now, Father? She asked, resting a ceramic jug on her hip.

"Come, Daughter!" said her father a few paces behind his men. "There is nothing left for us here."

Ne'uk looked back at Ham once more. She set down the jug and packed up a few belongings, then followed behind her father.

"I thought you wanted her," Shem whispered to Ham.

"Father would not allow it." Ham whispered back.

Noah called out to the men and waved goodbye. The woodsman gave one more look back to catch Noah's piercing, exhorting eyes, saying everything without a word. He reopened the pouch and stared at the many gold coins for a moment. He cinched it up, tied it to his waist cord, then pursued his trek across the valley toward Lake Sevan.

In the shelter of the ark's opening, Noah and Shem stood concentrating on the men as they walked across the bridge over the river.

Japheth sniffed sulfur in the air. "It smells like death. I hope they take your words to heart, Father."

Noah put his hand on Japheth's shoulders and watched as the men faded into the horizon. "That is my hope too."

"They will not and cannot," said Shem. "They are stuck in their old ways."

"Come, we need to finish moving in the seed. It will not be long now," said Noah.

Ham stared after the woodsmen and Ne'uk. "Father, do you think I should see if the quaking of the earth did any harm to the land?"

Noah hadn't considered the idea. "Why do you ask?"

"I wish to kill some more game and hoped they were not scared away."

Noah looked annoyed. "We have a season's worth of cured meat. I am not worried." Ham said nothing, but stood pretending to examine the sharpness of his spear. Noah peered over his nose at Ham. "If you think we should have more, then so be it. But return within the third night, for all will change from now on."

Ham picked up his spear. "As you wish, Father." He went inside to retrieve his traveling pouch, then headed off in the direction of the woodsman's party.

In the evening, the family sat around the fire to watch the stars in the heavens. The cloud of ash was long gone and the mountain was quiet. Shem stared up at the one bright light in the heavens that they had been watching for a week. It had grown in size, carrying its feather-like tail with it.

Shem turned to Noah. "Is death coming soon, Father?"

Noah looked down at the fire. "I am glad Father and Mother moved on to the heavens after the last growing season. What we have ahead of us will be a heavy burden." Noah stood up, poked at the fire with his walking stick. "It will not be long now. Get some sleep, people. For we will not rest from this day forth."

No one questioned Noah. His predictive words were as good as gold. The family sang a soft traditional song and called it an evening. They put out the fire and headed back to their homes. As much as Shem wished he knew what the future held for them, he was thankful knowledge of destruction was hidden from him.

* * *

It was a peaceful warm evening, good for sleeping, but not for dreaming. Noah felt himself moving above the earth like a bird watching over the land. A low voice entered his mind. "*Noah…*" Noah looked around while in the air of his dream. He flew over flora and fauna until he landed on a precipice. In front of him were all the animals of the earth. "*Noah…*" came the voice again. It was a grand, deep voice that penetrated his will.

Noah opened his eyes, sat up, and looked around. Naamah slept soundly. He wrapped a fleece around himself and walked out into the cool evening air. He inspected the area for someone, anyone, but no one else was awake. Noah pulled his fleece closer and stepped out into a full breeze. The wind moved around the rocks and trees with a beckoning moan. Noah was drawn up to the ark at the base of the mountain, which stood as a silhouette against the moonlit sky. When he came close, he could see the loading door and the sky hatches blown wide open. Gusts of wind blew through the ark, forcing the sound of a low voice whispering to him.

"*Nooooaaaah…*" Noah stepped closer to confirm what he had heard.

"Is, is that the wind?" Noah stammered. "Or…."

"*Nooooaaaah…I…Am,*" came a deep breath-whisper from the air.

Noah dropped to his knees. "Almighty One? What do you require of me?"

The wind blew in heavy gusts down from vents in the sky hatches, down through the stalls, out through the loading gate, and into the core of the patriarch's body. "*Nooooaaaah…it is time.*"

He raised his hand up to the void. "Time for what, Master?"

"*Maaaake ready…*" The wind whistled low out of the ark. "*…the beasts of the earth.*"

Noah peered into the ark, squinting for a view of the Creator. "I have but goats and sheep, my God."

"*Maaaake haste...the end is come*," said the wind of the night.

"How much time do we have, my God?" There was no reply. The wind had subsided. "Almighty One?" Still there was no answer. The wind had ended, leaving behind the buzzing of insects. Noah slowly stood up, stared at the ark for a moment, then turned and went back to his bed where Naamah rested soundly. Noah pulled his covers to his chin and gazed up at the ceiling.

The next morning, Noah told Shem and Japheth to gather all their belongings and transfer them into the ark. Moving their wares and clothing were the last of the move. Tons of hay from the recent harvest had previously been loaded into the upper level of the ship. Additionally, grain, fruit, and nuts now filled tall bins in the back of the ship.

As the family began their work, Noah looked on to the remaining Cainites encamped by the river. Many went about their business as if nothing had happened. Many more had left in fear of a reprisal from the god of the mountain.

The transfer of goods continued for two days, and Noah began to wonder about Ham. Extra food in a time like this was unnecessary.

At the end of the third day, Naamah scanned the landscape thoroughly. "Where is my son, Husband? He should be here by now."

"He will be here soon," Noah said, patting her arm. "It will be soon." He could convince her on this day, but in another day, he would have to convince himself.

On the fourth day, Noah woke up and was just about to send Shem out to look for Ham when the short, sturdy Sethite strode up to Noah's house, spear in hand and a deer across his shoulders.

"Father! Father!" Ham shouted, fully exhausted.

Shem and Japheth dashed outside from their homes when they heard their brother's voice.

Noah raised his hands in agitated concern. "Where have you been, Son?"

Ham dropped the carcass to the ground and pointed east. "Father, the river is blocked!" He gulped in breaths of air and leaned against the house.

Noah frowned. "What?"

"At the south canyon. I saw it with my own eyes. There must have been a great thunder in the ground, like the one we had the other day, for the hills on each side of the river have fallen in. A mountain of rock and soil has filled the canyon's river. The Aras now has nowhere to go. At the far end it is becoming a lake."

Noah stroked his beard in thought. "If it does not flow, then the water will back up."

"Could it reach our homes?" asked Ham.

"It does not matter now," said Japheth. "We have been moving our belongings into the ark. We can live safely up there."

Adataneses and Naamah heard the commotion and came out to investigate. "What is wrong, Husband?" asked Naamah. When she saw Ham, she ran and embraced him. "Where have you been? We feared for you."

Ham sighed. "Why do you worry, Mother? I am not a child."

"No, you are not. But you will always be my son."

"Well worry no longer. I am here."

"Let us not be idle," said Noah. "This mountain slide Ham speaks of is another sign for us to hurry." Noah looked across the river and into the hills. *But where are these beasts, Master? I cannot fulfill my duty if there are no animals. Do you want me to search the whole earth for them?*

Chapter 32
City Life Carries On
Six months before the end

In the renowned city of Tuball, the old truthsayer spied deeply into the tube with polished magnifying agates. He hummed to himself while he examined the newest star in the sky. Tural was known as the greatest of the magi alive. He had a long silver beard that touched his knees and a black wool cap on his bald head. The magus mumbled a bit then walked over to the celestial charts on the table.

His thin, eager apprentice had waited his turn to look into the spyglass then quickly planted an eye at the viewing port. "This one has a long tail," said the young man, trying to adjust the side knobs for a clearer picture. "What are the gods doing with it?"

"It is a bad omen!" shouted the magus.

The apprentice looked back with exasperation. "I can hear you, Master Tural!" he yelled back. "Talk softer, Master! The young man went over to see what the old magus had found in the charts. "You said the last star with a tail was a bad omen, and *it* never came."

"What?"

The apprentice reached over to the table and picked up the hearing cone. He handed it to the magus then asked his master again. "The last one with a tail did not hurt us. Why this one?"

The wise magus listened with the cone in his ear. "The ways of the heavens are constant. We depend on the stars to guide us on the earth. The first one is always a warning; the second one disturbs the harmony of the heavens and earth. This one is wild."

"What of all the falling stars? Why are they not bad omens?"

"Because their life is short and is apart from the order of things. They may be tears from the god El, or a sign that we are not obedient, or it may be…. This one will be with us for many days, and it will gain in size and strength." He pointed to the evening-sky and his voice grew in volume. "It could mean the end of us all!"

"I hear you!" the apprentice shouted back.

The old man shook his head. "I do not like it. The longer it stays in the sky, the longer it disturbs heaven's harmony. I must see the scrolls in the sanctuary."

"May I follow you, Master?"

He put the cone back to his ear. "What?"

"May I follow you?" the apprentice emphasized with his lips.

Tural shrugged with indifference. "Yes, but do not be a pest."

Four weeks before the end

As Tural had predicted, the comet had returned. He speculated that it rounded the sun's boundaries, flung around like a toy on an unseen string. He stepped away from the window, his thoughts drifted back to the early days of his youth when he met Shem on the steps of the ziggurat. Believing in the Sethite religion used to be a thing of fashion early into the quiet peaceful years of the unification between world tribes. Then time marched forward and restlessness set in. The Tuballites eventually became weary of the strict morality of the Sethite faith. Once Bulla's death permitted his grandson to be pronounced as grand elder, everything changed. The grandson reacquainted himself with the ancient gods. They provided the self indulgence he had been deprived of. As the grand elder behaved, so did his subjects. Longstanding pent up moral strictness was immediately replaced with carefree hedonism. And with pleasure as the new morality, so began the decline of a righteous people.

Tural's high position was nothing to him. He simply felt old and tired. At the sound of a commotion outside, he stuck a hearing cone to his ear and leaned out the window. The owner of the meat shop was beating a slave in the market with a stick.

"You will be put to death!" the owner yelled and continued to strike at the skinny man. It was evident that the slave had broken his chains and was trying to escape when the owner caught him.

The crowd chanted. "To the axe! To the axe!"

Hard work was seen as uncivilized, but still necessary to keep the wheel of prosperity rolling. The Sethites quickly became the easy target. Not wishing for the pious Sethites to judge them, the Tuballites convinced the grand elder to declare a law stating that the Sethites must accept their deities. Some of the Sethites agreed and, with open arms, were welcomed as comrades. Those not wishing to accept the city's gods were cast out of the city or allowed to stay—as servants. As the years progressed, the grand celebrations and declining revenues forced the grand elder introduce a new law that would bolster the monetary system. All Sethites and any dissenters of other tribes were forced into slavery.

Dulled to moral integrity, the crowds saw this punishment of a runaway slave as sport. In desperation, the skinny man suddenly made a dash toward away from his beater. An unexpected spear flew and pierced the man's chest squarely, stopping him dead in his steps. He fell limply to the stony street. A soldier at the gate grinned at the hit, raised his fist victoriously. All the people cheered…but one.

"You owe me!" The owner shouted at the soldier. "He was mine to deal with, not yours."

The soldiers scowled. "If you need to be paid, you can use my woman for payment. She is good that way."

"I do not need your woman. I have two of my own."

"Then you will not be needing payment." The owner of the slave cursed the soldier, and soon an argument ensued between them.

Steps away, male prostitutes were performing sex acts openly and unabashedly. Across the market place the yelping cry of a dog drew Tural's attention. It was running around in circles, its tail ablaze. Children with jugs of oil and fire-sticks were laughing at the torture they had inflicted upon the animal. The old magus looked to the sun and felt its blazing heat. It had been just two moons since Shem had come to the city and warned the people, but what good did it do?

The white-bearded magus observed the events until he had enough. He shook his head, went inside. "These people have become animals." He coughed a few times. "Why did I have to live so long as to see us fall into this filth?" He fanned out some charts on the table and took measurements with a thin rod. Tural made ticking sounds through the few teeth he had left.

The comet had arrived but was small through his looking tube. Tural knew it would grow in size. He went back to the window and looked down to the street where women of the night were roaming during the day as well. "You will see!" he shouted down to the women. "You will see and be afraid!"

The people in the market place looked up and laughed. "Go back to your scrolls you crazy old man!"

This was just another prediction of many they had heard of in the last few years. In their eyes, the soothsayer's wisdom had dwindled to foolishness. Insincere laughter filled their empty lives. Vacant goals directed their chaotic egos. Deaf minds ruled the day.

Three weeks before the end

Visible to the naked eye by day, at night the tailed star grew bright…brighter than all others, dragging its gaseous dust tail behind. Laced with rays and streamers caused by solar wind, those on the ground marveled at the spectacle as a gift from the gods. Tural knew otherwise.

However, on the other side of the earth, there was an event that wasn't predicted or known by Tural. It was the eruption of a volcano that would later be known as Mt. Mazama. It held a reservoir of hot magma that had waited a millennium to be spewed out. Rumbling and thundering earthquakes preceded the eruption around the region. The breaking of its top was cataclysmic. A huge volume of magma, gas, and smoke flew out of the mountain like an upward moving waterfall. The cloud of ash and smoke was ejected up into the troposphere for over six hours. The prevailing winds then carried the ash and smoke across the continent, over an ocean, and across another continent, until it passed over the city of Tuball.

On that day, the sun grew blood-red over the city. Bits of ash filtered down the face of the land. "How was this a gift?" grumbled the citizens of Tuball. Murmurs of discontent spread.

Tural stood atop of the city wall's viewing terrace with the spirit master. They debated the effects of the dark cloud.

Tural paced. "There is danger coming, my friend."

The spirit master gave a pitiful smirk. He had grown fat from an easy life. "There may be no danger. It could be another conflict between the gods." The spirit master raised his voice enough for Tural to hear. "We have seen storms and other oddities before, when there is a battle in the heavens. This could be a good or bad omen. We just do not know."

Tural shook his head despondently. "The ancient writings do not lie. This is trouble."

"Would you like to be the one to tell the people? That they should leave and stop their trade?"

The weather conditions had worsened through the decades. The region became hot and dry and many rivers poured more into the twin seas to raise the water level. The land bridge and its great road between the east and west had disappeared. Commerce to the east now relied on merchant ships to bring goods to the city.

Tural weighed out whether to alarm the public and cause a panic, or say nothing and accept a most certain death. In the end, because he had no solid proof, he submitted to the spirit master's assessment. "No. I cannot prove the city is in peril."

The spirit master squeezed his old friend's arms. "Then wait until we know more."

Unfortunately, rumors had run their course around the city and the citizens were certain a bad omen was upon them. The spiritual leader arranged a meeting with the masters to discuss the matter and quell their fears. With their allegiance, the city masters would be vital in stemming an uprising. The masters also had reservations about the stars and welcomed the meeting.

The spirit master greeted the others. "Many thanks for your presence, my friends. It always is encouraging to see—"

"Stop with your formalities," the stone master interrupted." We want to know what it means, this light in the heavens and this cloud of ash? Are the gods angry with us? Is this the warning that Shem spoke of?"

The shaman held up his hand. "Tural and I have decided that this is a good omen. We are not here to judge whether the Sethites' God is the reason for this or not. We are here to inform you that you can continue to make plans for the Harvest Festival." Tural sat with his hearing cone at his ear, his lips tight.

The metal master rose to speak. "If this is the same light in the sky that we saw in the cold season, we know that it did us no harm. But this cloud of death is another matter. The grey flakes cover everything."

The rotund master healer shook his head "Cloud of death?" he said with a scowl. "How could the gods not approve of us? We are thriving. The city is large and our enemies are few. The harvest has been good, and mothers are nursing more children than ever before."

"So we do nothing?" asked the water master. "You do not have to clean the fountains. Water from the mountains has been scarce. And we cannot drink the sea water, plenty as it may be. This ash will only further make the sweet water undrinkable."

The spirit master smirked at them. "It is up to you, good men. If you wish to alarm the people, so be it. I had hoped we would be as one and calm the fears of the people."

The water master stood up. "Where is the grand elder? Should he not be here?"

The spirit master sighed. "He is busy. We will inform him of the issue soon. It is up to us to make a decision."

The water master became flustered. "How do we know of the heavenly concerns? You and Tural are the all-knowing ones. It should be you that advise us."

Tural flushed slightly, wishing he could speak his own mind, but instead followed the spirit master's lead. He finally stood to calm them. "We know many things...not everything. Do not hold us to such a high standard. If you wish to leave the city and hide in a cave, so be it."

The trade master stood up and faced the other masters. "If we did that, it would disrupt trade in the city. And could we be certain the fields would be safe? If we tell the people there will not be a harvest festival, we may have an angry mob to confront."

A murmur of discussion erupted between the masters and continued for several minutes of organized chaos. Tural didn't hear most of the words spoken, and didn't care. He knew that the masters would follow the spirit master's views.

Eventually, the spirit master raised his hands to quiet them down. "You have spoken truly. Trade has slowed and you have lost profits and there are many angry citizens. Let me assure you the ash will stop and soon you will regain your profits and make ready for the festival. We do not want to panic the people, but neither do we want to anger the gods. We must believe they have given us their blessings. If I am wrong and it does not stop in three sunrises, we will talk again."

The men nodded and gave a muttering approval. They adjourned the meeting with the spirit master consoling a few dissenters on the way out. After the others filed out of the room, Tural sat quietly to ponder, then followed the spirit master out to the step pyramid.

A worried and disorderly crowd had collected in the public courtyard. Comments about the dreaded ash preceded by the burning star already had turned into threats against the hierarchy of the city.

The spirit master raised his hands to quiet the rabble. "Consider the star with the tail as a blessing from El! It is his affection on you! He is sending his glory over the earth by turning himself into a passing star! The ashes you see are sacred, and must cover and purify the land! Prepare yourselves, for El may visit you!"

The mob's anxiety was soon subdued with the shaman's reasoning. The people of the city listened intently to the spirit master's views and their fear changed to eagerness at the mention of a visit from the great god El.

But Tural knew that the spirit master wasn't letting them off so easily. There is always a price to pay for the visit of a god. While the spirit master placated the masses, Tural secretly hobbled up to the grand elder's chambers and requested his presence. The guards let him into the foyer, while a servant went to inform the leader. The servant led the Tural into the bed quarters where the grand elder was sprawled across his wide bed, two of his newest wives and a concubine next to him.

The grand elder sat up with a frown, then combed back his hair with his fingers. "What is it, Tural? Do you have some wisdom to sprinkle upon us?"

The women giggled.

Tural bowed. "It is the heavens, Grand Elder. They speak to us."

"I know of the new star. It will display itself and leave again, just as it has done in the past."

"It is more than that. The sun has turned red and ash is falling upon the city."

The grand elder huffed and slid off his bed. He wrapped an undergarment around himself and strode to the window. He put his hand out and felt the ash in his palm. "Will it pass?"

Tural leaned forward to hear better.

The grand elder shouted, "Will it pass?"

Tural glanced out at the falling ash. "Yes, Master."

The grand elder kept his voice raised. "Why bother me when I am being satisfied by my women?"

"I fear there may be other dangers resulting from the passing star. We may be punished for our misdeeds, and that heaven's wrath is upon us."

He scowled. "You sound like a worshiper of the '*one true god.*' Punished? For what? We are the greatest people on the earth. We have conquered the people of the north, south, east, and west. Even the common people have slaves now. Food has been plentiful." The grand elder crossed his arms. "But I sense there is more, Magi...yes?"

"Yes, Master. Shem and his father Noah, foretold of our doom because of our evil ways and belief in other gods. You must have heard Shem's warning when he was in the city last season. I am told his word is always true."

The grand elder laughed. "Noah? Ha! I am sick of the rumors about him. Even my grandfather, Bulla, believed in him. Noah is weak in the head. That old Sethite has spent many years building a boat…*in the mountains*. It is nonsense. You must calm the people, Tural. We do not need panic in the city. Fear will not do. I have made great plans for the Harvest Festival. Now go tell them what you told me—that it will pass."

"The spirit master is doing that as we speak."

"So be it. If *he* has no concerns, why should I? Now speak no more of this."

Tural bowed. "As you wish, Master." He exited the grand elder's chambers and walked to the top step. He gazed out at the umber colored horizon. The beauty of the once great city had turned ugly. *A dirty sunset for a dirty people.*

As morning broke in Tural's workroom, he went to his window. A thick layer of soot covered the city, but the air was clear. As the spirit master had predicted, the ash and dust had disappeared, and the air was dry and crisp. The star was even larger now, visible even with the sun nearby. Citizens could hardly tend to their work with the anticipation that the god El was to make an appearance on Earth. But not Tural. He poured over his charts and thought back to the warnings of Shem and Noah. The uneasy feeling in his stomach worsened.

Chapter 33
The Animals
Two weeks before the end

Shem climbed the top of the ship where Seda was sweeping off the last of the ash from the upper deck. It was their first morning to wake up on the ark. The mist covering the valley began to dissipate and light streamed into the clerestory slots above where Noah and Naamah slept on the upper level.

Shem put his arm around Seda. "I wonder what God has planned for us."

As the mist cleared, Seda pointed out into the distance. "Does that answer your question?"

Shem raced down the ladder, passed by Noah and went to the opening of the large door. "Everyone! Come and see!"

Shem heard Noah shuffle though straw on the wooden floor, then peek outside. "What is it, Son?"

Shem pointed east. "Look."

The waters of the river had widened and were now at the doorstep of their abandoned homes. Along the water's edge, hundreds of animal species were milling about and drinking. Roe deer, badgers, rabbits, wild cats—big and small, bears, various horse breeds, and more, filled the valley. It was a strange sight to take in.

Noah walked out next to Shem. "Thanks to you, my God! I see the beasts you promised."

"The water grows wide," said Shem. "If this persists, then the river will reach the ark in days."

Noah agreed. "We must finish moving our goods before it is too late."

The men were wary of the animals. Ham took it upon himself to stand watch. The others went back to loading the last of their provisions onto the ark. Their homes would have to be abandoned. Worry over the unknown future quickly began to sink in to the women and men alike.

Seda carried a basket of onions to the ark. "Look how the water covers the trunks. I will never be able to harvest the rest."

Shem smiled. "Woman, your two hands for planting are better than a hundred of mine. With your skill to nurture fruit, grain, and roots, we will never go hungry."

She brushed him aside. "There is never enough."

Shem laughed. "Wait!" He stopped her, held her shoulders, and looked into her eyes. "Many, many thanks for your hard work, my lovely one. Between the dried and fresh food, you could feed an army. It is enough." Her eyes dropped in humility, but he peeked under to see them. "We can only do so much and then it is up to the Almighty." He kissed her tenderly on the lips.

"I have to stay busy."

"You must not replace work for Cala. Please keep some room for me."

Seda patted his bearded face. "I will. And I will try to steady myself too. But that does not mean you can be lazy, Husband. Now get to work." She glared with jest and yanked on his beard. She turned and walked away with lighter steps.

Shem watched her with admiration, then trotted down to the homes where some small animals were poking around. He picked up the last wooden chest on his shoulder, and walked easily through meandering deer and lynx without even a concern.

He called up to Ham. "Why do you stand there like a warrior? There is nothing to defend us from. The animals have no interest in us. And soon we will be safe in the boat."

Ham spoke loud enough so all could hear. "The water gets closer. If it moves the boat, how do we know it will not fall apart? I think we should favor moving up the mountain. The water will never reach the high caves."

Shem said nothing, but secretly wondered the same thing. It had taken decades to finish the ark and it was doubtful to most that it would even float. Nevertheless, the family continued supplying the ship until the sun disappeared.

* * *

The following day, Shem was wakened from a peaceful sleep by his father's snoring. He stretched out some kinks from his back and climbed down the steps of the ark. When he reached the open door, Ham was already outside. Shem was stunned by the size of the river. In one day, it was wider by a hundred feet. By his calculations, the homes in the valley would look like islands by tomorrow. In two more days, the water would be at the boat.

Ham called up to his father. "There are more animals!"

Japheth walked out from inside the ark and stood next to Ham. Indeed there were more varieties of animals, and some that they had never seen. Elephants, rhinoceroses, mountain lions, as well as exotic birds; all lived peacefully among one another without incident. The strange had gotten stranger.

"Will we be safe here?" Japheth asked.

"We should not be fearful of the deer, but I do not trust the mountain lion," said Shem.

Ham used his spear as a pointer. "This is why I was worried. The water pushes more of the animals to us."

"We have the big boat to protect ourselves if they decide to attack," suggested Japheth.

"Or we could kill any that try to attack," replied Ham.

Shem pointed to the elephant. "That one is like the behemoth. You think we can kill that?"

"Yes! If we plan correctly," stated Ham indignantly. "He would make for many good meals."

"We won't be killing any animals," Noah declared.

Ham gave a pleading scowl up to his father. "Not even for food?"

"Not these animals," said Noah, calmly. "They all will be going inside the boat."

"What?" The three brothers spoke simultaneously.

Noah shrugged. "God wants it that way. Let us prepare." He turned and walked away without another word.

The sons glanced at one another with worried expressions.

"Father's mind is going," said Ham.

"But not my ears," said Noah, from around the corner.

Shem was annoyed at Ham. "Has Father been wrong before?"

Ham said nothing.

"Then let us get back to work. We must finish gathering our goods from our homes before the water takes them."

As they were speaking, one of the leaders of the Cainite camp approached them from behind.

"Greetings to you, men."

Japheth turned and took a step forward. "Greetings," he said, without offering his hand.

The man used his spear as a walking stick. He stepped closer. "I see you are moving your goods from your homes."

"Yes."

"I wish to talk with you about our families."

"What about them?" asked Japheth, suspiciously.

"As you can see, the river water will be at the steps of our home if it keeps growing."

Ham stepped forward. "You should have known better than to build your houses so close to the river."

"Let him speak," said Shem.

"You Sethites have more than plenty of room in this boat for a village of people. I am sure you can spare rooms for fifty of us."

Japheth's jaw tensed up. "You and yours have lived at the Aras for years taunting us. Now that the river rises, you want our help?"

The man raised his hand in peace to quiet Japheth. "Forget the past. Think of our families."

Noah stepped out from the shadows of the ark. "Why did you not go with the others of your kind, when the mountain sounded?"

The man bowed. "Master Noah, we were foolish not to leave, but the river is too wide for us to pass through now. We merely ask for a dry place to lay our heads. Surely you can provide room for us?"

"Surely I cannot. You will infect us with your small gods and foreign traditions. And, even more, my God has said no to others outside my own family."

The man boiled with anger. "You cannot do this to us!" he shouted, walking toward Noah with his spear.

Before the man could do any harm, Shem surged forward and kicked out the legs from under the man and sent him prostrate on the ground. Shem plucked the spear up before it fell and flipped it around. He stepped on the man's back with his sandal and jabbed the spear tip onto the man's neck.

"I believe it is time you left our company," said Shem, between gritted teeth. He stepped back.

The man got up with the help of his sons, then brushed the dirt off himself. "I will be back," he said, wagging his finger. His sons said nothing.

Once they were back to the river's edge, Noah lowered his head. "I wish I could take them. But the Almighty has not allowed it."

Ham became agitated. "He will return with the others. We must kill them before they kill us!"

Noah scowled at Ham. "What is this about killing? First the animals, now the Cainites. We will do nothing of the kind."

Ham thumped his spear to the ground. "Did you not hear his threats, Father? He would have killed you if Shem was not here."

Noah was calm. "I heard the man. But it is not our way. Now get back to your tasks."

As the brothers headed back to the houses, Ham spoke in confidence. "We must hit them before they hit us."

"Let it go, Ham," said Japheth.

Ham looked at Shem for support. "What do you say? Are we women?"

"I say, obey your father."

Ham cursed under his breath and lowered his voice. "I will not kill them. But Father did not say that I should not listen in on them." He left Japheth and Shem, then snuck down to the Cainite village.

Japheth turned to Shem. "Why is he so angry?"

"He thrusts his fury around, because he has lost his woman," suggested Shem.

"Ne'uk?" asked Japheth.

"Yes. You have Adataneses, I have Seda, and he has no one."

By evening the family had finally accomplished the transfer of goods. Exhausted from their chores, they rested in front of the ark. They tended a large fire, partially for cooking, but primarily for protection. Hundreds of animal eyes reflected the light of the flames like red fireflies. The Sethites were wary that at any moment an animal may decide to lunge at them. The family huddled together around the fire and sang songs to bring cheer.

Ham couldn't keep silent any longer. "Earlier, I listened in on the Cainites." The family turned to Noah for a response, but he hadn't one. "They plan to attack us before the second sunrise." Everyone kept silent. "Did you not hear me?"

Noah looked up from the fire. "Many thanks for your words, Son."

Ham pushed further. "What do you wish to do, Father?"

"Keep to our tasks at hand." Ham was ready to explode, when Noah stood and gave him a deadly stare. "Not another word on this."

Ham lowered his eyes, sat down. He kicked at a log.

Noah addressed the group. "We must be strong and fear nothing for the Lord our God is with us. Keep that in your thoughts when you sleep."

Murmurs of agreement echoed around the campfire. One by one, the members of the family left to sleep in their beds. Ham sat with Shem. They took the evening watch and kept the fire going. They gazed up to see the wandering star and its tail holding steady as the moon moved around it. Through the night, the star slowly began to break into several smaller segments and drift apart.

Shem put his hand on Ham's shoulder. "Brother, do you miss her?"

Ham gulped and stared into the fire. "Father is a fool!" he said jumping up. Ham turned and stomped away.

* * *

Shem peered out of the ship to see the morning sun crawl up the valley. Houses poked out from the wide river like rocks in a pond. Animals humorously stuck their heads out of the abandoned doorways as if they owned the place. The most unusual aspect of the animals was how muted the creatures were. All day long they drank quietly from the river and ate the grasses from the land. The upper floors of the boat were now full of wheat and barley for feed. Holes were strategically placed so as to easily distribute the feed below. All was ready as per Noah's instructions, and yet there were no animals inside.

Shem leaned on the bulkhead of the wide entrance. "We will need a thick rope to get the big ones in."

Japheth and Ham passed by Shem and stepped down the ramp. Japheth crossed his arms, and stared at the creatures. "There are so many. It will take weeks to capture them all."

Shem pitied his father. Noah walked slowly by the many empty stalls, with his hands clasped behind his back. At one point the patriarch paused in front of pen full of straw and stared. He turned and stepped toward the entrance of the ark.

"It is time we lead them in." Noah announced. "Japheth, Shem, bring some hay, berries and nuts, then set them at the opening."

Japheth and Shem gathered the feed, berries, and nuts, then placed them at the opening as their father said. Everyone stepped back so the beasts would eat, but the animals hardly glanced their way, but kept nibbling on the local foliage. Ham shook his head.

When that failed, Noah looked over at the pen where the sheep and goats were chewing their cud. "Ham, tether a ewe and walk her by the wild animals. Then bring her into the ark."

Ham followed his father's instructions with a roll of his eyes. He picked up some thin hemp rope, tied one of the sheep to the end. He then led it past the other animals and turn back to the ark. He and the sheep were hardly noticed. After several tries with no results, he led the ewe back to the stall.

Noah leaned on his staff with a contemplative frown. "Shem, you are good with animals. See if you can catch a fawn to bring in."

Shem glanced at his brothers reticently, but obeyed. He walked toward the animals and they scattered. Shem spotted a small doe and held out a root to entice the animal. The animal darted away. And so a comedic chase was on. Shem ran after the young doe bouncing through the throngs of animals. The other animals showed only a slight irritation. As Shem slowed down, his wife Seda ran over to assist in the chase. After many minutes of tripping over themselves, Shem and Seda returned, laughing and empty handed.

"We need a big net," suggested Seda.

"We need more than that," said Ham. "Why do we need any of the animals, Father? When the water rises, they will know to run up the mountain side—like we should do."

Noah closed his eyes to think.

"Those Cainites will be back tomorrow," Ham reminded.

Noah walked back into the ark and found a quiet spot to pray.

* * *

Noah knelt down on his knees and bowed on a bale of straw. *Father, God, what should I do? I do not doubt you, for you have brought these animals here. I doubt myself, for I do not know how to lead them in. When the waters rise, we will have to shut the door, and now have only our own sheep to claim.*

There was silence. Noah prayed until evening, but his prayers were not answered. With the sun setting, he stood and climbed the steps to the upper deck and looked one last time across the valley in the twilight. The fire reflected the silhouettes of the animals as they stood quietly *outside* the ark. Noah went to bed in frustration.

By morning, water was not even a stone's throw away and the animals practically hugged the ark. The men stood at the entrance, not daring to venture outside. Noah stood with his hands on the railing for an hour, trying to think of a way to bring the animals in without hurting man or beast. In the distance, he saw a large group of men with spears and axes approaching.

Naamah came to his side. "Husband, could Ham have been right about the Cainites harming us? Their homes are under water and they have no place to go."

Noah shook his head. "It is not our way to kill like that. It does not matter now. There are too many of them."

As the foreigners neared the ark, their faces turned white. For no apparent reason, the animals had closed to form a line and surround the ark. The leader of the Cainites stopped and turned to the others in a huddle. One of the men walked out from the huddle and approached the line of animals. He took a spear and lunged toward a roe buck. The animal didn't flinch. The man backed off and walked back to the huddle. The Cainite men talked some more then walked walked sullenly up the mountain slope, dragging their spears on the ground behind them.

"Why are they leaving?" asked Naamah.

Noah watched the men closely. "It seems that the animals have protected us from the Cainites."

She wrapped her hand around his arm. "Now the animals are our friends. So how do we get them to come with us?"

Noah rubbed his eyes with his hands. "I do not know, my wife. As you see, I have failed."

Naamah reached around to hug his plump waist. "Not in my eyes. You have done your best and I love you for it."

Noah kissed then caressed her head. There was little Naamah could say to convince him he wasn't a dismal failure. He had a mission to accomplish and it wasn't looking good. Finally, he closed his eyes and breathed deeply. *It is in your hands now. I can do no more.* When he opened his eyes, a big drop of water hit his forehead. Noah wiped the water from his face. He looked heavenward and saw a small cloud hovering alone in the sky. He looked back out to the animals and saw the elephants making their way toward the ark. Noah made his way down the ladder to the lower level.

Shem and Japheth stood at the opening. They flattened themselves against the hull of the boat as the elephants stepped up the ramp and lumbered passed them into the ark. Without prodding, the big beasts made their way through the main passage down to the largest pens that could hold them. It was as if they knew where their assigned stall was. Behind them were the rhinoceroses, also needing no guidance to their stall.

"What should we do, Father?" Japheth whispered loudly.

Noah walked to the far side of the entrance. "Stand away and let them come. It seems as though there was nothing for us to do all along."

Noah and the others stood aside, tentatively watching as the animals walked up and into the ark. The mountain lions entered the ship. They let out a guttural purr just as Seda was turning a corner with a plateful of berries. She jumped back in surprise and the berries flew across the room. She closed her eyes, and held her breath in fear of being eaten, but the big cats ignored her and sauntered over to their pens.

After they disappeared, she stood with her eyes still closed, her hands clasped close to her breast.

Shem came to her side. "It is safe, my wife."

She opened one eye and searched the area. A couple of foxes sniffed the floor near them. "I wish that all this be over."

Shem embraced her and chuckled. "It will be, soon."

Noah stayed at the entrance throughout the day. He watched and counted the creatures as they passed by. Every animal that had previously walked around the outside of the ark was inside and bedded down on the straw. The animals were unusually calm and quiet, peacefully caring for themselves and their own kind. The orderly boarding was such a success that no one dared to claim responsibility. Their hope was that the calm would last.

Chapter 34
Final Warning
The day of the end

It was the day before Tuball's Harvest Festival celebration. Tural stared up at the main portion of the falling star as it continued on its eastward course. Several pieces broke off and veered to the southwest. Excitement in the city grew, as word spread that that the largest fragment was the god El and that the smaller ones were Anat, Baal, and Mot with their servants. Tribes from every corner of the land had brought offerings to prepare for the full-moon festival. Pigs gathered leaves and straw, bulls and cows lay on the ground, and the crickets sang louder than they ever had before.

The spirit master had decided that this was an unrivaled event and that the tribes must pay homage to the gods in a special way. He sent out word of the price that El required. The people must sacrifice not only their first fruits, but also something of great importance. Each tribe was to sacrifice their most beautiful child on the altar of the ziggurat. If they disobeyed, then it would show disrespect to the gods and would lead to a horrific punishment. If the whole city participated in the plan, the gods would surely accept the sacrifices and bless the people.

The edict pierced the hearts of the Tuballite people. Human sacrifice? Yet no one spoke out. How could they offend the gods or threaten the good of the culture? Tural realized that this was the moment that Shem and Noah had predicted. He hobbled with the help of his walking stick back to his chambers and stopped to take a deep breath. He gazed across his table of charts and drawings of the heavens, then looked up at the bookshelf to see the many scrolls he had accumulated through the years. A pit of sickness hit his stomach.

"How can I pass on what I have learned? Will it all be lost?" He slumped over the table with his head in his hands.

His acolyte pounded on the door.

"Enter!" Tural shouted.

"Master, there are many lights over the city. Did you see them?"

"What?"

"Did you see the fire lights in the sky!" he yelled. "There are now seven!"

Tural rose from his seat. "You do not have to shout! Yes, yes, I know. Come here. I want you to gather..." Tural looked around at his favorite scrolls and pointed. "Those, those, and those. We are going to the sanctuary."

"Yes, Master." The young man started picking out the selected documents. "May I attend the Harvest Festival?"

"Yes, yes," Tuall said curtly as he reached for his walking stick. "If that is what you wish."

Tural waded through the throngs of people standing idle, staring and pointing up at the lights. His protégé followed closely behind with his arms full of scrolls. Excited yet nervous chatter ran wild. Tural and his acolyte fought through the crowd to get to the ziggurat.

The youth helped the old man up the steep steps until they arrived at the outer door. The two entered the pyramid threshold, and then walked down the passage and up to the doors to the sanctuary. Two guards stood at attention, spears at their sides. When they noticed the magi, they promptly opened the sacred doors. Tural acknowledged them with a quick bow of his head, and then proceeded to the treasure room. He twisted the handle on the wall and the access panel released. He ushered the boy inside and had him set the scrolls on the shelf next to the golden icons of the gods.

Tural stepped back. "If the gods honor the scrolls as much as I, this is the place where they should stay."

"May I have leave, Master?"

"Have any of my words of the Sethites' God sunk into your head?"

"Some. You have taught me many things, Master Tural. May I leave now?"

The magus sighed heavily. "Go."

The acolyte bowed and left his master. Tural stayed the night in the sanctuary to examine the vast history of the city that was written on the walls. It was cool and calm inside the room. Light reflected up from the passage to fill the room with a peaceful bliss. He relished the time there and fell asleep curled up at the foot of the gods.

* * *

The following morning, the festival had begun. The spirit master made certain that the mead was heavily laden with a powerful hallucinogen. It was important to him that when the strong drink was consumed, it would ensure two things: the people's urges would be heightened and, more importantly, any worries of sacrificing the lives of their children would be suppressed. The gods must be pleased with such a grand gesture and an honorable sacrifice.

As each tribe brought forth their special child, the executioner stood ready with an ominous curved knife at the ziggurat's main platform. Dulled of their senses, almost a hundred tribes reluctantly gave up their most cherished ones for the greater good. One by one, the children were brought forth and the executioner slit their throats so that their blood would empty quickly. Cries of the children and wails from mothers began to swell and put doubt into the populous. The children's blood ran in rivulets down the ziggurat steps, as a dream instead of a nightmare. The cries grew louder. Strong drink had little effect on parents offering their children as human sacrifice.

The spirit master strategically began a chanting mantra. He kept booming drums beating quickly to hurry the process and cover any sorrowful wailing. After the last child was killed, the spirit master initiated the final communion with the gods. He raped a young virgin on the steps of the ziggurat. The sexual frenzy could now begin.

With the narcotic fluid pulsing through their veins, the citizens steered away from pain and over to bliss. Flutes, cymbals, drums and other instruments sounded out, while wild dancing filled the streets. Soon, the people of the city and the region let go of any despair and indulged themselves in jubilant copulation with any and all. They ripped off one another's clothing to satisfy their crazed lusts—young and old—human and animal. With sexual passion rising to the pinnacle of ecstasy, no one would even care if good or evil would befall them.

But this day was like no other before. As the orgy progressed, the comet loomed closer. The collected mass of ice, mud, and ore was disintegrating. Small fragments of the comet burned up, vaporized in the atmosphere. Larger portions of the comet stayed intact until impact on the earth.

The largest segment headed directly into the ocean to the west with such ferocity, a tidal wave formed a several hundred foot wall in all directions. The Great Sea was hit with enough fury to force a colossal wave up north to the southern entrance of the Black Sea. For centuries, water had trickled into the Black Sea at a slow steady rate, but the thin fragile dam was no match for the approaching wave. The break was instant and devastating. Mountains of sea water poured into the Black Sea at millions of buckets per second.

The Vinca people fishing near the shore of the Bosporus River into the Black sea were submerged instantly. With the Black Sea rising over a foot an hour, fishing villages near the shore line were soon inundated and submerged.

The largest segment of the comet roared across the sky and over the city of Tuball with a thunderous roar and a billowing column of vapor trailing behind. It hit the eastern sea shore with an ear splitting *boom!* The earth shook.

The city people cheered, "The god El had made his landing on earth! All is well! El is here! All is well!"

The powerful blast at the eastern shore of the sea dug deep into the earth. The blow forced a huge swell a hundred feet high at a speed no one could avoid. Within minutes the wave curled up into a white-capped nightmare that dwarfed the western walls of Tuball. Guards atop the walls could only watch as the wave hit the city savagely. It flattened the thick stone walls. The bulk of the sea followed behind and flooded into the city. The huge obelisk toppled over, crushing any human or animal not already drowned. With moments, the population was erased—no one was spared.

* * *

Tural sat alone in the sanctuary of the ziggurat. He felt a shudder from within the sanctuary, but could not hear the screams and cries for help, or the devastation of the city. Tural could do nothing but wait as the light dimmed around him. He picked up a torch, walked to the opening of the sanctuary and observed that the guards had abandoned their post. When he heard water splashing up from the lower section of the passageway he went to investigate. Water had filled the entrance of the ziggurat and a pool grew before him.

Tural knew his own death was inevitable. He returned to the sanctuary and shut the doors so he could pray. But to which god? He held up his torch to look at the familiar gods of the city and gazed at their prowess for a moment. He walked over to the statue of the Sethite God and pondered the faceless statue. The light from the flame flickered, then sputtered out.

Chapter 35
Waters Pour Forth
Day 1

Shem inspected the gates on each of the animal pens. He quietly peered inside the lion pen with his oil lamp, but the lions only gave him a cursory glance. The same went for all the other creatures, great and small. Noah and Japheth worked to finalize the schedule for human and animal provisions with the women. Ham had finished his rounds and went topside to get some fresh air. A moment passed before he poked his head down through the sky hatch.

Ham was frantic. "Father! Brothers! Everyone! Come quickly!"

Shem and the other sons dropped what they were doing and climbed the stairs and ladders to the upper deck. Once outside, they saw Ham pointing over the rail. Noah, Shem, and Japheth went to the short rail and looked down the length of the vessel. The villagers had returned.

Ham stood back, with a cocky admonition. "Did I not tell you they would come? And now there are no animals left to stop them."

The villagers were well armed and dragging whatever they could carry that wasn't already underwater. The Cainite men had taken the lead and began a sprint toward the open door of the ark. The ramp to the ark was over sixty feet long and attached to the base of the fifteen foot high opening.

"Oh no!" Japheth exclaimed. "The door is open!"

"Oh yes," replied Ham, pompously. "I warned everyone."

Shem watched the men close in on the ramp. "Father, even if we could fly down there, it would be too late to stop them from getting in."

"It *is* too late," said Japheth.

"Is it?" asked Ham, twirling a rope in his hand.

Noah shifted his sight to the rope and raised an eyebrow. "What is that for?"

Ham chuckled. "For our own good."

Just as the men stepped on the ramp, Ham pulled hard on the rope. The other end of it was attached to the supports under the ramp nearest the boat. The supports buckled and the leading edge of the heavy ramp broke off at the lip of the opening. As the Cainites strode midway up the ramp, the wooden structure swayed to one side. They held on for dear life as it came crashing down to the ground. The men tumbled over, shielding themselves from the falling debris. Over twenty feet below the opening, a dozen men groaned and cursed their circumstance.

Noah watched the men pick themselves up from their fall. He turned back to Ham. "Well done, Son."

Ham bowed grandly. "It was my pleasure."

Japheth gazed down at the displaced Cainites with a slight displeasure. "I am sure it was, Brother."

Before Ham could bask in further praise, the northwest sky lit up. Across the valley and beyond, one of the sky lights shot over the mountains of Sevan. It headed east, a cloud column trailing behind it.

Everyone aboard the ark and on the ground gazed in amazement.

"It flies like a giant flaming spear," noted Shem.

Ham looked beyond the prow and pointed. "There is another smaller one coming this way!"

A gigantic comet splinter dragged its cloudy tail toward them from the northwest. It soared overhead with the roar of a wild animal, so close they could feel the heat. Everyone stiffened, captivated by the anomaly. It passed by them, crossed the valley, and careened into the mountainside. The explosion was deafening. They scrunched their eyes and covered their ears, yet it mattered little. The concussion seeped deep into their heads and bodies. Noah and his kin tried to gather their wits about them.

Ham pointed up to the sky. "Take heed! There are more!"

Thousand of bright little smoking lights filled the sky and flew in every direction. The sky lit up like a tremendous forest fire that rained fiery ice-balls down upon them. Everyone scattered like cockroaches.

"It is not safe up here!" shouted Noah. "Get below!"

They frantically climbed below and shut the sky windows just in time to hear what sounded like a hundred pounding fists above them. Shem ran to the rectangular portholes to get a better view. Heavy lumps of smoking ice balls the size of apples hit the hull in rapid succession. The river hissed as the hot hail peppered the surface into a thick, soupy mist. The rain of hail pocked the ground so extensively it formed a grid of holes across the land. Anything left alive in the open soon perished. Exposure was death.

Seda had moved down to the main entrance. She screamed, "Shem!"

Shem leaped from the second level to a bale of straw to get to her side. She clasped her hands together and stared out from the big opening of the ark at the Cainite people, bloodied by the hail balls.

In the middle of the storm, the Cainites had tried to erect a makeshift ladder to reach the opening. Hail continued to pelt the people. Those who hadn't found cover under support beams or the curved hull of the ship were knocked unconscious. Children wailed mournful cries, clinging to their mothers for safety. Water from the deluge inched up to touch the lower support beams and base of the ark. Seda agonized as galling ice rocks smashed a man and a woman trying to find cover.

Seda clutched Shem. "Husband! They will die! Do something!"

Shem stood paralyzed. "Why should I? Cala was killed by a Cainite," he muttered.

She shielded her eyes. "Husband! I cannot bear to see them die!"

Shem turned around with painful anger. "Then walk away, woman! My father would not approve."

"Please! It is not right!" she pleaded.

Shem lowered his head in shame. He looked down at the people being assaulted by the hail. He kicked the bulkhead. "I do this only for you, Seda."

Shem ran to a stall where a long rope hung. He tied it off on a stout crossbeam and strode back to the entrance. With the rope in hand, he twisted back, to gain momentum for a throw. Before he could throw, a gust of wind shot through the opening and the door of the ark. The heavy access door unexpectedly swung around on its heavy hinges and the wind forced Shem backward. He tripped and fell back on his rope. The thick heavy door slammed into the bulkhead with a booming *thud!* An iron latch on the inside automatically dropped into place and sealed the door snug to the bulkhead. It was pitch black, but Shem crawled to the door and reached up to feel for a release on the latch.

Noah came down from the second level with a lamp. "It is too late, Shem. I had the boat makers set it so that it could not be opened once it is closed."

The wailing of the women and children no longer could be heard, but muffled pounding against the outside of the bulkhead continued. Seda put her hands to her ears and cried. Shem consoled her. Noah felt around the edge of the door to check for a tight fit, then left them. The pounding on the hull decreased, but Seda could not bear it any longer. She ran back to her sleeping quarters.

* * *

The hours passed slowly as devastation continued to move across the earth. Splinters of the comet drifted over the planet, waiting their turn to enter the lower reaches of the atmosphere. One by one the house-sized splinters of ice, mud, and rock sped to earth. Water from the cosmic heavens rained down upon the earth such as men had never before seen.

The Aras River swelled up around the ark at an exponential rate. Higher and higher the water rose up the sides of the vessel, until the boat began to shift away from the ground. It creaked and groaned from the support beams that held the vessel upright for so long. In another moment a wall of water rushed down from upstream and crashed against the ark's aft end with a roaring splash. Like a giant hand, the surge of water forced the ark off its supports and into the current of the river and away from the foot of Mt. Ararat.

What seemed impossible for decades was now proven true…the ark could float. Noah's sons were sent out to inspect the vessel for leaks. Japheth opened the hatch to the bilge and used a lantern to inspect the hull. It was dry as a grain house. Shem and Ham also took lanterns and walked throughout the vessel to inspect the bulkheads on every floor.

Seda caught Shem's arm on his return. "What will befall those who stood up to the evils of the grand elder? Would they not be spared?"

"We have other things to worry us."

"Surely the Almighty will look with favor upon them. Yes?"

Shem sighed. "If they did not turn their hearts to Him, then they will be punished." He caught Ham's lamp moving to the upper level. "I must go."

Seda dropped her head. "We could have saved those people."

Shem squeezed her hand. "It is all up to the Creator. He gives and He takes. He is terrible in His love and yet is also merciful. We must trust all will be as it should."

She looked into Shem's eyes. "God's love can be hard."

"Yes it can." He kissed her forehead, then trotted back up to join Noah and Ham.

The pelting hail had stopped, but the rain was left to strike endlessly on the roof. Noah sat on the edge of his bed tapping his foot, when his sons returned. Ham was stoic, Shem still absorbing the latest events.

Noah held onto the side of his bedpost. "I take it all is well?"

"The insides of the boat are dry and sound," said Ham.

Noah called out for the rest of the family members to join them. While the ark rocked gently in the current of the broad open river, they huddled together and prayed for safety.

After their prayer, Noah recommended the others secure themselves in their rooms. He wanted to verify the upper deck was intact. He climbed the ladder to the roof and peered through the narrow rectangular slit below the sky hatches to watch the storm. Shem sent Seda to their room and climbed up next to his father.

The river was now raging eastward and sweeping the ark along with it. Rain continued to rattle on the roof as the ark began to gain speed. It glided downstream for an hour and passed by mountain trees until it entered a snake-like canyon. It pitched left and right as it moved near the cliff walls, missing rocks by a finger.

Noah called down the steps. "It does not look well. Put out the lamps and find a place for safe keeping!"

Shem started back and found Ham on the second deck pacing nervously. Shem approached his brother and whispered gently. "Ham? Father told us to bed down. Why do you keep walking?

Ham stared straight ahead. "I do not wish to."

Shem blocked Ham from walking further. "What is it?"

Ham looked to the floor boards. "We should have gone to the caves."

"Your pride is great," rebuked Shem. "You must let go of your own ideas. He is our father and we must obey."

Ham choked up, then looked into Shem's eyes. "I told Ne'uk to meet me there."

"What?" Shem replied in a loud whisper. "Why did you tell her to do that?"

"I was hoping I could convince Father to abandon this silly boat and stay on dry land." Tears dropped down his cheeks.

Shem groaned. "Oh no." The ark rolled and creaked. "But we cannot stand here now. Go bed down and we will talk of it later."

Ham stood trembling. "What is there to live for?"

Shem put his arm around Ham and walked with him back to their chambers. Lamps were extinguished and it became pitch black. The aft end of the boat tipped up. They held on for the unknown.

* * *

Noah kept watch from above. A huge wave had formed behind and began to push the ark at a rapid rate. The wave sucked the ship in and funneled it through the channel, missing the canyon walls by a whisker. He took a breath and held it. Once the narrow channel broadened, he let out his breath and peeked through the slit to see where they were headed. Lit up by lightening, he saw a dead end. The light flashed through the cracks in the sky hatches, followed by a horrific blast. Chunks of debris from the comet careened into the mountain side. Huge boulders split from the mountain and tumbled down into the water next to the ship. The ark tipped starboard and held steady at a ten degree list until it eventually realigned. Their greatest concern was not the boulders. They were headed directly toward a sheer cliff wall.

Noah shouted below. "Prepare yourselves. All will be well…pray!"

Noah knew that even the sturdy ark could not withstand a frontal blow into a cliff. As he braced for their demise, a huge wave moved from behind and split around each side of the vessel, lifting the ark upward as the wave swelled beneath. When the ship dropped into the well of the passing surge, his stomach turned. The wave pushed ahead of the ship and heaved up against the stone wall, only to curl backward. With seconds to spare, the return wave crashed back into the ark, sparing it from a collision into the rocks. The vessel pitched upward over twenty degrees until it hit the wave crest. At the crest the ark paused, then slipped over and onto the backside of the wave. It pressed into the cliff, splitting off a chunk of the decorative prow.

The ship's momentum propelled it still forward. It screeched along the cliff side and landed on a clay bank with a heavy *bump*. Rocks let loose from the cliff and pounded the roof. The ark was wedged into the grip of the bank. Water spilled down from the hillside and through the upper windows.

Animals and humans were thrown against the bulkheads. The women wailed. Men were terrifyingly quiet. All waited in desperation for the inevitable. The force would have split apart any smaller a vessel built with less than thick old-growth trees.

A series of waves buffeted the cliffs, then returned to the ark to shake it, twist it, and squeeze it. Creaking and cracking of wood sent chills through the Sethites. It looked hopeless.

In the chaos, Noah clung to a post and looked upward. "No, Master! You promised! You promised!"

* * *

In the high mountain cave, Ne'uk sat on the ground with her arms tightly wrapped around her knees. She rocked and rocked, knowing this was the end of days. "God of Ham! God of Noah! Spare me!" she cried out between sobs.

The water line, still far below the cave, inched its way closer to the opening. Rain and hail splattered ferociously in front of Ne'uk. Lightning flashed across the night sky, blazes of hot stone shot like spears down to the earth. She ran back to a little dugout boat in the cave and crawled in. She lowered her head between her legs and moaned. "Let me live, let me live," she wailed. "Please, let me live!" She moaned and sobbed as she never had before.

* * *

Water cascaded from the hillside and carved soil away from the area. Loosened from the bank, the ark slipped backward into the sea of chaos. As the ark slid away from the rocks, it rolled to port, then starboard, and again to port. It wobbled, but was moving away from the shore quickly. Moments later, *Screeeeeech!* Man and beast were thrown forward. The scraping echoed throughout the ship as it moved over an obstruction. Soon the ark bottomed out and sat solid in one place. An immense quiet followed.

Noah let go of his grip on the post and rested his hand on the bulkhead. "Please do not split apart on us." He listened to the women's frightful weeping. Noah called out into the darkness. "When we have doubts, we see fear! When we have faith, we see God! Have faith!" The cries lessened to whimpers.

Rivulets of water continued to pour down from the mountain, as if it was giving drink to a hungry animal. Eventually the vessel rose up from the obstruction. The ark moaned and creaked as it rocked away from the obstacle.

Noah gripped the post till his knuckles turned white. He waited for another collision. Nothing. He loosened his grip and felt his way to the sky hatch. He took a peek outside.

Lightning filled the sky. The ark had floated backwards toward open waters. Random thumps of stones on the roof had given way to steady raindrops. Lingering flashes of lightning spilled light through the sky hatch, followed by claps of thunder.

After an hour, the ark still held together. Noah cracked open the sky hatch to see what awaited them. What was once a slender river, now was an immense lake. A dark, low cloud lay over the lake, obscuring the mountains and their cliffs. The sky rained down over the waves. The ark rocked and drifted aimlessly. He listened to the drumming of the rain on the roof.

Noah closed and locked the sky hatch. "Sons! Light the lamps! Look for leaks!" he shouted.

Naamah looked up to Noah. "Are we safe now? Never have I seen that much water. Could it rise over the mountain tops?"

Noah took a deep breath. "If the Creator wishes it. I pray the worst is over. We must ensure we will not sink. If all is well, we must try and sleep."

Japheth found a small leak and pressed in straw and pitch to stop it. Once it was determined that the ship was stable, everyone went back to their beds.

Noah took out a knife and made a notch in the beam close to his bed.

"What is that, Husband?" asked Naamah.

Noah set aside his knife. "That is the mark of our first day. May the second be better than the first."

Day 2

By midday, Shem couldn't contain himself. He had to see what was happening outside. He went to a port hole and removed the block to see a dismal grey seascape. Clouds, rain, and water spread out as far as the eye could see. Rolling swells and wind had turned the ark so that it floated westward. The clouds had descended to the water line and it was impossible to know their position. One thing was sure, the rain kept coming. The hard patter on the roof was ubiquitous and disquieting.

Shem was about to give up identifying their location when he thought he saw something. The clouds parted momentarily over the water just long enough for him to see a boat. Shem shut the block, opened the sky hatch, and carefully stood up to get a better view.

It was a small boat with a covering over it. "There is someone out there!" Shem shouted down into the ark.

Ham ran to the bottom of the second level stairs. "Did you say you saw something?"

Shem's eyes were wide, his head sopping wet. "I think someone is out there. But they will not live long."

Ham climbed up next to Shem and looked out. "Please, God," he whispered.

"It is coming closer," said Shem.

The gap between the two vessels narrowed. It wasn't long before the ark and the little boat were within a stone's throw of each other. The boat bobbed up and down the huge waves like a seed in a pond. The craft was as wide as it was long, sealed by an animal skin. The two brothers couldn't take their eyes off it. Their curiosity piqued when the two vessels touched. Then the skin was pulled back and a woman sprang up and waved. Rain poured in and began to fill the small boat.

"Help me!" the woman shouted.

"Ne'uk!" Ham whispered loudly. "Ne'uk!" he shouted and waved.

In a flash Ham bolted down the steps, grabbed a rope on the bulkhead, and sprinted back to the sky hatch. He tied off the rope to a beam. He let out several arm lengths of it then tied a length around his waist. The remainder of the line slipped over the side. Ham started his descent from the sky hatch. Shem grasped his wrist.

"Should you be doing this? Remember what Father said."

"Leave me be!"

Noah stepped up from below and reached out and pulled Ham back. "No! It is not permitted," he shouted, wiping the pouring rain from his face.

Ham pleaded with sorrow in his eyes. "We must save her, Father."

"I tell you, no!"

"She will die!"

"So be it!" said Noah painfully.

Ham snapped. "I have listened to you my whole life and never asked for anything. Now leave me, old man! I am saving her!"

Ham yanked himself away and slid across the wet deck to the short rail that ran around the top deck. He descended to the edge of the ark and checked the rope around his waist. Once at the short wall, he dangled the rope and signaled the woman to clasp the rope. A huge jagged swell rolled ominously across the water and drew the little boat into a deep trough out of Ham's view. As the swell passed by, the boat reappeared but was capsized.

Ne'uk had been thrown from the boat and was groping around in the turbulent water, gasping for air. She went under and resurfaced, frantically trying to find a grip on the slippery rope. Ham had his feet planted on the rail, ready to pull her up. He cried out in agony as he watched the woman go under for the second time. The sea took down the small boat and smacked it against the ark with crushing blows.

"You do not think he would jump in for her do you?" asked Shem.

"If you see him start to undo the rope from his waist, we must pull him in," Noah replied.

The woman resurfaced, spitting out water, and gasping for breath. For a third time, she reached for the rope and wrapped it around her wrist, then pinched her inner thighs against the line for support.

Ham immediately arched his back and used his legs to pull her up. Shem held onto the upper section of the rope to make sure Ham didn't fall off the edge. After several pulls, the woman appeared over the edge and Ham embraced her. The ark then shifted from the blast of a rogue wave, causing Ham and the woman to fall on their bellies. They slid down to the edge and almost off it when the ark shifted back.

Noah and Shem didn't wait for another wave. They quickly pulled Ham and Ne'uk up to the sky hatch. They laid at the opening, holding one another. Shem untied the rope from Ham.

Ne'uk clung to Ham, burying her face into his chest. "I knew your God would save me," she sobbed through tears of joy. "I knew He would."

Ham held her tightly, then kissed and stroked her head through his tears. "Come, Ne'uk, we must get below."

Once all had climbed through the hatch, Shem shut the panel and the four of them sat on the planked floor, dripping wet and exhausted. Naamah climbed up to the third level with an oil lamp to see what the commotion was about. She brought the light around and gaped at the stranger.

"You are the daughter of the woodsman," said Naamah.

Noah scrutinized the woman in the lamp light. "It is Ne'elatama'uk, is it not?"

"Yes," she said, coughing and wringing out her hair.

Shem thought his father may throw her back into the sea. "Father, I will not let you send her away."

Noah scratched at his bearded chin. "I have to do what is right in the eyes of God."

Shem glanced at Ne'uk cringing behind Ham. "This is not right."

Noah held up his hand. "Ne'elatama'uk. Do you take this man, Ham, to be your husband?"

Her mouth dropped open, she froze in the middle of hair wringing and looked toward Ham for instruction. Ham peered at his father with disbelief.

Shem frowned with astonishment. "What are you doing, Father?"

"What I am doing," he announced to everyone present, "is allowing this woman to live." Noah looked back at the woman. "Do you?"

She nodded, "Yes," she replied, without further hesitation.

Noah looked over to Ham. "Do you wish to have Ne'elatama'uk as your wife?"

Ham nodded. "Yes, I do."

"Then, as God the Almighty is our witness, the two of you shall be joined as one."

Naamah wiped her eyes, then wrapped her arms around Ne'uk. "Three daughters! This is such a blessing."

Ne'uk was still in shock. "What does this mean, Ham?"

Ham wriggled in between Ne'uk and his mother. He placed his hands on her cheeks and kissed her on the lips, then embraced her. "It means that you are my wife. Father has allowed it." He smiled back at Noah. "My greatest thanks, Father."

Noah cracked a smile and shook his head. "You must have much love for this woman, to risk your own life for her."

Shem patted Ham on the back. "So is this the only way you can expect to get a wife?"

Ham chuckled tearfully. "Maybe so." He led Ne'uk back to his cubicle to dry off and rest.

Naamah leaned into Noah. "This is meant to be, yes?"

Noah nodded. "Yes. It is all in God's will."

"You are a good man, Husband."

Noah raised a finger. "There is one more thing, Naamah. Would you please tell the others so we can celebrate the union with food and dancing?"

"Now?"

"Yes, woman! Is it not our custom after a bonding ceremony? The storm has let up and we have nothing better to do."

Naamah clasped her hands for joy and went below to organize the event.

The reception was splendid despite their circumstances. They skipped and danced to songs of joy on a floor full of straw. All was in order. The sons of Noah were bonded with their women. All was safe. Truly a blessing sheltered within a cursed storm.

Day 3

Ham woke the next morning with Ne'uk under his arm. He caressed her face. Her eyes opened, and her lips parted into a grin.

"Your God is a good God, Ham. And I must give thanks to Him...and your father."

"I thought I would never see you again, Ne'uk. How did you find us?"

She stroked Ham's bearded face. "I hid in the cave above the ark, like you told me."

"Why did you not come to us before the rains fell? Father would have wed us then."

She smiled up at Ham. "No he would not. Not if he knew that I did not follow your God."

Ham nodded. "That may be true."

"The waters came up to the cave and I had to leave. I did not think I would live, but I prayed to your God and He brought me to you."

Ham smiled. "Yes He did. But why does He always make things so hard on us?"

Days 4-28

Noah developed a daily routine: He got up each morning and made a notch in the beam near where he and Naamah slept. He then made his rounds through the ship to see if any of the animals were sick or restless. Next, he would assign his children their tasks, such as feeding the animals and cleaning the ark. At some point, Noah would peek out the slotted portholes to determine the weather conditions. And at the end of the day, he would pray for the safety of the passengers.

At the beginning of their voyage, the chores were accepted willingly—all thankful to be alive. But as the days wore on, some chores became drudgery; removing animal waste being at the top. Fortunately, with the exception of rank odor, the dried animal feces made good fuel for cooking and acted like cement for filling cracks in the bulkheads.

In many ways, the ship was ingeniously designed. When oil lamps burned their dingy light, the smoke and excess heat floated up through slats in the decking on each floor and eventually exited through air vents. The vents were located in the high elongated structure at the front of the ship. Another feature was the high structure at the bow. It acted like a wind rudder to keep the ship aligned with the wind and reduce broaching.

Noah walked through the ship proud of the design, and proud of the men that helped him build it. It truly was a marvel. Inspection of the animals made him nervous at first, but most of them were very quiet and slept for days without stirring. This put him at ease and gave him time to examine the countless species of creation. Even so, the others kept a safe distance away from the animals, their eyes sharp for any disturbance that might require some retaliatory action.

Day 29

Time seemed to stand still. The days were dreary and gloomy, hardly lighter than the nights. The only relief from boredom came when racing footsteps and giggling flooded corridors of the ark. Ham would chase Ne'uk and then she would chase him. The others looked on with seasoned recollections, wagering how long their bliss would last.

Noah carved another notch into the pillar that held up his room and counted. "Twenty-nine," he said with a sigh. "Twenty-nine days and the rain still has not let up," he grumbled.

Noah squinted through the slit to see something, but the pouring rain and mist blanketed the earth. He took a deep painful breath. "Will this never stop?"

It did not matter. He and his family did what had to be done.

Day 41

Another twelve rainy days had passed when Noah woke up in the early hours of the morning with a start. He nudged his wife. "Naamah, wake yourself."

Naamah groaned a little. "What is it, Husband?"

"I do not hear anything," he whispered.

"Then why did you jab my side?" she asked half awake.

"It is too quiet. I believe the rain has stopped."

Naamah sat up for a moment to listen. "Yes, yes it has." She flopped back down and snuggled into the fleece. "That is nice."

Noah got up, dressed himself, made another notch in the wood, and climbed up to the roof window. He opened it and put out his hand. He looked skyward to see a star next to the moon in the waning blackness. *Aah! They still hang in the heavens.* A blast of cold air caused him to reel back. *It is as cold as the devil! But at last, the rains have paused!*

The rains had indeed stopped, and yet the ark still drifted through thick layers of fog. For just a moment, the icy cloud dissipated long enough for Noah to see water stretch out to the edge of the horizon. He braved the cold and watched as the morning light appeared across the water. It was only for an instant, then the clouds returned. It had been dark and dreary for many of the days. Oil torches burned constantly during the waking hours. With the rains behind them, the upper sky windows were opened to allow light to reach down to the lower levels of the vessel and to assist in service and cleaning of the vessel. Noah closed the openings in the afternoon to keep the heat in and ensure future rain did not enter.

Day 150

Many days passed, and the morning fogs slowly gave way to scattered blankets of cumulus clouds that touched down to the water. A dry westerly wind blew the ship gently across the sea. By midday, the cloud formations began to open up pockets of blue. Shafts of sunlight, like pillars of gold, reached down and touched the surface of the sea. For the first time in months, the sun showed itself.

Seda and Shem lay on the upper shelf just below the sky hatches for hours. They peered through the rectangular port holes, anticipating wonderful changes in the weather. Even though the peaceful quiet would sometimes be interrupted by a distant rumbling thunder, these moments became one of the few cherished diversions from monotony.

* * *

The blockade at the end of the Aras River began to form cracks. Water trickled through the small openings of the earthen dam of ice and stone. Cracks widened into crevasses. Trickles grew into brooks, then into streams. Eventually, gushes of water poured out. It wasn't long before the rock and mud and ice loosened enough to compromise the dam. It was on this particular day that the barrier suddenly gave way with a blast. A huge surge of water burst through the opening like an enormous waterfall. In a matter of days the dam collapsed completely and thousands of tons of water emptied into the valley below. All the water around Mt. Ararat and the surrounding mountains was receding.

Day 224

The ark continued to move wherever the wind took it, until one day, the large vessel glided to a stop with a loud *thud!* The gentle rocking had ended. Curiosity got the better of Noah and his family. One by one, they filed up to the main deck to see what had occurred. The clouds were so thick, they could see but a few feet before them. There was just a brief moment when the vapor moved enough for them to see a mountain peak—or was it?

"We hit the ground!" shouted Ham. "I am sure of it."

"Where do you think we are, Father?" asked Japheth.

Noah shook his head. "We could be anywhere on earth."

Shem covered Seda with a fleece as she shivered from the cold. "Father, we have hit some land, but the water still surrounds us. And it is too cold to even think about leaving."

Noah shrugged. "Then we will wait."

"Wait for what?" asked Shem.

He chuckled. "I do not know. But when I know, I will tell you."

Day 264

The following days were clearer and produced more warmth from the sun. Seda spent more and more time on the top deck of the ark. She was able to tend to her garden on a regular basis. On this day, the clouds lifted fully from the horizon.

"The mountains!" Seda announced down into the ship's hull.

The rest of the family piled out of the vessel. They stood and gazed at the panoramic view. The clouds had lifted high enough to reveal the vast mountain range encircled them north and south.

"Praise the Almighty, God!" Noah shouted with raised hands.

"It is beautiful, is it not?" asked Seda.

Shem put his arm around her waist and patted her pregnant belly. "Not as beautiful as some things," he muttered.

"The waters *must* be dropping," Noah surmised. "Wait here." He disappeared below and, moments later, came back with a raven. He stroked the bird's feathers. "I wager you have been cooped up long enough," he said to the bird.

Noah released the raven into the air and it flapped its wings until it was out of sight. Everyone watched intently as the bird disappeared.

Noah then addressed the family. "It is my hope that it will bring back a nut or a berry. Then we can be sure that there is a place for us."

Day 271-?

Seven days went by and it was evident that the raven would never return. Noah decided to try again by sending out something more trustworthy—a dove. He had used his doves for communicating with others in far off lands and they always made a reliable return. After the bird was released, it flew for many hours and came back by evening, breathless and weary, but with nothing to show for its exertion. After seven more days, Noah sent out the dove again, and this time brought back a twig in its beak.

The receding water near the ark continued to drop at an accelerated rate of more than a foot a day. The expanse looked less like a lake and more like a valley with a river. Within a week, the valley was close to what Noah had remembered. The exception were the trees, bushes, and grass stripped of their green. It was a muddy, mucky, barren land. Could it ever recover from something as traumatic as the deluge? The earth was not ready for them.

Day 314

Eventually, the water receded. The vessel rested at a seven degree angle to port, cradled next to a huge boulder on the mountain slope. Both humans and animals fought to tolerate the angled floors. Leaving the ship was still not an option. The animals spent their time resting against the easy wall, while the humans managed the tilt of the floors and ladders as best they could. Nevertheless, mountains ranges could be seen from base to peak, the rivers were back to their normal levels.

The animals began to stir and make noise as if it were time to leave. With the earth continuing to dry and the food stores almost gone, the large access door had to be opened. Shem and Ham took turns breaking the latch on the door with axes. Once they broke the lock, the door swung open and the sunshine blazed in. Cumulus clouds covered the landscape in awesome beauty, with a magnificent rainbow that touched down somewhere at the end of the river. The fields were yellow and brown. But hopeful tips of green had sprouted.

Fortunately, the access door was adjacent to the uphill side of the mountain and an arm's length from the ground. With the doors open, wild creatures of all kinds ventured out from the ark gingerly and cautiously. Once outside, they quickly bounded across the land to find new homes to bed down. The family watched in amazement as the animals took turns leaving their stalls to exit the ark. It couldn't have been more orderly if they had led the animals out in sequence.

Day 370

Noah had kept his family inside until he knew it was time to leave. After enduring the chaos of the deluge, Noah had thought he would fear nothing. With the exception of the domesticated sheep, goats and some birds, the food stores were almost out and he could take grumblings from his sons for so long.

Noah went to bed that night with trepidation. *What holds me back? Why do we not leave the ark? Is it because the land is in no condition to start a new life?*

In the darkness of Noah's dream, God spoke to him. "Noah, it is time. As you walk the earth again, I vow that your descendants will be many. You have seen the sign of my promise in the sky. I will never flood the earth, or mankind and animals again."

The following morning, Noah stood at the entrance of the ark and gawked at the rainbow. He leaned on his staff and put his arm around his wife. "Woman, we have much work to do." He turned around. "Ham, Shem, Japheth! Bring the clean animals; it is time!"

Ham hopped off the ark with Ne'uk. "Thank the Almighty, we are at the end! No more cleaning after animals."

Shem helped Seda step out of the ark with her bulging belly. "Ha! There is no chance for that. We will always have to clean up after something. It's our lot in life."

Ham tested the soil. "Better to be on solid ground than in that boat."

Shem patted Seda's belly. "It will be a new beginning. And we can start with our children."

Noah stepped forward with his staff. "I pray we do better than those before us. "Come all of you, we must build an altar and give thanks to our God."

Chapter 36
Beginning Again

And so, Noah built his altar and they gave thanks for their survival. Hanging over them was the question of why only their family was given life…but it was time to move on. They saw the rainbow and would remember God's covenant. A new mission was in store—a duty to care for nature and man, to bring up their children with righteous goals, and to always follow the ways of their Creator.

With haunting memories of the Aras Valley, they ventured back to their land near the Tigris River to start anew. To their surprise, the land had healed remarkably well. With rich sediment coating the field, wheat sprouted up as if it were planted.

A year later, Noah, and his sons, Japheth, Shem, and Ham, and their sons and daughters, brought in the first harvest. The wheat was full and golden.

Shem strolled through the fields with Seda at his side. She held their baby boy in her arms. At the edge of the field they stopped and looked out at the beautiful vista. The blue river wound through the golden grain on land that stretched out to the horizon.

Seda cooed at the baby in her arms. "Hello, Elam." The baby giggled. "I love you. Yes I do."

Shem wiggled his finger and the boy went for his father's hand. "His grip is a good one. He will plow the land like an animal."

Clutching his father's finger, the boy opened his mouth with a toothless grin.

Shem pulled against the firm grip the boy had on his finger. "Yes, you will."

Seda gasped. "Husband. Did not all things perish in the flood?"

Shem moved his attention away from the baby and up to Seda. She brushed back her hair from her face then pointed at something behind him.

Shem whirled around. He covered his eyes from the sun's rays and squinted to see in the distance. Shem's heart beat faster, his throat dry. He took a drink of water from his flask. "This cannot be!"

He wiped his mouth slowly, then rubbed hies eyes in disbelief. "How is it there are others?"

Descending from a knoll at the edge of the field came three men with walking sticks, wearing traveling robes and hoods. The sun's brilliance shined behind the men, obscuring their faces. Their steps were steady and fixed.

Shem blinked to make sure they were real.

The three men kept coming.

Shem's heart skipped with anticipation and a glint in his eye as he looked to the heavens. *All Knowing One, what new marvels do you have in store for us?*